HALLOWEEN: Magic, Mystery, and the Macabre

Other Anthologies Edited by
Paula Guran

Embraces
Best New Paranormal Romance
Best New Romantic Fantasy
Zombies: The Recent Dead
The Year's Best Dark Fantasy & Horror: 2010
Vampires: The Recent Undead
The Year's Best Dark Fantasy & Horror: 2011
Halloween
New Cthulhu: The Recent Weird
Brave New Love
Witches: Wicked, Wild & Wonderful
Obsession: Tales of Irresistible Desire
The Year's Best Dark Fantasy & Horror: 2012
Extreme Zombies
Ghosts: Recent Hauntings
Rock On: The Greatest Hits of Science Fiction & Fantasy
Season of Wonder
Future Games
Weird Detectives: Recent Investigations
The Mammoth Book of Angels & Demons
The Year's Best Dark Fantasy & Horror: 2013

HALLOWEEN:
Magic, Mystery, and the Macabre

Edited by Paula Guran

PRIME BOOKS

HALLOWEEN: MAGIC, MYSTERY, AND THE MACABRE

Cover design by Sherin Nicole.
Cover art by Sandra Cunningham.

An extension of this copyright page can be found on page 383.

Prime Books
www.prime-books.com

For more information, contact Prime Books:
prime@prime-books.com

ISBN: 978-1-60701-402-7

Again, for My Kids

May the magic of Halloween
always be part of your lives.

Contents

Contents

INTRODUCTION: NEW BOO

> Hark! Hark to the wind! 'Tis the night, they say,
> When all souls come back from the far away—
> The dead, forgotten this many a day!
>
> —"Hallowe'en," Virna Sheard

While researching and compiling the anthology *Halloween*, a treasury of reprinted stories published by Prime Books in 2011, I felt there was a need for some fresh tales for the old theme. *Halloween: Magic, Mystery, and the Macabre* is the result: eighteen new works of Halloween-inspired fiction. Happy Halloween!

Since I provided a lengthy essay about the holiday and its history as an introduction to *Halloween*, I won't repeat myself here. (That introduction is available online here: www. prime-books.com/an-introduction-to-halloween.) But I will reiterate a few ideas pertinent to this volume.

Until fairly recently, we humans were much closer to nature and our lives far more dependent on the annual cycle of the seasons. For most of the northern hemisphere, autumn meant crops had to be harvested and stored, livestock slaughtered or secured for winter months. Survival during the upcoming darker colder days of winter must be considered and assured. But we couldn't simply depend on nature, hard work, or even a bountiful harvest when it came to such matters of life-and-death; the season begat celebrations, ceremonies, rituals, religious beliefs, and the working of magic.

In Western European tradition—particularly that of the Celts—fall also marked one of the two times of the year (the other was the beginning of summer) when the mundane world was supposedly the closest to the "other world." The friendly dead could commune and visit with the living; less-than-friendly supernatural entities could cause harm. Beloved souls traveled abroad, but so did fairies, vengeful ghosts, and malign spirits. One did one's best to appease all.

Christianity gave the English language the word *Hallowe'en* sometime during the sixteenth century: a Scottish contraction of *All Hallows' Eve* (evening)—the night before All Hallows' Day, set by the Church on November 1. The "hallows" being the "hallowed"—the holy—commemorated on that feast day, also known as All Saints Day, The Feast of All Saints, and Solemnity of All Saints.

Long before the word was coined, however, Christianity's efforts to dampen pagan belief in the extramundane had to be augmented to accommodate ideas that refused to disappear—concepts that are, perhaps, ingrained in our psyches. (After all, one of the defining elements of any religion is a belief in supernatural beings and forces. And most cultures develop mechanisms to help the living cope with the mystery of death.)

The connection with the dead and the supernatural was too powerful to be obliterated by merely honoring saints, so All Souls Day—also known as the Commemoration of All Faithful Departed—was established on November 2. The living could remember and pray for the souls of all the (Christian) dead; prayers offered for souls in Purgatory could alleviate some of their sufferings and help them reach heaven.

This was all well and good, but the older ways and beliefs persisted. Folks still believed the dead and supernatural beings wandered on All Hallows Eve; they were still—at least for that one night—part of the living world. Rituals and traditions were adapted . . . and continue to endure and evolve.

This—combined with other superstitions, bits of ancient and newer religions, different regional undertakings to prepare for winter and harvest, a hodgepodge of ethnic heritages, diverse cultural influences and practices, and various occult connections that seem always to be associated with the season—eventually became a celebration of otherness when scary things are acceptable, disguise is encouraged, and everyone can become anyone or anything they wish.

The season has always offered us an opportunity to consider or confront the coldest, darkest, deepest, most primal of our fears: death. In a multitude of ways the basic meaning of Halloween and the symbols and practices that have become associated with it—pranks, pumpkins, treats, bonfires, masks and costumes, the supernatural, the frightening, the fun—are ways of dealing with or even mocking that which comes to us all.

We might have faith or theory or hopes about what comes after death—a 2013 HuffPost/YouGov poll showed forty-five percent of American adults believe in ghosts, or that the spirits of dead people can come back in certain places and situations; sixty-four percent believe there's a life after death. But no one *really* knows, do they?

Of course there's always the chance that Halloween truly is a time when magic is possible, that forces beyond our ken are present, that the living and the dead can interact.

Magic, mystery, and the macabre—elements that inspire thoughts of the fantastic, the enchanting, the supernatural, the horrific, that which is not explainable, and so much more involved with the holiday. When soliciting stories for this anthology, I asked the writers keep that in mind. "Scary" was not necessarily the goal, but is a natural part of the mix. Nor did stories need to adhere to customs associated with the primarily North American Halloween as we know it today. Other—real or imagined—holidays and rituals that coincide with or parallel the Halloween season, or have connections to it could also be themes. Sometimes the fact that it *is* Halloween became the linchpin of a story.

The remarkable results are contained within. These tales are each a treat; no tricks involved, but there are certainly some very interesting twists. In Laird Barron's "Black Dog," a Halloween date in a whistle-stop town leads the protagonist far beyond its Catskills location. A small-town legend combines the sinister spells of a certain silver screen and Halloween in Stephen Graham Jones's "Thirteen."

In Dunhaven, Brian Hodge's isolated town of "We, the Fortunate Bereaved," Halloween is a school holiday and genuine dark magic occurs on All Hallows Eve. Jonathan Maberry's "Long Way Home" takes us back to his mysterious town of Pine Deep, Pennsylvania, on Halloween as a soldier returns from war. Brenda Cooper also revisits a fictional site she previously introduced—a truly enchanting place on the other side that is more or less analogous to Laguna Beach, California—in "All Hallows in the High Hills."

The season's thin veil between the living and the dead is gently breached and a soul does some traveling in Melanie and Steve Rasnic Tem's "Lesser Fires." "Angelic" by Jay Caselberg also brings a family together for an annual get-together, but one fraught with far more meaning than one relative is aware. A strange multi-generational alliance in 1930s Kansas culminates with a Halloween harvest in Laura Bickle's "From Dust."

A modern witch copes with trust issues and Beggars' Night in Nancy Kilpatrick's "Trick or Treat." Another witch manages some challenges of contemporary life by moving into a man's new home—uninvited and accompanied by her cat—for the month leading up to All Hallows Eve in "For the Removal of Unwanted Guests" by A. C. Wise.

Both Norman Partridge and Carrie Vaughn take monsters whose popular tropes began in 1930s movies and are now connected to Halloween—the mummy and the werewolf—and add their own imaginative components: human trauma and psychosis in Partridge's "The Mummy's Heart," and the World War II Nazi SS in Vaughn's "Unternehmen Werwolf." "Pumpkin Head Escapes" by Lawrence Connolly creates an entirely new boogeyman by combining theatrical and Halloween magic.

A visit to a haunted house unexpectedly takes the ghost hunters to a cemetery and a strange encounter in Barbara Roden's "All Souls Day." A hospital's emergency room staff deals with Saturday night, the full moon, Halloween, and the weird in Chelsea Quinn Yarbro's "Quadruple Whammy."

In John Shirley's "And When You Called Us We Came To You," a young Chinese factory worker making products for the huge commercial U.S. Halloween market calls for aid from those who wait beyond the darkness, and they answer—thousands of miles away amid American teenagers. "Whilst the Night Rejoices Profound and Still" by Caitlín R. Kiernan takes us to a far future, another planet. and a strangely evolved festival with roots in our ancient celebration. Maria V. Snyder's "The Halloween Men" are enforcers in a strange time and place far different than our own.

I'm sure that our All Hallows Eve brew will help make this a happy Halloween for those who consume it. With some luck—and maybe the casting of a magic spell or two—perhaps *Halloween: Magic, Mystery, and the Macabre* will become part of the season itself.

Paula Guran
Beltane 2013

BIG CHIEF

THIRTEEN

Stephen Graham Jones

Here's how you do it, if you're brave enough.

First you go down to the Big Chief theater. That's the old one behind the pizza place nobody goes to any more, the one my dad says he used to work at in high school, each of the ovens so deep, like a line of mouths to Hell.

The tops of his forearms have these smooth scars to prove it.

I've always wanted to write a word on that burned skin, then wait, see if it's one of those prayers that make it through, get answered.

But this isn't about him. This is about the Big Chief.

It's just got two screens, and they're right beside each other. If you're in the first one and there's a war movie in the second, you can hear the machine guns and dogfights and heroic last words bleeding through. It's one big room, really, you can tell. They just hung a thick curtain right in the middle so they could show two movies, double their money.

My dream's always been for them to roll that curtain up one night, show us the big picture.

Maybe someday.

It's been there for forever, the Big Chief. According to Trino's uncle, a kid got castrated there about fifteen years ago. In the last stall of the bathroom.

Maybe that's why this trick works.

See, first you go there, get your ticket, your popcorn, and settle in. It doesn't matter what row, or which theater, one or two. And if you're watching a horror movie—it's supposed to *only* work with horror movies—what you do is, right when it's most scary, right when whoever's with you is probably going to make fun of you for closing your eyes, you close your eyes. And hold your breath. And don't let any sound in, kind of by humming all your thoughts into a dial tone.

And then you count two a hundred and twenty.

Two minutes, yeah.

That's the real trick.

And if you're getting scared, if you can feel it starting to work, you can breathe out all at once, even though you could have gone five or ten seconds longer.

It's safest to do that, really.

Just breathe out, laugh, maybe hunch over into a coughing fit. Spilling your popcorn's an especially good tactic, even—who would do that on *purpose*, right?

And then look back up to the screen through your tears. See that the movie's still up there, right where it should be.

Your laugh'll be kind of forced, but your smile, that's a hundred percent true.

That's where the movies should be, up on the screen.

If you make it to a hundred and twenty, though, *then* open your eyes?

The screen'll look just exactly the same. And your friends'll still be sitting there by you, waiting for you tell them what it was like. To see if it worked.

How it works is that, when you're not looking, or listening, or breathing—it's like how you're supposed to hold your breath when your parents are driving by the cemetery. If you don't, then you can accidentally breathe in a ghost.

That's sort of how it works at the Big Chief.

With you not breathing, playing dead like you are, it makes like a road, or a door, and the movie seeps in. Way in the background, like at the edge of town, not everything changing all at once. Nothing that dramatic.

But the movie's there. It's there because you invited it. Because you left a crack it could come through, because you made a sound like a wish, and the darkness just washed that direction, to cover it up.

Ask Marcus Tider.

If you can talk to the dead, that is.

Marcus moved here last year, but he didn't come to eighth grade with us in the fall. If all the girls' collected hopes and dreams had anything to do with it, though, it would have been one of us in his place. Just so they could have him to take them on dates all through high school. Just so they could pin all their hopes and dreams on him, bat their eyes every time he passed, and then sigh into their lockers.

But Marcus—at his last school, it had been big, like 4A, and they'd been a rich district, the kind that has a pool. Meaning they had a swim team. And Marcus was too blond and too perfect not to have been captain.

He could hold his breath forever.

It was only a matter of time before he ended up at the Big Chief.

He wasn't even scared of the movie, either, said horror was stupid, all make-believe. We were all there to watch, except for right at the end, when me and James ran out to the parking lot, to see if we could catch the movie starting, off on the horizon. Just see one star dimming out, another winking on.

There was nothing.

Inside—we heard later, had forgot our ticket stubs, couldn't talk our way back in—Marcus just opened his eyes, looked around at everybody waiting for him to say how scary it had been.

He'd just shrugged, looked back up to the movie, and, like he'd timed it all out, that was when the monster lunged close to the camera, its tentacles whipping all around.

Everybody but Marcus flinched back into their seats.

City kids always think they know stuff we don't, all the way out here. And maybe they do.

But we know some other things.

Two weeks later, we all figured he'd cheated somehow. That he'd peeked, or sneaked a breath using some swimmer trick. Or that he hadn't believed right.

The Big Chief doesn't care if you believe or not, though.

For Valentine's Day four months later, Marcus threw blood up into his construction-papered shoe box, already floating with secret admirers.

None of us said anything.

He had a tumor inside him. Mr. Baker explained it in Life Science right before spring break. He hauled out the movie to show us, finally got the projector going, and when we saw it, that tumor, it was what we were already expecting: a tentacled monster, lashing out for whatever it could grab onto, pulling that bit of meat towards its center. But it could never get enough.

By Memorial Day, he was dead.

We sat in our back yards and ate the hamburgers and hot dogs our parents had grilled for us, and they didn't ask us about Marcus.

His parents moved away for July fourth, their rearview sparking with the fireworks we felt compelled to light.

Their house is still empty.

And now that movie's over.

This is a double-feature, though.

Marcus was just the example, the test case.

Grace, though.

Everybody loved Grace, me most of all. You know how when you know you're going to grow up and marry somebody? That's who she'd always been for me, all the way since fourth grade. I would have stepped in front of a truck for her. And I wouldn't have closed my eyes, either.

We were supposed to have gone to homecoming together, but I got sick, then ended up locking the door to my room, my Exacto knife hovering over my stomach, because I'd been too close to the Big Chief that night Marcus held his breath, I knew. I had a tentacle monster inside me too.

I never cut deeper than a scratch, though.

My parents went on to homecoming without me—it had been their first date, fifty-thousand years ago—then knocked on my door when they got home, so I could knock back on my wall, and the next morning I was fine. Mom drove me over to Grace's to give her the three-streamer corsage I'd been saving for since summer.

"There'll be bumps in the road," my mom said, pulling us away from Grace's house. "You've just got to keep going, right?"

I nodded, hated myself.

To make up for it, two weekends later I saved up enough to take us both to the movies, and get a medium popcorn.

This was going to be *our* story, I told myself. Not my parents'. That's why I'd gotten myself sick. Fifty-thousand years from now, Grace and me were going to come to the Big Chief, to remember. It was going to be better than any stupid football game.

Her mom dropped us off, slipped Grace a five for concessions, then went home to sit at her kitchen table some more. According to Grace, since her dad left five months before, all his money mounded in front of the television like that was going to make up for him being gone, that's mostly what her mom did: sit there and stare, like she was trying to backtrack to where this part of her life had started.

My parents felt sorry for her, they said, and then would hold each other's hands, like to show they were different, they were better.

I held the door of the Big Chief open for Grace, already had our tickets.

It wasn't a horror movie, either.

After Marcus, none of us went to the horror movies any more, even though it was almost Halloween and there was always one playing. We were still watching them after lights out at home, of course, but on videotapes we'd smuggle from our big brothers' rooms, handle with extreme caution, like, if we dropped them, if that plastic cracked, the blood was going to come out.

We were still getting our scares, I'm saying.

But, with Grace, it was a love movie, where the girl looks and looks like she's not going to get the guy, then, surprise again, she does.

I could sit through it. For her.

Maybe it would give her some ideas, even.

The theater was just usual-full for a Friday showing. Maybe six or eight seats between everybody, some movie with screaming playing next door.

I sat between Grace and that scary movie—her word—and held the popcorn on my knee for us, and, I admit, I kind of got into *our* movie. The girl's dad in this one was trying to find her the perfect husband. He felt he owed her or something, because her mom wasn't around to help her. But he was overdoing it, was pulling in everybody from his office, where he was boss, and then his friends' sons, and on and on, when the guy the girl really loved was the guy who fixed the copy machine at her dad's office.

I mean, I got into it, but I was also tracking the movie next door, of course. Trying to time to the screams. Trying to imagine if we were over there, how tight Grace would be clinging to me. How her knee would probably be up on my thigh and she wouldn't even be aware it was happening.

But this wasn't bad, either.

She kept having to bat the tears from her eyes, and had pretty much forgotten the popcorn altogether. Not me. I never forget the popcorn.

With the Big Chief, too, if Willard's working the counter, he'll even slip you a free refill if you promise not to make a mess he'll have to clean up later.

Right when the movie was winding up for its final pitch, I whispered to Grace about our empty box, slithered out to the lobby for more. Willard fixed me up, and even let me peek into the other theater.

It was mayhem in there. Chainsaws and werewolves, it looked like—no, werewolves *with* chainsaws. The chocolate and peanut butter of the horror world. I didn't even realize I was holding my breath until my eyes started burning.

It was all older kids in there, though. If I'd taken Grace in there, there would have been a timer over my head, just counting down to when the first senior leaned forward, whispered advice to me that Grace would have to pretend not to hear. And then things would just get worse and worse, and it's not like I could fight any of them and win, so it would be a coke-throwing thing, and I'd probably get banned for the month again.

No, the love movie was the better choice for us. Definitely.

I got back just in time for the end.

Instead of a marriage, it was back to the office. The dad had hired the copy guy into the office, and now, with everybody watching, was promoting him up and up and up, to next in line to run the place, the girl just standing there beaming, crying, her whole world coming together just the way it should.

Grace was crying right along with her.

From where I was I could see her cheeks, shiny and wet, her eyes closed to try to hold the rest of the happiness in.

When I brushed her arm, climbing back into my seat, she jumped, and started coughing like she was going to throw up.

She ran out hiding her face and I followed, and Willard fixed her up with water and she hid in the Ladies until just before the horror movie let out.

And that was it.

My dad was waiting for us at the curb like every time, the car filled with his menthol smoke, and I held the door for Grace again and she just kept batting her eyes.

"Good movie?" my dad asked back, meaning completely different things, and I nodded just to shut him up.

Two weeks later it was Halloween.

Because we were in eighth grade, none of us dressed up, of course. And because the Big Chief was the Big Chief, none of us went there either. Not yet. Soon we'd be high schoolers, though, we knew, and none of the high schoolers ever died from holding their breath.

The kid who got castrated, he was supposed to have been thirteen or fourteen. Maybe that was why they were safe. Why we weren't.

Anyway, because of what happened at the last Halloween party for our class (my dad's menthols, Lucas's dad's beer, some light bulbs in the basement somehow unscrewed), this year the guys were going one way, the girls another. Most of the girls had signed up to chaperone the first- and second-graders trick-or-treating.

Where the guys went was the old graveyard behind the convent. Of course.

I called Grace before, to just mention it casually, where we were headed, so she could get how brave that made us, how we might not be making it back, all that, but she was already gone with her second-grader.

"Look for Bo Peep," her mom said, instead of goodbye. Because she wanted us to be happy, I knew. Because she remembered how your heart can swell when you're in eighth grade.

I met up with everybody in the alley ten minutes later and we were gone, my dad's menthols safe in my chest pocket. I'd sneaked one at a time all week.

The graveyard, as it turned out, was still the graveyard. Crooked headstones, weeds as tall as us, and, when we first got there, a couple of sophomores making out on the concrete bench. We ignored them, or pretended to pretty well, but I guess they could tell. Then it was just us and the grossest cigarettes ever invented. And the town, spread out before us.

Marcus was buried back wherever he'd lived before. Not here. And it wouldn't have been in this graveyard, anyway. This was just for people who died a hundred years ago, before the convent got condemned and haunted.

According to the seniors, there was a zombie nun who still carried a candle around in there.

We didn't believe them even a little bit. But we didn't get any closer than the graveyard, either. The reason we knew the nun wasn't in there was that she'd been in our dreams already for years, her candle going out right when she got close to us.

So we sat on the headstones like they were nothing, and we blew smoke up into the inky-purple sky, and, squinting like outlaws at the full moon, we held our cigarettes up to Marcus, wherever he was. Like we'd even really known him.

We were pretending he'd been the best of us, that he was some tragedy.

We'd been the ones who paid for his ticket that night, though.

Soon enough, like always happened, I took a drag too deep, that green smoke filling my lungs, and I had to stagger off into the bushes, to throw up. Because it had to be some kind of bad luck to throw up on a hundred-years-dead person. It might be like giving them a little bit of life. Just enough.

I fell through the trees, finally got to the little cliff we'd used to drop our action figures from to test our bandanna parachutes, and I splashed my dinner all down that scar of white rock.

When my eyes could see again, what they saw was the east end of Saginaw Street, right before it hits St. Francis.

Five years ago, this was the best candy street of all. It was all old people, who only got to see kids on Halloween, pretty much. Better, they'd forget you almost as soon as you left, so you could go back to that same well again and again. Sometimes we'd trade masks, mix and match costumes, but I don't think they'd have busted us anyway. Or cared.

Saginaw Street was still doing good business, too. Was still the place to be if you hated your teeth.

I stood up to go back to the graveyard, and, if I'd just done that half a second sooner, I'd have never seen the shepherd's crook cresting over the Frankensteins and ghost heads. It was navigating through them, moving down the sidewalk.

Bo Peep.

Grace.

I smiled, nodded to myself, pinched the hateful menthol back up to my lips.

There she was, all right. Her second-grade robot holding her hand. Cars moving slow and heavy alongside her—all the parents who were driving their kids instead of walking them. That's cheating, though. If you want the candy, you've got to earn it.

I waved my arms as big as I could then remembered one of them was glowing. I balanced my cigarette on a rock behind me then stood up again, waving bigger, and yelling.

By now Grace's second-grader was moving up a sidewalk, his silver-tubed arms and legs making him look like he was going to topple over with every step.

And she heard me, somehow.

Because of love, I think.

At first it was only her head angled over, like being sure, but then she turned around, her lungs filling with hope.

I jumped, jumped, but what she fixed on instead of me was one of the parents creeping past.

She leaned forward as if she hadn't heard something all the way and the dad behind the wheel leaned out the open passenger window, holding out a white bow, the kind that goes on a good Bo Peep costume.

Grace looked back to her second-grade robot, still cued up for some grandparent candy, and the way she looked I could tell she was timing it. That she felt she had to, because what was this dad going to do with a Bo Peep bow, right?

Right.

She lifted the front of her big skirt, kind of ran out to the car, and, because I was a good almost-boyfriend, I kept my eye on her second-grade robot for her, watched him stiff-arm his plastic pumpkin up to Miss Massey, who used to teach English, and always tied verses of poetry to her candy.

Once upon a time the poem on my candy had told me the fields were white, the fields were long, the fields were waiting, and I'd always wanted to ask her for the rest of it, but never had the nerve.

By the time I looked back to Grace, she was in the passenger seat of the car, and it was pulling away slowly, no rush at all. Just melting back into the parade.

"*No*," I said—what about the robot?—and started to step forward but my foot stabbed into open space and I had to balance back hard, my arms windmilling in space.

I fell back, ran along the cliff for the next break in the trees, the last piece of road before the highway opened up, and I got there just in time for the driver to look right through the bushes at me, and nod.

It was the dad from the movie, the one Grace had wished into our world.

He smiled his winning smile, his trustworthy smile, his smile with the sharp, sharp corners, and that was the last time anybody ever saw Grace Lynn Andrews, except as a photo on the news for two states in every direction, and it was the last cigarette I ever smoked, too, and it was the last year Halloween was the same for any of us.

It was also three months to the night before I crept out my window one Wednesday after lights out, and filled one of my mom's good glasses with kerosene from the lamp her mom had given her, balanced it all the way downtown in the cold.

It wasn't cold for long, though.

The Big Chief had just been waiting for somebody to burn it to the ground.

I stood there beside it and I held my breath as long as I could, the skin of my face drawing tight in the heat, my heart shaped exactly like two hands holding each other, and when I finally turned to go home, Lucas was there, and Thomas, and Trino, and they hid me, and they never told, and I'll never leave this town, I know.

Not for the usual reasons, though.

In the flames that night before anybody got there, I saw a boy, the front of his pants wet with blood, and I saw Marcus, wearing his swim goggles, and I saw a pale white shepherd's crook ahead of them, leading them through, leading them on.

Someday she'll come for me too, I know.

I'll be waiting.

Stephen Graham Jones is the author of sixteen books now. Most recent are *Zombie Sharks with Metal Teeth* and *Flushboy*. Coming up soon are *The Least of My Scars* and *The Gospel of Z*. Jones lives and teaches in Boulder, Colorado. More at demontheory.net.

THE MUMMY'S HEART

Norman Partridge

Who knows how dreams get started.

But they gear up in all of us, maybe more than anything else. Waking . . . sleeping . . . sometimes it's hard to tell the difference. Sometimes dreams are sweet little ghosts, dancing in our heads like St. Nick's visions of sugarplums. Other times they're a hidden nest of scorpions penned up in a bone cage they can never escape, digging stingers into soft brain-meat hour after hour and day after day.

Sugarplums and scorpions. Take your pick. Or maybe grab yourself a full scoop of both. Because we all do that, don't we? Hey, I plead guilty. I've had my share of dreams. Most of them have been bad, but even a guy like me has had a few sweet ones. And every time I've bedded one of those and snuggled up close, a monster movie scorpion came crawling from beneath the sheets and jack-hammered his king-sized stinger straight into my brain.

That's why I don't trust dreams.

That's why I'd rather have nightmares.

Nightmares are straight up. They're honest—what you see is what you get. Dreams are another story. They don't play straight. They take your nights, and they take your days, too. Sometimes they make it hard to tell one from the other. They make you want things and want them bad, and every one of those things comes with a price.

Of course, no one thinks about the price of dreams on the front end of the deal. We all figure we'd pay up, but that's because the price is never self-evident going in. So we spend more time dreaming, as if the act itself will turn the trick. A few of us work hard, building a staircase toward a dream—but people like that come few and far between. Most of us look for a shortcut. We toss coins in a fountain or go down on our knees and say a prayer. We look for a quick fix from some mystic force, or one god or another.

After all, that's the dreamer's playbook. Dreamers don't take the hard road. We look for instant gratification. We make a wish, or two, or a dozen . . . as if something as simple as a wish could be a vehicle for a dream. But you never know. The universe is deep, and odds are that someone has to get lucky taking the short road sometime. And wishing only takes a second. Like the man said: *Nothing ventured, nothing gained.*

Nothing. It turns out that's a key word, because the thing most dreamers end up with is a fistful of nothing. And for most of us, that's when the whole idea of *dreams becoming reality* disappears in the rearview mirror. For others, that's when the longer road comes in. It's not a road taken by realists, or workers, or builders. No. It's a madman's road. It's built on books of mystic lore, most of them written by other madmen. It's built on half-truths and faulty suppositions and twisted logic that (by rights) should be nailed through with a stake, boxed up, and buried in a narrow grave. It requires a certain brand of blind faith codified in stories and legends, and it demands a high level of trust in things that are beyond fantastic. Wizards and witches, monsters and myths. The power of an eye of newt, a jackal's hide, or even a child sacrifice.

Most of the time, it's a twisted trail that leads nowhere, except maybe to a cozy rubber room or not-so-cozy prison cell, or (if we're going gothic) a locked attic in the home of some rich relation. But that doesn't happen all the time . . . and it doesn't happen for all madmen.

I say that because I know it's true.

I've seen where those roads can lead.

The night I first walked a madman's trail I was in the wrong place at the wrong time, no more than a passerby in the darkness. It wasn't my own dream or my own trail, but it was one I took.

Walk any trail and you're bound to soak up the scenery. Might be there's only one way to go, so you follow it. And you put one foot in front of the other, the same way as those who have gone before you, and sometimes the darkness takes hold of you as it did them. Sometimes it draws you in.

You might stay on that trail a long time, always looking for a way off, sure you'll find one eventually.

But walk anywhere long enough, and that place becomes yours.

Especially if you walk alone.

The trail I'm talking about was cut by a mummy.

He did the job on Halloween night in 1963. He was mad as a hatter, and he came out of a plywood pyramid that was (mostly) his own making. And no, he wasn't really a mummy. But that night, he was definitely living the part. Even in the autopsy photos, that shambler from the darkside was a sight to behold.

His name was Charlie Steiner and he was nearly twenty-three years old—too old to be trick-or-treating. And Charlie was big . . . football-lineman big. If you know your old Universal Studios creepers, he was definitely more a product of the Lon Chaney, Jr. *engine of destruction* school of mummidom than the Boris Karloff *wicked esthete* branch. But either camp you put him in, he was a long way from the cut-rate dime-store variety when it came to living-dead Egyptians.

Because this mummy wasn't playing a role.

He was embodying one.

Which is another way of saying: He was living a dream.

Charlie's bandages were ripped Egyptian cotton, dredged in Nile river-bottom he'd ordered from some Rosicrucian mail-order outfit. He was wound and bound and wrapped tight for the ages, and he wasn't wearing a Don Post mask he'd bought from the back pages of *Famous Monsters of Filmland*. No. Charlie had gone full-on Jack Pierce with the makeup. Furrows and wrinkles cut deep trenches across his face like windblown Saharan dunes, and the patch of mortician's wax that covered one eye was as smooth as a jackal's footprint . . . add it all up and drop it in your treat sack, and just the sight of Charlie would have made Boris Karloff shiver.

And you can round that off to the lowest common denominator and say that Charlie Steiner would have scared just about anyone. Sure, you'd know he was a guy in a costume if you got a look at him. But even on first glance, you might believe this kid was twenty-three going on four thousand.

Look a little closer, you'd see the important part: Charlie Steiner was twenty-three going on insane. There was no dodging that if you got close enough to spot the mad gleam in his eye—the one he hadn't covered with mortician's wax. Or maybe if you spotted his right hand, the one dripping blood . . . the one he'd shorn of a couple fingers with a butcher's cleaver. And then there was his tongue, half of it cut out of his mouth with a switchblade, its purple root bubbling blood.

Charlie wrapped those things up in a jackal's hide he'd bought from the back pages of a big-game hunting magazine with Ernest Hemingway on the cover. Who knew if that hide was real but Charlie believed in it, same way he believed in the little statue of a cat-headed goddess he added to the stash, along with a dozen withered red roses, his own fingers and tongue, and a Hallmark Valentine's Day card.

The same way he believed in the dream those things would deliver to him.

The same way he believed in the madman's trail he was about to travel.

Charlie tossed all those things in the back of the family station wagon (along with one other important ingredient), and he drove down to the local lover's lane, which wasn't far from his house. At that time of year, the place was deserted. By the time Charlie had things set up to his satisfaction, he had swallowed so much of his own blood that he might as well have eaten three raw steaks. But he kept on moving—readying his incantation mummy-slow . . . sure but steady. Just the way you'd expect a mummy to do business, moving like the sands of time.

Just the fact that Charlie could do that was a little slice of a miracle all by itself. Whittling himself down like that, how'd he even keep walking? Chalk it up to drugs he stole from the VA hospital. All through high school, Charlie worked in an after-school program up there, pushing guys around in wheelchairs. He learned about pain management during that time, and he'd continued working as a part-time attendant after he graduated. In other words, Charlie knew what he was doing with the needle and the knife.

So Charlie Steiner was walking on a cloud that night. Or an imaginary dune overlooking an Egyptian oasis, with jackals howling in his head and a mad priest's plan in his heart. On this single night, at long last, he'd finally become the sum of his dreams . . . or maybe a dream *personified*. And what wasn't locked up in his own skin was wrapped in that mojo hide . . . or waiting, bound, beneath a blanket in the back of the station wagon.

Put it all together and it was an offering, a single wish boiled up, and Charlie had a place for it.

Not in the plywood temple he'd abandoned. No. His place was out in the night and under the Halloween moon . . . just a stone's throw from lover's lane.

Beneath the same stars that shone down on Egypt.

If you've seen those old mummy movies, you know something about mummies and their dreams. And Charlie knew that, too. He knew those movies backwards and forwards, and he knew that mummy was always after the same dream. Kharis was looking for a reincarnated princess, Ananka, who died on the altar of a dark Egyptian god and left Kharis alone to pay the price for their twin blasphemies. Which, when you strip the Hollywood mysticism and curses and *high priests of Karnak* window-dressing off the tale, means one thing: Kharis died for love, and he came back from the dead looking for a second eternal helping of the very same thing.

Pure love. Eternal love. Love that didn't backslide.

That's what Kharis was after, and almost every knockoff mummy who came in his wake wanted the same thing. That's what Charlie Steiner was after, too, and his madness started on the day he wrapped his needs in the bandages of the most accessible mythos he could find. And while that's a ticket that buys us an egress to Charlie's story, it's a long way from the whole deal, because there was a lot of other mumbo jumbo that Charlie Steiner believed. But eternal love was the final destination Charlie had in mind, and the path that led to it traveled through Egypt and Hollywood. As crazy as he was, that's all Charlie really wanted. The quest for same lay beneath the insanity, and the magic, and the bad things he'd done and was about to do.

Who knows.

Maybe the whole thing came to him in a dream.

Of course, I didn't understand any of that back then. That's because I was just a kid, out on the prowl on Halloween night in 1963, looking for candy and ready (or so I thought) for whatever came my way.

We were out trick-or-treating for the very last time before our teenage years closed the door on the holiday. My brother Roger and me and Roger's best friend. On the loose without the parents, or any adult supervision at all. I was twelve, Roger was thirteen. We were a pair of Irish twins, as they used to say back in the day, brothers born just eleven months apart.

Me, I was dressed up like a soldier—mostly courtesy of the local army surplus store, but with a coat my dad had worn in Korea. Roger was a baseball player. Yankee pinstripes just like Roger Maris, and a Louisville Slugger, too. The preacher's kid who lived next door to us was a vampire. Hair slicked back with Brylcreem, he looked like the greaser son of Bela Lugosi himself.

Of course, our parents had given us ground rules for the night. Stay on the streets. Don't go anywhere the street lights don't shine. But we had our own agenda, and we got down to business with it once our treat sacks were full. And that put us on the edge of town, where the blacktop ended at a rust-flecked twenty-foot stretch of guardrail capped with a NO TRESPASSING sign.

Beyond that was a dirt trail that twisted through a eucalyptus grove. And beyond the grove was a cattail-choked hollow, a place called Butcher's Lake. Maybe that was the only place for us to go that night, because by then we wanted to find out if there was something more to Halloween than knocking on doors and getting candy. We were looking for something a little more exciting.

Butcher's Lake seemed like the best place to find it. Though there were a few ghost stories about the place, it wasn't named for a murder spree or anything quite that exciting. No. The far side of the lake just happened to mark the border of a couple of neighboring cattle ranches, and that's how it got its name. The only other thing about Butcher's Lake was that it was the local lover's lane, but by the time Halloween rolled around that action had pretty much shut down for the season.

That night, it was ghosts we were after.

So Butcher's Lake was where we went.

That's where we found Charlie Steiner.

Or the thing he'd become on Halloween night.

Or the thing he most wanted to be.

As soon as we climbed over that rusty guardrail, Roger's friend, the preacher's kid, said, "I don't know, Rodge." He said that practically right away, before we took a single step on that trail that led through the eucalyptus grove, as if he was already primed to turn tail and head for home. But my brother gave him a look. "We've been planning this for weeks," Roger said. "We're not turning chicken now."

Rodge meant it. Every word. Like I said, he was only thirteen, but he'd grown up on John Wayne movies and TV cowboys and that was how he operated. If you didn't grow up back then, it seems impossibly archaic now. But in those days, they built us to do what we set out to do, and finish the job. Or, as our old man always said, "If you talk the talk, you walk the walk."

So we set out, putting one foot in front of the other. Roger took the lead on that snaking path through the eucalyptus grove. He had a flashlight, but he didn't turn it on—we were counting on the moon that night, and we didn't want to spook anyone who might be down by the lake Anyway, the trees grew close in the grove. Straight. Thick-bodied. Tall. And the moon was full, but you wouldn't have known it. Those eucalyptus trees blocked out the light and made everything you heard seem twice as loud.

The castanet rattle of dry leaves.

The soughing wind tearing snakeskin flaps of bark from straight, smooth trunks.

The short whispering breaths of three kids on the prowl.

Ahead, near the lake, the sounds were moist and alive. Crickets cut their music in the night. Frogs croaked a hundred yards away, where the trees gave ground to a muddy little patch of beach that rimmed the first wall of cattails.

And there was another sound just ahead . . . one that hung over the night like a shroud. It was enough to make us slow our pace as we approached the last stand of eucalyptus trees, and I remember telling myself that it was probably just the sound of the wind cutting through the cattails.

It might have been . . . but it wasn't.

Chanting. That was the sound waiting for us down by the water.

Bright moonlight shone over that muddy little beach. It washed in waves, as if buffeted by the winds and the clouds—silver light lapping over the dark water and the sandy banks of the lake, each little glimmer of moonlight washing in rhythm to the sound that I'd mistaken for a soughing wind.

Because now I knew what that sound was. Someone was down there, ahead of us in the night. He stood before the lake and the swaying cattails, silhouetted by the glow of the moon, watching the water. We didn't know it then, but he was watching for a sign.

Of course, there were a lot of things we didn't know then. All we knew was what we saw, and we couldn't believe it as the moonlight spilled over the figure and turned that silhouette into something we could recognize.

A big thing pacing back and forth along that shore. Wrapped in bandages.

Gray and silent as a mountain of cobwebs.

A mummy. At Butcher's Lake. On Halloween night.

The preacher's kid said something, and Roger cut him off with a sharp whisper. The monster didn't see us. We stood frozen at the edge of the grove. Every once in a while he'd stop and stare at the water, but there was nothing waiting for him except the sound of his own chanting rolling over the surface. The moon washed over it and spilled a reflection on the murky waves like a spotlight that could open a hole into a black brimming pit. And that mummy would stare at that white hole in that black sky, and the white hole in the water, and the emptiness of both seemed to drive him mad. He stared up at the heavens, and he swung his free arm like a crane, and the wrinkled fist on the end of it was like a wrecking ball ready to tear down the universe.

Of course, we didn't know the reason for that then. We had no idea that it was Charlie Steiner beneath those bandages. We didn't know he was casting a spell to that dark water and that bright moon and whatever gods or demons worked their magic in it, tossing the contents of his jackal-hide mojo bag into Butcher's Lake. We didn't know he was waiting for a sign that would tell him it was time to conduct the most difficult and dangerous part of his spell. We didn't know he was trying to raise a dream woman from the depths of Butcher's Lake. All we knew was that his pendulum wrecking-ball fist was swinging in a way that told us he was coming up empty, and he wasn't happy about it, and that there was going to be hell to pay.

From some god we hadn't heard of. Or some devil. Or the universe itself.

Or maybe us.

Then Charlie Steiner started screaming, and it got worse.

I'll never forget the sound of that tongueless scream. Even though we were hidden from view in the tree-line twenty feet away, I'll never forget the sight of it, either. The mummy turned toward us, and his cobweb lips opened into a black hole that even a full bucket of moonlight couldn't illuminate, and more black spilled out of it, dripping blood that ran in rivulets through the irrigation-ditch wrinkles that covered his chin. And then came the sound—a buzz-saw screech that descended into a roar so heavy with anguish it could have made a deaf man jump up and take notice.

"Oh, God," the preacher's kid said, and just that fast he was gone.

We didn't even hear him running back to the road. The mummy was coming toward us now, still screaming, taking one sloughing step after another. At first I thought he'd spotted us for sure, but then he suddenly reversed course and headed toward the deep shadows near a thick stand of cattails.

At that moment, we had no idea what he was up to. But it came clear later. With his three-fingered hand, Charlie Steiner was ready to grasp for the final straw that might seal the deal he'd tried to cut with the powers of darkness.

That meant he'd gotten down to the portion of night that was really bad business.

The worst.

The mummy stopped at the rear of a station wagon. Swaying just a bit, as if it were fighting gravity itself. Then his fist swung down, and the tailgate dropped, and a light came on in the rear of the vehicle.

We couldn't see much by that light, but we could see the mummy bending low. He reached inside, grabbing for something. There was a muffled scream as he took hold of it, and something tumbled to the sand.

"Sweet Jesus," Roger said. "It's a little girl."

The mummy bent low, staring down at the prone figure before him.

He wasn't chanting anymore.

Three words crossed his ruined tongue and bubbled over his bloody lips, and they were the only words he said that night that we truly understood:

"Dream . . . wish . . . *sacrifice!*"

The girl was nine, maybe ten. In the moonlight, I could see that her ankles and wrists were bound with ropes. And she wore a princess mask—the cheap plastic kind you found at a drugstore. Expressionless, with black hair cut straight across in bangs, and lips as red as red could be. That mask was taped to her head, thick swatches of sticky plastic stuck to her own black hair as if she'd been mummified herself.

If she hadn't screamed, I would have thought she was dead. She lay there on the ground, gasping now, the breath knocked out of her. She couldn't have moved if she wanted to. I stared at her, still unable to move myself. Roger was staring at her, too.

"We've got to stop him!" Roger said.

He wasn't whispering, and he was moving forward, flicking on his flashlight as he advanced.

"Hey!" Roger shouted. "Stop!"

The mummy whirled, holding up a hand against the bright beam. For the first time we saw that he truly was as gray as a grave, except for the places he was black-red. One hand was missing a couple fingers and dripped blood. More gore spilled from the thing's mouth—it looked like he'd been chewing razor blades.

Given all that, it was amazing how fast he moved when he saw Roger coming. One big arm swung down, and he snatched up the girl, and his bandaged feet kicked up gouts of sand that hissed against the October wind as he walked toward the edge of the lake.

His back was to us now, and he raised the girl over his head.

"He's going to toss her in!" Roger said. "He's going to drown her!"

I started across the beach, following Roger. He'd already covered ground. He'd dropped the flashlight and was closing on the mummy's back with his Louisville Slugger in his hands.

Someone else was coming, too. At least I hoped there was, because I heard police sirens rising in the distance. But I couldn't be sure they were headed in our direction, and there was no time to waste. The mummy already had that girl over his head, and before we knew it she was sailing through the dark night.

A hollow splash, and the lake took her. All I could think of as the water closed over her head was the black and bloody pit of that mummy's mouth snapping closed. And then the mummy whirled. Perhaps it was the sound of the sirens that brought him around, or maybe he heard Roger racing toward him. But that wrecking ball fist of his swung out, and it banged my brother to the side.

For a moment, Roger was airborne. He hit the sand rolling. Then he came up, but he'd lost the baseball bat in the fall. By that time I was already halfway across the beach, splitting the distance against the mummy to come at him from the other side.

"No!" Roger yelled. "Get the girl! She'll drown!"

I was close to the mummy now. Close enough to see the crazy gleam in his eye. People have asked if I realized that he was a man in a costume, or if I thought he was real. To tell the truth, I can't remember any of that. I only knew that he was dangerous, and that if he had a chance he'd kill both my brother and me.

And that's what he tried to do. His fist flashed out again. I ducked and dodged the blow, trying to give Roger a moment to recover the bat. The mummy lurched forward, gaining ground for another strike, but I'd given my brother the moment he needed. Roger was up again, charging the mummy with his Louisville Slugger. As I turned toward the lake I heard it land once, and the mummy grunted. Another blow struck home and the mummy groaned, but I couldn't afford to look behind me. I already had my eye on the water and the dull moonlight washing those little bands of wave.

I searched the surface for a ripple . . . any sign of the girl as I tried to remember where she had gone under.

I should have had my eyes on the shadows.

Because the mummy was still coming for me, even as Roger struck him again with the bat.

He was coming with one fist raised like a wrecking ball.

And the sirens were louder now. Definitely coming our way. I was skirting the shore, moving quickly, when I realized that I had almost run into the rear of the station wagon. I got my hands up before I slammed into it, and then the mummy's fist cut a path through the shadows.

I never saw it. I never heard it. I can't even remember the first blow striking me. I know it caught me from behind, and low on the base of my neck, because I still get a little *click* in my top vertebrae anytime I turn my head to the left. Anyway, I staggered and spun on my heel like a drunk.

Roger bashed him again, but it didn't do any good. The next blow crashed against my forehead, just above my left eyebrow. It opened a two-inch gash. Not that I knew I was bleeding . . . or falling. I don't even remember falling into the lake. But the next thing I knew, I was underwater. I came up coughing a mouthful of sludge that tasted like something a frog had vomited up. For a moment I thought the mummy's fist was coming at me again, but I realized it was only a clutch of cattails waving in the wind.

The moonlight shone down, riding black ripples. My stomach roiled, and I retched. The sound of prowl car sirens still rode the night, but

I saw no light cutting through the eucalyptus grove, and no light on the beach.

I didn't see Roger or the mummy. Apart from the sirens, there was no sign of activity behind me. It was as if they'd disappeared. And then I heard a splash out there in the darkness, somewhere near a large stand of cattails that cut in from the shore, and I thought maybe it was Roger.

Sure. It had to be. Maybe Roger had dropped the mummy with his bat. He'd dived in to join the search, and now he was out there in the lake, looking for the girl.

"Roger!" I shouted. "She went in over here . . . over by the road!"

I didn't get a reply. Maybe the splash I'd heard was Roger going under, looking for the girl. One thing was for sure, if I was right and he'd found her, he would have called out. But I hadn't heard anything. And I didn't hear anything now, except for the sirens drawing near.

Quickly, I pulled myself onto the muddy bank and kicked off my shoes. Then I shucked my father's jacket and sucked a deep breath, and dove back into that cold water.

The girl was still out there.

Maybe my brother was, too.

Hitting that water the second time was like swallowing an iceberg. My chest froze up, but my thoughts cleared as that icy black water shocked my brain alive. I didn't know how much time had passed between the mummy tossing the little girl into the lake and the time I went in after her. All I knew was that enough seconds—or maybe minutes—had been burned off the clock that the little girl couldn't have too many left.

I knew some other things, too. As big as he was, the mummy couldn't have thrown the little girl far. I had a rough idea where she had to be, because I'd made my dive from the spot where I thought the mummy had been standing when he heaved her in. But the water was deeper there than I'd expected. The sand didn't slope down from the water's edge the way a beach does. It was a sheer drop-off from sandy shore into murky lake—maybe a foot or a foot-and-a-half drop in some places—and the water was deep enough that I barely skimmed the sludgy bottom when I dove in.

I couldn't see a thing, of course. Even on a sunny day, that water was nothing but thick murk. I swam forward, my hands sweeping before me, but all my fingers found was slick bottom and broken cattail shafts. I covered ten feet that way—maybe fifteen. Then I came up for air, turned, and immediately dove again.

This time I reversed course, swimming back towards the shore, covering the area to my left. My hands sweeping out, sure I'd hit something solid any second. I didn't find anything—not even a junked spare tire. Just that sludgy bottom and rotting slime a catfish wouldn't want in its belly.

Again I came up for air, breathing harder now. I was closer to the shore, and I could stand. A case of shivers rattled up my spine, and I was shaking now. The cold . . . the blows to the head . . . whatever the reason, I nearly lost it and passed out.

But I caught myself. I wasn't going to let that happen.

"Roger!" I called. "Are you out there? Did you find her?"

No answer.

I sucked another deep breath, but it came up in a wet cough that seemed like a slap against the quiet night. I cleared my throat and got another breath down and held it. It was only then that I realized the sound of sirens was gone.

Just that fast another sound replaced it.

The sound of a shotgun blasting away in the night.

I didn't have time to listen.

That little girl was down there somewhere.

I had to find her.

She's alive, I told myself, and even in that moment I knew it was a wish as much as a prayer.

She's alive.

Apart from that wish, I can't say what I thought about as I searched for the girl. Diving, coming up for air, diving again. It happened a long time ago, though I still dream about it sometimes. Over the years, those dreams have come and gone, but they always seem to come around . . . the same way that night has never left me.

Sometimes I dream about that mummy, too. And sometimes

I think about him in the light of day. The mummy . . . Charlie Steiner . . . in my head, they're a pair. I don't know what emotions were squirming in Charlie's guts by the time he found his way through the eucalyptus grove. He certainly wasn't walking out of there with a black-magic dreamgirl on his arm, the way he'd imagined. I'm sure anger and betrayal boiled in his crazy brain . . . maybe even fear. But all that's speculation. The only thing I know for sure is that by the time Charlie turned his back on Butcher's Lake his fate was sealed, and in more ways than he could ever imagine.

Because the preacher's kid hadn't chickened out. He had more stones than Roger or I had imagined. He'd run to the nearest house, banged on the door, and told the owner to call the cops because there was a crazy man loose in the woods.

God knows how the sheriff and his deputy reacted when they rolled in and caught their first glimpse of that bloody mountain of cobwebs coming out of the trees. Of course, I've heard the stories over and over. And, like I said, I've had dreams, too. And it's the dreams I see when I picture the scene in my mind's eye: *The mummy staggering backward when the patrol car lights hit him, then realizing he had nowhere to retreat because the cops were already out of the car. Sheriff Cross and Deputy Myers barking orders, drawing down. The mummy's black pit of a mouth opening like a sinkhole, and words and blood spilling out that no one ever remembered because his wrecking-ball fist was rising in the air as he lumbered forward, charging the cops. Then the sharp bark of gunfire, and the thunder of shotgun blasts, and a rain of blood and bone and flesh slapping against a straight and tall eucalyptus trunk as that bloody mountain of meat avalanched to the ground, leaving a wake of shotgunned Egyptian cotton fibers floating on the October wind like its very own ghost.*

You kill something that dead, you don't worry about it getting up again no matter what it looks like. At least, that the way Sheriff Cross and Deputy Myers saw it. They weren't going to worry about a dead kid in a Halloween costume. And that's what they saw when they looked at Charlie Steiner's corpse. That's all they saw. A dead kid in a Halloween costume.

But that didn't mean they were done for the night. Cross and

Myers worked their way through the eucalyptus grove, guns raised, not sure what they'd find when they reached Butcher's Lake. And the first thing they found was me, still diving in that black water, still looking for the girl in the princess mask. Sheriff Cross jumped into the water and grabbed me, and he always tells me I put up one hell of a fight, even though I was just a kid. I didn't want to give up the search. I told him the whole story. Practically screamed it in his face. The mummy . . . the little girl with the princess mask . . . Roger and I fighting the mummy. All of it.

The sheriff went into the lake himself that night, and he found nothing. Later a diver went in, and the next morning they dragged the bottom. But they didn't find any trace of a little girl, dead or alive.

They did find a body, just after dawn, but it wasn't underwater.

It was a boy's body, and it was hidden in a stand of cattails.

The kid was wearing a New York Yankees uniform. It was my brother Roger, and he'd been beaten to death. *Blunt object trauma* was the phrase they used.

That could have meant a wrecking-ball fist had taken him down.

Or it could have meant the mummy had used Roger's own Louisville Slugger to finish the job.

They found the Slugger just a few feet from my brother's dead body.

It's the one thing of Roger's that I still have.

Once people learned what Charlie Steiner had been up to in the weeks and months before that fateful Halloween night, they discovered he sure enough fit the m.o. for a kid who'd gone nuts enough to dress up like a Halloween boogeyman and charge a pair of fully armed cops.

Behind Charlie's house—which was just this side of the boondocks, and not too far from the dirt road that skirted the lake—Sheriff Cross discovered a path chopped through heavy brush. It was a little wider than a deer run, and it snaked up a hill. At the top of that hill was Charlie's own private temple. Google the name of this town and the word "mummy," and you'll find pictures of it. Some people say Charlie built it, that it was some kind of plywood pyramid, but I've seen it inside and out and I can tell you that's an exaggeration. It was (and still is) a simple A-frame design—that's how the pyramid stories got started—but it had four sides. And, sure, Charlie did paint Egyptian-style pictures and hieroglyphs on it back in the day, but all that stuff faded away a long time ago.

To tell the truth, there wasn't much *inside* to the place at all, then or now. One large room with a narrower loft cubby up above, the kind of place that used to sit in a far-off corner of a large property so the owner would have a hideout with just enough space to get into some trouble out of sight of the main house.

And maybe that's what the place was in the old days, when the A-frame had been in better repair. The whole property had made the slide to rack and ruin by the time Charlie's folks bought it. But in the old days—who knows? I've heard the old road along the swamp was once used by bootleggers who wanted to skirt the two-lane county highway on delivery runs. Hey, anything's possible. Histories get lost—for houses, for places . . . even for people.

But the little slice of history made by Charlie Steiner in his A-frame hideaway wasn't lost at all. No, after the incident at Butcher's Lake, the contents of Charlie's own private temple were photographed, cataloged, and filed, using the best police science of the day. Examine that stuff today and it looks like it belonged in a clubhouse for an obsessed monsterkid. The walls were papered with one-sheets from the old Universal creepers, and there were lobby cards and eight-by-tens of Lon Chaney, Jr. doing his thing as Kharis. Comic books featuring an army of Kharis wannabes, too. Paperback novels, plus a couple magazines tipping monsterkids to Hollywood makeup secrets. There was even a stack of 8mm monster movies and a cheap projector. Remember, this was 1963—a long time before VHS, let alone DVD.

There was other stuff, too. Charlie had taken Woodshop 1, 2, and 3 in high school, and he'd learned enough to build himself his very own Egyptian sarcophagus. A couple professors from the State U came out and looked at it, and they said Charlie might have made something of himself as an archeology student if he'd taken another path. They analyzed some other Egypt-ware he had in his little hideaway, too. There was a brazier that looked like a real-deal museum piece, a collection of little jars with odd-smelling oils, and a box with a bunch of leaves the guys at the local nursery couldn't identify. The profs from State U fingered the brazier as a knockoff piece of bric-a-brac from the days of the King Tut craze in the 1920s, and the carved box came from the same era, but they didn't have any more luck identifying those leaves than the nurserymen did. A rumor spread that Charlie had himself a stash of marijuana, but surely the profs would have known what that was. Even though Mickey Spillane always bumped Jack Kerouac out of the paperback racks around here, we weren't that far off the map. There's no doubt a couple of college guys would have known reefer when they saw it.

But it wasn't the drugs (or possibility of same) that kept the story pot bubbling. No. The mummy mythos did that job. Of course, there weren't too many people around here who knew much about Kharis and his eternal search for a reincarnated princess, but that changed PDQ. The local all-night TV station took a clue and started running those old movies on the *Late Late Show*, and a lot of folks stayed up watching, looking for answers. Not long after that, we had a town full of experts. You'd hear people sitting around in coffee shops discussing reincarnation, black magic, and all the rest of it. A couple of tabloids picked up the story, too. One of them ran a piece called "The Terror of Butcher Lake." That's where the name came from, and it stuck.

Sheriff Cross and Deputy Myers became mummy experts, too. Just like everyone else, they coffee'd up and watched those Universal movies on the *Late Late Show*. After the mummy marathon aired, Cross even borrowed the prints from the TV station and ran them on the big screen at the local Bijou for some of the guys from the D.A.'s office, the state shrinks, and a few other invitees. God knows what that crowd made of them. I've always wondered if they just sat there stunned, or if they ate popcorn and had themselves a ball. I especially wonder about Sheriff Cross—after all, he'd gunned down the thing. It must have been something to see its twin take loads of buckshot and keep on coming, even if it was just a Hollywood shadowshow up on the big screen.

Of course, the Hollywood part of the equation was just the sizzle for the story, not the steak. The inventory of Charlie's temple didn't stop there, because there was more locked up in his personal madhouse besides the movie stuff. There were books about black magic, too. A stack of them. And there were notebooks Charlie had written with lots of missing pages, and other books with whole chapters cut out.

But by then, it really didn't matter.

After all, Charlie Steiner was dead.

For the next few weeks, I told the story over and over. My parents didn't let me talk to any reporters, of course. It's hard to believe with the way things are now. These days people spill their guts anywhere and everywhere, but that didn't happen back then. You kept your business to yourself unless the cops told you otherwise, and that's the way we played it. I talked to a couple of doctors, and I talked to someone from the district attorney's office. Of course, I talked to Sheriff Cross, too.

I told all of them the same story. How Roger and me and the preacher's kid had come across the mummy—or Charlie Steiner. How he seemed to be working some kind of magic spell, and how he'd tossed a bound girl into the water after saying something about dreams, and wishes, and sacrifice.

It really was a simple story, and it didn't change. But every time I told it, the whole thing always came back to one question that punched a hole in the whole deal: Where was the little girl? They never did find her body in the lake. And, sure, there had been a couple young girls reported missing in neighboring towns during the preceding months, but that didn't mean anything. After all, if Charlie had tossed a missing girl into Butcher's Lake, they should have found her body. Drowned girls didn't just disappear into thin air.

Pretty soon, that girl in the princess mask was all the doctors wanted to talk about. I can't really blame them. After all, I'd been busted up pretty good that night. I had a concussion. I was still having headaches several weeks after the fact. My sentences would run off to nowhere, and my thoughts would run to places I didn't like. I wasn't sleeping too well and I admit I had problems putting things together after a while.

Not the story, but other things.

The story was always there in my head.

The story was always the same.

I knew what I saw and heard that night, and I was sure it happened just the way I remembered it.

But, in the end, it didn't matter what I thought. The doctors brought in a headshrinker from upstate, and he put the word out that I was having trouble separating reality from fantasy. Something about disassociation, or misassociation, or something like that. All this, because I stuck to my story about a little girl who no one could find. That, and the fact that sometimes I talked about a mummy, and didn't talk about Charlie Steiner at all.

Like it mattered.

Like that thing hadn't been real for me on Halloween night.

For most people, that delivered the entire episode to the closing gate. Sure, something had happened out there in the darkness, and my brother was dead. But as far as the state shrinks and the D. A. were concerned, they already had the culprit responsible for my brother's murder. That kid's name was Charlie Steiner, and Charlie wasn't talking to anyone. He'd died in his very own boogeyman suit. The undertaker didn't have to do much work on him—Charlie's belly had been hollowed out by the sheriff's shotgun, and there weren't enough guts left in his carcass to fill a whore's nylon. So they sluiced the blood off Charlie and scraped off his makeup and dressed him up in a suit that had already been a couple sizes too small on him a few years before. Didn't matter, because there was less of Charlie now. His family (such as it was) didn't even hold a funeral. They wanted Charlie in the ground double-quick, and they didn't have any money anyway. So the county took care of things, and they did a first-class, bang-up job.

I've heard that some of Charlie's wounds leaked so bad you could hear the formaldehyde sloshing around in his plywood coffin when they hauled him off to the local Potter's Field. They dropped him in a hole and covered him over. They didn't even put a tombstone on Charlie's grave, though it didn't take long for most of the kids in town to figure out where it was.

Pretty soon guys were daring each other to climb the wrought-iron fence and take a piss on old Charlie, the trick being to do the job without the terror of Butcher's Lake reaching up and pulling them down to hell by the short hairs. And not too long after that . . . well, people have short memories, don't they?

They forget.

They forgot the Terror of Butcher's Lake.

They forgot Charlie Steiner.

They forgot my brother Roger.

And life moved on.

For most people, anyway.

For most people, that's the way they like it.

The story ends, and they turn the page.

So life moved on, the way it does. I finished junior high and started high school. But everything I did, I figured Roger would have done better. It made me feel kind of like a shadow, two steps behind a guy who wasn't even there to cast it anymore.

Fresh out of high school, I got drafted. Uncle Sam sent me to Vietnam, and I stayed there four years. That was the first thing I felt I did on my own, so it didn't seem like such a bad deal to me. Of course, I couldn't leave everything behind. I took Roger's Louisville Slugger with me. Sometimes I used it on scruffy baseball fields . . . most of the larger bases had ball fields. Sometimes I took it into the jungle, but I never used it there. It was just something to help me keep away the bad dreams.

Funny to be in a jungle and dream about a desert, or a mummy, but it happened.

Over and over, night after night.

But after a couple years, I stopped dreaming about the mummy. I dreamed about the jungle instead, and the war. I was crazy enough to think that marked some kind of progress, but looking back on it maybe all I did was trade one bad dream for another.

Then I came home and slipped back into the world. I borrowed a car, drove around. Started doing some of the same things I'd done before I left. And then the dreams started to change again.

I dreamed about my brother, and Butcher's Lake.

And the girl in the princess mask.

And the mummy.

I'd wake up sweating, with my head feeling like it was ready to crack. Finally one morning I didn't go for a drive. I started looking at the newspaper classifieds instead. Figured it was time to find work, something new that would put the past behind me. For a while I even thought about college, because I could have used my G. I. Bill benefits.

But that whole plan changed one morning with a couple of knocks on the front door. It was Sheriff Cross. Older and grayer, but still built like a guy who could hold his own with just about anyone.

"Hey, Sergeant. Welcome home."

"Thanks." I knew I should have said more, since I was practically a kid the last time I'd seen him, but I couldn't think of anything else to say.

"Got a minute?" he asked. "I've got something here I'd like to show you."

"Sure."

Sheriff Cross had a new leather wallet. He flipped it open. There was a deputy sheriff's badge inside. He flipped the wallet closed and handed it to me. I took it from him.

"I think you're the guy I'm looking for," he said. "What do you think?"

"I don't need to think. I'm in."

"That's what I like to hear. We've got some paperwork to fill out. An application . . . some other stuff. You'll have six weeks up north in the training academy. You'll have to pass a physical, some other tests. You can talk to the other guys about that. They can let you know what's coming."

"Sounds good."

"I thought it would. Now let's go down to the cop shop and I'll introduce you around. This is going to work out fine."

The town had changed while I was gone.

Actually, that's an understatement.

What had really changed was the whole damn country.

It seemed like a century had passed since the lockstep America of the fifties. The sixties had definitely made their mark. And even though it was 1973, the sixties were holding on, the same way the fifties had right up until the time that JFK took that bullet down in Dallas. Even in our little corner of the world, it might as well have been the Summer of Love. Grass and acid and downers had come to town. Hair got longer; guitars got fuzzy. No one remembered Elvis or Mickey Spillane. Truth be told, most of my contemporaries didn't remember Jack Kerouac, either.

But in the heart of the town, and the heart of America, not much was different. Same stores, same people, same crew cuts on the older guy who held the keys to the store. Every now and then some kid got hired, and there were a few twentysomethings checking groceries at the market or selling TVs over at Sears or working down at the bank in the teller's cage. But they came and went. They didn't stick around long enough to wear out the linoleum or pocket the keys to the store, like the old guard had. For them, it didn't seem like ringing up corn flakes was a lifelong ambition, or moving a weekly quota of Magnavox consoles, or stamping deposits in the Christmas Club accounts. No. The twentysomethings would catch a whiff of sweeter possibilities and move on, and the old guys would grind out their cigs and put up a HELP WANTED sign, and some fresh face would take the bait and give the forty-hour grind a test-drive while the old guard grumbled about training another kid who wasn't going to stay the course.

So, in that way, things were pretty much the same, it was just that the faces changed more often. Tote things in those terms, and you'd say that all that had really changed were the clothes and the haircuts and the vices. But around the corners, the town had gotten a little frayed.

Take Charlie Steiner's house. Charlie's mother had passed away when I was in high school. Then one day his father packed up his pickup and left the place behind. The house sat vacant the whole time I was in 'Nam, and it was the "20" for one of the first calls I rolled on after Ben Cross pinned a badge on my chest.

I still remember that night. Wind rustling through overgrown trees around the place as I pulled up the drive, no lights inside but a fire in the fireplace that cast flickering ribbons against windows dull with grime. I killed my lights as I cut off the dirt road that went out toward Butcher's Lake, and I killed the patrol cruiser's engine ten feet after that. We'd had reports of stoners using the place as a crash pad, and I didn't want to leave them a way out if they had wheels.

The walk to the house was a long one. Not because I was worried about what I'd find inside. For the first time since the jungle I felt edgy. I mean, really edgy. I had a .38 strapped to my leg, but what I wanted in my hand was an M-16, or even Roger's Louisville Slugger. Something familiar, something I could trust. It was a weird feeling, as if yesterday's baggage were ready to bury me as deep as Charlie Steiner, right along with the new future I was building. I felt like I was on Charlie's turf, and even though I knew he was six feet under in Potter's Field, that night he cast a long shadow.

Lucky for me, Charlie's shadow got shorter once I took charge of the situation. I banged through the front door and hit the occupants with my flashlight beam. A couple of the stoners rabbited through a back window, and two girls spread out on a mattress in front of the fireplace were so toasted on downers they didn't even wake up. It was almost comical. Right away I forgot all about Charlie. I nudged those girls and shook them, and after about ten minutes I even got them up walking, but it was tough to manage the both of them. Before I could do anything about it one would wander off and find her way back to the mattress, and when I went to grab her, the other stumbled out the door and fell asleep in the weeds in front of the place.

I called it in to Jack Morrison, who was on duty back at the cop shop. He said he'd roll out and give me a hand with the girls. In the meantime, he told me to check out the rest of the place. Right away I knew what he meant.

He didn't mean the house.

He meant Charlie Steiner's pyramid.

By that time I'd cooled out. Still, you never know what you'll find, and I'd tangled enough with Charlie in my dreams that I wasn't looking forward to a walk up his own personal madman's trail. But it was my job. So I checked behind the main house and found the little deer run path that led up to the A-frame. No lights out there except my flashlight, and the wind had died. If there had been a noise, I certainly would have heard it. A mouse skittering across the porch. A mummy's padded footfall. Anything. I would have heard it.

But I didn't hear anything that night.

I walked up to the A-frame.

I swung open the door.

I didn't know what to expect.

My flashlight beam skittered across the floor and over the walls. But it was just an empty room. There was nothing there at all. And that taught me something . . . at least for a while. Even though it was a lesson that didn't stick, I held onto it—and that moment—for a few months.

For a while, it convinced me everything would be okay.

For a while, I actually believed that dreams were ephemeral.

About a month later, the sheriff called me up on a Sunday morning and asked me to go to breakfast down at the diner. Ben told me he'd bought the old Steiner place, and was thinking he'd fix it up and turn it into a rental. Maybe even look into moving into the place himself when he hit retirement age and was ready to get a little farther out of town. He said it seemed like a good investment, and that he'd make some money if nothing else.

"Sounds like a sweet deal," I said. "I'm going to bank as much of my check as I can this year. Maybe one of these days I'll have enough to start looking around for a place myself."

"That's a good plan," Ben said. "Can't be easy being under your parents' roof again."

"Well, I'm probably going to grab a studio apartment after I get a few more checks, but paying rent will definitely cut down on the savings. Can't have it both ways, though."

"Maybe I can help you out with that."

"How do you figure?"

Ben took a sip of coffee. "The Steiner place needs a lot of work. I'm looking for someone to help me out with it. Way I see it, you could live there rent-free. Clear the brush around the place. Do some carpentry. Some painting. I'd come in on the weekends and help out. How's that sound?"

I didn't know what to say, but I knew I had to say something.

"Well . . . hey, it's hard to turn down free rent."

Ben nodded and set down his coffee cup. "Look, I know you have a history with Charlie Steiner, and this was his house. Maybe this isn't the best move for you. If you have any second thoughts—"

"I know what you're saying, Ben . . . but I'll probably always have second thoughts. But I can't bury the past, and maybe I shouldn't try. Maybe what I need to do is confront it. You know, come to terms with it. And maybe working on that house will help me do that."

"Okay . . . but if it doesn't work out—"

"Then we'll cross that bridge when we come to it."

We shook on the deal, and that was that. I moved into the Steiner house, and fortunately the night with the crash-pad girls was still fresh in my mind. I told myself everything would be okay, just as it had been that night, and if it wasn't . . . well, I'd find a way to tell Ben that it wasn't going to work, even if that was the last thing I wanted to do after the conversation we'd had.

The first week, I lay awake at night listening to every creak and moan the old house made, and it seemed like those old fears had moved in with me. But eventually, spending so much time in that old house made the worries I'd had about moving into the place seem as out-of-style as a teenager with a crew cut. And it got easier once I started to work on the place. I took one thing at a time, and focused in on each project. A few weeks went by, and I'd cleared all the brush around the house, even chopped a wider path up to Charlie's pyramid so I could get up there with a wheelbarrow and some tools. I figured I'd use that pyramid as practice before I started on the main house.

To tell the truth, at first I was tempted to talk to Ben about knocking the pyramid down. After all, that had really been Charlie's place. But if part of this deal was about confronting Charlie Steiner, then I knew I couldn't do that. So I decided to work on it first.

I replaced a few broken windows, then gave the place a coat of paint inside and out. The further I got with work on the A-frame, the less I thought about Charlie and the past. Instead, maybe for the first time ever, I started to think about myself and what lay ahead of me. I didn't know what that was going to be. Sometimes it was scary to think about it and sometimes it was exciting, but in the end it didn't matter.

In the end, I didn't think about myself for very long at all.

I was working with Ben Cross the night the call came in. Since starting at the cop shop I'd been on day shift with the sheriff, and by this time he was breaking me in to work swings. That way, I'd have my mornings free and could work on the house before clocking in at three, and Ben could come by and do some work of his own after he clocked out without having to worry about crowding my space. That way we could double-shift projects during the week. The plan was to work together on weekends on stuff that took two pairs of hands, and we'd get the place in shape faster. It made sense, and I knew going in that I'd take swing shift over graveyards any day. I'd pulled those shifts a few times and they made for a long night of patrolling empty streets, rattling doorknobs, and (mostly) trying to stay awake until the sun came up.

It was July. Not too hot for that time of year, with the possibility of a summer storm blowing in. It was around ten p.m. and neither one of us had had any dinner. We were talking about where to catch a bite when the main line rang. Ben wasn't on the phone more than a minute. And he didn't say much besides "yeah" or "uh-huh" before he finished with the important one: "I'll check it out."

He cradled the receiver and shot me a look.

"What's the deal?" I asked.

"You know that guy who owns the dairy farm out by the county two-lane?"

"You mean Vince Kaehler?"

"Yeah, that's the one. His ranch backs up against Butcher's Lake on the north side. He found a stretch of downed barbed-wire this afternoon. Turned out some of his stock got loose. A couple cows wandered up the dirt road that skirts the lake, and Vince spent the evening rounding them up. He just got back to the house after fixing his fence. Says he saw a campfire down there by the water, heard some loud rock 'n' roll and some screaming, like a party was going on."

"Loud rock 'n' roll? He actually said that?"

"Well, what he really said was *goddamn loud hippie music*, but that's close enough."

"Yeah. Well . . . Vince is a Merle Haggard kind of guy."

"Uh-huh." Cross smiled. "And he didn't say *party*. He said *orgy*."

"You're kidding."

"No . . . not even a little bit."

Quiet hung there between us, but just for a second.

"So you want to roll with me on this one?"

"Sure, boss," I said, and we strapped on the hardware.

Of course, at that point it hardly seemed worth it. I mean, strapping on our guns or rolling on the call at all. I figured I was in for an instant replay of crash-pad night at Charlie Steiner's. Maybe I'd even find those same two stoner girls who'd been asleep on the mattress in front of Charlie's fireplace that night, only tonight they'd be snoozing on a couple of air mattresses out in the middle of Butcher's Lake.

Man, was I ever wrong.

Dead wrong.

I killed the lights before I pulled up to the rusty guardrail by the eucalyptus grove. The night really wasn't that much different than that Halloween back in '63 when I'd met up with Charlie Steiner. But I wasn't really thinking about Charlie on this night.

Part of that had to do with living in his house. It seemed the creep factor around the place had reached the point of diminishing returns, as if the work I'd done there had exorcised his spirit. The other part was easier to explain, because it didn't have anything to do with a ghost of the past—it was all sensory input and gut reaction as Ben Cross rolled down his window and a couple specific varieties of noise spilled up that black little path that led to Butcher's Lake.

Laughter. Lots of it. And all of it male.

And music. A transistor cranked up to ten, playing Iron Butterfly.

"Goddamn," Ben said. "It *is* hippie music."

I couldn't argue. I couldn't return the joke, either.

Because I wasn't listening to the music. The sound of that laughter reached down and grabbed me by the balls. It was over the edge and more than a little mad, reminding me of party sounds I'd once heard in the jungles of Vietnam. We'd run across a village another platoon had raided looking for Cong. We'd come upon them at dusk, tipping back bottles of Cutty Sark, partying with VC soldiers who were dead and others who wished they were.

Those weren't good memories.

And the laughter I heard that night at Butcher's Lake brought them back.

Of course, I didn't mention any of that to Ben Cross.

There was only time to size up the situation and move forward.

That's what we did. We didn't take the trail through the eucalyptus grove. We figured we'd cut around to the dirt access road that led to the lake and block it with the cruiser, just in case the laughing crew had wheels. That way we'd pen them in, because there was only one way out of there.

I backed up, then started down the dirt road. I thumbed the lights, pushing in the knobbed rod until the headlights died. That left the parking lights, which were just bright enough to get me down the road. I knew where I was going: this was the same road I took to the Steiner house. When I hit the forked cutoff down to the lake itself I knew I'd gone far enough, because there was a solid-panel Dodge van parked about halfway down the fork, alongside a couple of choppers.

"Bikers," Ben said. "Shit."

We ran the plates. The Dodge had been reported stolen three days before, more than two hundred miles away. The choppers were registered to a couple of bikers with gang affiliations and rap sheets a mile long. With my Spidey senses already tingling, this didn't surprise me. I don't know if Ben had a clue before the hard news came over the squawk-box, but he didn't look happy. Any way you sliced it, the idea we were in for an easy time of it rousting a bunch of partying teenagers had definitely gone south in a big way.

We got out of the car.

That laughter was still there, hanging on the wind like a coming storm.

Ben said, "Watch yourself."

I said, "You do the same, boss."

That about covered it. Cross unlocked the shotgun from the rack. He jacked a shell into the chamber. My left hand slid toward my holster, and I unsnapped the leather strap that ran over my .38.

Then we walked around the Dodge van and moved into the darkness.

The young woman screamed just about the time we spotted the campfire.

She was down by the water. Naked, wearing nothing but mud. The bikers stood between her and the fire, backlit by the flames. And since one of them wasn't wearing his pants, it wasn't hard to figure out what had been going on.

Mr. Bare Ass brayed like a billy goat. Then he said: "You don't want to play anymore, babe, then we ain't got no further use for you."

His hand came up, rising like a fistful of molten lava.

It jerked out, shot back. Then repeated the action.

The woman screamed again. The bikers laughed, and her hand shot out, slapping Bare Ass across the face.

"Whoa. She's a live one!"

"Not for long," Bare Ass said. "This bitch is just another rack of ribs ready for the grill."

"Burn, baby, burn!" one of the bikers yelled.

Those words sent a chill up my spine. Just that fast another biker raised his fist. More molten fire, this handful so bright it made me squint.

That's when I realized what the bikers had in their hands.

They'd sparked a bunch of road flares.

They were using them to herd the young woman into the water.

The flare jabbed against her arm, and she screamed like she'd swallowed a bucket of brimstone. Ben was way ahead of me, advancing toward the fire with the shotgun shouldered and the barrel trained on the bikers.

"County Sheriff!" he shouted. "Freeze. Now!"

I knew they wouldn't. Ben probably knew it too. And to tell the truth in that moment we had as much going against us as we had going for us. The pack started to turn, and I had the feeling at least one of them was going to end up with something more than molten fire in his hand. At the same time, I doubted Ben was going to let loose with the street howitzer unless he absolutely had to—after all, the woman was right in the middle of the pack, and the scattergun would sure enough do a job on her, too.

The best thing going in that moment was that none of the bikers had thought to grab the woman and use her for a shield. Apart from the gap between two of them, she was almost standing behind them. Two of them were holding burning flares, and one of them let his loose, throwing it in Ben's direction. In the time it took Ben to sidestep the flare, I drew my .38. The fire was between us and the mob; the flares were blazing; there was light. But there were shadows too, and night pouring thick around the edges of every damn one of them, and there was no way to judge everything without making a dozen guesses that could be dead wrong.

One sound took all that second-guessing away.

I heard a .45 chambering a round, and I let loose.

The .38 bucked in my hand. Once. Twice. One of the bikers fell like a slaughterhouse steer. Another stumbled a few steps and dropped on his knees in the campfire before pitching face-first across the flames. That cleared enough ground to see that the young woman wasn't in the picture anymore. Just about the time I thought we were about to tighten the cinches on the deal, another shot rang out.

It wasn't mine.

It was the .45. I hadn't dropped the man who held it after all.

The biker fired again. This time, the sound hit me just as someone laid a red-hot poker across my shoulder. At least, that was the way it felt.

The .38 dropped out of my hand.

By then, it didn't matter.

Because Ben Cross let loose with the shotgun.

A couple ticks of the second hand, and the whole thing was as over as over can be.

* * *

At least, we thought it was.

Four of the bikers lay on the ground. Still. One of them face down in the fire. Smoke billowed up around him, and he was finished. I didn't give him a second glance, because I was only thinking of one thing.

The woman.

Had to be she'd gone into the water to escape the gunfight. It had been the only way out.

I dropped my gun belt and kicked off my shoes. I didn't say a word to Ben. Didn't have to. The sheriff was standing next to Mr. Bare Ass, who was the last biker standing. Only now he was down on his knees, with his hands behind his head. Ben had the shotgun near the biker's head, and I know he wanted to pull the trigger. After what the bastard had done, he sure enough deserved it. But all Ben did was touch that shotgun barrel against the biker's cheek, and he let out a howl as the hot metal scorched him. Then Ben put a knee to his spine, and he was flat on the ground as the sheriff snatched the cuffs from his gun-belt and proceeded to truss up the turkey.

I was headed for the water by that point. The smoke from the dead-man fire drifted between me and the lake, giving the heavy moon above a black cataract. But I was through it in a second, and the cataract was gone, and a familiar white glow pooled on the still water before me.

Black water.

And beyond the expanse of darkness, out there where the moon's reflection floated, a glimmer of movement.

I heard a splash, and spotted the woman.

I dove into the darkness.

I swam towards the light.

It had to be her. That's what I told myself as my hands cut furrows in that cold water and I stroked toward the moon's reflection.

By that time, you'd think I would have been flashbacking like a son of a bitch. Seeing visions of a little girl taped up in a plastic Halloween mask. Seeing her disappear underwater all over again. Only difference from that Halloween night back in '63 was that I wasn't a kid anymore . . . but the girl in the water wasn't a kid, either.

Other than that, my heart was pounding exactly as it had ten years before—same lake, same hope, same fear, same desperation. That's how far I'd put Charlie Steiner's memory behind me . . . or maybe it was just how deep Charlie was buried.

At least that's what I thought. That's what I told myself.

Whatever the case, I wouldn't give the past a window. I felt no pain; didn't even feel the bullet wound trenched in my shoulder. Everything that was with me was in my head. The things that had just happened most of all—each one of them was a flashbulb pop that waited for me every time I closed my eyes and dipped my head into that water.

Ben walking with the shotgun.

The naked woman getting prodded with the flares.

The gunfight.

The corpses on the beach.

The man facedown in the fire, and the stink of burning flesh.

And then I'd gulp a clean breath, open my eyes, catch my bearings, and see that spot of moon on the water, and the streak of light that stretched across the lake between it and me—

—and the woman. There she was. Paddling away from me, arms splashing the water in hard slaps, a black wake left behind by her kicking feet.

She had to be terrified. That was it. Had to be she didn't even know what had happened back at the beach. If that were true, she was still trying to get away. Hell, she might think I was one of the bikers, and—

She coughed. Hard. Like she'd swallowed water. Again, as if she was spitting up a bellyful.

"Hey!" I yelled. "It's over! It's okay. I'm with the sheriff. Tread water. Stay in one spot. We'll take care of you!"

Another cough. A few frantic splashes in a streak of moonlight.

She was going under.

My head was above water as I stroked forward. Watching, keeping my eye on the woman so I'd know exactly where to dive if it came to that.

A gasp for breath, and then her head went under.

And her arms followed. And her fingers.

That's when the past slammed me hard, right between the eyes. And it wasn't the woman disappearing beneath the surface of the lake. It was a sound, from behind me.

I knew it was only the campfire, stirring in a gust of wind.

Or the rising wind carving a path through those old stands of eucalyptus.

I knew it was. It had to be.

Because it wasn't a mummy, swinging his wrecking-ball fist, roaring in the darkness.

It wasn't a mummy, cursing loneliness, and dreams, and wishes, and magic . . . and fate.

So I ignored it, and I swam fast, and then I started diving.

Underwater, there was silence. My heart pounded with desperation, but there was nothing else to do. I dove once, twice. And the second time down I thought my fingers were passing through a tangle of weeds. At first I did. But it had to be the woman's hair. Because as I pulled my hand free, the strands were pulled in the other direction, and a torrent of bubbles came up at me from below, brushing my face as they rose to the surface.

I wished I could gulp one down. My chest was burning, but I pushed further, deeper. She had to be close. But there was nothing but black. Nothing to see at all. My hands pulled at the water, as if straining to part a pair of locked doors. And this time I touched flesh, and my fingers passed over lips and an open mouth.

And next I found a hand.

It seemed small. Not like a child's hand. But frail, like something you'd brush against in an old woman's coffin.

For a moment I thought it was something long dead.

But I grabbed it, and five fingers closed around my own.

And we rose to the surface together.

The whole department ran on adrenaline for the next few days as we put the investigation together. Everyone pretty much had to double-shift it, questioning the perps and doing the crime scene and handling anything else that came our way.

The crime scene itself wasn't much to sweat over. We were prepared to bring in a drug-sniffing dog from upstate if we had to, but the bikers weren't that clever. Once we got a look, we knew we'd have an open-and-shut case. There were several baggies of cocaine inside the van's spare tire, more in the gas tank of one of the choppers. A couple of sawed-off shotguns rolled up in a rug in the back of the van. Besides that, it turned out that there were two .45s down by the campsite, both which had been in the hands of convicted felons. The biker who went facedown in the fire had a .357 Magnum tucked into his pants, and Ben and I both knew we were lucky he hadn't managed to pull that cannon. So even without rape charges, and the double-shot possibles of kidnapping and attempted murder, we had those boys cold.

At least, we had the one who was still alive.

For his part, Mr. Bare Ass lied up one side and down the other. About everything. Swore he didn't know anything about the drugs, or the guns. Swore he was just along for the ride with some friends of his who maybe once in a while got a little bit out of hand. All he wanted to do was party. That was his sole mission in life.

The only thing he'd admit straight up was that, sure, he liked to smoke grass. Who the hell didn't? And the girl? Hell, she was down by the lake. That's where they found her. She was nineteen, maybe twenty . . . just another stray. She wandered up to their campfire, shivering, covered in mud and naked as a little spring daisy. Connect the dots, and she was just some misplaced flower child who got herself dosed up on acid and was left behind on life's long and lonesome highway. Wasn't that a pity. And what the hell were they supposed to do, with some naked chick showing up like that? They weren't Boy Scouts, and this wasn't the annual jamboree. So they gave her a blanket and a couple pulls on a bottle of screw-top red, and then she took herself a few hits of herb. What was supposed to happen next? Didn't the same thing happen, everywhere? Nature took its course.

When he finished up his tale, Ben hit the STOP button on the little cassette recorder we used for interviews. I escorted Mr. Bare Ass back to his cell, then met up with Ben in his office.

"That guy couldn't shut himself up if you gave him a rubber plug and a roll of duct tape," Ben said.

"Yeah . . . but when I think about what they did to that girl. Man. Sometimes I just don't know. Talk about a guy who deserves a beating. Walking him back to his cell, it was all I could do to stop myself from ramming his head into the wall. Take my badge if you want to, but I really wanted to knock the teeth right out of his mouth."

"Oh, he'll have his beating coming . . . and worse. You can bank on that. I'm sure he's got a full-course menu of pain and humiliation ahead of him."

"Where?"

"In prison." Ben smiled. "They've got plenty of experts in there."

He grabbed his keys off the table.

"Now let's go check on that girl."

And that's what we did.

Walking into that hospital room with *Jane Doe* taped on the door, it was almost like seeing her for the first time. The night I'd rescued her was a blur, and there were really only two things I remembered about her—her eyes, which were wide and terrified. And the trail of bloody burns the bikers had left on her body with those road flares, as if they'd wanted to leave her with a set of brands that marked a trail of pain she'd never forget.

Ben had already called an ambulance by the time I got her out of the lake. We carried her up the access road and met the paramedics where we'd blocked the road with the police cruiser. Maybe two minutes later, the ambulance doors closed and she was gone. That was the last we saw of her until the hospital visit.

A couple days rest had done her some good. She actually smiled at us as we came through the door. We talked for a while, just chit-chat. *Nice day . . . nice room . . . oh, you've got a great view here . . . and look at that little birdbath out on the patio. That's nice.* I was surprised to find how pretty she was. Especially her eyes. They were dark pools, deep brown, and they shone beneath long bangs that were the same color.

Ben asked her some questions. He was patient. He had to be, because she really didn't have any answers. After a while she said, "I'm sorry I can't be more help. I'm still kind of tired. The doctors say things might be better after I get some rest."

"Okay," Ben said. "You take care of yourself. If there's anything you think of, just give us a call." He handed her his card. "Anything you need, too. We'll be right here if you need us."

After that, there wasn't much else for Ben to say.

But she had something to say, and she looked at me when she said it.

"They tell me you saved my life, and I remember that."

I nodded.

"It's the one thing I do remember. I didn't forget you."

She stared at me.

"I won't ever forget you."

She didn't blink. I was about to say something stupid, like I was just doing my job, but then she said something else.

Something I'll never forget.

Her eyes were bright pools beneath those dark bangs as she spoke. "I tell myself there are other things I'll remember," she said. "Right now I'm waiting for them, like I was waiting for you. Underwater."

And maybe that's the way it was. I didn't know. There was a lot we didn't know about the young woman in the hospital room with *Jane Doe* on the door. Some of the hospital staffers thought she knew more than she was saying. Not so much the doctors, but a couple of the nurses definitely felt that way. One of them even said the girl was in on the dope deal, and that she was just putting on an act until she could get free and clear. Ben and I didn't buy any of that, and for one simple reason—our Jane Doe just didn't act like any biker chick we'd ever seen.

The doctors weren't much help. One dealt the *amnesia* card on the table; another wouldn't even use the word. He said that diagnosis was out of his league. And, who knew, it could have been that foul-mouthed biker wasn't far off the mark. Maybe the young woman was some cast-off flower child, left by the side of the road after a literal and figurative bad trip of epic proportions. Or maybe the bikers had snatched her off some college campus, dosed her up and kept her that way until she couldn't even see straight. We could have speculated until the wheels came off, but no amount of guessing was going to get us to the truth.

Me, I found another answer. It came in a dream . . . or it might have been a nightmare. I wasn't sure which.

It was 1963 again. That same Halloween night. I was a kid all over again, battling a mummy, trying to save a little girl. She hit the water, and I dove in. Only this time, things ended differently.

This time, underwater, I reached out and found a hand. It seemed small, but not like a child's hand. I took hold of it and kicked to the surface, and I came up in sunlight.

In that moment, things changed.

We weren't kids, either of us.

It was a woman I'd saved, and I was a man.

I carried her to shore. We were all alone.

"I didn't forget you," she said, looking up at me. "I won't ever forget you."

And then our eyes closed, and our lips met, and we were like that, together. The wind rose around us. I could smell the clean, cold scent of the eucalyptus grove, hear the dry leaves rattling in the breeze. And when our lips parted, I felt calm . . . as calm as I'd felt in a long, long time.

Then I looked behind me and saw the dead thing standing at the edge of the eucalyptus grove, watching us. Charlie Steiner smiled, and blood bubbled over his lips. He was still dressed up in his Halloween clothes. Still playing the part of the thing he wanted to be . . . and the thing that would get him what he wanted.

His words were slurred around the bloody remains of his tongue. "It takes a long time for a dead girl to grow into a princess," Charlie said, "and this one is mine."

Then he raised his bloody hand.

And he started forward.

My shoulder healed up fast, but that dream stuck with me. Sometimes it made it tough to be in the Steiner house, though I tried to stay busy and wear myself out with work. I tore out drywall, started on the electrical. That kept me going. A lot of nights, exhaustion kept the dreams at bay. Other nights I'd go to bed, and I wouldn't sleep at all. I'd listen to the wind outside, waiting for a sound that didn't belong. And when I did sleep (and sleep deeply), it didn't turn out well, because Charlie Steiner was waiting for me.

"She's my dream," he'd say, his mouth bubbling blood. "Not yours. Mine."

And so I'd get up and work. I'd walk around the house, listening to the floorboards creak, wondering if they'd creaked that way for Charlie when he was on the road to insanity. That wasn't a good way to think. Sometimes I'd grab Roger's old Louisville Slugger and use it to take out some drywall. That made a mess, but at least it worked off some energy, and it felt good. Then I'd clean it up and do some real work. And, eventually, I'd sleep.

Sometimes working with the Slugger, I'd imagine that I bashed in a wall and found the missing pages from Charlie Steiner's notebook tucked between the wall studs. I'd wonder what those missing pages would say, and what they'd tell me, if they told me anything.

I'd wonder if it would be anything I didn't already know.

I didn't think so.

See, by then I understood Charlie Steiner pretty well.

There wasn't really anything I could do about any of it. I didn't think talking would be a good idea. I wasn't good at talking. The way I was built, I figured there wasn't much to do but ride it out.

So that's what I tried to do. But maybe I wasn't the only one pushing my way through a bad patch. I didn't see Jane Doe again after that day at the hospital, but I heard a lot about her. For a few weeks her picture was in all the papers. The story even made the national news a couple of nights running. But no one came forward to ID her. No relatives, no friends, no co-workers. It was as if she'd come from nowhere.

Or out of a dream.

That's when the gossip geared up. A tabloid ran an article, "The Lady in the Lake." That got them through the first week. By the second, they'd dredged up the old Terror of Butcher's Lake stories about Charlie Steiner. A few of them even mentioned me. They ran with that until the story cooled off, and then they found something else.

Of course, that wasn't the end of it around here. The local chatter started up, and it was running strong by the time the young woman was released from the hospital. Some of the nurses had taken to calling her "Ananka" behind her back. And maybe she'd heard them. Maybe that's why she took the name "Ana Jones."

Anyway, Ana walked out of the hospital. She walked into town and found a studio apartment with some money a few of the doctors had raised for her. Pretty soon she was working at a roadhouse out by the state highway. A place called The Double Shot.

She worked swings, same as I did. Mornings she had to herself. Nights, too. Sometimes I'd drive by The Double Shot toward the end of my shift, thinking I'd stop in and say hello. See how she was doing. Then I'd remember what she said to me, and how her words had frozen me up. I'd remember the look in her eyes, and I'd remember Charlie Steiner's words. And I wouldn't stop. I don't even know why, exactly, but I wouldn't.

I felt like I had to figure things out before I could talk to her again. Sometimes it seemed things were coming full circle, and other times I felt like I was just going around and around like a cat chasing its own tail. Maybe life (and fate) were doing the same things. Which is another way of saying that the wind blew in different directions, and it definitely had me in its grip.

I don't know how those times were for Ana. For me, the nights remained the worst part. Even if I didn't dream, Charlie Steiner was waiting there behind my eyelids. Some nights Ana was waiting there, too.

Things stayed that way for a while. Some mornings I'd get up early and go for a run on the dirt road that ran along the lakeshore. Sometimes on my way back I'd take that familiar cutoff down to the water, just to stare out at the lake. I'd listen to the wind whispering through the eucalyptus, and try to convince myself that there was nothing there at all.

Sometimes I'd take that road and find that there was already someone else down by the water.

Sitting, watching, listening.

Ana Jones.

I didn't talk to her.

I left her alone.

I left most everyone alone.

Things settled into a routine. Not a pleasant one, but a routine. Six weeks like that, maybe seven. I still wasn't sleeping much, and I wasn't really trying anymore. It just didn't feel right, and like I said, I didn't like what was waiting in my head when I tried to sleep.

So I'd bang nails during the day, replacing dry rot around the doors and windows. Then I'd go to work at the cop shop. Walked in one afternoon, and Ben Cross was waiting for me.

"How's your shoulder?" he asked.

"Ancient history, Ben. The bullet didn't dig deep. I'm all healed up."

"Really?"

"Well, I don't sleep on it, if that's what you mean. But, hell, Ben . . . I'm fine. It's not like I ended up face down in a campfire, like that biker did."

"Let me be straight with you: I'm thinking you should take yourself a couple weeks off. Rest. Relax. Rehab. We'll take a break from working on the house. I won't come around, and you won't bang nails."

"C'mon, Ben—"

"No arguments. Go to the gym. Drink some beer and eat some barbecue. Get laid. Do whatever it is you young guys do these days."

"Really, Ben. It's no problem. If I'm screwing something up, I'll fix it. Just give me some time."

"If you were screwing up, we'd be having a different conversation."

"Fair enough."

"The thing is, I don't want you screwing anything up . . . and I think we're getting to a point where you might."

"Okay. That's plain enough. But—"

Ben put up a hand. "No 'buts.' Two weeks off, pardner. Sick leave. You get paid, and you hang on to your vacation time. As far as I'm concerned, that's doctor's orders, and the clock starts ticking right now."

"All right, boss."

"That sounds better," Ben said, and we shook on it. "Like I said,

I'd better not catch you pounding any goddamn nails, either. Get out of that goddamn house."

Of course, I didn't take Ben's advice. I went right back to the Steiner place. I holed up there like a grizzly with a toothache. It wasn't the best move I've ever made. I might as well have barricaded the door.

Around that time, my phone started ringing more often. I didn't answer it. Ben and I had hooked up a police radio in the house, so I knew it wasn't someone calling from the cop shop. If Ben wanted me, he would have called on the squawk-box.

For my part, I didn't really want to talk to anyone . . . especially another tabloid reporter. I was even avoiding my family. You could get away with that in those days. It was easier to check out of the game for a while. People didn't walk around with phones in their pockets. The phone hung on a wall in your house, or sat on a table. It was easy to ignore. If it rang and you didn't answer it, you'd have no idea who called. No caller ID. No muss, no fuss.

My phone didn't ring a lot, just enough to tell me there was someone out there who wanted to talk to me. Just enough to tell me they were going to keep trying.

And then one day it didn't ring at all.

It was a Saturday. I'd been off for a full week, and I was trying to figure out what to toss on the barbecue.

That was the evening Ana Jones knocked on my front door.

"Take a walk with me?" she said. "I'd like to talk."

So we walked. It was a crisp night coming on after a sunny day, the kind of day that makes you think of spring more than fall. Ana wore a long dark skirt, sandals, and a flannel shirt over a tight top—the kind dancers wore. As we walked the road toward Butcher's Lake, sunlight trickled through the branches and shone against her long black hair. Wherever she went that night, I would have followed.

She wanted to go down to Butcher's. I wouldn't have suggested going there. I would have thought she'd never want to see the place again, but she said she needed to. So we went down to the lake, neither of us saying a word. I was carrying a couple of blankets and a bottle of wine. I thought the wine was the least I could do for putting her off, because I was sure it was Ana who'd been calling. Besides that, I figured a little wine might help loosen my tongue. Hell, I probably could have used a case of wine and a shoebox full of dynamite, too. But there were things I needed to know. I didn't know if Ana had the answers, but I knew I needed to find some before I skidded into a really bad place.

We sat, and we watched the sunlight on the dark water. That wasn't exactly a conversation starter, considering. So I took out my knife, flicked the corkscrew out, and opened the wine.

The sun went to orange and started to set.

"I guess I forgot cups," I said.

"That's okay." Ana smiled. "I think there's enough history between us to share a bottle."

It was easier after the bottle went back and forth a couple of times. Ana talked about her job, and the town, and what it was like settling in. She even talked about the gossip that was going around.

"Have you heard the latest? Some people are saying you shouldn't have saved me. They say I'm a witch, and that I would have sunk to the bottom of that lake like a stone."

"People." I stared across the water. "That's why I like to be alone."

"Yeah. I kind of figured that out."

"Look, it's nothing personal. I've been having a tough time of it. Nothing like you've had . . . but it hasn't been good for me lately. Ever since that night with the bikers some old ghosts have come knocking at the door. I'm trying to handle them."

She handed me the bottle, and when I took it she caught my arm and my gaze.

"Am I one of those ghosts?"

"I don't know, Ana. You're the only person who can answer that one."

"I wish I could. Sometimes I think I'm so close to figuring things out. I feel like I'm scratching at the surface of a real memory. I wish I'd never read any of those tabloid articles or listened to any of the gossip. It gets in there, too . . . and sometimes I can almost see some of it happening—even that whole thing on Halloween night all those years ago. I wonder if I really could have been there. And sometimes I have these nightmares—"

"I have a few of those, too."

"About Charlie Steiner?"

"Yeah."

I handed back the bottle and she tipped it against her lips—a short, sharp swallow. "Last night was the worst. I dreamed of Egypt. I was standing near a pyramid, and Charlie was there . . . fresh off the autopsy slab. He didn't say anything. Every time he tried, blood spilled out of his mouth and splattered the sand like rain. But it didn't matter that Charlie couldn't speak. There were a dozen dead roses in his hands, and I knew what he wanted. I couldn't get away from him. I tried, but he just kept coming. And then he cornered me, and he peeled the petals off one of the roses with a three-fingered hand, and he pressed them against my lips, and he opened my mouth with a pair of withered fingers, and—"

"Don't torture yourself. It was just a nightmare."

"You really believe that?"

I looked at her, realizing what I'd said. We might have laughed then, and maybe we should have, but we couldn't.

Something else happened.

She put down the bottle.

And she reached out and took my hand.

"This isn't easy," Ana said.

"For me, either," I said.

"You know, sometimes I think that maybe they're right. The ones who say I popped out of some warlock's bubbling cauldron. Maybe that's the reason I took that princess's name, or at least part of it. Like the poet said: *Such stuff as dreams are made on*. Sometimes I think it could be true, and I'm just a shadow of someone else's dream. I was nowhere for such a long time. Forever, almost. And then you came along and—"

"Don't read too much into me. I'm no knight in shining armor."

"Maybe not. But if it is true—and let's just say it is—then you're the one who tried to save me the first time around and paid a price for it. You lost your brother. And you're the one who came back all those years later and did the job the second time, and you're paying still."

I didn't say anything. I looked across the water.

"And I just want you to know. I have to tell you: When you swam out there and took my hand, that's when life started for me. I was underwater, and you saved me. But part of me feels like I'm still underwater. And I'm never going to get to the surface unless you pull me through."

Her grip tightened, and it was strong.

"See, it doesn't matter who I was," she said. "It doesn't matter at all. It only matters who I'm going to be."

She moved closer then, and my arm slid around her shoulder. We kissed, and our kiss deepened. And it was so quiet out there by the lake. The wind was still, and so was the water, and the tall eucalyptus covered us in long shadows.

It was so quiet. I could almost hear her heart beating. I could feel it beneath my hand. And in that moment I wouldn't have cared if the worst of it was true. It wouldn't have mattered if Ana was a witch, or a dead thing born in Egypt five thousand years ago. Because in that moment I believed what Ana believed, that none of it mattered, that what really mattered was ahead of us.

I held her tight, and I held her close, and I told myself I'd pull her through.

I wasn't going to let her go.

That was what she wanted.

That was what I wanted, too.

I didn't work on the house the next day. To tell the truth, I didn't do much of anything. I had a big breakfast and then I went for a walk, following the dirt road until it connected up with a county two-lane on the other side of the lake. I thought about what Ana had said, and I thought about the past and the future. Then I came back to the house, ate lunch, and fell asleep.

No dreams came my way, and that was a very good thing.

At dusk, a knock came on the door. I got up, running a hand through my hair, and went to answer it, expecting that Ana had cut out of work early and come back.

I opened the door, and a mummy was standing there.

A small one.

He held out a paper bag and said, "Trick or treat."

I didn't have any Halloween candy, so I grabbed a bag of cookies out of the cupboard and gave a few of them to the kid in the mummy costume. He thanked me, and I watched him walk across the yard, alone. He made me think of Roger somehow, and that last night we'd gone trick-or-treating so long ago. For a second I wanted to call out to him and ask his name, but I didn't. Still, it felt right somehow, remembering Roger. It felt good.

I closed the door. I didn't know how the date had slipped by me, but the circle had come around again. But for the first time in as long as I could remember, Halloween seemed different. It wasn't just Ana, though she was a big part of it. Things were changing. I was different. The Steiner house was different. And maybe those old ghosts could finally get some rest.

I poked around the kitchen. It turned out I had a couple candy bars in the house, but that was it. I didn't figure to get much action since the house was down a dirt road and a good piece off the beaten path. But I also knew the Steiner place was as close to a haunted house as we had around here, so it was hard to tell. After a few more knocks, I drove down to the grocery store, grabbed a couple bags of Snickers and enough goods for a late supper with Ana, and then I headed back home.

By eight-thirty, maybe ten Snickers were gone.

After that, the only ones that disappeared were the ones I ate.

And then, just past eleven, there was another knock on the door.

I have to admit, that knock gave me enough of a jolt that I set my .38 on the side table next to the door . . . just in case.

Then I answered the door.

An Egyptian princess was standing there. Diaphanous gown. Little tiara. Lots of eyeliner.

Ana said, "That bastard down at The Double Shot made all of us dress up in costumes tonight."

She tossed the plastic tiara on the floor as she came in.

"I think I'm going to quit that job."

I picked up the tiara and threw it out the door.

"I think that's a good idea," I said.

I'd bought a bottle of wine, a loaf of sourdough, and fixings for pasta. We never got to it. A few Snickers, and we were out of there. The bedroom was too strong a draw.

Later I slept deeply, and I didn't dream, and I didn't wake.

Two hours passed.

And then I woke sharply.

I thought I'd heard a knock at the door.

Ana was still asleep. I slipped on my jeans and grabbed a flannel shirt. I was halfway down the hall before it hit me.

I didn't want to answer that door.

Not at all.

Certainly not without a gun in my hand.

And suddenly I wondered if I'd imagined the whole thing. Sure. Maybe that knock was just a leftover shard of dream jackknifed in my brain. By the time I reached the end of the hallway that opened into the living room, I'd almost convinced myself of that. But I'd also remembered that I'd left the .38 on the side table next to the door, and I planned to grab it before I checked things out.

But like they say, plans change.

I came around the corner. The lights were out in the living room, but I could see.

Because the front door was open.

And dull moonlight spilled across the hardwood floor.

I waited for Charlie Steiner to follow that moonlight through the doorway. And I thought of those bikers I'd killed, too—after all, they had friends who might be looking for revenge. All that flashed through my brain in a couple ticks of the second hand, but no one was there.

I didn't wait for someone to make an appearance. I was moving. Toward the door, and the side table. I snatched up the .38 and flicked on the living room light. I hit the porch light at the same time and scanned the front yard.

Nothing. No one there. No sign of movement. Just my pickup truck parked on the gravel drive, and Ana's beat-up Toyota parked next to it.

I closed the front door and set down the pistol. I was just about to turn around when I caught a flash of reflection on the living room window. Something against the far wall behind me, a dark smear waiting in the corner. Whatever it was, it didn't belong there.

It wasn't moving . . . yet.

I spun, staring across the room.

The thing that stood in the corner wasn't a mummy.

But it was Charlie Steiner.

All trace of the Hollywood monster was long gone. No costume, no bandages, no Lon Chaney, Jr. frightface. Charlie wasn't a rampaging mountain of cobwebs anymore. No. He was just a thing that had lain in a leaking plywood box for ten long years. Shrunken and black. Desiccated and degraded. His corpse had rotted in the wet earth, then dried and baked in the heat of summer, then rotted some more when the next rains came. It had been like that month after month and year after year as the seasons ran their circles and ran them again, until all that was left of him was bone and gristle and the black jerky that held it all together . . . along with a little bit of a very old dream.

What remained couldn't have weighed more than fifty pounds. Charlie stood in that corner, looking more like a giant marionette than anything human, a pile of tottering bone. Empty-eyed, he stared across the room at me, death's eternal grin on his skinless face.

I expected him to collapse if he moved so much as an inch.

But he didn't.

He still knew what he wanted.

He still knew what he needed.

He came after it, faster than I ever could have expected. He skittered across the room like a giant insect, and his bones clicked against the hardwood floor, percussion for a nightmare dance. His arm came up just as I raised the .38, and as I turned to face him I thought that arm had become thicker and whiter as it descended toward me.

But the thing I saw wasn't Charlie's arm at all.

It was Roger's Louisville Slugger, and it came at me in a white-ash blur.

The bat slammed my wrist, and I lost the pistol. Charlie's jaw clacked open and closed, and the sound was castanet laughter as he whirled and slammed the Slugger against my skull. Next thing I knew I was on the floor, and as I rolled away the bat came down on the meat above my collarbone.

That burst of pain hard-wired me.

The pistol was right there, by my other hand.

I snatched it up. Charlie stood above me, Roger's bat raised over his head with both skeletal hands. He opened his mouth, and I swear I actually heard him take a breath. Blood bubbled over his black teeth, and he started to say something, the way he always did in my dreams.

"No," I said. "This time you don't say a word."

Six times I pulled the trigger. And I thought of Roger, and a missing little girl, and a woman who was down the hall.

And Charlie Steiner fell. His bones clattered to the floor. The lights started to flicker, and then the room started to spin. A black hole opened up in the middle of it, and I remembered the mummy's cobwebbed mouth opening all those years ago at Butcher's Lake, and I remembered his buzz-saw scream.

But there was no scream this night. There was only chanting. There on the ground, with gunfire echoing in my skull, I know I heard it. Distant. Indistinct . . . as if it came from a place far below or far above. And then I started to fade and the lights went out, and the black hole went away, and the moon seemed to hang above me in the darkness. It shone on me and the dead thing at my feet like a spotlight that could open a hole into a black brimming pit. And there was no way to fight it, not when the moon shone down and that black hole returned at my feet. Charlie's wrecking-ball fist had already crumbled, and I was slipping into unconsciousness, and everything was suddenly slipping away except for me and the whisper of my own breath.

Wherever I went next, I didn't hear anything.

It was a quiet place, and empty, and I was alone there.

I awoke the next morning, and I was alone still.

* * *

The Louisville Slugger lay there on the floor. My pistol was next to it. But Charlie was gone. The only trace of him was a set of scratches that started in the far corner of the living room and ended at the front door. Looking down at them, I remembered the clicking percussion of his bony feet as he came after me the night before.

I searched the house for Ana, but she was gone, too. All that was left was a beat-up Corolla parked in my driveway, and a princess costume on the bedroom floor—a gown that smelled of Ana's vanilla perfume. I went down to Butcher's Lake, hoping I'd find her there. I drove to her apartment, and then I went to The Double Shot, but by then I knew she wouldn't be there . . . or anywhere.

I kept it to myself for a few days, hoping the phone would ring, hoping it would be Ana. But the phone didn't ring. Finally, I worked up the nerve to call Ben Cross. He came over to the house, and I told him the whole story. God knows what he thought of it. But after I finished, Ben asked me to get in the car and we went for a little drive.

To Potter's Field.

To Charlie Steiner's unmarked grave.

"We thought it was kids who did it," Ben said staring down at the open hole and the broken box at the bottom. "You know—Halloween night, taking a dare to buck the town legend. We expected we'd find Charlie's bones hanging in a tree somewhere. But after what you've told me, I'm not so sure."

Ben kept the story out of the paper. That was fine with almost everyone. The town fathers didn't want any more tabloid reporters sniffing around. The next day, a county work crew used a backhoe and filled in Charlie's grave. They tamped down the earth and rolled a couple strips of fresh grass over the top of it. Next thing you knew, Charlie's unmarked plot looked like it had never been disturbed at all.

Ben didn't really want me in the Steiner place anymore, but we worked it out. I had nowhere else to go. Now it's my home. More than anything, it was the place I'd been with Ana. That's what I wanted to remember about the house by Butcher's Lake, and that's why I stay there.

As for Butcher's, I still go down there. Not often, but often enough. Usually at sunset. Sometimes I'll take a bottle of wine and walk along the shore. One night the wind was up, blowing through the eucalyptus, making the cattails dance. It was almost dark. And I thought I saw someone down near the water, staring at me from a gap in the cattails.

I hurried to the spot.

Someone was there. In the cattails, watching me.

I moved closer.

My hand reached out.

It was a Halloween mask. A little princess with black hair and red lips. The mask was hung up in the cattails. I didn't want to think about how it might have gotten there. I really didn't need any false hope. But I took the mask home with me, and I put it on the mantelpiece right next to the plastic tiara Ana had worn that Halloween night.

Of course, I didn't tell anyone about it.

No one, except Ben.

"Maybe she'll come back," he said. "She was a dream, that one. I guess she really was."

I don't know anymore. I really don't.

Like I said, I don't like dreams. I don't trust them.

But that doesn't mean I don't have them.

I have them, still.

Norman Partridge's fiction includes horror, suspense, and the fantastic—"sometimes all in one story," according to Joe Lansdale. Partridge's novel *Dark Harvest* was chosen by *Publishers Weekly* as one of the best one hundred books of 2006, and two short-story collections were published in 2010—*Lesser Demons* from Subterranean Press and *Johnny Halloween* from Cemetery Dance. Other work includes the Jack Baddalach mysteries *Saguaro Riptide* and *The Ten-Ounce Siesta*, plus *The Crow: Wicked Prayer*, which was adapted for film. His work has received multiple Bram Stoker awards. He can be found on the web at NormanPartridge.com and americanfrankenstein.blogspot.com.

UNTERNEHMEN WERWOLF

ϟϟ

Carrie Vaughn

October 31, 1944

The boy, Fritz, had only a few hours to assassinate the collaborator.

He had completed the first part of the mission the night before, crossing over enemy lines into occupied territory. This was the easy part; he'd done it a dozen times before. But this time, he carried a gun in his pack, not the messages and supplies he'd couriered previously.

As usual on these journeys, he awoke in the morning, safe in a copse of autumn shrubs he'd found to hide in, hidden by fallen leaves and tangled branches. He was naked, but he was used to that. After giving himself a moment to recall where he was, to reacquaint himself with his human limbs, his grasping fingers instead of ripping claws, he untangled himself from his pack, looped around his shoulders so it wouldn't slip off when he was wolf. Inside, he found a canteen of water, a day's rations, and common workmen's clothes and boots so he could travel unnoticed. And the gun.

Dressed and armed, he set off. He'd memorized the maps and the description of his target. The village had been occupied by Allied forces for several weeks, and the woman, Maria Lang, a nurse, had not only surrendered to enemy forces, she had been assisting in administration of the village, supplying the American soldiers with aid and information. The village might or might not be recaptured in coming battles, that wasn't his concern. Right now, the woman must be punished. Executed.

Not murdered, they told him. Executed.

He balked, when they told her his target was a woman. That did not matter, his superiors in his SS unit told him. She was a collaborator. A traitor, not worthy of mercy. And Fritz was seventeen now, ready for such an important mission. He ought to be more than a letter carrier. And so here he was, trekking across abandoned farmland toward the edge of a wooded stretch where the collaborator's cabin was said to stand, using his preternatural sense of smell to detect the scent of treachery.

A wolf could cross enemy lines when a man in a uniform could not. When even a man in disguise could not. A wolf traveling in a forest did not draw suspicions. And a wolf could be trained to follow a certain route, certain procedures. To return to a certain spot on schedule. A wolf was wild, but the man inside the werewolf could learn.

Fritz had been a shepherd boy, like in one of the old fairy tales, tending sheep in pastures at the edge of a Bavarian forest. Still living the old ways, with the old fears. Then, he cried wolf, and no one heard him.

He survived the attack, and the bite marks and gashes on his legs healed by morning, and everyone knew what that meant. He knew what to do, and on the next full moon he spent several nights in the woods alone. Howled to the sky for the first time. When he returned, friends and family said nothing about it, did not ask him what he felt or what he'd experienced. He learned to live with the monster, but he no longer looked after his family's sheep.

The war came, and he was too young to be recruited as a proper soldier, but a man from the SS found him. Said he was forming a special unit, and that he'd heard rumors about these forests. About the shepherd boy who no longer looked after sheep. Colonel Skorzeny had a job for him, and you did not tell men like that no, so Fritz went with him.

His new home, a compound fenced in with razor wire—steel edged with silver, he was told—had normal barracks and storage buildings and such. There were also cages, for those who had not volunteered, or who had changed their minds. The soldiers carried knives and bayonets laced with silver. Silver bullets loaded their guns. A mere knick from one of those blades, a graze from one of those bullets, would kill him. Fritz did as he was told.

Fritz had never met another werewolf before joining Skorzeny's special unit. The SS colonel had found a dozen of them across Germany, and he made more, finding soldiers who volunteered to be bitten, and a few who didn't. Fritz was the youngest, and his instinct was to cower, to imagine a tail folding tight between his legs, to lower his gaze and slouch before the older, fiercer werewolf soldiers. Skorzeny would shout at him for weakness because he didn't understand, but the others recognized the gestures of a frightened puppy. Some looked after him as an older wolf in a pack would. Some took advantage and bullied.

Fritz was a monster from a fairy tale. He shouldn't be afraid of anything. What, then, did that say about the SS soldiers he cowered before? Who were the greater monsters? He told himself he deferred to them because he was loyal to the Fatherland, because he fought for the Führer, because he believed. But when he returned from a mission in the pre-dawn gray, lying naked at a rendezvous point as soldiers waited to escort him back to the barracks and the silver razorwire, he knew the truth: he was afraid. Even him, near invulnerable, a monstrous creature haunting dark stories, was afraid. This was the world he lived in.

Tonight was the full moon. He had two choices: to stay human and shoot the woman before night fell. Or to wait until the light of the moon transformed him, and let his wolf do the work with teeth and claws.

In the forest some miles outside Aachen, he did not trust his wolf to do what needed to be done. The wolf worked on instinct, on gut feeling, and in the end Fritz could not tell his wolf what to do, especially on a full moon night. He had tried to argue with the colonel, who wasn't a wolf and didn't understand. But the colonel said this mission must happen now, and must be completed tonight.

The Allies were gaining ground and a message needed to be sent to other would-be collaborators, that death awaited them.

So Fritz went. *He* would have to complete the mission, not his wolf, because he suspected his wolf would follow his instinct and run to safety. Away from Germany. He and his wolf had been having this argument for months, now.

He found the house; it wasn't hard. As the description said, it stood alone, isolated, and the woman lived by herself. She walked to the village several times a week, but she rarely had visitors. The place seemed oddly comforting: an old-fashioned white-washed cottage with a thatched roof, a garden plot that still had a few odd remnants left over from the fall harvest, a well lined with stones and a wooden bucket beside it. He circled the place, smelling carefully, and only smelled a woman, Maria Lang. And she was at home.

He camouflaged himself behind a tree on a small rise some hundred yards away and watched for the next hour until she opened the front door. He had good vision, a wolf's vision, and even from the hilltop he could see his target. Standing on the threshold of her doorway, she wrapped a woven shawl more tightly over her shoulders and looked out. Not searching for anything in particular, not bent toward any chore. Just looking.

When her gaze crossed the hill, her eyes seemed to meet his, and he started.

Smiling before she ducked her face, she went back inside and closed the door. She had seen him—or she had not. If she had, perhaps she believed he wasn't a danger. Some hunter lost in the woods. A boy from the village.

If she did not believe he was a danger, he could simply knock and shoot her when she opened the door. In loyal service to the Fatherland. Keeping low, moving quickly, he made his way toward the cottage.

He could not explain the feeling of dread that overcame him as he left the shelter of the trees and approached the clearing where the garden plot and semi-tamed brambles spread out. The setting still appeared idyllic. A curl of smoke rose from the leaning stone chimney, indicating warmth and comfort inside. These were like the cottages at home. This should be easy. But he took a step, and he could not raise his foot again. As if the ground had frozen, and his boots had stuck to the ice. As if his bones had turned to iron, too heavy to shift. The cottage before him suddenly seemed miles away. The sky grew overcast, shrouded with clouds, and a wind began to murmur through the trees.

His wolf scented magic and told him to run.

The memory of Colonel Skorzeny and his silver bayonet urged him on, and Fritz forced another step. Forward, not away. Only a few steps, a knock on the door, and he could finish this. The gun was already in his hand.

Next came the voices, a scratch-throated chattering descending over him like a fog and rattling his ribs. He put his hands over his ears to cut out the noise, and looked up to see ravens. Glint-eyed, black, wings outstretched and blurred as they flapped over him, and their nearly-human croaking seemed to call, *away, away, away*. They banked and swooped and tittered, brushing his hair with wingtips before dodging away. He snapped at them, teeth clicking together, and swatted with fingers curled like claws. Wolf would make short work of them. But he had vowed to stay human. The gun sat coldly in his hand.

He ignored the ravens, which settled in surrounding trees and cawed their commentary at him. They smelled like dust and spiders.

He shifted a leg to take another impossible step, but again he could not move. Vines had come, thorny brambles reaching from the solid hedge to take hold of him, to dig into the fabric of his trousers, and under his skin. The pain pricks of a thousand little needles. A growl caught in the back of his throat. A threat, a show of anger. Wolf, wanting to rise up. Wolf could escape this, if the human was too stupid to.

Teeth bared, Fritz jerked his leg forward, then the next. His trousers ripped, as did his skin. Blood trickled down his legs. Still the brambles climbed, reaching for his middle, grasping for his arms, pulling him away from the cottage. He twisted, lunging one way and another, hoping to break away, and it worked. Vines ripped, he progressed another foot or two, and his momentum carried him full around—and when he faced away from the cottage, the brambles vanished.

For a long time he stood and looked across the clearing to the straight pines of the forest, all quiet, all peaceful. He could move freely—as long as he moved away from the cottage. It was all illusion. His breath caught.

He really had no choice about what path to choose. He could not fail in his mission. He could not take the coward's route. But when he turned back to the cottage, the brambles returned, the battle resumed. His wolf's strength let him fight on when a normal person would have been overwhelmed, succumbing to the blood and pain of the thorny wall. He wrenched, pushed, twisted, and growled, until the last strand of vine broke away, and he was through, close enough to the cottage to touch.

His wolf's agility meant he sensed the ground give way a moment before it did. A hole opened—no, a trench, or a moat even. A cleft in the earth, circling the cottage, splitting open and falling to darkness. Fritz sprang back, balanced as if on a wolf's sure paws, to keep from falling backward into the vines, or forward into the pit. His toes pushed a stone and few bits of brown earth forward, and the pieces rattled down the sides to some unseen bottom.

Colonel Skorzeny had not told him that Maria Lang was a witch.

The cleft widened, the edge nearest him crumbling further, forcing him to inch away until the brambles with their reaching thorns threatened to claw into his back. This was impossible. This also made him furious. He wasn't a boy, a feckless common soldier, he was a wolf. Hitler's werewolves, the colonel called them, and they saluted with their heils and expected victory.

Fritz dug his booted toes into the earth, called on wolf's strength, imagined the light of the coming full moon filling him further, giving him power. He took a single running step and jumped. Crashed to the ground on the other side of the pit, rolled once, hit the cottage's front door, and slumped to a rest. His ears were ringing, his muscles ached. He'd only traveled a few feet but felt as if he'd run for miles. For a moment, he couldn't remember why he'd come here at all.

The door opened, and the woman stood on the threshold,

looking down on him. His information said she was in her thirties, but he couldn't decide if she looked old or young. Her hair was black, tied under a blue kerchief. Her lips were full, but pale. Laugh lines creased her eyes. Her hands were thin, calloused.

"Boy, would you like some tea?" she said. Her voice was clear, amiable. Something like an aunt, not so much like a grandmother, and nothing like a witch.

"But I am a werewolf," he blurted, perhaps the first time he had ever stated this aloud.

"Yes, I know," she answered.

He looked over his shoulder at the way he'd come. The clearing, the garden, the forest and hill beyond—all were normal, utterly ordinary, the way they had been when he arrived. He looked at the gun in his hand, and the woman who didn't seem at all afraid. Sighing, he climbed up off the ground and followed her inside.

She showed him to a straight-backed, rough-hewn chair, and obediently he sat. She had an old-fashioned open hearth with a fire burning, and already had a kettle set to boiling water. He watched as she used a dishcloth to move the kettle from the fire, pour water into a teapot, and scoop in herbs from an earthenware jar.

He looked around. The place was filled with herbs, jars of them lined up on a shelf, bundles of them hanging from roof beams, mortars and pestles sitting on a work table in the center of the room, all dusted with herbs. The pungent smell, strong as a Christmas dinner, made him sneeze. Stairs led up, probably to an attic bedroom. The whole cottage was as cozy as one could wish for, insulated and warm, filled with signs of home. Fritz was surprised that his wolf wasn't complaining about the closed space and the shut door. His wolf did not feel trapped, but instead had settled, like a puppy curled by a fire.

He blinked up at the woman, confused. "They told me you were a nurse."

"Healer, not a nurse. They couldn't tell the difference, I'm sure."

"You're a witch."

She smirked at him. "You are very young. Here, have some tea."

And just like that she presented him with a teacup and set it in his hands as she slipped the gun away from him. He didn't even notice until he'd taken a long sip. The tea warmed him, and the warmth settled over him. Citrus and cinnamon, and hope.

Then he stared at his hands, his eyes widening. She set the gun on the worktable out of his reach and left it here as she poured herself a cup of tea.

"What have you done to me?" he cried.

"I haven't done anything." Her smile should have been beautiful, full lips on a porcelain face, but the expression held wickedness. Mischievousness. Tricks. "I have nine layers of protection around my home, knowing people like you would come to kill me. You should have dropped dead—even you, with your half-wolf soul—should have dropped dead before you reached my door. Do you know what that means?

"You never truly meant to kill me. You thought you did, perhaps. You might have held the gun in your hands and pressed the barrel to my chest, but you could not have killed me. Everyone would call you a monster if they knew what you were. But you have a good heart, don't you? What of that, boy?"

He didn't know. He took another sip of tea and kept his gaze on the amber surface of the liquid. She wasn't even wolf, and he was showing her signs of submission. He was useless.

"Then what am I to do?" he said. He knew what happened to those the SS no longer had use for. Skorzeny knew how to kill werewolves.

"It's the night of the full moon," she said.

A window in the front of the cottage still showed daylight. The ghosts of his wolf's ears pricked forward. No, it wasn't quite time, not yet.

She said, "They wanted you to come tonight, on the full moon, because they thought your wolf would make you a killer. Make murdering easier."

"I tried to explain to them, it doesn't work like that—"

"Especially when they have made us a world where men are the monsters, and the wolves are just themselves. Would you like one?" She offered him a plate piled with sugar cookies, wonderful, buttery disks sparkling with sugar, and where had she found butter and sugar in the middle of the war? He recalled the story of the witch who fattened children up to eat them.

"No, thank you," he said. Smiling, she set the plate aside.

"Do you know what tonight is, boy? Besides a full moon night?"

He thought for a moment and said, blankly, "Tuesday?"

"All Hallows Eve. The night when doors between worlds open. And a full moon on All Hallows Eve? The doors will open very wide indeed. Where would you like to go? This is a night when you might be able to get there."

I want to go home. That was a child's wish, and he was ashamed for thinking it.

She might have read his mind.

"The home you knew, you will never see again. Even if I could transport you there this moment, home will never mean what it did. Germany will never be the same. We might as well all have landed on another planet, these last years." She went to the table, wiped her hands on her apron, and began to work, chopping up a sprig of some sweet-smelling plant, scooping pieces into a mortar, grinding away, adding another herb, then oil to make a paste. The movements seemed offhand, unconscious. She'd probably done them a thousand times before. She spoke through it all. "They, your masters, are intent on harnessing the powers of darkness, but they do not remember the old stories, do they? The price to be paid. They have forgotten the lessons. They put werewolves in cages and think because they have a bit of silver, they are safe."

He leaned back in the chair, sipping his tea as worry fell away from him. He was a child again, listening to the stories of his grandmother, the old ones, about dark woods and evil times, bramble forests and wicked tyrants. He was sure he didn't close his eyes—he remembered the fire in the hearth dancing, he watched her hands move as she chopped, mixed, ground, and sealed her potions up in jars. He saw his gun sitting at the corner of the table and remembered he had come for a reason. But he no longer cared, because for the first time in ages, the wolf inside him was still.

"Some of us still have power, and some of us can fight them," she said. "We do what we can. Your masters, for example. Just seeing you, here, I've learned so much about them. They think their werewolves will save them. Even without the true wolves like you, they think that they can act like wolves to strike at their enemies. They think that they can control the monsters they've created. But I will curse them, and they will fail. Keep this in mind when you decide what to do, and which way to run."

He saw an image in his mind's eye of endless forest, and the strength to run forever, on four legs, wind whispering through his fur. His voice tickled inside him, not a snarl this time, but a howl, a song to reach the heavens.

"Boy." He started at her voice, suddenly close. She stood before him, arms crossed. "The moon's up. It's time for you to fly."

The world through the window was dark, black night. The trees beyond the clearing glowed with the mercury sheen of the rising moon. Both he and his wolf awoke. Marie took the teacup from him before he dropped it.

He could change to wolf anytime he liked, but on this night, this one time each month, he had no choice. The light called, and the monster clawed to get out, ribs and guts feeling as if they might split open, the pinpricks of fur sprouting from his skin, over his whole body. His clothing felt like fire, he had to rip free of them. His breathing quickened, he turned to the door.

She opened it for him. "Goodbye," she said cheerfully as he raced past her.

He ripped off all the clothes before he crossed the clearing, left his satchel behind, never thought again about the gun. By the time he reached the trees he had a hitch in his stride, as his back hunched and his bones slipped and cracked to new shapes. His vision became sharp and clear, and the scents filling his nose made the world rich and glorious. Tail, ears, teeth, a coat of beautiful thick fur, and nothing but open country before him.

The doors of All Hallows Eve had opened, and the boy's wolf knew where to go, even if he didn't. West. Just west, as far and as fast as he could. Armies and soldiers and checkpoints and spies didn't stop him. No one fired on him. All any of them saw was a wolf, a bit scrawny and the worst for wear perhaps, racing through the night, a gray shadow under a silver moon.

Later, Fritz would remember flashes of the journey, woods and fields, a small stream that he splashed through, the feel of moonlight rising over him. For decades after the smell fireworks would remind him of the stink of exploded artillery shells that filled his head as he crossed the site of a recent battle. The memories made him think of a hero in a fairy tale, the boy who had to fight through many hardships to reach the castle and rescue the princess. The knight with his sword, slaying the dragon. Never mind that he was a monster, like the monsters in the stories. Perhaps he didn't have to be a monster any more. Not like that, at least.

He ran all night, collapsed an hour or so before dawn, not knowing where on the map of Europe's battlefields he'd ended up, not caring. He'd run as far as he could, then he slept, and the wolf crept away again.

He'd run all the way to France.

The American soldiers found him naked, satchel and gun and clothing long gone. Hugging himself, he hid behind a tree trunk, torn between fleeing again or begging for help. When they leveled rifles at him, he didn't flinch. He didn't imagine the Amis had brought silver bullets with them. They could not kill him, but they didn't know that. He waited; they waited.

He read confusion in their gazes. He must have looked like a child to them: thin, glaringly pale against the gray of the woods and overcast sky. Lost and shivering. Ducking his gaze, a sign of submission, he crept out from behind the tree. He licked his lips, needing water, but that could wait. Still, they didn't shoot. He decided to step through the door that had opened.

"I . . . I surrender," he said in very rough English, and raised his arms.

Carrie Vaughn is the author of the *New York Times*-bestselling series of novels about a werewolf named Kitty, the most recent of which is *Kitty in the Underworld.* She's also the author of young adult novels (*Voices of Dragons*, Steel) and contemporary fantasy (*Discord's Apple, After the Golden Age*). *Dreams of the Golden Age*, the second Golden Age novel, will be published in January 2014. A graduate of the Odyssey Fantasy Writing Workshop, she's a contributor to the Wild Cards series of shared world superhero books edited by George R. R. Martin, and her short stories have appeared in numerous magazines and anthologies. An Air Force brat, Vaughn survived her nomadic childhood and managed to put down roots in Boulder, Colorado. Visit her at www. carrievaughn.com.

LESSER FIRES

Steve Rasnic Tem & Melanie Tem

Right at sunset, when the big bonfires snaggled the hilltop like pumpkin teeth, reflecting both ways through the veil that was so thin tonight between the worlds you might think there was no veil but everybody knew there was, Clara tripped over the hem of her costume and fell. It was embarrassing. Also, it hurt.

She'd just crossed the bridge between the lesser fires that marked the path, on her way to the party. Before then she'd been feeling pretty good, pretty proud, feeling like the witch/fortuneteller/farseer of impending doom she'd tried to make herself up to be. With all the school she missed, and all her trips to the hospital and the doctors, and all the meds she took, and the way her body moved, people thought she was weird anyway, and some of them avoided her and some of them wanted to be her friend just because of it, which she didn't much like, either.

She couldn't get up. She wasn't sure why. She felt like she'd broken something, but she always felt like she'd broken something. One of these days she wouldn't be able to get up at all, and that would be that—whatever "that" was. She'd always sort of imagined that was how she'd die, but maybe she'd have to be carried or pushed or dragged around for the rest of a long life. Whatever.

At the moment she could barely raise her head. Just enough to see the legs in costume walking by. She caught herself trying to figure out what the rest of the costume must look like based on the legs, but stopped herself because that was being dumb. It wasn't solving the problem. A couple of people stopped to help her up but she said no in kind of a mean way in order not to act as helpless as she actually was. "I'm fine. Just go on. Don't be late for the party," she sort of snarled at them, and then when they did go on and leave her there she was mad and hurt. No wonder people thought she was weird. *She* thought she was weird.

Being late to the party would not be good. Clara couldn't exactly sneak in; Clara couldn't sneak anywhere. The whole family would stare at her while she clunked to her place. Ma would have that OMG-I-can't-believe-this-is-my-kid look on her face, and she'd be drinking too much of what she never called just "ale," always "Pa's good amber ale" that she looked forward to all year and Clara could manage just a tiny sip of. And Pa—she'd never please Pa no matter what she did. The cousins would be laughing behind handfuls of crumbly cakes for the dead, which were really dry cookies Clara could hardly swallow, especially when it was Auntie Reba's year to make them. In a few years Clara would be expected to take a turn. She hated cooking and was terrible at it and saw no reason to learn just so she could make cakes for the dead who couldn't eat them anyway.

Great-grandma Beryl had been invited home for this year's party, west windows left open for her for weeks in the October chill, so that it was as cold and bleak inside as out, the empty place set for her at table. When Great-grandma Beryl had been on this side of the veil Clara had never been able to figure her out, and it wouldn't be any easier now. Great-grandma Beryl was a scary lady, alive or dead. But Clara didn't want to miss her.

Waiting for her body to decide if it was going to get up this time or not, Clara worried about Great-grandma Beryl's crystal ball in her backpack. Lucky she'd fallen forward instead of back. You had to take luck where you could get it, especially when you didn't get much of it. The backpack pretty much ruined the costume but at least it was behind her so people didn't see it right away. If she was a fortuneteller she needed a crystal ball, right? But this one was so heavy. She remembered it just sitting on a shelf in Great-grandma Beryl's house, dusty, not doing anything. She'd heard the clink when she'd hit the ground. There was probably a crack in it now. Would it work if it was cracked? That was dumb. Crystal balls didn't work. They weren't how you told the future. It was just a prop. She'd promised to take extra special care. Ma would be furious, or sickeningly understanding, depending on how much of "Pa's good amber ale" she'd had by now. The most Pa would do was shake his head, if he noticed at all.

Falling hadn't been in Clara's plan. It should've been. She should've known. She should've been more careful. She should've worn something that fit her better—not that anything really fit her—instead of this old tie-dyed dress of her mother's that they'd only been able to take up so much. But she liked the colors and the way it felt, and it hid her legs and made her movements look kind of mysterious instead of just clunky. She liked the dress. She liked Great-grandma Beryl's crystal ball. She hated always having to be careful, and then falling anyway.

The ground was cold, like the glass in her bedroom window when she put her cheek there to see what was down in the yard. Except during the weeks when the lesser fires burned, she never could see much, but she held her cheek there as long as she could, until it hurt so bad there'd be tears in her eyes and her face so frozen she couldn't smile or frown or do much of anything with it at all except stare at her dumb self in the mirror: weeping eyes above a stiff red and white face.

Here on the ground, under the red-green-purple-orange tent the big dress made over her, it was warm. As hard as her heart was beating, she knew she was making lots of heat. In fact she was sure she'd be too hot soon. Part of your body too hot and part of you too cold—wasn't that what gave you pneumonia? Sweat was sliding off her skin like Auntie Reba's "special" oil that was maybe a little less disgusting than her "cakes" for the dead.

"Clara."

Somebody had stopped beside her. Who was that? The voice was really familiar and strange at the same time, a girl's voice, and Clara's name didn't sound quite right in that voice. The girl had on a green and purple and orange dress that covered her shoes and dragged on the ground. A lot like Clara's. It sucked that when you tried to fit in you just made yourself look more different, and when you deliberately tried to be different somebody else showed up in the very same costume.

"Clara."

"That's my name, don't wear it out." Clara managed to sit up, leaning on the backpack and probably doing more damage to Great-grandma Beryl's crystal ball. Her head hurt and she was dizzy.

The girl was circling around her, far enough away that her edges faded into the firelight and then so close that Clara'd have felt her body heat if she hadn't been so hot herself. The girl moved like Clara, jerky and clumsy. Was she making fun of her? Or were all the same things wrong with her body that were wrong with Clara's?

The girl leaned down toward Clara on the ground and held out her hands, then pulled them back out of reach so that Clara couldn't grab them even if she wanted to, which mostly she didn't. The girl's face looked red and white and kind of stiff. Any minute now she was going to fall on top of Clara or drift away.

"Dance with me."

"Yeah, right."

"Dance with me." In the big flowing dress, with the oily shine, with the drumbeats and the sunset and the greater and lesser bonfires in the background, what she was doing did sort of look like a dance.

"Duh. I can't dance." But if this chick who looked so much like her and moved so much like her could dance, could Clara, too?

"Duh. Sure you can." Clara found herself reaching for the outstretched hands, though she didn't want to. Her hands were so cold she didn't really feel the girl's hands, but somehow the girl was helping her up, and the two of them danced a few steps together to the music from the party that she was already late to. Then the other girl was gone and Clara was dancing by herself, and she accidentally kicked the backpack and the crystal ball clinked and clunked again, and her mother was yelling at her to hurry up. Clara hurried as fast as she could, which wasn't hurrying by anybody else's standards except maybe, she thought, that girl's.

Clara stumbled a little but made it to her house and inside and to her place at table. Great-grandma Beryl's place was at the other end where she could barely see it, but there was a shimmer around it. Here next to her was the empty place for her cousin Spencer who'd been killed in Afghanistan. Clara didn't miss him. He'd never grown up enough to quit being mean to her. Last year, just before he deployed, he'd played this bizarre trick on her where he claimed he wasn't Spence, he was Spence's ghost, and then he'd said he was the living Spencer again and he'd seen his own ghost, and he acted scared, all wide-eyed like a cartoon of scared.

She'd thought she was the only one he'd done that to, just messing with her mind, and it'd made her mad. She might be sick but she wasn't stupid. Then, after they got the news, she'd heard Pa tell Ma he'd known Spence would die within the year because he'd met his own ghost. That gave Ma something to use against Reba. Clara wondered if she had.

Now Reba was crying and making everybody eat her cakes for Spencer. Ma teased loudly that Reba never got the recipe right, and the two of them got into one of those sibling arguments that made Clara glad she was an only child. Having tons of cousins was exhausting enough. She couldn't tell if Spence was here or not. Maybe Reba hadn't left the westward window open right for him, either. Reba was sort of a ditz.

Clara passed the zucchini casserole. Zucchini was disgusting.

Maybe that chick she'd danced with had been somebody's out-of-town visitor here for the party. But she didn't see her at table, and she reasoned that it wasn't very likely the girl had been a stranger; strangers didn't come here without being approved and introduced all around, and, besides, she'd known Clara's name. Maybe it had been some cousin dressed up in costume and make-up. She had looked so much like what Clara thought she herself looked like: same crooked body, same face both younger and older than she was, same boobs getting bigger every day so that Clara couldn't bring herself to look at herself in a mirror.

The backpack was getting uncomfortable between her and the chair, but getting it off would mean leaning and twisting and turning and creating even more of a scene. The big bright dress ballooned out around her, and she felt ridiculous. She drank a tiny bit of Pa's good amber ale when the bottle came around. Busy chatting and laughing, Ma wouldn't notice anyway, so she let herself make a face.

Ma called out to Auntie Reba, "He doesn't have to come, you know. I bet he's not coming."

Reba howled, jumped up, grabbed the plate of her gross cakes for the dead that nobody would eat any of, dashed around the table crashing into people and chairs, and dumped the whole thing including the plate on her sister's head. Like practically everybody else, Clara laughed. These fights between Ma and Reba were pretty ridiculous. But they were also embarrassing, and somebody always got hurt. Pa moved in to break it up, and then both of the sisters were fighting him, and then other people got into it, and everything just sort of blew up. No wonder Spence didn't want to come home. She saw the shimmer that maybe was Great-grandma Beryl leave the empty chair at the end of the table, too.

Clara started to feel sick. Her head swam, and her hands and feet felt as if they'd come loose from her body and were floating around like sparks and smoke. She was going to faint. She was going to throw up. That would be embarrassing. She struggled to her feet, swayed, steadied herself on the back of Spence's empty chair, started on her own version of hurrying out of the room. Ma yelled after her, sort of absent-mindedly. The good amber ale made Clara's name sound weird coming loud out of Ma's mouth, and she was more interested in fighting with Reba and kissing Pa than finding out what was going on with Clara.

Clara kept going, not fast and not steady, but determined. She was relieved that nobody tried to stop her or ask what was wrong. It also hurt her feelings.

She almost fell a couple of times, and she banged the backpack with the crystal ball in it against the door frame, but she made it outside. The cool air and quiet cleared her head a little, but she still felt sick. It was probably just Pa's good amber ale and the cakes for the dead. She'd probably feel better pretty soon.

The cool air did clear her head a little. Darkness had come down like a tent over the town. The big toothy bonfires on the hilltop grinned. Clara followed the lesser fires away from the house. She was cold and hot, shivering and sweating. Her face was stiff.

Going up the hill, she stepped on the hem of the too-big too-bright dress again and fell. The crystal ball in the backpack clunked and felt like two or three jagged pieces now pressing against her back. She couldn't keep track of where all the pain was, leg and back and head and stomach.

"Don't worry your little head about it," Great-grandma Beryl said. "It ain't real."

Clara's head was swimming so she wasn't sure, but it seemed to her that Great-grandma Beryl was shimmering in one of the gentle, flickering lesser fires that could show the way if you didn't trip over them and catch your costume on fire. "Are you real?" She couldn't believe she was asking that. Ma would have a fit. Being sick was her excuse. Everybody knew that ghosts were real, and the veil between the worlds was real, and when the veil was thin like this, ghosts were realer than ever, realer even than the living.

"You betcha." The fire that was Great-grandma Beryl was steady and low to the ground and warm but not too warm. Clara let herself lie down by it. "So's Clara real."

"Well, yeah," Clara managed to say. "Never thought I wasn't."

"Clara," said Great-grandma Beryl. "Meet Clara."

The chick with the body like Clara's and the over-sized tie-dyed dress like Clara's was squatting beside her. Their costumes drifted over each other's knees. "We met," the girl said. "Clara just didn't recognize me. I don't know why."

Great-grandma Beryl hissed and crackled. "They never do. Mine didn't at first neither. It shouldn't be that hard, we look just like 'em. I mean, who else would we look like, I ask you."

"Didn't expect me, did you?" The girl named Clara nudged Clara, but she didn't feel it.

"They never do. Not yet." Great-grandma Beryl sort of sputtered. "Not ever yet."

Clara was too hot and too cold. High up on the hill the great bonfires snagged the edges of the thin thin veil. She wondered which west window they'd leave open for her next year, if it would have to be low and wide so she could get through it or if that wouldn't matter anymore. Would she have to walk in front of everybody to get to her empty place at table? At least it wouldn't be Auntie Reba's turn to make the cakes for the dead so they'd probably be okay.

Clara might come back if they invited her right. Or, she was sorry, she just might not.

Steve Rasnic Tem's newest story collection is *Celestial Inventories* (ChiZine), to be followed by *Twember* (New Con Press) in October. Next year will see publication of his new novel *Blood Kin* (Solaris) and the novella *In the Lovecraft Museum* (PS Publishing).

Melanie Tem's work has received the Bram Stoker, International Horror Guild, British Fantasy, and World Fantasy Awards, and a nomination for the Shirley Jackson Award. She has published numerous short stories, eleven solo novels, two collaborative novels with Nancy Holder, and two with her husband, Steve Rasnic Tem. She is also a published poet, an oral storyteller, and a playwright. Her stories have recently appeared in *Asimov's Science Fiction Magazine* and the anthologies *Supernatural Noir*, *Shivers VI*, *Portents*, *Blood and Other Cravings*, and *Werewolves and Shapeshifters*. The Tems live in Denver. They have four children and four granddaughters.

LONG WAY HOME
A Pine Deep Story

Jonathan Maberry

Author's Note: *This story takes place several years after the events described in the Pine Deep Trilogy, of which* Ghost Road Blues *is the first volume. You do not need to have read those books in order to read—and hopefully enjoy—this little tale set in rural Pennsylvania.*

-1-

Donny stood in the shadow of the bridge and watched the brown water. The river was swollen with muddy runoff. Broken branches and dead birds bobbed up and down—now you see 'em, now you don't—as the swift current pulled them past.

The river.

Jeez, he thought. *The river.*

He remembered it differently than this. Sure, he'd lived here in Pine Deep long enough to have seen the river in all her costumes. Wearing gray under an overcast sky, running smoothly like liquid metal. Dressed in white and pale blue when the winter ice lured skaters to try and cross before the frozen surface turned to black lace. Camouflaged in red and gold and orange when early November winds blew the October leaves into the water.

Today, though, the river was swollen like a tumor and wore a kind of brown that looked like no color at all. It was like this when Halloween was about to hit. You'd think a town that used to be built around the holiday, a town that made it's nut off of candy corn and jack-o' lantern pumpkins and all that trick or treat stuff would dress up for the occasion. But no. This time of year the colors all seemed to bleed away.

The last time he had seen the river was on one of those summer days that made you think summer would last forever and the world was built for swimming, kissing pretty girls, drinking beer, and floating on rubber inner tubes. It was the day before he had to report for basic training. He'd been with Jim Dooley, he remembered that so clearly.

Jim was going into the navy 'cause it was safe. A red-haired Mick with a smile that could charm the panties off a nun, and a laugh that came up from the soles of his feet. You couldn't be around Jim and not have fun. It was impossible, probably illegal.

They'd driven twenty miles up Route 32 and parked Donny's piece-of-shit old Ford150 by Bleeker's Dock. The two of them and those college girls. Cindy something and Judy something.

Cindy had the face, but Judy had the body.

Not that either of them looked like bridge trolls, even without makeup, even waking up in Jim's brother's Boy Scout tent in the woods at the top of Dark Hollow. They were both so healthy. You could stand next to them and your complexion would clear up. That kind of healthy.

And with Jim around they laughed all the time.

Nothing like pretty girls laughing on a sunny day, as the four of them pushed off from the dock and into the Delaware. Way up here, above the factories down south, way above the smutch of Philadelphia, the water was clean. It was nice.

On that day, the water had been slower and bluer. It hadn't been a dry summer, but dry enough so that in shallow spots you could see the river stones under the rippling water. Judy swore she saw a starfish down there, but that was stupid. No such thing as freshwater starfish. Or, at least Donny didn't think so.

Didn't matter anyway. That was the last time Donny saw Judy. Or Cindy or even Jim for that matter. The girls went back to college. Jim went into the navy.

Donny went into the army.

It all seemed like a long time ago.

Way too fucking long.

It was no longer summer. October was burning off its last hours. Even if the river looked like sewer water at least the trees were wearing their Halloween colors.

Donny stood by the bridge and watched the brown river sweep the broken, dead things away. There was some message there, he thought. There was at least a Springsteen song there. Something about how nothing lasts.

But Donny was no more a songwriter than he was a philosopher.

He was a man who had spent too long coming home.

Donny climbed up from the bank and stepped onto the creosote-soaked planks of the bridge. It was a new bridge. The old one had been destroyed in the Trouble.

He'd missed that, too.

He'd read about it, though. Probably everybody read about it. That shit was how most people first heard of Pine Deep. Biggest news story in the world for a while. Bunch of militia nutjobs dumped all sorts of drugs into the town's water supply. LSD, psychotropics, all sorts of stuff. Nearly everybody in town went totally ape shit. Lots of violence, a body count that dwarfed the combined death tolls of Afghanistan and Iraq. Eleven thousand six hundred and forty-one people dead.

So many of the people that Donny knew.

His folks.

His cousin Sherry and her kids.

And Jim.

Jim had come home on leave from the navy. He hadn't taken a scratch in boot camp, had been posted to an aircraft carrier, was halfway through his tour and filling his letters with jokes about how the worst thing that happens to him is the clap from getting laid in every port in the Pacific.

Jim had been stabbed through the chest by a drugged-out corn farmer who claimed—swore under oath—that he was killing vampires.

How fucked up was that?

The massacre in Pine Deep changed the world. Like 9/11 did. Made the great big American paranoia machine shift its stare from everyone else in the world to its own backyard. Domestic terrorism. No one was safe, not even at home. Pine Deep proved that.

Eleven thousand people dead.

It had happened ten years ago. To the day. The militia goons had used the big Pine Deep Halloween Festival as its ground zero. Thousands of tourists in town. Celebrities. Everyone for miles around.

If the militia assholes ever had a point, it died with them. The press called them "white supremacists," but that didn't make sense. Most of the people in Pine Deep were white. WASPs, with some Catholics and a handful of Jews. Except for a few families and some of the tourists, there wasn't enough of a black or Latino or Jewish or Muslim presence to make a hate war point. It never made sense to Donny. The people in town were just caught up in the slaughter. Either they wound up taking the same drugs, or the red wave of insanity just washed over them.

Donny had been in Iraq, midway through his second tour.

He'd been over there, killing people, trying not to die from insurgent bullets or IEDs, fighting to protect the people at home. But the people at home died anyway.

Donny never did figure out how to react to it, and standing here now on this new bridge didn't make it any clearer. The death of so many at home, neighbor killing neighbor, felt like a sin. It felt like suicide. Even though he knew that with all those drugs in the water no one could ever be held responsible for what they did. Except those militia dickheads, and Donny wished there was at least one of them alive that he could hunt down and fuck up.

"Damn it, Jim," he said to the air.

He stared across the bridge to the thick stands of oaks and maples and birch trees. From here, in the sun's fading light, it was hard to tell if the trees were on fire or if it was just the red blaze of dying leaves.

Donny adjusted the straps of his backpack and stretched out one foot. Somehow taking this step would be like crossing a line.

But between what and what, Donny had no idea.

He was no philosopher.

He was a soldier coming home.

-2-

It seemed to take forever to walk across the bridge. Donny felt as if his feet were okay with the task but his heart was throwing out an anchor.

He paused halfway across and looked back.

Behind him was a million miles of bad road that led from here all the way back to Afghanistan and Iraq. He was amazed he'd made it this far home. Donny always figured he'd die on a cot in some dinky aide station in the ass-end of nowhere, way the hell out on the Big Sand. God knows the world had tried to kill him enough times. He touched the row of healed-over scars that were stitched diagonally from left hip to right shoulder. Five rounds.

Should have died in the battle.

Should have died in the evac helicopter.

Should have died in the field hospital.

Lost enough blood to swim home.

The dead flesh of the scars was numb, but the muscle and bone beneath it remembered the pain.

And beneath that suffering flesh?

A heart that had ached to come back home, when there was a home to come back to. Now that heart beat a warning tattoo as if to say, *this is not your home anymore, soldier.*

This isn't home.

All the way here, with every mile, every step, he wondered why, after all these years away, he was coming back here at all.

He closed his eyes and felt the river wind blow damp across his cheeks.

The house he grew up in wasn't even his anymore. Attorneys and real estate agents had sold it for him. His parents' stuff, his sister's stuff, and everything he'd left behind when he joined the army had either gone to the Salvation Army or into storage.

Donny realized he didn't know where the key was for that. A lawyer had sent it to him, but . . .

He gave himself a rough pat-down, but he didn't have any keys at all.

No keys, no change in his pockets, not even a penknife to pry open the storage bin lock.

Shit.

He turned and looked back as if he could see where he'd left all of that stuff. Did someone clip him on the bus? Was it on the nightstand of that fleabag motel he'd slept in?

How much was gone?

He patted his left rear pocket and felt the familiar lump of his wallet, tugged on the chain to pull it out. He opened it, and stared at the contents.

Stared for a long time.

Donny felt something on his cheeks and his fingers came away wet.

"Why the fuck are you crying, asshole?" he demanded.

He didn't know how to answer his own question.

Slow seconds fell like leaves around him.

A car came rumbling across the bridge, driving fast, rattling the timbers. Crappy old Jeep Grand Cherokee that looked so much like the one Jim used to drive that it tore a sob from his chest. Sunlight blazed off the windshield so he couldn't see the driver. Just as well. Maybe it meant the driver couldn't see a grown man standing on the fucking bridge crying his eyes out.

"You pussy," he told himself.

The car faded into the sun glare on the other side but Donny could hear the tires crunching on gravel for a long time.

Donny sniffed back the tears, shoved his wallet back into his pocket, took a steadying breath, and then raised his head, resolved to get this shit done.

He crossed the bridge, paused only a moment at the end of the span, and stepped onto the road.

In Pine Deep.

Home.

-3-

Donny walked along Route A32.

Unless he could thumb a ride it was going to take hours to get into town. There were miles and miles of farm country between here and a cold beer. So far, though, no cars. Not a one.

As he passed each farm he thought about the families who lived there. Or . . . used to live there. Donny had no idea who was still here, who'd moved out after the Trouble, or who hadn't made it through the war zone the militant assholes had created. He'd gotten some news, of course. The Tyler family was gone. All of them. And the Bradys.

The farm to his right, though, was the old Guthrie place. One of the biggest farms in town, one of the oldest families. Old man Guthrie had died before the Trouble. Or, maybe at the start of it, depending on which account he'd read. Guthrie had been gunned down by some gun thugs up from Philly. Donny couldn't remember if the thugs were hiding out in Pine Deep, or they broke down there, or whether they were part of the white supremacist nut-bags. Either way, one of them popped a cap in Mr. Guthrie, and that was a shame 'cause the old guy was pretty cool. Always ready to hire some town kids to pick apples and pumpkins, and pay them pretty good wages. Always smiling, he was. Deserved better than what he got.

Beyond the rail fence the late season corn was high and green, the thick stalks heavy with unpicked ears. Two crows sat on the top bar, cawing for their buddies to join them, but the rest of the birds were way up in the air, circling, circling.

What was it they called a bunch of crows, he wondered? He had to think back to Mrs. Gillespie in the third grade. A pod of whales, a parliament of owls, and a . . .

A murder of crows.

Yeah, that was it. So, what was it when there were only two crows? Attempted murder?

Donny laughed aloud at his own joke and wished Jim was here. Jim usually came up with clever shit like that. Jim would have liked that joke, would have appreciated it. Would have patted him on the back, fist-bumped him, and then stolen the joke for his own repertoire. Which was okay. Jokes are free and everyone should take as many as they could, that's how Donny saw it.

Smiling, Donny walked along the rail fence. Up ahead he saw an old guy on a ladder wiring a scarecrow to a post. The scarecrow was dressed in jeans and a fatigue jacket, work gloves for hands, and a pillowcase for a head. Straw and shredded rag dripped from the sleeves and pants cuffs. Shoes were mismatched, a Converse high-top sneaker and a dress shoe with no laces. Donny slowed to watch the man work. The man and the scarecrow were almost silhouetted by the sun. The image would have looked great on a Halloween calendar. A perfect snapshot of harvest time in the American farm country.

He liked it, and smiled.

"Looks great," he said when he was close enough.

The old guy only half-turned. All Donny could see was grizzled white hair and wind-burned skin above pale eyes. He nodded at Donny's fatigue jacket.

"Afghanistan?"

"Yes, sir," answered Donny.

"You left the war," said the old man.

"No, sir . . . I reckon the war left me. It's over. They're cycling most of us home."

The old man studied him for a few long seconds. "You really think the war's over?"

Donny didn't want to get into a political debate with some old fool.

"I guess that's not for me to decide. They sent me home."

"Did they?" The man shook his head in clear disapproval and said, "The war's not over. No sirree-bob, it's not over by a long stretch."

Donny didn't know how to respond to that. He began edging further up the road.

"Son," said the old man, "some folks join the army to fight and some join to serve. What did you join for?"

"To protect my home and my family, sir." It sounded like a bullshit platitude, even as he said it, but in truth it really was why Donny enlisted. Ever since 9/11, he was afraid of what might happen here at home, on American soil. Donny knew that he wasn't particularly smart and he was far from being politically astute, but he knew that he wanted to do whatever he could to protect those who couldn't protect themselves. In school, it had been Jim at his back, who kicked the asses of bigger kids picking on the geeks and dweebs. Donny hated a bully. As far he saw it, terrorists were just bullies of a different wattage.

"Gonna be dark soon," said the old guy, apropos of nothing.

Donny glanced at the angle of the sun. "Yeah. In a while, I s'pose."

"We all got to do what we can."

With those words, the old man nodded to himself then turned back to his work. After half a minute Donny realized that there was nowhere to go with that conversation.

Gonna be dark soon.

Yeah, well, sure. Happens a lot around nighttime.

Crazy old fuck.

Donny walked on.

When he was just at the end of the Guthrie fence he heard a sound and turned to see a man riding a small tractor. Far, far away, though. Way on the other side of a harvested field. The tractor looked like one of those really old kinds, the ones that looked a little like a 1950s hot rod. It chugged along, puffing smoke but not really making much noise. At least not much of it reached Donny. Only an echo of an echo.

He cupped his hands around his eyes to try and see who was riding it. But all he could see was a man in coveralls with hair that could have been white or blond.

Even so, Donny lifted his hand and waved.

The man on the tractor waved back.

Maybe another old guy, but not an old fuck.

It was a simple conversation between strangers a mile apart. Donny wondered if it was a stranger, though. Might have been another of the Guthries. Or it might have been someone working for them. Or, hell, maybe it was whoever bought the farm if the surviving Guthries sold it after the Trouble. Didn't much matter. It was just nice to see someone.

Anyone.

The Guthrie farm ended at Dark Hollow Road, and Donny lingered at the crossroads for a moment, staring down the twisted side road. Not that he could see much, certainly not all the way to the Passion Pit where everyone went to get high or get laid, but it was down there. That's where he and Donny went with those two girls. Last place he went in town before he climbed onto a bus to go learn how to be a soldier.

That last good night and day. All those laughs, the snuggling, cuddling sex in the tent with Judy, while Jim and Cindy screwed each other's brains out in a sleeping bag by their campfire. A great night.

But then he thought about Judy. She hadn't written to him, not once in all the time he was away. He never heard from her after that night.

That was strange. It felt bad. For a long time it made him wonder if he was lousy in the sack, but over time he realized that probably wasn't it. Judy had gone to college and that was a different world than a war half a world away. Maybe the sex and the pot they'd smoked was some kind of close-one-door-open-another thing. Like he and Jim were doing with their last blast weekend before going to war.

Maybe.

He'd written to her, though.

Four letters with no replies before he got the idea that she wasn't ever going to write back.

In some way he supposed she was as dead to him as his folks and town. And Jim.

"Jesus, you're a gloomy fuck, too," he told himself. He turned away from Dark Hollow Road and the dead memories, disgusted with himself for thoughts like that.

On the road, the traffic was still a no-show, so he drifted into the center of the two-lane, liking the sound his heels made on the blacktop. A soft but solid *tok-tok-tok*. The echo of it bounced off the walls of trees that divided one farm from another.

At the top of a hill he looked down a long sweep and the beauty of his town nearly pulled more tears from him. The farms were not the geometrically perfect squares of some of the agricultural areas he'd seen. Some were angled this way, others turned that, with hedgerows and fences and rows of oaks to create borders. Cornfields swayed gently like waves on a slow ocean. Pumpkins dotted green fields with dots of orange. Autumn wheat blew like marsh grass in the soft breeze.

High above, a crow cried out with a call that was so plaintive, so desperately sad that the smile bled away from Donny's features. With the distortion of distance and wind, it sounded like the scream of a baby. Or the banshee wail of a woman kneeling over the body of a dead child.

Donny had seen that image, heard that sound too many times. In Iraq, in Afghanistan.

He touched his shirt over the scars, remembering pain. Remembering all the dying that went on over there.

But it went on here, too.

While he was gone, his town died, too.

Except for the one car that crossed the bridge, there hadn't been a single vehicle on the road. A tractor in a field hardly counted. And only two old sonsabitches at the Guthrie place. All of the other fields and the whole length of Route A32 were empty. It was Halloween. The road should have been packed with cars. Jeez . . . had the Trouble totally killed the town's tourism economy? That would seriously blow. Just about every family in town had their income either tied to farming stuff like Indian corn and pumpkins or to attractions like the Haunted Hayride, the Haunted House, the Dead-end Drive-in, and other seasonal things. Had the Halloween Festival not been revived? Could he have been wrong about the town starting to come back from the Trouble?

It was weird.

Donny felt suddenly scared. Where *was* everyone else?

Had the town died for real?

Had he come home—come all these miles—to a ghost town?

High above the far row of mountains he saw a white cloud float between him and the sun. Its vast purple shadow covered most of the horizon line and as it sailed across the sky toward him, it dragged its dark shadow below, sweeping the land, brushing away details with a broom of darkness.

The belly of the cloud thickened, turned bruised and was suddenly veined with red lightning.

A storm was coming.

He hadn't noticed it building, but at the rate it was growing it was going to catch him out here on the road.

He suddenly wondered if that's what the old guy on the ladder was trying to say.

Gonna be dark soon,

He looked over his shoulder at the road he'd walked. It was a black ribbon fading out of sight as the shadows covered it. Up ahead was eight miles of hills between him and a bar or a Motel 6. He chewed his lip as he debated his options. The breeze was stiffening and it was wet. It was going to rain hard and cold. And soon.

Maybe he could go back and ask one of the guys at the Guthrie place for a ride into town. Or a dry spot on a porch to wait it all out.

He could have done that.

Didn't.

Instead he let his gaze drift over to the thick wall of oaks and pines beyond the closest field. He could haul ass over there and stay dry under the canopy of leaves. Yeah, sure, you weren't supposed to stand under trees in a lightning storm, but you weren't supposed to stand out in a cold rain and catch pneumonia either.

Thunder snarled at him to make up his mind. The first big raindrops splatted on the blacktop.

He cut and ran for the trees.

-4-

As he ran he thought he saw the car again. The Jeep Grand Cherokee that looked like Jim's. It bumped along the rutted length of Dark Hollow Road, a dozen yards to his right, beyond the shrubs and wind-bent pines.

The car was heading the same way he was. Going away from the main road, following an unpaved lane that only went to one spot. The Passion Pit that had long ago been carved out of the woods by generations of hot-blooded teenagers so they could try and solve the mysteries that burned under their skin. Donny had lost his cherry there. So did most of the guys and girls he grew up with. Getting popped at the Pit was a thing, one of those rite of passage things. It was cool. It was part of being from this town. It was what people did.

That car, though, why was it heading here right now? Wrong time of day for anything but a quickie. Wrong weather for anything at all. No tree cover over the Pit. Rain would sound like forty monkeys with hammers on the roof of an SUV like that.

The car kept on the road, going slow like it was keeping pace with him.

Eventually it would reach the Passion Pit, and so would he.

How would that play out?

If it was a couple looking for privacy, they weren't going to be happy to see him. But, Donny thought, if it was someone who took a wrong turn in a heavy rain, then maybe he could leverage a ride in exchange for directions.

Worth a shot.

But the car pulled out ahead of him, bouncing and flouncing over the ruts, splashing mud high enough to paint its own windows brown. Donny watched it go.

"Nowhere to go, brother," he told the unseen driver.

Donny angled toward the road, thinking that if the car was going to turn around at the Pit then he wanted to be where he'd be seen.

He jogged through the woods, staying under the thickest part of the leafy canopy, sometimes having to feel his way through rain-black shadows.

When he got to the edge of the clearing he jerked to a stop.

The car was there.

Except that it wasn't.

It was the wrong car.

Same make, same model. Same color. The muddy tire tracks curved off the road and ended right there. Those ruts were only just now filling with rainwater.

But it had to be the wrong car.

Had to be.

"What the fuck . . . ?" Donny said aloud.

The car sat there at the edge of the Pit.

Maybe not "sat." Hunched. Lay. Something like that. Donny stared at it with a face as slack as if he'd been slapped silly.

The car was old. Rusted.

Dead.

The tires were nothing but rags, the rims flecked with red rust. There were dents and deep gouges in the faded paintwork. Spider-web cracks clouded the windshield. The side windows were busted out; leaving only jagged teeth in black mouths. Creeper vines snaked along the length of the SUV and coiled around the bars of the roof rack.

The car was dead.

Dead.

Cold and rusted and motherfucking dead.

He didn't know what to do. He didn't know how to think about something like this. His mind kept lunging at shreds of plausibility and reason, but they were too thin and slippery to grab. This made no sense.

No goddamn sense.

He stood just inside the wall of the forest. It was thinner here and rain popped down on him. Hitting his shoulders and chest and forehead like a big wet finger jabbing him every time he tried to concoct an explanation for it.

He turned and looked at the curving tire tracks. No chance at all that they belonged to any other car than this. He looked at the car. No way it had driven past him. He looked at the road. There was nowhere else to go. The Pit was the only destination on that road. The Pit was the only place wide enough to turn around and go back, and besides, Donny had been close enough to the road to have definitely seen something go past him.

It made no sense.

No sense.

No sense.

Donny didn't realize that he was crying until the tears curled past his lips and he tasted salt.

"Oh, man," he said as he sagged down into a squat, buttocks on heels, palms over his face, shoulders twitching with tears that wanted to break like a tide from his chest. His voice sounded thin, like it was made out of cracked glass. "Oh shit, oh shit, oh shit."

"Yeah," said a voice behind him. "It's all total shit."

Donny almost jumped out of his skin. He whirled, rose to his feet, fists balled, heart hammering, ready to yell or fight or run.

Instead he froze right there, half up, bent over, mouth open, heart nearly jerking to a halt in his chest.

A figure stood fifteen feet away. He'd managed to come this close without making a sound. Tall, thin, dressed in a Pine Deep Scarecrows football shirt. The shirt was torn, with ragged cloth drooping down to expose pale skin beneath; the material darkened as if by oil or chocolate, or . . .

Donny felt his own mouth fall open.

The world seemed to fall over sideways.

The figure had a big shit-eating grin on his face.

"Hey, Donny," said Jim.

-5-

"What the fuck?"

It was all Donny said, and he said it five or six times.

Jim laughed.

"No," growled Donny, "I mean what the fuck?"

"Guess you're the fuck," said Jim. "Christ on a stick, you should see the look on your face."

"You can't," began Donny. "I mean . . . you just can't. You can't . . . "

"Yeah," agreed Jim. "But I guess I can."

"No."

"So can you."

"Can what, man?" screamed Donny. "This is crazy. This is totally fucked,"

Jim spread his hands in a "what can I say" gesture.

Donny pointed an accusing finger at him. "You died, you stupid shit. You *died!*"

A shadow seemed to pass over Jim's face and his smile faded a bit. Not completely, but enough.

Enough to let Donny know that Jim didn't really find this funny.

Somehow, in a way Donny couldn't quite identify, that realization was worse.

Tears burned on Donny's face. It felt like acid on his skin.

Jim stepped closer, and with each step his smile faded a little more. He stopped a few feet away, the smile gone now. Donny saw that Jim's face was streaked with mud. His skin gleamed as white as milk through the grime.

"You died," Donny said again, his voice less strident but no less hurt.

"Yeah," said Jim, "I did. Kind of blew, too."

Donny said, "What . . . ?"

"The whole death thing? Blows elephant dick."

"What are you . . . ?"

"For one thing, it hurt like a bitch." Tommy touched his throat. "Nothing ever hurt that much before. Not even when I busted my leg when I fell off the ropes in gym class and the bone was sticking out. Jeez, remember that? You almost hurled chunks."

Donny said nothing. He wasn't sure he could.

"They had to carry me out of school. I was crying and shit 'cause it hurt so bad."

"That was when we were kids," said Donny weakly. "Fourth grade."

"Yeah," agreed Jim. "Long time ago. Lot of ships have sailed since then, huh?"

Donny just looked at him.

"But the day I died? Man . . . that was something else. The pain was red hot. I mean red fucking hot. And all the time it was happening I kept trying to scream." His voice was thin, almost hollow, and Jim's eyes drifted away to look at something only he could see. Memories flashing on the inside walls of his mind. It was something Donny understood, even if he could understand nothing else that was happening.

"Help me out here, Jim," said Donny slowly. "You remember . . . dying?"

"Sure."

"How?"

Jim gave him a half-smile. "I was there, dude. I was paying attention to that shit."

"No, assface, how do you remember dying? How can you remember dying? I mean, how's that even possible?"

Jim shrugged. "I just remember. The pain in my throat. How hard it was to try and breathe. The air in my lungs feeling like it was catching fire. Shit, there's no part of that I'll ever forget." He glanced at Donny and then away again. More furtive this time. "I remember how scared I was. I pissed my pants. Imagine that, man. Me dying and pissing my pants and even with all that pain I think I felt worse 'cause I gave myself a golden shower. Isn't that fucked up? I mean, how pathetic is that? I'm dying, some motherhumper is tearing my throat out with his teeth, and I'm worried about what people will think when they find out I juiced my shorts."

Donny looked at Jim. At his neck.

"That's not how you died? he said.

"What?" asked Jim.

"That's not how you died. That's not what happened."

"Yeah," said Jim, "it is."

"The hell it is. I read about it in the papers, saw it on the Net. Heard about it from people in town who lived through that shit, the Trouble. Some drugged-out farmer stabbed you in the chest."

Donny jabbed Jim in the chest with a finger, right over the place where his friend's shirt was torn. He jabbed hard. Twice.

"Right there, man. They said you got stabbed with a big piece of wood right there."

Jim stepped back out of poking distance. There was a look on his face that Donny couldn't quite read. Annoyance? Anger? And what else? Shame?

"Oh," said Jim. "Yeah, well, there was that."

"That's how you—"

"No," Jim said, cutting him off. "It's not how I died."

"But . . . "

"When that happened," continued Jim, "I was already dead."

-6-

Donny said, "What?"

Jim touched the spot on his chest where he'd been poked. He

tried to push the torn material back into place to cover it, but the shirt was too ragged.

"Um," he said, and strung that word out for as long as he could.

"What the hell are you trying to say?" demanded Donny. "You got to start making sense out of this shit."

"Sense? Damn, man, you don't ask for much." Jim shook his head. "I was killed, man, but not by that ass pirate with the stake."

"'Stake,'" said Donny, tasting the word and not liking it one bit.

"It's all part of the way they look at us. They think that stakes and all that shit really works."

"W-what?"

"Stake. It's just bullshit man."

"What are you talking about? C'mon, man, don't do this to me," pleaded Donny.

"Dude," said Jim sadly, "it's already done. I died when I got bit. I was already dead when I got staked."

"Already dead . . . ?"

Jim nodded.

Donny stared at him, his mouth forming words, trying to shape sounds out of broken echoes of what Jim had just said.

"You got . . . *bit*?"

"Bit, yeah."

"By . . . what?"

"The fuck do you think bit me? The tooth fairy?"

"But are you trying to say that you were killed by a . . . a . . . ?"

"Go on, man, nut-up and say it. Put it the hell out there."

Donny licked his lips and tried it, forced the word out of his gut, up through his lungs, and out into the world. As he struggled to say it, Jim said it with him.

"A vampire."

"Yeah," said Jim, "I got bit by a goddamn vampire. How totally fucked up is that?"

They stood there staring at each other as the heavens wept and the trees shivered.

"Before you totally lose it," said Jim, "just think about it. All those stories about the Trouble? All that wild shit everyone was saying about how when everyone got stoned from the drugs the militiamen put in the water they started seeing werewolves and ghosts and vampires. You read about that, right?"

Donny said nothing.

"Well, there really wasn't any white militia . . . not like the papers said. There was a jackass who was a racist prick, but he was working for someone."

"Who?" asked Donny in a ragged voice.

Jim shrugged. "Doesn't matter. A big bad mothergrabber from Europe somewhere."

"A vampire?"

"Oh yeah. He started killing people, turning 'em into vampires and shit. Then there was a big-ass fight and people started killing each other, killing the vampires, vampires killing civilians. It was totally fucked up."

"And . . . you?"

"Oh, they got me like ten days before the shit hit the fan. I was home on leave and I was on the way over to Jessie Clover's place. You remember her from school? Brunette with the ass? I started banging her the day I got home and I was tapping that every night. I was on my way to her place for some pussy when someone grabbed me and dragged me over a hedge."

"A vampire?" asked Donny.

"Shit yeah it was a vampire, but here's the nut-twister . . . the vampire was that kid, Brandon Strauss. You know him, fourteen or fifteen, something like that. Hung out with Mike Sweeney all the time."

Donny nodded numbly.

"Kid's half my size, but he's got all these vampire super powers and shit," said Jim. "I tried to beat the shit out of him, and I got some good shots in, too, but . . . like I said, he's got that strength and speed. That part of the vampire legend is true. Speed, strength. Hard to hurt. Hard to kill. And . . . always hungry."

Donny took an immediate step backward.

"Hey," said Jim, "no, man . . . don't be like that. You're my road dog. I'm not going to hurt you."

"You're a fucking vampire, man," said Donny.

"Yeah, well, that part sucks."

They stood there, cold and awkward as the rain fell. Donny pointed to his friend's chest.

"You did get stabbed though, right?"

"Yeah, and that hurt, too. Hurt like a bastard. That's the thing . . . even being, um, like dead and all? We still feel pain. And that hurt. Not as much as Brandon killing me, but it was bad."

"What happened?"

Jim's eyes darted away again. "He was alive," he said. "Even though he was looped on drugs from the water, he was alive. I was hurt . . . and I was hungry."

"Oh, shit . . . "

"Yeah," said Jim. "It kind of blows. I mean . . . it's evil and all that, but for some reason I don't really seem to give much of a shit about that. It's nasty. It's messy, and even though I have to kill, I really can't stand the fucking screaming. Oh, man, you think it's bad when you're like at a concert and everyone's yelling? For me, it's like that but like ten times worse. All that heightened sense of hearing crap . . . it sounds good, it sounds like superhero shit, but then when you actually hear a full-throat, balls-to-the-wall death scream, you go about half deaf. Your head wants to explode and the pain drives you bat shit."

He stopped as if considering the kind of picture his words were painting.

He sighed.

"Long story short, man," he half-mumbled, "I only died that one time. And if I'm careful and smart and follow the rules, I won't ever die again."

Donny echoed those last four words. "Won't ever die again."

"Yeah."

"But you're killing other people?"

Donny looked momentarily surprised. "Oh, the vampire thing. No, man, that's yesterday's news. I don't hunt like that."

"What do you mean?"

"What I said. I haven't made that kind of kill in years, man. Not since right after the Trouble."

Donny narrowed his eyes. "You expect me to believe that?"

"Shit, man, you can believe what you want. But it's true. I can live off of animals. There's a whole state forest right here. As long as I feed every couple of weeks, I'm good to go. The taste blows, but I figure it's kind of like being a vegan. It may not taste good but it's better for my health."

"Why? What made you stop?"

"The Big Bad got killed. That night when the town burned, somebody must have killed the vampire that started all this."

"Who?"

"Shit if I know. I wasn't there when it happened. I was, um . . . doing other stuff."

"Killing people?"

Jim looked away once more. "You don't understand how hard it is. The hunger? It screams in your head. Especially back then, especially when the Big Bad was alive. It was like he juiced us all, amped us up. You couldn't fight it. And when he died? Christ, it was like a part of me died, too. I wanted to die. Really, man, I wanted to kill myself."

"But you can't die."

Jim snorted. "Everything can die."

"But you said that you couldn't die."

"No, I said that if I was careful I wouldn't die. Not the same thing."

Donny frowned. "You can die?"

"Sure. That night, when we had the Trouble? Couple of hundred of us died."

"There were that many?"

"Yeah. Would have been thousands if the Big Bad had his way. But we almost all died that night."

"Almost all? There's more like you?"

Jim didn't answer that, but that was answer enough.

"This is bullshit," grumbled Donny. Then he corrected himself. "This is nuts."

"It's the world, man. Bigger, weirder, badder than we ever thought. And lately it's started to get worse. There's more . . . of them, of people like me."

"Vampires," Donny supplied.

Jim flinched. "Yeah. More vampires and maybe something coming—something like the Big Bad we had—coming back. People . . . or something . . . are starting to hunt. Not animals, like we been doing . . . but humans."

"What do you mean something's coming? What's coming?'

Jim said, "Bad times are coming, Donny. Bad times are here. It's getting dark and there's something coming. I . . . can feel it. I can feel the pull. It's Halloween, man. Stuff . . . happens on Halloween. Halloween kicks open a door. You're from here, you know that. Something's going to take a bite out of town."

"No," said Donny, dismissing all of this as if it was unreal.

His gaze drifted over to the rusted out car. Jim followed his line of gaze.

"Is that yours?" asked Donny.

"Yeah. I miss that old heap. We had some fun with that."

"It's a wreck."

"Well, yeah. Been like that for years."

"But I saw you driving it."

Jim frowned.

"No, man."

"I did. On the bridge and then ten minutes ago."

"Really," said Jim, "that car's deader than me. It's *dead* dead, you know?"

"No, I don't know," snapped Donny. "None of this makes sense. I finally manage to get home, and you want me to just accept all this shit?"

Jim shrugged.

"It's bullshit," snarled Donny suddenly. "This? All of this? It's bullshit."

"It is what it is."

Donny stepped forward and suddenly shoved Jim. "Don't give me that crap, Jim. We went to fucking war, man. We enlisted to fight for this, to protect all of this." He waved his arms as if to indicate the whole of Pine Deep and everyone in it. "And while we're out there fighting real bad guys—terrorists, the Taliban, Al-Qaeda and shit—you're trying to tell me that vampires came in and killed everyone I know? You want me to believe that?"

Jim spread his hands again.

Donny shoved him again. "No! I fought every day to get back home. I bled to get back home. Do you have any idea how many firefights I've been in? How many times I was nearly killed? How many times I got hurt? Do you have any idea what kind of hell I went through?"

"I know, man."

"No you don't. You went into the navy, Jim. You played it safe. But I went to fucking war. Real war. I fought to protect . . . to protect . . . "

Fresh tears ran down his face. They felt as cold as the rain.

Colder.

"And it's all for shit. There are more like you out there. They're going to keep feeding on my town. They're going to make a punk out of me because they'll just take away everything I fought for."

Jim looked at him, and there was a deep sadness in his eyes. "Donny . . . believe me, man, I do know what you went through. I know all about it. Everything."

"Oh yeah? And how the hell are you supposed to know that shit? You get psychic powers, too?"

"No, man . . . I read it."

Donny blinked. "Read it?"

"Yeah."

"Read it where?"

A single tear broke from Jim's right eye. It carved a path through the grime on his face. "I may sleep under the dirt, dude, but I do read the papers. I read all about you."

"What are you . . . ?"

"They did a whole big story on you. Donny Castleberry, Pine Deep's war hero." Jim shook his head. "Donny . . . I read your obituary, man."

Donny said nothing.

"They had the whole story. You saving a couple of guys. Getting shot. They played it up, big, too. Said that you killed four Taliban including the one who shot you. You went down swinging, boy. You never gave up the fight."

Donny said nothing. What could he say? How could he possibly respond to statements as ridiculous as these? As absurd?

The ground seemed to tilt under him. The hammering of the rain took on a surreal cadence. None of the colors of the forest made sense to him.

He touched his chest, and slowly trailed his fingers slantwise across his body, pausing at each dead place where a bullet had hit him.

He wanted to laugh at Jim. To spit in his face and throw his stupid words back at him. He wanted to kick Jim, to knock him down and stomp him for being such a liar. He wanted to scream at him. To make him take back those words.

He wanted to.

He wanted.

He . . .

He fought to remember the process of recovering in the hospital in Afghanistan, but he couldn't remember a single thing about it. Not the hospital, not a single face of a nurse or doctor, not the post-surgical therapy. Nothing. He remembered the bullets. But it seemed so long ago. He felt as if there should be weeks of memories. Months, maybe years of memories. His discharge, his flight back to the States. But as hard as he tried, all he could grab was shadows.

After all, he couldn't remember how he came to the bridge that crossed the river to Pine Deep. None of it was in his head.

None of it was . . .

Even there?

"God . . . " he breathed. If, in fact, he breathed at all.

"I'm sorry," said Jim. "I'm so sorry."

Off away in the woods there was a long, protracted shriek. It was female. Cold and high and completely inhuman.

It's getting dark.

"What is that?" he asked.

Jim shook his head. "I don't know. Not really. Whatever it is, it's not right, you know?"

Donny said nothing.

"When it screams like that, it means that it's starting to hunt."

"It's a vampire, though," said Donny hoarsely.

"Yeah," said Jim. "I think so. Some . . . kind of vampire. Something I haven't seen before. Something bad."

Donny turned and looked toward the road. “And it wants to kill Pine Deep.”

“It doesn’t care about the town. It just wants the people.”

“No,” said Donny. He wiped at the tears on his face. The wetness was cold on the back of his hand. As cold as ice. “I didn’t fight and . . . ”

He couldn’t bring himself to say the rest.

Fight and die.

“I didn’t come home . . . come *back* . . . just to see terrorists destroy my town.”

“Terrorists?” Jim almost laughed. “They’re not terrorists, man, they’re . . . ”

But his words trailed off, and it was clear from his expression that he was reevaluating the word “terrorists.”

“Donny?” he asked.

“Yeah?”

“I don’t have any inside track on this shit,” Jim began, “but I wonder if that’s *why* you’re back.”

Donny said nothing.

“What if the town needed you and you were . . . I don’t know . . . *available?*”

Donny said nothing, but inside his head something went *click*.

“You said that you can die,” he murmured.

“Yeah.”

“Can you tell me . . . how?”

Jim only paused for a single second. “Yeah,” he said.

The scream tore the air again. Deep in the woods, hidden by the rain. But coming closer, angling through the darkened forest and the pounding storm, toward Pine Deep.

“Maybe you’re right,” said Donny. And as he said those words he felt a smile force its way onto his mouth. He couldn’t see it, but he knew that it wouldn’t be a nice smile. Not pleasant, not comforting.

He turned to Jim.

“All bullshit aside, Jim, we both signed up to serve. To protect our homes and our folks and our town, right?”

Jim nodded.

“So . . . let’s serve. Let’s be soldiers,” said Donny. “You tell me how to kill them, and I'll bring the fight right to them. Right fucking to them."

"Are you serious?" asked Jim.

A third scream slashed at the air.

Donny touched the dead places on his chest.

"Yeah," he said, and he could feel a small, cold smile form on his mouth. "Dead serious."

Jim looked at him and his eyes filled with fresh tears. Not of pain, nor of fear. There was love there. And joy. And something else, some indefinable quality that Donny could not label.

"Okay," said Jim. "Dead serious."

The scream came again, louder and closer than before.

Donny stared in the direction of the approaching monster.

And he smiled.

A soldier's smile.

Jonathan Maberry is a Bram Stoker Award-winning author, writing teacher, and motivational speaker. Among his novels are *Ghost Road Blues*, *Dead Man's Song*, *Bad Moon Rising*, and *Patient Zero*. His most recent novel for adults, *Fire & Ash*, fourth in the Benny Imura series, was published earlier this year. Maberry's nonfiction works include *Vampire Universe*, *The Cryptopedia*, *Zombie CSU: The Forensics of the Living Dead*, and *They Bite!* His work for Marvel Comics includes writing for series such as The Punisher, Wolverine, DoomWar, Marvel Zombie Return, and Black Panther.

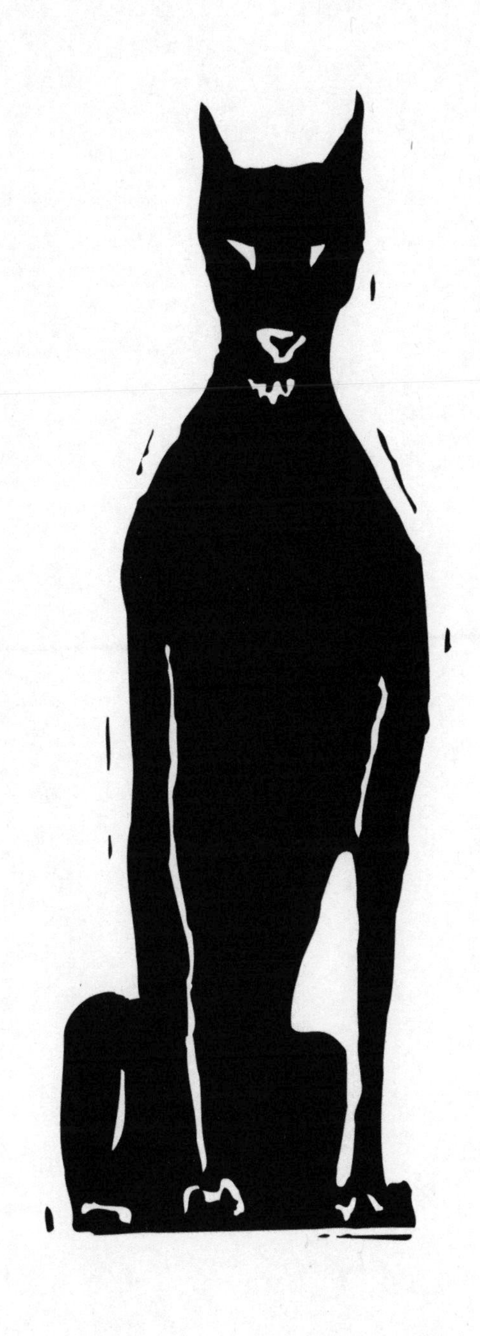

BLACK DOG

Laird Barron

While waiting at the table and watching the door he found himself humming "Love Will Tear Us Apart" under his breath.

She walked into the restaurant two minutes late. She dusted cigarette ashes off the sleeve of her coat and hugged him and accepted the rose he'd brought. First date and the rose was the nicest of the bunch, wrapped in baby's breath and pink tissue paper. He'd destroyed some other pretty nice flowers to get this sucker out of the refrigerated cabinet at the store. He'd also gotten stabbed by a thorn, and it made him wonder if this might be a sign from whatever gods watch over the chariot races of the Hippodrome of Romance.

They sat across from one another for a few moments without speaking. Her eyes were brown. No, her eyes were green. The glow from the lamps changed them moment by moment. Looking into their depths disoriented him as if the building might be rotating upon the crest of a wave. He noticed two things: the top button of her blouse was undone and his collar felt a little tight. Also, the room seemed warm. He gulped some water, but the ice had melted and the water went down his throat like blood.

"Your eyes change color," she said.

"I get lizard eye. When I'm tired. Or in a mood."

"In the mood?"

"A mood."

She raised her brow and tried her water. Her throat moved and he regarded the patterns in the canopy overhanging the walkway.

Dusk was upon the world again. It was All Hallows Eve. The sky glowed as softly as the belly of a wine bottle. Street lights and lights in shop fronts were flickering to life along the slope of the avenue. The breeze through an open window tasted of wildflowers and moss and dying leaves. Her scent was lilac in his nose.

He'd been drinking. Scotch on the rocks. Probably not enough of it, though. When she removed her coat, he noted that the flesh of her arms was bruised purple. He breathed in the smell of her and observed how her skin shone, how her breast rose and fell, how her lips curved enigmatically, and nope, definitely not enough with the drinking for him.

"Wasn't something there a minute ago?" She pointed to the sidewalk and the sandwich board sign that advertised the restaurant.

"A big fucking black dog," he said. He'd seen the dog all right—huge and shaggy, black as the heart of night. Foam curdled its muzzle. Its tongue had lolled as it grinned at him from where it reclined at the foot of the sign. "Red eyes. Kinda spooky."

"Red eyes like in a photograph, or red eyes like the wolves in a Disney cartoon?"

"Red eyes like a vampire in a motherfucking Hammer flick." Wow *fucking,* then *motherfucking,* no less, and in under the first twenty seconds. A personal best. He finished his scotch and loosened his collar and stared at the patch of sidewalk where the enormous black dog had lain moments ago. Had there been a leash? A master? He couldn't picture the scene anymore. He remembered the last of the sunlight in its eyes, however. Those eyes were suddenly coals ignited by a breath, and its wide, friendly smile hinted at a sort of knowingness.

"That's not good," she said.

"It's gone now. I've got no problem with dogs. Seemed friendly. Just odd, is all."

"No, no, it's bad luck. Or, wait. Not bad luck—a bad omen. To see the black hound means death for you or someone close to you."

"Oh. Where do you get that?"

"Britain. A legend from over there. My dad went and lived on the moors when he graduated from school. He photographed mounds and menhirs, pillaged tombs. That sort of thing."

"He's an archeologist?"

"Dad?" She laughed. Soft and lovely. "Hell no."

"What does he do?"

"He's dead."

"May I have another?" He quickly raised his empty glass to the passing server. "I'm sorry."

"Makes one of us."

"Ma'am, a double on that scotch, eh?" Yeah, his collar just kept cinching in like a noose.

"What about you?" She studied him now. Focused upon him with an intensity that caused his heart to flutter.

"My old man is alive and well and living in Lincoln, Montana. He races huskies. We don't talk."

"Lucky you."

"Trust me, it ain't luck. Years and years of effort."

"Any kids? Wife? Girlfriend?"

"One dog, an ex, my work. Back at you."

"A cavalier King Charles spaniel. I've never been married. What kind of dog is yours?"

"A pit bull. I rescued her. She's sweet and gentle."

She nodded. "That's what everybody says right before their darling takes off an arm."

"Don't care for them, eh?"

"I had a bad experience. Where did you grow up?"

"Alaska," he said. "My dad was a hunter."

"Yes . . . and so the huskies. I think it's cruel to put a harness on an animal."

"How about a saddle?"

"Ha. Screw the Kentucky Derby. Horse racing should be abolished. Don't you agree?"

"Nice weather, isn't it?" He studied his place setting.

"Totally. I spent the day looking at houses for my mom. She's in Florida."

"She's moving back north. How nice for you."

"Nah. She just likes to shop online. Takes one of those video tours and convinces me to see the joint in person and report. She put in a bid on a place last month and then canceled it. Decided the staircase was too narrow to lug her king-sized bed up to the second floor. Jesus Christ. No way she's coming back to New York. She'd freeze."

"Why does she send you around to recon then?"

"She's a sweet old bird. Who the hell knows why she does what she does?"

The server came with another scotch for him and more ice water for her. They ordered dinner. She requested noodles and something else. He chose the fried rice without giving a damn.

"You're divorced, huh? What went wrong?"

"I was a neglectful bastard."

"Really? You seem different."

"I'm working on it."

"Good."

"Are you seeing anyone?" he said because she'd deflected the question earlier. It seemed impossible that she wasn't. For the love of God, just look at her. He'd already decided not to involve himself in any triangles, had resolved to get up and walk out depending upon the answer. A brief, early sting was easiest in his estimation.

"Am I seeing anyone . . . Huh. Two months ago, my boyfriend left me for his ex. That one broke my heart." She glanced at her hands, toying with the rings, then swung back to meet his gaze. "At the moment it's you, only you."

He still wasn't certain whether that was a yes or a no. Another sip, another moment spent lingering upon the lines of her jaw and neck, the sweep of her clavicle, and the strength to move drained from him. He wished like hell that he enjoyed mysteries.

What did he know, then? She was in her thirties. She clerked at the library. She was a karate instructor at a local school—thus the bruised arms from being thrown down on a mat. That's where they'd first met a couple of years back. He'd flown into town to visit friends, a whistle-stop before driving down to his book signing at a literary bar in the city. His friends, who also attended the school, dragged him to their dojo to meet the gang. She arrived on the scene, knotting her second degree black belt and wham, he was smitten. He'd been married at the time, so he shook her hand and smiled and ignored the sparks that shot out of their fingers and into each other.

A lot had changed in three years. But not her.

His pulse thrilled and that worried him. Married forever and a day, then suddenly alone again, and absorbed in his writing, he'd almost forgotten the rush that accompanied the new and the unknown. He felt a curious and unwelcome sense of vulnerability that reminded him of his youth, of plowing headlong into a towering blizzard. Since the divorce he'd spoken to many women. Here was the first one to get his heart beating faster.

So, he tasted his drink and gloomily acknowledged that the tremor in his hand, the faint sickness in his soul, meant she was getting under his skin in a big way. He sighed and smiled at her and vowed, for the umpteenth time so far, not to say anything stupid, or misanthropic, or inane.

The angel on his shoulder laughed and laughed at that one.

Full darkness arrived. They migrated outdoors.

She took a pack of Camel No. 9s from her coat and lighted one. She smoked and watched him from the corner of her eye. He stood on the sidewalk and breathed heavily. He felt as winded as a prizefighter who'd survived into the later rounds. A cold breeze dried the sweat on his brow. The moon drifted over the black curve of the horizon. Full and radiant as a searchlight, the moon smoldered in the void, frozen as close to them as it would be for another million years.

The couple moved on after a while, stepping through bands of shadow cast by the interlaced branches of lithe potted magnolias and oaks. Many of the shops were locking up. The watchmaker and the baker hunched behind cold display cases, counting tills. A girl in an apron pushed a broom and smiled wistfully. Small groups of college kids drifted between the soft neon oases of bars and restaurants. There were fairy wings, a toga, some glitter and face paint, but few had bothered to get dressed for Halloween. A man played a violin in a second floor window over a darkened bookstore. The musician was a brawny, shirtless lad. Sweat wisped from his glistening shoulders. He nodded gravely and sawed with vigor as they passed.

"Love it," she said. "My brother plays the cello. Damned good. Make you cry." Her shoulder bumped his. "Ah, now check it. This used to be a swell art gallery." She indicated a deserted shop front. The placard promised the impending advent of a chain Irish pub. "Alas, the poor Krams. I knew them, Horatio. Lived here their entire lives, had local artists and poets in all the time. Robert Creeley read here, once. *The* Robert fucking Creeley. Nobody wants art, though. Nobody wants poetry. What they want is another bloody pub the same as every other cookie cutter pub. I hear the Irish mob had a hand in running my friends out."

"Where'd the owners go?" he said, thanking God she'd taken the pressure off him by cursing. He put his hands into his pockets, then took them out again. He wished he'd remembered to bring gum. His bum knee hurt. A panel van rolled by, slow as a shark on the cruise. Its plates were splattered in black mud.

"Yonder." She waved in the direction of the Catskills.

"That reminds me. There are caves nearby."

"Caves everywhere around these parts. Why do you ask?"

"Something about the mafia or Prohibition I overheard. Maybe the War of Independence. My memory is shot."

"Hm. There's also the Iron Mountain facility. They store all kinds of documents in some limestone caves in Rosendale. Hush-hush stuff."

"Aha." He watched the van's taillights dwindle. "I also heard some murders happened here in town. Gruesome was the word."

"Sure. Those are still going on, though. Have been since the '70s. Cops never bagged anybody. Never will."

"Serial killer?"

She stopped. Her face was luminous as if animated by the prospect of blood. He fell in love, just a little bit, then and there. "Uh, huh. Creepo snatches hikers and joggers and street people. Leaves them in the woods. Maybe seven, eight years ago, a Boy Scout troop stumbled upon eleven decomposed corpses in a cavern along the Wallkill. What kinda merit badge do you get for that, I wonder?"

"Hold up a sec. The seventies? Forty years, give or take. That seems like a long time for one guy to be about this sort of business."

"I bet it's a family thing," she said. "Pop passes it down to the eldest son the way tradesmen did during the agrarian era. Some kind of whacked traditionalist."

"Lurid as lurid can be, yet, it never made the national news . . . "

"It made the news. Twenty-four hour cycle is the problem. Today it's a mass grave, tomorrow it's back to celebrity meltdowns and the peccadilloes of the rich and the beautiful."

He stared at the moon and thought about her explanation.

"Are you here to research the case?" she said.

"No. My book is about an ornithologist. He dies in a valley in the mountains. Birds eat him."

"Ah, you're researching birds."

"I'm here for you."

Her turn to scrutinize the moon and not say anything.

They kept on. Residential houses now—old, Gothic models that he'd noticed were common here in the Hudson Valley. Iron fences and lushly neglected yards. Televisions flickered blue in certain windows, projecting phantom lovemaking, train wrecks, explosions, murder. Fires glowed inside jack-o'-lanterns. Lawn gnomes crouched with feral aspects in the long, wet grass.

He loved how she walked. Somewhere between a sway and a shuffle, arms swinging loose, head turning on a swivel in the manner of every professional fighter he'd ever known. She possessed a sort of animal grace that wasn't conscious of itself, but alert to everything occurring within its environment. Heat emanated from her in waves.

He shivered. "Do you go armed, considering the situation?"

"Yeah, sometimes. When I'm not sure of where I'm headed or who I'm meeting. Then I carry a blade."

"Got it on you now?"

"Nope." She kind of smiled and patted his arm. "Didn't figure I needed it. Besides, *I'm* a weapon. You're safe as houses with me."

"I'm sure."

"Ask me where I got the knife."

"The knife you should be packing, but aren't?"

"Yep. Haha, I did carry it this afternoon when I met the realtor."

"Okay. Where did you get the knife?"

"From the Sneaky Fucking Russian."

"Let me guess—he's a karate guy."

She grinned. "Right on. Speaking of the mob, this dude's got the swagger. Broken nose and gin blossoms, wears heavy jewelry and a track suit. Thick accent. Eyes like pennies. A scowl mean enough to make a Spetsnaz drop his AK. Kinda skulks around. He asked me out about a hundred times when he first arrived at the dojo. He got more and more belligerent about the whole thing. Finally he exploded and demanded to know what was wrong with me that I wouldn't date him. Shouting and stomping his foot, the whole routine. I told him this was unacceptable behavior and to piss off before he got kicked out onto the street. Very tedious."

"Ah, an old school eastern gentleman. I like those guys all right."

"Do you?"

"Yeah. They tend to be tough, loyal, no nonsense types. I got a soft spot for that. He'd probably make a great boyfriend after you slap him around a little."

"Sure, it isn't you he's trying to feel up when you're sparring."

"Fair enough. Does he know you call him the Sneaky Fucking Russian?"

She snorted and laughed. "Uh, no. Are you going to listen to the rest of the story? I'm not finished."

"Tell me."

"So, right. A couple of months go by. The Sneaky Fucking Russian keeps training, but he avoids me like the plague. Won't so much as glance in my direction. One night he comes over to me with flowers and a small box wrapped in a bow. I'm thinking, oh shit, here we go again, but he holds up his hand and says, 'No, no, I was wrong to speak to you in that manner. You are strong American woman and I am the dirt under your shoes. I am not fit to kiss your foot.' Then he gives me the box . . . "

"Thus the knife."

"Yep!"

"What kind is it?"

She shrugged. "What do you mean? It's a knife."

"I mean is it a Randall, a Gerber, a Ka-Bar . . . ?"

"Oh. Well, I don't know. It folds."

"You should get a fixed blade and keep it on you."

"Thanks, Dad. I told you, I'm a weapon." She was quiet for a long moment. "Death doesn't frighten me. I've died plenty of times."

"How does that work?" He squeezed her hand and let it go. "You feel warm enough."

"*Everybody* has died. When I was six I went sledding and hit a concrete retaining wall under the snow. Felt my neck crack and everything faded to white. When the world came back into focus I was right as rain, but . . . "

"I understand," he said. The booze made him a bit giddy. He remembered a long ago storm on Norton Sound, the rasp of diamond-bright snow scouring the ice, a universe of white; his hands were blurred shadows groping for purchase, and all around him, inside him, a constant dull roar. "And for a few hours after you came to, everything was in too sharp focus. Everything was too real."

"Yes! Too shiny, too present. I felt like a ghost floating through a world that had materialized just to accommodate me. By the next day I'd forgotten. Sometimes it comes back when I dream, or at odd moments."

"Like tonight."

"Maybe a little." She gave him a sidelong glance. Her eyes were ringed like a raccoon's and they shone with wary innocence. "The portal opens on All Hallows. Tonight is the night to do a séance or summon a spirit, if that's what floats your boat. All possibilities are viable."

"How many times has it happened? The return from the dead bit?"

"Three. You?"

He considered. "Eleven or twelve."

"Jeez, dude! What the hell were you doing before you started writing?"

"Misspending my youth. Drinking, fighting, whoring around. Tramping across ice packs and climbing mountains. The usual for where I grew up."

"Can't leave it there. Tell me a story."

"Oh, how about I do that on our next date? Give you something to look forward to."

"What makes you think there's going to be another date?" She smiled. "Come along, tell."

"I drowned once when I was a kid," he said. "Fell in the creek. Dad had to press the water out of my lungs and get me going again. Another time, very late in the winter, I was training a string of huskies on the Susitna River. The ice gave way under my sled and I went into the black water as deep as my chest before the team somehow dragged me free. There wasn't any bottom to that river. That current is strong and it'll just plain suck you under. Basically a miracle I survived. Got shanked in a bar fight in Dutch Harbor. A deckhand stuck me with a big ass filet knife. Except that's not quite what happened—damned if the point didn't bounce off my chest. Not even a bruise, but I saw my life go pouring out onto the sawdust floor anyhow. There you go. Three stories for the price of one."

She chewed her thumbnail and kept walking, half a stride ahead. She said, "I'm a bitch after you get to know me."

"How many dates in is that, would you say?"

"Usually halfway through the first one. I like my space. Everything tends to be about me, me, me."

"Everything?"

"I'm all I've got."

"You've been fucked over. That's coming through loud and clear."

"With a vengeance," she said.

"Okay," he said.

"Thought it might be useful information. I'd hate to disappoint you down the road."

"That doesn't sound so selfish."

"I like to make people smile, but I hate them too. Ah, the essential dichotomy of me. It might drive you crazy. You'll love me, but you'll be a mad dog."

He chuckled. "The damage was done long before we met. Are you happy?"

"I'm happy and I'm never bored. I've always thought I was meant for great things. But, all that happens is I keep getting older."

"You're in a rut. Press your face to the grindstone and that's all you can see. Same friends, same colleagues, same scenery. The years roll over into one another. Happiness and misery become intertwined."

"I like my rut," she said.

"People always think they do. It's either that or slit your wrists."

Streetlights stretched farther and farther apart. The night deepened. They came to a bridge with rusty girders. The water below gleamed in moonlit streaks.

"I've lived in this town for twenty years and never walked across this bridge," she said.

"Tonight is the night?" he said. "For séances and a bridge crossing?"

"Yeah. Watch out for the ghost of the Hessian." She pulled her collar tight and winked.

He counted sixty-six steps, measuring each stride with the precision his father, a Marine, had instilled within him. Being slightly drunk concentrated his mind, oddly enough. Seventy-six steps saw them atop a gravel embankment that functioned as a turnout for cars. A heavily trodden path began just off the white line of the road and immediately forked. One path descended to the river; the other climbed a hillock toward a copse of gaunt trees and a jumble of rocks. She plucked his sleeve and led the way upward.

The largest, flattest stone shone white. She brushed aside a litter of dead leaves and primly seated herself upon its surface and beckoned him. For a time they sat, shoulder to shoulder; she smoking, he watching the lights of the town and the headlights sparkling along the road. The wind rose in brief gusts and branches moaned in the surrounding woods.

"This is romantic," he said, putting his arm around her. She didn't move one way or another.

"They say there was a grove here once," she said. "During colonial times those white settlers who followed the Old Gods cultivated this hillside, planted oak and sage and conducted rituals. Naturally, the Christians eventually squashed them. Hanged the 'witches' from the trees, or drowned them in the river. The grove was razed to ash and this stone became known as the White Spot."

He raised his head to examine the few scraggly trees that poked from the dense soil, claws raking free of a grave. "Nothing good grows here, I take it."

"Stunted, emaciated shadows of the grand oaks of days gone by. The ground is supposedly cursed, but I come here all the same. I feel drawn like a flake of metal hurtling toward a giant magnet. There's a current in the earth, a conduit. It speaks to my blood."

The moon floated across the near pane of sky, visibly traveling like a golden sail on the night sea. She inclined her head toward him and they gazed into each other's eyes. A charge arced from her and into him. His vision doubled. He beheld himself kneeling before her naked form, lips pressed to her sweet hip while the great and deathly blizzard that nearly killed him once raged against the walls of a landlocked cabin. He had the sense of the moon plunging toward the earth, the dissolution of himself within the following shockwave. As he dissolved, the lilac taste of her was the last artifact of his being to go into that good night. A dog or a wolf howled.

She touched his neck and her hand was cool. She said, "What's wrong?"

"Must be the Great Conjunction, or too heavy on the booze," he said, shuddering free of the illusion.

"No conjunctions tonight. Plenty of single malt, though." She laughed and kneaded his arm. Her fingers were very strong.

"I like your bruises," he said. "Sexy as hell."

"You are a little nuts, aren't you?" she said and kissed him on the mouth. She was sweet with lip gloss and smoke and spearmint gum.

His toes curled. He thought of the Stevens poem about the wind in the hemlocks and the tails of the peacocks and the dead leaves turning in the fire as the planets aligned and turned outside the window. Fear and exultation turned within him. The wind and the cold in his chest receded, growling.

She separated from him slightly and said, "*And I remembered the cry of the peacocks.*" She licked her lips. "Sometimes I can read minds. Ever since that sledding accident."

He caressed her cheek with the back of his hand. "Precognition. Usually during dreams, but occasionally when I'm walking down the street or chatting on the phone . . . Zaps me like a bolt from the blue. Too unpredictable or else I'd hop a plane to Vegas and rake it in. Eerie, though."

"That explains your perspicacity."

He kissed her again.

Finally, she said, "All night I've had a feeling of impending doom."

"I'd say everything has turned up aces so far."

"Maybe, maybe. Can't last. Romance with me is fraught with peril. Consider yourself duly warned."

Clouds rolled across the stars and covered the moon.

"Hm, the gods agree," he said, noticing the abrupt and precipitous chill that slithered over his flesh and into his bones. He felt her breath against his face, but could barely see the shine of her eyes.

She trembled and tightened her grip on his arms. "All the lights are out. Everywhere."

The chill intensified as he realized that she was indeed correct. While they'd been distracted, a vast, cosmic hand had erased the town below them with a sweep of darkness. Fog and cloud covered the world. The rock vibrated beneath them and small stones cascaded away toward the water. In the near distance a metallic shriek rent the silence. Its echoes died quickly and the land stilled.

"What the hell?" he said.

"Earthquake," she said. "We get them now and again."

He stood and smiled with faint reassurance. "The witching hour is upon us. Let's start back. I can see pretty well in the dark."

They inched along the path, and gradually were able to discern just enough of the landscape to make out the road and approach the bridge.

"You've probably already written a story about this while we walked down the hill," she said.

"Of course," he said. "Although, I don't have an ending."

She took his hand and led him onward.

The shadowy lines of the bridge materialized amid the bank of fog that boiled up from the river. As they stepped onto the partitioned walkway, his heart began to drum. He imagined the previous tremor had sheared the bridge in twain and that in a few more paces he'd swing his foot over murky nothingness and fall. There wouldn't be a cold river awaiting his plunge; only the endless void between stars.

Behind them and on a steep grade in the road, a pair of headlights clicked on and pierced the gloom. He understood this was the panel van he'd seen cruising town. He knew with absolute infallibility *who* inhabited the idling vehicle and *what* they intended to do with their ropes and machetes and plastic bags. The dog, or wolf, howled again. Its cry bounced from the fog and could've originated anywhere.

She turned to him and her expression was hidden. "We're not going to die tonight. I promise." Then she released him and stepped backward and vanished. Somewhere in the town ahead, a distant solitary porch light winked into existence.

"What about your sense of impending doom?"

"Melted away by the power of love. Come on."

A pair of red eyes flashed low to the ground and were gone. If they'd ever been.

"I felt afraid," he said, meaning it in every sense of the phrase.

"We're not going to die. Trust me, trust me." Her voice was faint and fading. She laughed a ghostly laugh. "Probably something worse."

He waited for a time, standing on the bridge, listening to the night and preparing for the inevitable. But nothing happened.

In a while he squared his shoulders and began to walk toward the light that flickered and receded with each heartbeat.

Laird Barron was born and raised in Alaska, did time in the wilderness, and raced in several Iditarods. Later, he migrated to Washington State where he devoted himself to American Combato and reading authors like Robert B. Parker, James Ellroy, and Cormac McCarthy. At night he wrote tales that combined noir, crime, and horror. He was a 2007 and 2010 Shirley Jackson Award winner for his collections *The Imago Sequence and Other Stories* and *Occultation and Other Stories* and a 2009 nominee for his novelette "Catch Hell." Other award nominations include the Crawford Award, Sturgeon Award, International Horror Guild Award, World Fantasy Award, Bram Stoker Award, and the Locus Award. His first novel, *The Croning*, was published in 2012; his latest collection, *The Beautiful Thing That Awaits Us All*, is due out soon. Barron currently resides in Upstate New York and is writing a novel about the evil that men do.

THE HALLOWEEN MEN

Maria V. Snyder

Two Halloween Men paused in front of our shop. Crouched in the dark window display, I froze, hoping they wouldn't notice me among the merchandise. My navy blue merchant's robe blended in with the black velvet mannequin heads, my simple mask was unremarkable in the midst of the elegant and colorful masks on display.

Despite the *Closed* sign hanging on the door, the Halloween man on the left twisted the knob. My heart crawled up my throat as metal rattled. I'd just locked it. His partner held a box in his gloved hands. They both wore wide-brimmed leather hats to keep the rain off their full-face Bauta masks. Drops of water beaded on their black robes, resembling little globs of molten glass as they reflected the weak yellow light from the street lanterns.

Go away. Please go away.

But he knocked. Each bang of his fist sent a spike of fear right through my chest.

I squeezed my eyes shut as I huddled in my dark corner. *Go away. Please go away.* But the knocking turned into a pounding that reverberated throughout the building.

They'll break the door down. Memories from childhood flashed—being jerked from a sound sleep by boots hammering up our staircase, voices shouting, my mother screaming as she disappeared in a sea of black hats.

Opening my eyes, I banished the nightmarish images. Only two stood outside. *How bad could it be?*

"Antonella, answer the door," my father roared from the back room unaware of the importance of our visitors. "Tell them to return tomorrow during business hours."

My body refused to obey even though the half-face, Columbina mask I wore met all the legal requirements.

My father shouted again as the thumping continued. The curtains parted and he stomped into the showroom, drew in a deep breath—to unleash a tirade on either the offending customer or me—and threw open the door.

The tirade failed to erupt. Not even my father would dare speak harshly to the Halloween Men.

"Master Salvatori, may we have a moment of your time?" the Halloween Man holding the box asked.

My father stepped back, allowing the men inside the showroom. Masks for every occasion hung from the walls and were stacked on the shelves. A few of the more expensive ones graced smooth-headed velvet mannequin heads to best display them. Beads and sequins sparkled even in the dim light.

The men dripped on the floor, making a puddle while Father lit a couple more lanterns on the counter. Trapped and uncertain, I remained in my crouched position.

The Halloween Man placed the box on the counter and opened it. He removed a bright glittering heart-shaped Columbina party mask cut from leather and decorated with red feathers. "Do you recognize this?"

Daggers of fear pumped through my body.

"No," my father said.

"How about this one?" He pulled another Columbina from the box. This one had been cut to resemble a butterfly.

"No."

"Are you sure?" the Halloween Man asked.

Father wore his usual navy Bauta with the small silver beads, but a hardness shone from his eyes. "Yes."

They stared at each other. My heart tapped a fast rhythm,

drowning out the rain pelting the windows. I stifled the desire to bolt.

The Halloween Man looked away first. "What can you tell us about these masks?" he asked.

Father picked up the green and purple butterfly and examined it. Sequins outlined the wings and it had small peacock feathers for antennae. He measured the length and width and checked the back. He did the same for the red one.

I held my breath.

"Aside from their unconventional shapes and overly ornate embellishments, they are legal," Father said, setting it down.

The man huffed in disgust. "They make a mockery of the law! Proper masks are essential to societal order, not—"

His partner put a hand on his arm. "Tell us something we *don't* know."

"Have you checked—" my father said.

"Yes, we talked to the other *mascherari*. They believe the quality of the craftsmanship points to you."

Father waited. I bit my lip. Would they arrest him?

"And you, of all people know *this* is how it starts." The man stabbed a finger at the box. "We want to stop it before it begins. Before we have to teach another young *mascheraro* a lesson."

"I'll keep an eye out," Father said.

His words seemed to satisfy them. They returned the masks to the box and left. Father re-locked the door.

"Antonella," he said.

I jumped as Father focused his hard gaze on me. *Did he suspect?*

"What happens when the Halloween Men come for you?" he asked.

Yes, he did. "They arrest you?"

"Are you asking me or telling me?" he demanded.

"They take you into custody."

"And then what happens?"

Depending on the severity of the crime, punishment could be a public whipping, being locked in the stocks for a few hours or many days, being forced to wear a metal Bauta mask, and many more things

I did not want to think about. Getting caught in public without wearing a mask had the worst consequences. So horrible, no one spoke of them. My father never told me for fear of giving me nightmares.

Father saw the answer in my eyes. "Don't give the Halloween Men a reason to suspect you of wrongdoing. Understand?"

I longed to ask what reason Mother had given them, but he never talked about her. Instead, I nodded.

"Good. The deliveries are ready, get moving or you'll be out after curfew."

"Curfew?" I hadn't had one since I turned eighteen last year.

"Yes, curfew. And tell Bianca that you will not be able to attend her Halloween party. You have work to do."

"But—" I clamped my mouth shut. There was no arguing with my father. Even the Halloween Men had backed down. They appeared to be satisfied with his answer. *I'll keep an eye out.* Was he spying for them? That would confirm the rumors about him, which just increased my desire to move out.

And as long as I lived in his house, I had to follow his rules. My masks didn't sell as well as Father's, and my recent attempt to supplement my income had just brought the Halloween Men to our door. I shuddered at the memory. "Yes, sir."

I hurried to the back room to load the cart with the boxes.

Father followed me. "Mister Bellini gets two and Mistress Fiore ordered four party masks for her daughters." He handed me the list and their corresponding addresses.

I scanned the sheet, memorized it, slid it in a pocket of my robe before pulling the two-wheeled cart behind me. Rain continued to pound the windows so I paused to draw my hood up, tucking my long black hair underneath. Then I strode out into the wet streets. Raindrops struck my chin and drummed on the waterproof boxes. Everything had to be sealed against the frequent rains. Even my robe resisted soaking in the water. But in this downpour, it wouldn't last long.

The wheels of the cart splashed through puddles and sprayed against my boots. Tied up for the night, the boats in the canals bobbed in tune with the choppy water. No one else walked the streets, only the Halloween Men stood in their dark corners, watching for law-breakers. I yanked my hood lower even though my navy Columbina with the sedate silver trim met all government regulations. My back burned as I imagined their gazes piercing my skin and searching the depths of my soul for guilt.

Normally my forays into the city were a welcome break, but not tonight. I hustled through the city, delivering the special-ordered masks. On my return trip, I took a shortcut through the food district. At the bakery, a lantern glowed behind the closed curtains.

I pushed opened the door.

Bianca yelped in surprise and reached for her Columbina sitting on the counter. But then she relaxed. "Don't scare me like that, Nella! I thought you were a Halloween Man. Your soaked robe looks black."

"You wouldn't have to worry if you wore your mask." I averted my gaze from her exposed face. Nineteen like me, we'd been friends since I delivered a mask for her mother two years ago.

"I don't have to wear it, we're closed for the day." She leaned on her mop.

But this was a public area. And the image of the Halloween Men still burned in my mind.

"Besides," she said. "It was digging into my temple."

I crossed to the counter, leaving behind puddles that Bianca mopped up without comment. Her half-mask matched the color of her buttery yellow robes, marking her as a member of the confectionery class. Brown, orange, and red beads outlined the edges and around her eyes. I turned it over. The velvet had worn off along the one side, exposing the leather underneath. I dug into my pockets and found a patch, fixing the problem.

"Here." I held it out to her. "You can put it back on."

She laughed and waved me off. "Put it on the counter."

When I didn't move, she strode to the door, locked it, and drew the shades. "Better?"

A little. I set it down.

"Relax," she said. "Your stodgy father isn't here. Master-follow-the-rules-to-the-extreme Salvatori." She huffed with derision. "Not letting you take off your mask in your very own home is a form of abuse."

Not bothering to correct her for the hundredth time, I settled on the stool behind the counter. I was allowed to remove my mask in the privacy of my bedroom, but she never remembered that detail. Plus I suspected I resembled my mother and seeing me was painful for my father. At least I hoped that was the real reason, otherwise Bianca might be correct.

Unaffected by my silence, she continued, "Once you have your own home, you can do whatever you want. Oh! I almost forgot." She handed me an envelope stuffed full with money. "They loved your masks, Nella. I sold every one."

Fear mixed with pride—a strange combination. "You didn't!"

She waved away my concern. "No, I didn't tell anyone you made them. They bought them because they're fabulous, not because of your family name. I've orders for a dozen more!"

Overwhelmed, I said, "I can't . . . "

But she didn't hear me. She prattled on about our future shop—a place that would provide all your party needs: cakes, confections, food, decorations, and themed masks to match. Even though parties were held inside homes, the Halloween Men considered them public events and all guests had to wear masks. Wealthy hosts provided masks for their guests as a party favor.

Unless it was Halloween, of course. The only day the citizens could go out in public without their masks on. The day the Halloween Men retreated to . . . no one quite knew where. Rumors speculated they disappear back to hell where they'd come from. Who else but demons would conquer our city and force us to wear masks as a punishment? Others claimed they ascend to heaven. That they were angels sent to discipline us for our vanity and shallow nature. And a few people were certain the Halloween Men took off their masks and enjoyed the day among us.

It was the biggest day of the year with the grandest parties, parades, and entertainment on every street corner. Which reminded me . . .

I interrupted Bianca's dreaming to tell her about the Halloween Men's visit. "And since I have a curfew again, I can't stay and make more masks."

"They are *legal*, Nella. They can't arrest you because they don't like your designs."

Guess her father hadn't terrified her with stories about the Halloween Men since she was little. Mine did. All because of my mother. Had she broken the strictest law?

"Bianca, do you know what happens if you're caught without a mask on?"

She plopped the mop into the bucket. "I've heard they drown you in the Grand Canal, but Mister Cavella says they lock you in the dungeons forever."

"You don't know?"

"No one does. No one has ever returned. Now stop fretting, Nella. *You* of all people will never be caught without a mask on, plus no one but me knows *you* made those masks. And they'll only be worn at private parties. Besides, I've already bought the material and supplies for you. They're in the icing room."

"My father knows." And that was more than enough.

"Oh, Nella, don't let your father ruin your life."

"He's—"

"Lonely and doesn't want you to leave him like your mother."

I understood why she'd think that—the rumors claimed she left him. The truth was too hard to explain. And if I could just move out on my own, the pressure of those past sins would no longer haunt me.

"I'll find a way to make them." I promised.

"Yay." She ran to the back and returned with a box.

When I returned to the shop, my father was already upstairs in our apartment. I stashed the box of supplies in the workroom and then joined him for a late supper on the second story that housed our living area. Our bedrooms were on the third floor, and an attic occupied the entire fourth floor.

After Father retired for the evening, I snuck back downstairs and carried the box and a lantern to the attic. Careful not to make any noise, I cleared an area in the far corner—the one over my bedroom and as far away from my father's ceiling as possible. I set up a work area.

As sleet tapped on the roof, I cut leather into butterflies, snails, cat faces, and diamond shapes. I let my imagination run for hours.

Finished for the night, I considered. My father never came up here—the boxes were full of Mother's belongings, but just in case . . . I remembered putting a box of old sheets up here . . . somewhere. I dug around and opened one promising box.

Instead of sheets, I found clothes, then cookware, and then a box full of bright colorful masks. Odd. I examined one in the lantern light. Not my father's elegant conservative style, more brassy and bold. More like my true style. Mother's?

I sat back on my heels in shock. She had been a *mascherara*, too.

The glass bead rolled across the table. I bit back a curse and lunged for the escaping purple bauble before it fell. The sound of a bead hitting the floor would be enough to cause Father to look up from his work and with a single glance convey his extreme irritation over my clumsiness. The bead clung to my sticky fingers. I fumbled in an effort to glue a line of them along the edges of a basic black funerary Bauta. Most customers purchased the traditional somber color for their deceased loved ones.

Tired from working late the last three nights, I struggled to concentrate on the task at hand.

The bell jingled, signaling a customer. Father stood, smoothed the few wrinkles that dared to crease his midnight blue robe, and parted the curtains separating the back workroom with the rest of the shop.

No longer feeling as if under a microscope, I relaxed and concentrated on the pesky beads. I'd wanted to use the bigger size, but Father refused to let me add expensive materials to my masks. Very few customers purchased my creations when they sat beside a master craftsman's. Which was another reason why I decided to keep making those other designs. The Halloween Man's words, *before we have to teach another young* mascheraro *a lesson* replayed in mind.

I banished those thoughts—they wouldn't find out—and held my newest creation at arm's length, examining it with a critical eye. Not nearly as edgy as my masks for Bianca, it met all the government requirements for a funeral mask, but it had my own personal . . . flair.

The curtains parted with a snap of fabric. "You have a customer," Father said from the threshold.

I stared at him. *Did he just make a joke?* No. Standing, I wiped my hands along my robes, earning a stern glare. I adjusted the Columbina on my face, checking to ensure it hadn't moved while I worked.

"Hurry up," Father said. "They're waiting."

I slipped pass him and entered the storefront.

Sleet pelted the big display windows and the wind howled outside. Two men wearing the gray robes of the manufacturing class stood in the center of our showroom. They wore charcoal-colored business Columbinas trimmed in gray and red. The man on the right examined one of my funeral masks.

Aware that Father remained in the doorway, I asked, "May I help you, sirs?"

The man holding the mask said, "Master Salvatori tells us you designed this?"

Was he a spy for the Halloween Men? "Yes, sir."

"We'd like to order one just like it except trimmed with our family's colors."

Shocked, it took me a moment to find the proper words. "I'm sorry for you loss, sir."

He nodded and although he kept his lips pressed in a thin line, amusement sparked in his deep blue eyes. Odd.

I retrieved the order sheet from the desk. "What colors, sir?"

"Red and gray, miss. And we'd like them on a white base."

White? I glanced up. While still within regulations, the color was . . . unconventional for a funeral mask. "When do you need this by?"

"Two days. Will that be a problem, miss?"

"No, sir." I'd finish it by tomorrow. "Where should it be delivered?"

"One forty-two Canal Street."

In the heart of the factory district—no surprise. I noted it on the sheet.

"How much?" the man asked.

"Oh, my father . . . er . . . Master Salvatori will assist you with the price."

The men glanced at each other as if I'd said something significant. My slip earned me another stern glare from Father before he turned cordial for the paying customers. Well as cordial as my father managed. He had a reputation of being gruff, but his masks were sought after by all the elite. Of course these men would get a discount since they chose one of my designs. Still, every bit helped.

Father shot me a look and I hurried to the back room. I abandoned my current project to work on the special order, pulling a piece of white velvet from the shelf.

When Father joined me, he said, "I expect that mask for Mister Cattaneo to be your very best."

I glanced at him. Did he purposely steer the customers to one of my masks? Was this his way to lessen the blow of trying to prevent me from making more masks for Bianca? Hard to tell.

The row of homes along Canal Street fronted a narrow waterway and even narrower sidewalk. Water sloshed over the edge. My cart's wheels barely fit as I navigated the broken pavement and dodged the waves.

The four-story-high houses appeared to have been squashed together by a giant. One forty-two no exception. However, its windows remained dark unlike its neighbors. I knocked on the door. Gray paint peeled off the thick wood and the bottom third was bloated and warped by the constant soaking from the canal.

After banging again, this time with more force, the door swung open, revealing a young man with short black hair and deep blue eyes. I started at him a moment, taken aback by his sharp nose, handsome features and welcoming smile. Realizing too late he wore neither mask nor robe over his clothes, I glanced down at the box in my hands. Heat spread down my back.

"Your order, sir," I said although he had to be only a few years older than me.

"Ah yes, Miss Salvatori. Do come in." He cupped my elbow and drew me inside, closing the door behind me with a thud.

Panicked, I raised my head. Lanterns blazed in a sitting room to my left. The scents of pine oil and wet muck dominated.

"This way." He headed down a hallway.

Clutching the box to my chest, I hesitated. This was unusual.

He returned. Amusement glinted in his eyes, but he remained polite. "My mother wishes to inspect the mask before we pay the balance. She's waiting in the back parlor."

Understandable. I didn't have my father's reputation for quality. *Not yet, but someday I will.*

As we walked down a tight corridor, the wood squeaked and flexed under our boots.

"The water is intent on reclaiming its territory," he said. "Most of the neighbors have moved all their furniture up to the higher levels because of the frequent flooding."

The reason they hadn't retreated to the upper floors sat in an oversized chair. The woman's large girth and misshapen legs were a bad combination for walking, let alone climbing stairs.

The young man handed the box to his mother. When she pulled out the mask to examine it, I glanced around the room. Two ladies who resembled the young man—probably his older sisters—sat on a lumpy couch. His father sat in the wooden rocking chair. The runners had warped and it moved in fits and starts. Thump, thump, thud, bang.

None of the family wore masks. I stared at the floor feeling almost scandalized even though this was their home. Bang, thud, thump, thump.

"Excellent work, Miss Salvatori," Mistress Cattaneo said in a high-pitched musical voice.

"Thank you," I said, uncertain.

Thump, thump, thud, bang.

"She's the one, right?" her son asked.

"Yes, Enzo. You did well." She set the mask on a nearby table and reached for another box by her chair, setting it in her lap.

Enzo smirked at the ladies on the couch. They scowled back at him.

Bang, thud, thump, thump.

Unease swirled in my chest. Abandoning politeness, I said, "The balance is due on delivery, Mistress."

"Of course. Enzo, pay her."

He strode to a desk and yanked on a drawer. It squealed and then stuck tight.

Thump, thump, thud, bang.

"We'd like to place another order," she said.

"Certainly, just stop by the shop—"

"Not for *those* masks." She tsked. Opening the box, she held up one of my butterfly-shaped Columbinas. "I need two dozen more of these."

Expecting the Halloween Men to jump out of the shadows, I backed away. "I . . . they're not . . . I don't . . . Eep!"

Enzo blocked the doorway. Was he this muscular and tall before?

"Relax, we'll keep your secret," he said.

"I . . . "

Bang, thud, thump, thump.

"I didn't want to work through your agent, who refused to name you. We have a big New Year's party planned," Mistress Cattaneo said. "We'll pay you three times what your father charges."

"How did . . . ?"

"Each of the *mascherari* has a distinctive style," Enzo said. "We checked every shop in town, looking for yours. Imagine our surprise when you turned out to be Master Salvatori's daughter."

And imagine mine. If he found me so easily, so could . . . "The Halloween Men won't—"

"Let us worry about them," she said, waving away my concern. "We've invited all our clients, including the Medico Della Peste and once *he* sees your unique creations, the whole city will be clamoring for them. Your anonymity will only add to the allure."

Thump, thump, thud, bang.

I paused. The Medico Della Peste ruled over the city. If he was a client, it meant this family didn't work in the factories, but owned them. This meeting was a setup. Did they even live here?

Bang, thud, thump, thump.

Scanning their faces, I considered. They didn't appear apprehensive about the Halloween Men. Bianca's family was the same way. They followed the laws so they shouldn't have to be terrified. Neither should I.

And now was the perfect time to shed the fear. I gathered my courage. "I'm interested, but I can't make them in my father's shop."

"We have plenty of space you can use," Mistress Cattaneo said.

My thoughts raced. I'd still have to follow my father's rules and I couldn't keep up with the late nights. I drew in a breath—time to be bold. "I'd like a sponsorship to set up my own shop."

Thump, thump, thud, bang.

The details had been easy to work out. The Cattaneo family would become my patrons, setting me up in the house on Canal Street to start. They owned the entire row of homes and had used the currently empty one forty-two to make me feel more comfortable—apparently I had a reputation for being . . . skittish.

Once I'd made enough money to pay them back and be self-sufficient, I'd open my own shop. The deal seemed too good to be true, but Mistress Cattaneo assured me she didn't need interest on her investment, she wanted my masks.

The hard part would be telling my father.

I waited until after Enzo brought me the paperwork to sign a week after they'd agreed to sponsor me. His family had cleaned out the moldy furniture in one forty-two and converted the upper three stories to a workroom and living quarters for me. The speed of the renovations impressed me and confirmed the Cattaneo family was well connected. Surely, the Halloween Men would never arrest them.

Filling a box with my masks that had languished in my father's showroom—getting rid of the evidence, according to my conscience—I summoned my courage. As expected, he came out from the back room to see what I'd been doing. I blurted out my plans in a gush of words.

"You're a fool," he said. "The Cattaneo family will not be able to protect you."

"From what, Father? I've broken no laws. I'm of age and it's a legal agreement."

His gaze burned right through me, reminding me of the Halloween Men on the street corners. Sweat dripped under my mask. The desire to flee from his anger pulsed through my body, but I stayed, determined to see this through.

"Haven't you been listening to me all these years? They don't need evidence to arrest you. Suspicion and rumors are all they need."

"Suspicion and rumors about what? Other than telling me of crimes and punishments, you never give me details. Maybe if you told me why Mother was taken, I'd understand."

He jerked back as if I had just slapped him.

"I saw them. What did she do?" I asked.

"You saw . . . ?" He recovered a bit. "What did you see, Antonella?"

"I saw enough." I yanked off my mask. Cool air caressed my hot skin. "You should be happy I'm leaving. Then there's no chance of seeing my face. Of seeing what you lost."

Openmouthed, he stared at me. I returned to packing.

A pounding on the door shattered my concentration. I jerked in surprise, knocking over a container of beads. My heart beat extra fast as I peeked out the window of my workroom. Bianca pressed against the door. Relief coursed through me. When would I be able to hear knocking without panicking?

Bianca banged again with her free hand. She held a white box in the other and she'd hitched her robe up to avoid soaking the hem in the ankle-deep water. I hurried down two flights of stairs to let her in.

She surged in with a wave of water, sputtering with exasperation. "You could have warned me to wear my waders."

I closed and locked the door behind her. "You said you'd be here this morning. That's low tide." Then when she continued to gaze at me, I added, "Sorry."

"It's worth the soggy socks to see your face, Nella."

I ducked my head. The desire to cover my cheeks and nose flared. It would take more than a week for me to get comfortable with being with people without my mask on. "You saw me last Halloween at your party."

"Barely. You arrived with your mask on, and then after an hour of hiding in a dark corner, you left."

"I wasn't hiding."

"So you say. This year you are to leave your mask at home and you *must* mingle. I invited Enzo Cattaneo and he accepted."

"Bianca!" My fingers itched to tie on my Columbina and hide the flush of heat in my face. Enzo had visited me every day since I'd moved here. Each time I had my mask firmly in place.

She held up two fingers. "You have two weeks to get used to the idea." Then she handed me the box. "Here are the pastries for Mistress Cattaneo to sample. They're all colored and shaped to match the butterfly masks, and the decorator will have examples of the complimentary decorations for her soon." Bianca twirled. "Our first client!"

In my head, my father's voice muttered, *if this party is a failure, she'll be your last*. I gritted my teeth. It had been easier to move out of his house than evict him from my thoughts.

After Bianca left, I settled my favorite Columbina on the bridge of my nose and tied the ribbon. The familiar pressure helped me concentrate on my work and kept Master-follow-the-rules-to-the-extreme Salvatori at bay.

The squeaky left wheel of my old rusted cart didn't quite cover the click-clack of boots following me. I tried hard all day to ignore the Halloween Men. Their interest in me was no different than the other masked citizens shopping in the crowded market piazza in the misty drizzle. Plus they all dressed the same, no way to confirm a certain two took particular notice of me. I was being overly fearful.

But after I left the busy downtown and headed for the quiet rows of homes, it became difficult to ignore my fears. In fact, they lingered and grew until sweat caused the cart to slip from my grip, spilling its contents onto the wet pavement.

I scooped up my packages in a panic, but it didn't matter. Mere steps away, the Halloween Men stopped to help.

"Good evening, Miss Salvatori," the shorter Halloween Man said as he righted my cart.

All moisture fled my mouth. I rasped. "Good evening, sirs."

"Returning home?" he asked.

"Yes."

"We noticed you moved from your father's house. I hope under pleasant circumstances?" He took the bundles from me and stacked them in the cart while his partner picked up the remaining mess on the ground.

My insides twisted. They'd been watching me. "Ah . . . yes. I'm starting my own mask shop." I touched my Columbina, ensuring it remained in place.

He aimed a soul-burning stare at me. "We haven't seen any paperwork . . . "

"Eventually. I've a patron right now." But they already knew all this. So why bother to ask?

"Ah, yes. The Cattaneo family. An interesting . . . choice for a patron. Their reputation is . . . well known. Perhaps you should resume your apprenticeship with your father. His reputation is . . . well regarded."

"I will think about it, sirs."

"You should do more than think. He'll keep you out of trouble, Miss Salvatori."

In a blur of motion, the Halloween Man pulled on the end of one of my ribbons holding my Columbina in place.

"No," I cried as the silky material slid then held tight, jerking my head to the side. I'd double knotted it, but I still pressed my hand to my mask in case he tried again.

"See? He has already taught you well. Most of the citizens are trusting fools. With one yank on their ribbons we have cause to arrest them. Understand?"

Fear swept through every part of my body. "Yes, sir."

They touched the brim of their black leather hats with tips of their right fingers in what might have been a salute before heading toward downtown.

My heart resumed beating in a sudden rush. If my mask had fallen off . . . Could they really arrest me if they were the ones who caused it? That would be cheating, even illegal. But I suspected they didn't care.

Once I calmed down, I analyzed the Halloween Men's comments and didn't like what they'd implied. After I dumped my supplies in my workroom, I rushed over to my father's shop. The showroom was empty, but he heard the bell and came out from the back room. We stared at each other in the semi-darkness for a moment.

"What happened?" he asked. Neither anger nor annoyance colored his tone.

I told him about my encounter with the Halloween Men. "Did you tell them about my masks?"

"Of course not. You are my daughter."

It took a moment for that simple sentence to sink in. The feelings behind it were more than just a statement of fact. They implied . . . affection. "Why are the Halloween Men so against my masks?"

"Because they will become popular. The other *mascherari* will copy you and even our everyday masks will transform into exotic shapes and designs. The Halloween Men don't want that. When they invaded hundreds of years ago, they used the masks to remind us of our sins. Masks were once used to cover those who had been deemed ugly by our citizens. Beauty had been valued above all else and those considered unworthy had been forced to wear a mask in public. Due to our ancestors' vanity, the masks are a burden we must all bear, a punishment. They'll arrest all the *mascherari* and those who survive will return to making stark utilitarian masks."

"How do you know all this?"

"You're not the first to embellish masks. Every generation has at least one of the *mascherari* who goes against convention. The Halloween Men have learned this and now stop the cycle before it can even begin."

And then it clicked, explaining that box in the attic. "Mother did it, too."

"No."

"But she—"

"The Halloween Men came for *me* that night, Antonella. Your mother left me after. She could not . . . I don't blame her. You were so young at the time, I thought you didn't remember."

Shocked, I stared at him. "Why didn't you tell me this before?"

"It is . . . difficult to talk about."

"What did the Halloween Men do to you?"

His lips pressed together and he held his arms straight down by his sides. The familiar posture meant I'd get no more information about that no matter how hard I tried.

I switched topics. "How did they find you?"

"I didn't hide. My masks filled the shelves."

The knot in my chest eased a bit. They didn't know about me.

Father watched me. "They suspect you, Antonella. That's enough. Come home."

"I can't. I have a patron. I signed a contract."

"I can fix that for you."

I crossed my arms. "Are you working for the Halloween Men?"

"I aid them on occasion."

Horrified, I stepped back.

"You've no idea what they're capable of, Antonella."

"Actually, I do. You've been telling me for years." I headed for the door. With my hand on the knob, I turned. "Just stay out of it. I can handle it on my own."

I strode out into the rain. My brave words fueled my steps. But as I passed more and more Halloween Men, my courage wavered.

"Do not worry, Nella," Enzo said after I told him about my visit with my father. He picked up one of my masks from the drying rack in my workroom and inspected it. "You're an employee of my family's business and under our protection. That's why they told you to return to your father. He can't protect you."

"Has your family ever . . . had trouble with them."

Enzo laughed. "All the time. We manufacture goods and sell them beyond the city's limits. My family gives the Halloween Men some extra . . . wine to look the other way." He returned the mask to the rack. "I have something important to ask you." Enzo took my hand in his. "Will you accompany me to Bianca's party?"

A strange and unfamiliar emotion pushed out my fear. I grinned. "Of course."

"Ah, you do know how to smile." He reached up and cupped my cheek. "Take off your mask, Nella. You don't need to hide from me."

True. With a sudden surge of courage, I untied the ribbons and placed it on the table. And even though I wanted to duck my head, I gazed at Enzo.

Enzo tucked a strand of my hair behind my ear. "It's a shame you have to hide such beauty under a mask. Even the Halloween Men would fall in love at the sight of you!"

My heart spun in my chest. "Don't be silly."

"I'm serious, Nella. Every man is going to envy me at the party."

And then he pulled me close and kissed me. New sensations surge through me, buoying me up like a boat at high tide.

Halloween festivities started at midnight. Most citizens gave up sleep for this once-a-year chance to be outside without a mask and robe. Enzo collected me and we walked through the piazzas hand in hand. I'd worried my skittish nature wouldn't allow me to enjoy the day, but with the streets filled with people without masks, I just blended in. I relaxed.

Jugglers, comedians, and acrobats entertained the revelers. Young children collected candy from those who stayed inside. We sipped wine and ate linguini mixed with a white clam sauce. The sun peeked out from time to time.

By mid-afternoon, we collapsed onto a bench exhausted.

"You're so fun to watch," Enzo said. "It's like all this is new to you."

"It is," I confessed. "My father never let me go out on Halloween until I was eighteen. And that first year . . . " Bianca had told the truth about me.

He laughed over my hiding in a dark corner. "This year is already better."

Yes. Much better. My life had started and I planned to embrace it.

"Come on." Enzo pulled me to my feet. "The Harlequins are putting on a show in Piazza Piccione. You don't want to miss that!"

He was right. I haven't laughed so hard . . . ever. My sides hurt and tears rolled down my cheeks. Afterwards, we ate in a sidewalk café and then headed to Bianca's party.

Since the rain held off, her family set up in the street outside their bakery. A band played and pyramids of pastries filled the tables.

Bianca squealed when she spotted us. "You came!"

"Don't act so surprised," I said.

"I was talking to Enzo," she teased.

"Wouldn't miss it," he said.

After she introduced us to a few of her friends, Enzo asked me to dance. The evening flew by as we stuffed ourselves with creamy cannoli and burned off the sweets on the dance floor.

Despite the party, I couldn't completely shake my worries. During one break, I sought Bianca for a private chat, pulling her inside the bakery for a moment.

"Have the Halloween Men asked you about me?" I inquired.

"No. Since I stopped selling your masks no one has asked. Why?"

"Just checking." Relief raised my spirits. The Halloween Men hadn't taken any more notice of me since that time when I spilled my cart.

Enzo and I left the party with barely enough time to reach my house. At midnight the Halloween Men would return to the streets. We ran through the city, laughing and jumping over puddles.

Slipping inside one forty-two, we gasped for breath. Mere minutes later, the bell tolled midnight.

"Looks like I'm stuck here," Enzo said with a sly smile. "I left my mask at home."

I opened my mouth to remind him I had a dozen of them upstairs, but clamped it shut as he closed the distance between us.

Enzo wrapped his arms around me and kissed me. Heat spiked, shooting to my core and igniting another new, but wonderful feeling. I desired more.

He broke away and gazed at me, questioning.

"Guess you'll just have to spend the night," I said.

"Rotten luck," he murmured, tangling his fingers in my hair.

"The worst." I slid my hands under his shirt.

After that we didn't talk.

* * *

It wasn't until late the next morning that we'd discovered someone had stolen all my butterfly masks for the Cattaneo's New Year's party. I blinked at the empty tables and drying racks in shock, thinking if I closed my eyes longer, all my weeks of hard work would reappear. They didn't.

Enzo checked the other rooms, looking for the culprits. He found nothing. Not even evidence of burglary. When he returned he asked, "Who knew about these?"

"Bianca, your family, my father, and according to him, the Halloween Men suspected."

"We can rule out my family and the Halloween Men. They wouldn't bother to steal the masks."

"Why not? You said your family has dealings with them. Perhaps they thought this was the best solution. We can't prove they took them."

Enzo shook his head. "It's not their style. They'd arrest you and then we'd bribe them to release you."

"You'd do that for me?"

The hard anger in his face softened. "Of course."

"Would it work?"

"It has in the past. How do you think the Halloween Men are able to afford new masks and robes every year?"

I'd never thought about it. Along with many other things.

"We can rule out Bianca, too," I said. "She would profit from the party's success."

"I'll talk to my mother," Enzo said. "We have a rivalry with the Farina family who is also having a big New Year's party." He swept his hand out. "If they knew about the masks, this might be a form of sabotage."

Which left my father. Which made the most sense to me especially if he wished to protect me. But I wouldn't tell Enzo my suspicions until after I visited him.

The rain faded the bright Halloween colors from yesterday, coating everything in dark gray. A few people hustled along the slick sidewalks, while the rest probably slept off their hangovers. Water sloshed and slapped. Empty bottles and confetti floated on the rough surface.

My boots tapped out a steady rhythm as I debated. Should I be angry that he interfered or glad that he cared for me enough to go to such extremes? Both feelings swirled inside me.

I entered the shop without a plan. The bell jangled. Instead of my father, four Halloween Men stepped from the back room.

"I . . . " I inched toward the door.

"Miss Salvatori, we were just discussing you," the closest Halloween Man grabbed my arm, pulling me away from my escape route.

"I . . . " My thoughts buzzed into a jumble.

"We're not very happy with you or your father." His grip tightened.

"Master Salvatori lied to us," the second man said as he clamped a hand on my other arm.

"And you've been very busy creating things that offend us, Miss Salvatori," the third man said.

"But they're legal." My voice squeaked and fear liquefied my muscles.

"In size and coverage, yes. But offending us is the greater crime," the fourth man said.

"The Cattaneo family—"

"Not to worry," the fourth man said. "Your patrons will pay for your return. Once you've been punished." He jerked his thumb toward the back room.

The Halloween Men dragged me through the curtains because my legs stopped working. They strapped me down on a table. Arms, legs, torso, and my head all immobilized. Then they stepped back, revealing my father. I pressed my lips together to keep from crying out.

"You're in luck," the second Halloween Men said. "Master Salvatori has agreed to do the punishment himself."

I screamed at my father. "You betrayed me."

"Not him. Miss Bianca Sommerso was most obliging this morning and her hands should heal, for the most part, by the new year."

Oh no. Poor Bianca! I wanted to scream at the Halloween Men, but Father approached the table and met my gaze.

"I tried . . . " Father's shoulders slumped. "I failed." He reached behind his head and untied his mask.

I sucked in a breath. It was an awful time to finally show me his face. Except when he removed his Bauta, there was a plain navy Columbina underneath it. Confused, I stared until I noticed the mask wasn't tied on. Metal wire punctured his scarred skin around the edges of the mask.

The mask had been sewn onto his face.

Shock and horror and revulsion boiled up my throat, rendering me speechless.

"This is what the Halloween Men did to me fifteen years ago. What made your mother leave. I should have told you, shown you . . . the truth. I was trying to protect you," he whispered. "Instead, it is your fate as well." Father picked up a simple half-mask and placed it on my face.

I screamed and struggled against the straps until I puffed from exhaustion.

A Halloween Man leaned over me. "Keep still and it won't hurt as much. Besides, you should be grateful your father agreed to help us. He *is* a master with a needle and thread."

Meteorologist turned novelist **Maria V. Snyder** has been writing fantasy and science fiction since her son was born. Eighteen years, ten published novels, and a dozen short stories later, Maria's learned a thing or three about writing. She's been on the *New York Times* bestseller list, won a half-dozen awards, and has earned her MA degree in Writing from Seton Hill University where she's been happily sharing her knowledge with the current crop of MFA students. She also enjoys creating new worlds where horses and swords rule—'cause, let's face it, they're cool—although she's been known to trap her poor characters in a giant metal cube and let them figure out how to get out. Check out her website (www.MariaVSnyder.com) for excerpts, free short stories, maps, blog, and her schedule.

PUMPKIN HEAD ESCAPES

Lawrence C. Connolly

With its concrete floor, brick walls, and ductwork ceiling, the space looked more like an artist's loft than a theatre lobby. Indeed, everything about it suggested the kind of disregard for convention that Elle had told him about on the phone. "The New Immersion Theatre isn't about taking performance to a new level, Glenn. It's about transcendence . . . moving beyond convention . . . rethinking the entire concept of character and story."

Posters hung throughout the space, mounted on foamcore and suspended from wires. They seemed to float in air, turning slightly as Glenn walked among them.

The tag lines said it all:

No Boundaries!
Breaching the Divide!
Beyond Audience Participation!

He paused to consider the more interesting ones, coming at last to a splash of black and orange, a carved face leering beneath a jagged title:

PUMPKIN HEAD ESCAPES!

A jack-o'-lantern head dominated the poster, crowning a body that tapered to slender hips and vine-like legs. The feet resembled roots, spreading through a mass of fallen buildings, broken bridges, smashed cars. There were people too, running in terror, eyes wide, hands in the air. Some wore Halloween costumes: ghosts, vampires, fairy-tale princesses—all screaming from cartoon balloons:

"IT'S REAL!"
"IT'S ALIVE!
"IT'S COMING OCTOBER 31!"

At the bottom of the poster, a line of duotone stills showed highlights from the play: Pumpkin Head smashing through a door, Pumpkin Head lurching through a city neighborhood, Pumpkin Head standing before a burning skyline and beating back a hail of bullets . . . or were they missiles? The art left the scale open to interpretation.

Each picture had a caption, bold letters in jagged frames:

YOU . . . see it!
YOU . . . live it!
YOU . . . are it!

"You made it!"

The voice spoke from beyond the posters.

Glenn stepped from the maze of a hall and into view of a familiar face. It was Elle, dressed in sweater and jeans, a little heavier than he remembered, but looking much better than she had on their last night together.

Her face had healed.

She offered her hand. "You're looking well."

"You too."

Now what? A long-overdue apology for causing the accident that had laid her up while he tripped the light fantastic out of town? He'd thought long and hard about the things he might say when he saw her again, but maybe it was best to leave the past behind them. Elle seemed ready to do that. Why shouldn't he?

"Been a while," he said.

"Too long."

An awkward silence.

"You know—" They spoke it together, almost in harmony.

She laughed. "Sorry."

"Guess I'm still stepping on your lines."

"No, Glenn. You never—"

"I'm afraid I did."

"Anyway. You were saying?"

"Doesn't matter, really. You go ahead."

"All right." She released his hand, glanced at her watch. "I should show you the getup. Make sure you're up for filling in."

"The show's really tonight?"

"Like I said."

"And there're no lines to memorize? You said that too, right?"

"Right. No lines. It's all about movement and improv . . . and a rather unusual suit that should fit you just fine." She stepped back, looked him up and down. "You've kept in shape."

"The demands of Broadway cattle calls. I've been focusing on dance. Safer than acting."

"Thirty waist?"

"Thirty-two, actually. Thirty in a pinch."

"Shoe size?"

"Eleven and a half."

"Eleven okay?"

"I'm sure I can manage."

"Hat size?"

"Ah, now that . . . I'm not sure."

She produced a tape measure.

"Always prepared," he said.

She measured his crown. "Seven and a half."

"Is that good?"

"Hold still. Couple more." She checked the circumference of his face, then the distance between his eyes.

"So this is my audition?"

She returned the tape to her pocket.

"Have I passed?"

"Flying colors." She took his arm. "Come on. I'll introduce you to your character."

She led him away from the posters, past a plywood partition, toward a narrow stairwell. "This building used to be a church. It was gutted and subdivided before we took it over. The stage is through there." She pointed to a door in the partition wall. "Control booth's upstairs." They entered the stairwell. "Wardrobe and props are down here, in the basement." She led him into darkness, pausing to hit a switch when they reached the final step. Lights came on, bare bulbs in a drop ceiling, three doors in a foamcore wall.

"The guy you're replacing was a lot like you, physically at least." She opened one of the doors. "I don't think you'll have much trouble stepping into his skin." She hit a switch. Fluorescent lights flickered, illuminating a jack-o'-lantern monster in the room's corner, head resting on brackets, body dangling from a hook.

He followed her in.

"The body is formfitting." She took it down, handed it to him. It was a black unitard, almost like a wetsuit, but with extra padding along the chest and waist. "You can put your stuff in here." She crossed to a closet with a sliding door, opened it to reveal hangers and shelves. "Clothes, briefs, socks—everything. The suit's made to be worn over skin. I'll step outside while you put it on." She was making it clear that their days of casual intimacy were behind them. "The seam goes in the back. I'll fasten it when you're ready. And the headpiece . . . don't touch that. It's more than you can handle on your own." She left, closing the door behind her.

He glanced at Pumpkin Head as he undressed: oval eyes, triangular nose, wide grin with jagged teeth. It seemed to watch as he pulled the unitard over his legs. "Couldn't they make you any uglier?"

The eyes just stared.

He looked away, tried focusing on what he was doing.

The costume felt a little tight around the waist at first, but the fit adjusted as he pulled the top up along his shoulders. The suit stretched with him when he stood, conforming as he moved, hugging him like a second skin. He tried a couple dance steps, then a few more. He was coming out of a spin when Elle reentered the room.

"You still got the moves, Glenn."

"I don't know. I'm getting old."

"Twenty-nine isn't old."

"It is for a dancer." He spun toward her, gave her his back. "Zip me up, dear?"

She tugged the seam. "Not a zipper. Micro clasps. At least, that's what the designer called them. He studied wearable tech in college. He's the one who came up with this design. We based the show around it." She pressed her hand against the small of his back, slid it toward his shoulders, closing the seam. "That should do it. Turn around. Let me see." She glanced at his chest. Then his crotch. Nothing personal. Just business. "The fit's good." She pulled a chair from a dressing table. "Have a seat. I'll get your feet and hands."

"Shoes and gloves?"

"No." She opened a cabinet, took out a pile of twisted things. "Feet and hands." They looked like roots and branches that had grown into talons and claws.

"I'm supposed to dance in those?"

"Not dance exactly. I wouldn't call it dance. But the other guy managed some pretty good moves before breaking his ankle." She pushed one of the rooty things onto his foot, secured it with another set of micro clasps, then did the other. "It wasn't these feet that caused the accident, though. It was him. He wasn't used to taking chances. There was always a kind of . . . I don't know . . . like a hesitance about him."

"Not like me?"

"I always admired your willingness to inhabit your characters . . . take things to the edge . . . *beyond* the edge." She secured the second foot, giving him a clear view of the back of her jaw in the process. The scar was there, a pink thread running from ear to chin, a reminder of the last time they'd shared the stage.

"Looks good!" She was talking about the feet, of course. "Now the hands." She picked them up. "You'll want to be careful what you touch with these." She helped him put them on. "They're not as sharp as they look, but with enough force . . . well, just be careful."

"This is quite a costume."

"More than a costume, actually."

"Creepy."

"Yes, that's the idea."

"But what exactly do I do with it?" He glanced at the head. It still seemed to be watching. He looked away. "What's the story?"

"*Pumpkin Head Escapes*."

"But what's the *story*?"

"Not really a story, per se. I got tired of that sort of thing after you left town. Healing from the accident made me realize I was through with acting, that I need to try something new. I got into a couple of improv groups, hooked up with an investor interested in audience integration, and now I'm here—Total Immersion Theatre!"

"So what you're saying—"

"We're not about story."

"But you said we'd have time for a walkthrough."

"Right. But you're going to need your head for that." She helped him up. "Come on. I can't bring it to you."

His feet clicked as he walked, toes coming down in uneven arpeggios. *Clickety-clack. Clackety-click.*

The monster watched, the darkness behind its eyes following him as he drew nearer. He turned his attention to the rubber-rimmed opening in the base of the head. The space within was completely dark, no light from eyeholes. Once inside, his head would be locked up like a canned ham.

"You've got to be kidding," he said.

"Think of it as a space helmet."

"Space helmets have visors."

"Right, but you get something better." She pushed her fingers into the one of the carved eyes. "Mini cams, one in each socket. They're mounted way back, completely hidden, and each one's connected to an internal viewer. Audio has a similar set up, outside mics, inside speakers."

"Wouldn't it be easier to just drill some holes."

"Not for this show. The stage manager needs to see what you see, hear what you hear. She'll give you instructions as needed, make sure you hit your marks before each improv. And if you have questions, there's a vocal mic near your chin. She talks to you, you talk to her, and the audience never hears a word."

"I'll be hermetically sealed."

"Pretty much. Your head, anyway."

"How do I breathe?"

"Right! That's the coolest part. There're intakes in the back of the mouth."

"Holes?"

"Not just holes. There's a series of resonators between the intakes and you."

"I don't get it."

"Resonators. Distortion chambers. That's how the monster gets its voice." She ducked under the headpiece. "Here, I'll show you." She grabbed the support brackets and pulled them down until the head rested on her shoulders. Her chest rose, inhaling. And then the monster screamed. Terrible sounds: cats in heat, lambs in slaughter, nails on slate.

He winced.

She lifted the headpiece, peeked out, grinned. "All you have to do is talk, and the resonators do the rest." She pushed the headpiece higher along its track, giving him room. "Now you."

The carved face waited, staring with a darkness that seemed larger than the head itself. He wondered about the mini cams. Were they on? Were they the reason he kept feeling like the thing was looking at him, studying him?

"Come on, Glenn." She took his arm, pulled him into position. "Can't do the show without your head."

The rubber-rimmed opening was above him now. He tried making out what waited within, but it was dark inside—impossibly dark.

"Face front, Glenn. Straighten your neck. That's it." She tugged the brackets. The headpiece came down, snagged on an ear, then eased into place, enveloping him in a moment of complete darkness before the view screens came on.

Elle appeared, face glowing with the hyper-clarity of digital video. She donned a headset, adjusted her mic. "Test your vocals, Glenn. Say something."

"Something."

"Sounds good. Can you see me okay?"

"Crystal clear." He heard Pumpkin Head's voice coming back at him through the earphones, words transformed into distorted moans.

"I'll secure the seal." She reached for his neck. "You won't be able to release it yourself . . . not with those prosthetic hands. When you need to take it off—" She raised a finger. "Hold on." She turned away, apparently listening to something in her headset, a voice he couldn't hear. "Right!" she said. "Sorry. I should have introduced you. Glenn, this is Lauren, our stage manager. She'll be taking you through your paces."

"Hello, Lauren." He waited for an answer, didn't get one. "I don't hear her."

Elle frowned. "Hey, Lauren. Try again. Channel B."

Static.

"Just noise," he said.

"All right. We'll deal with that in a minute. First things first." She gripped the clamps beneath the head. "Brace yourself. Releasing the brackets." The clamps swung away, transferring the full weight of the head to Glenn's shoulders. "You all right? It's a little heavy. Nearly thirty pounds, but you'll get used to it. Now hold still." She yanked something from the back of the head. The video went dark, flickered, came back on. "You're on battery now. Fully charged."

The video brightened. A strange face appeared, transparent as a ghost, hovering between him and Elle. It was there for a moment. Then gone. "Your stage manager?" he said. "Does she have red hair?"

"Why?"

"I think I just saw her."

"In your viewers?"

"Yeah. Gone now."

"All right. It's the relay. "

"Is that bad?"

"No. It's an easy fix, but I can't do it from here. Can you walk?"

He tried. The head was heavy but balanced. He stepped away from the wall, turned in place. "Not too bad."

"Can you sit?"

He eased into the chair.

"Will you be all right if I run to the booth for a few minutes?"

"Sure." He tried getting comfortable. "I'll just sit here. Get into character."

"The suit's the character, Glenn. You're in it. That's enough for now. No need to go Stanislavsky on me yet" She turned, headed for the door. "Just stay in the chair."

Then she was gone, leaving him alone with all the things he knew he should have said to her, all the things he would have said if she had only given him the proper cues. Life, like acting, was about reacting . . . but she had given him nothing to play off of, only business, as if the past hadn't happened. He wondered about that. A minute went by. Then another. He wondered what she was doing, if she was up to something other than checking relays. It was as if—

"Glenn? You there?"

He straightened up. "Yeah."

"Do . . . me . . . okay?"

"You're breaking up."

"How about now?"

"Yes. That's better."

"I'm in the booth. Think I've found the problem. Lauren's out back checking the router. Shouldn't take long."

"Is she online with us now?"

"No. Just me and you. But listen, there's a chance your video might go dark again. If it does—" Her voice cut out, then returned. "Sorry. That was me. I bumped a switch. Easy to do up here. We need a bigger space."

"Listen, Elle. There's something—"

"How's that head. Not too heavy?"

"I'm all right."

"You can stand and stretch if you need to. I know I said to stay in the chair, but—"

His video went dark.

"There go my eyes."

"Video go out?"

"Just like you said it might."

"Hang tight."

He waited.

Hang tight.

"Elle, listen. There're things . . . I feel there're things we're avoiding. Things about us." He expected her to interrupt again, but this time she seemed ready to let him go. *All right. Go on! Tell her!* "There are things I should have said when you called. About the accident, about the way I left town without you. That was wrong. I'm sorry." He wanted to stop there. That was enough. But something about the darkness took him back to their nights together, back to his flat where the only window faced a brick wall and the only light had come from their charging phones. They'd done a lot of talking then, sharing dreams, making promises that he wished he had been able to keep. "I guess I forgot myself. I always seem to do that . . . even when I'm not acting. And when I am? Well, you know about that." He was rambling now, but so what? It felt good. He kept going. "We never should have been cast as Iago and Emilia. Those roles . . . all that rage . . . it was like—" He was crying now. Not audibly. But enough to overflow his eyes, wet his cheeks and lips. Salty tears. And he couldn't wipe them. What a mess. But it felt good. The weight lifting even as the headpiece bore down on his shoulders. "What I mean . . . what I'm saying is . . . I'm sorry. Okay? Can you forgive me?" He paused, giving her space to reply. But something was wrong. "Elle?"

The video flickered. Came on a moment. Went dark again.

"Are you there?"

Silence.

"Do you hear me?"

Nothing.

Had she heard any of it?

The darkness closed in.

She puts me in this thing. Then she leaves.

It didn't feel right. Or maybe . . . it fell *too* right. Almost staged.

What if she's paying me back? Getting even!

It was an irrational thought, but there it was, and in the darkness . . . in the silence . . . it had the resonance of truth.

What if the whole thing was a setup, a get-even scenario devised the moment she'd heard he was back in town? Was there even a Total Immersion Theatre? He hadn't heard or read anything about it until Elle had called with her proposition. "Look, Glenn. I know this is last minute, but I've started my own company, and if you're looking for work, we might be able to use you."

Use me!

Why hadn't he noticed the edge in her voice?

"I've started my own company."

But had she? Had she really? How much effort would it take to furnish an old church with a barebones lobby and dressing room? No need for a stage or control booth. All she had to do was mention those.

" . . . stage is through there . . . booth's upstairs . . . "

Was he thinking rationally? Would these thoughts have occurred to him if he weren't locked up in a padded headpiece, sensory deprived, stewing in guilt and regret?

The video flashed.

"Elle?"

The room came back into view. Same as before. Just him and Pumpkin Head's shadow staining the floor in front of him: elongated body, giant head.

What's she planning? What's her next move?

He reached for the micro clasps about his neck.

Got to get out of this thing.

He tried detaching the headpiece. No good. It was just like she'd told him. His hands were useless, couldn't even move his fingers.

Trapped!

He got up, stumbled to the closet, got out his clothes. His phone was in the jacket. He clawed at it, ripping the pocket. The phone toppled out, landed on the floor.

Now what?

He doubted he could pick the thing up let alone work the touch screen with his tree-branch hands. And even if he placed a call, what then? Hold the phone to Pumpkin Head's mouth and scream like a horny cat?

Just go. Get out of here before she gets back.

He wasn't thinking clearly. Part of him knew that, but the panic was winning.

Get out. Now!

He grabbed his clothes, crossed the room, and threw himself against the door. It shuddered in its frame, thin and flimsy, plywood over a hollow center: the kind used to dress a set. He backed up and rammed it with his thirty-pound head, smashed it to hell and stumbled into the hall.

The lobby stairs rose to the right, but an exit sign marked a closer flight to his left. He went that way, ascending until he reached a fire door. He kicked the panic bar and lurched out into a city neighborhood: working-class homes, narrow sidewalk, parked cars, open-air restaurant across the way. It was cold for alfresco dining, but the patio had pole-mounted heaters, basking the diners in an orange glow. They were all looking right at him.

Trick-or-treaters approached to his left: a ghost, vampire, wicked witch, and a pair of zombies—all led by a rock-n-roll queen with a blue mane of electric hair.

He dropped to his knees, grabbed his head, gesturing. *This head. Help me get it off!*

The kids stopped.

The girl leaned forward. She seemed to understand.

Her friends watched.

He gestured again, more frantic this time . . . maybe too frantic.

The girl backed away.

"No! Please!" He reached for her. "Help me!"

Bags of candy hit the pavement. The kids took off, tripping over each other until they reached a home a few doors away. The porch was decorated with orange lights, polyester cobwebs, electric jack-o'-lanterns. The kids careened up the stairs. Porch light came on, front door opened, a woman looked out. Then a man.

Meanwhile, the people in the café were stepping back from their tables, raising their phones, taking pictures, placing calls.

In the distance, sirens wailed, coming closer.

The theatre's fire door had closed behind him. No exterior latch.

No way back in from this side of the building. And where were his clothes? His wallet? Phone? Had he dropped them?

His video pixelated as he looked around, finally focusing on a man coming toward him from the decorated porch. He carried a baseball bat, smacking it against his hand. . . .

Glenn turned and ran, around to the front of the building and up the stairs to the lobby. He didn't try working the latches. He just used his head to smash through. The first time didn't work. The second time Elle's voice came back on line, screaming in his ears: "Glenn. *Glenn!*"

He rammed once more.

The door flew open.

He entered the lobby, stumbled through the hanging posters, and passed through the partition door to find himself in the back of a small performance space: no chairs, just a stage dressed with the backdrop of a burning city.

People streamed in through the partition door. Some carried guns, a neighborhood militia of hunting and assault rifles. The people from the café came next, then the trick-or-treaters. But were they the same kids? They seemed younger, with the rock-'n'-roll queen looking almost like a fairy-tale princess. He noticed that for an instant. Then the girl was gone, blocked by the advancing militia.

A light came on behind him, tossing his shadow against the floor: slender body, giant head. And that's when it happened. Something turned inside him, the darkness that was always there. Sometimes he controlled it. Other times it took over, when a character's rage became his rage, when the walls came down between the man he was and characters he portrayed. No boundaries then. Total immersion!

He crouched.

The militia stopped.

"Glenn!" This time it was Lauren, the stage manager. "Glenn. Back away! Head for the stage. Elle's coming!"

But Glenn was no longer in the suit. He was Pumpkin Head now. And the Pumpkin was pissed!

The guns swung toward him, taking aim.

He charged.

The guns fired.

The first shot struck his shoulder. The others ripped into his chest and torso. He lost balance, slipping first on blood, then on a trail of ropy things that spilled across his loins. He dropped to his knees, body in shock. He raised his arms once more, released a bellowing roar, and toppled backward. And now, at last, the micro clasps opened. The headpiece shifted, someone pulled it free. A moment of darkness as the rubber padding slid past his eyes, and then there she was, leaning over him. "My, god, Glenn!" It was Elle. She helped him to his knees.

The room rang with applause.

"Amazing," Elle said. "Just amazing!"

The guts dangling from his suit were rubber, inflated and released in sync with the gunshots. And the guns? They weren't real. One of the vigilantes stood close by, leaning with his hand over the barrel, grinning like an ingénue.

"I knew you'd surprise us!" Elle leaned closer, indifferent to the smears of blood. "You missed a couple marks, but we hadn't gone over those. We'll hit those next time—after we've put you back together!"

Part of him wanted to feel relieved. But his head was on fire now, swelling from within. He didn't need to be put back together. He was right where he needed to be.

"Come on, Glenn. Take your bow!"

He looked at his gloves. So heavy. So sharp. But they weren't gloves any longer. They were part of him.

Elle's walkthrough might be over.

But Pumpkin Head's escape was just beginning.

Lawrence C. Connolly's books include the novels *Veins* (2008) and *Vipers* (2010), which together form the first two books of the *Veins Cycle*. *Vortex*, the third book in the series, is due out in late 2013. His collections, which include *Visions* (2009), *This Way to Egress* (2010), and *Voices* (2011), collect all of his stories from venues such as *Amazing Stories*, *Cemetery Dance*, *The Magazine of Fantasy and Science Fiction*, *Twilight Zone*, and *Year's Best Horror*. *Voices* was nominated for the Bram Stoker Award for Superior Achievement in a Fiction Collection. He teaches writing at Sewickley Academy and serves twice a year as one of the residency writers at Seton Hill University's graduate program in Writing Popular Fiction.

WHILST THE NIGHT REJOICES PROFOUND AND STILL

Caitlín R. Kiernan

Remember thee!
Ay, thou poor ghost, while memory holds a seat
In this distracted globe. ~ Hamlet

-1-

Of course, the first colonists brought their own sacred days and traditions with them. When their Bussard ramjets and shimmer sails descended from the black into the orange Martian atmosphere, they carried with them the religions and celebrations of Earth. But Mars is not Earth, and beliefs erode as surely as anything. One or another belief adapts to the needs of those who need them, or the belief dies off altogether, to be supplanted by a new, more useful, more appropriate *weltanschauung.* So it was with the colonist's children's children's children and with the generations that followed after. Worlds turned—one hundred years for earth, hence two hundred for Mars—and the old ways were duly supplanted. Meanwhile, across the void, the cradle of mankind rotted away under the weight of half-recollected calamities, and the supply freighters ceased their comings and goings. No one was left to remind the colonists, who were now Martians, of the world their ancestors had forsaken hoping for better lives so far away. The elaborate terraforming schemes of corporations and governments were only ever half-implemented, at best, and outside the sanctuary of the domes, the planet stayed more or less as it had been for three and a half billion years.

Beáta is thinking none of these thoughts as she sits at her gourd stall halfway down the dusty boulevard. She is thinking only that it has been a good year for the farms and the foundries, and that the people of Balboa have coin to spend on the march, which means they have money to spend on her gourds and candles and wards. It will be a proper Phantom March, which is never a guarantee. Beáta is always prepared for the lean times.

The boulevard smells of incense, sweeting cooling in candy molds, the leafy hydroponic wares of the greens merchants, modest cauldrons of precious, bubbling sugar. And the starchy meat of her gourds, two of which she's split long ways so that customers may see for themselves she is offering the best on the row.

"Buy'em dry, buy'em raw," she calls out over the clamor. "Fresh for stew or holl'er for the light. Buy'em dry, or buy'em raw."

If all goes well in the scant hours remaining before the march, she'll have sufficient roll to cover both rent on her stall and on her one-room coop five blocks over in the genny district, where the hundred plus wind turbines raised above the dome's roof run day and night, night and day, twenty-four months a year. She'll still owe some back rent, but who in the genny district doesn't? The landlords know well enough to tolerate a modicum of tardiness or watch the empty coops pile up, empty and even less profitable than tenants who only pay when they can.

"Buy'em dry, buy'em raw . . . "

The customers come and go, glittering and painted in their march finery, and Beáta happily watches as her stock of gourds diminish. At this rate, the lot will be gone an hour *before* the march. Which means she'll be able to close shop and climb onto one of the balconies, or squeeze into the press filling up the bleachers. As a gourd seller, she has a certain status among the citizens of Balboa, and respectful folks wouldn't begrudge her that much.

Two women stop and carefully survey her wares, then she sells them a pair of yellow-brown gourds, dried, hollowed, already fitted by beeswax tcandles, already fitted at their tops with jute loops. The two women immediately attach the gourds to their rosaries of olivine and hematite beads strung on strands of transgen hagfish silk. The women have likely inherited the rosaries from their mothers, who inherited them from their mothers before them, and so on. New strings can be purchased at stalls along the boulevard, but the oldest are the most prized, and Beáta can tell by the cut of their clothes that these are women of tradition. They do not even haggle over her asking price, and they tip. For Beáta, tips are rare as blue turnips are to sugar-beet farmers, as they say. The women thank her, offer well wishes from the Seven Ladies of the Poles and the Seven of the Wells, and then vanish once more into the crowd. Beáta grins, which she rarely does, because she's ashamed of the teeth she's missing right up front and all the rest going lickity split. But even a gourd merchant hasn't the cachet to land a health patron, not in times like these, so she makes do with teeth she has left, and only smiles when she can't help herself.

"Fresh for stew or holl'er for the light. Buy'em dry, or buy'em raw."

Beáta Copper's first Phantom March—well, the first she can recall—she was five years old, and her mothers took turns holding her up on their shoulders so she could watch the mummers over the heads and hats of the other celebrants. To her eyes, the boulevard seemed to have caught fire, all those lanterns swinging side to side, twirling roundabout, the gourd lanterns in the march and those scattered in amongst the crowd. It was not so simple to put her at ease when the rods came along, but then they were *meant* to frighten the children. The worst of the four was Famine, three stories tall, it's many-jointed limbs and its toothsome jaws worked by twenty puppeteers. Famine, its hungry gaze blacker and colder than a winter's night on the Niliacus. Not even Old Man Thirst could trump Madam Famine. Beáta wanted to look away, but her mothers wouldn't permit it. Yes, the march is celebration and reverence, but it is also a grim reminder of the gifts and of the frailty of day-to-day existence in this and any dome.

"Buy'em dry, or buy'em raw."

At her Phantom Eve tuition in the week before, she'd been *taught* of the famines that had gripped Mars in the long seasons after contact with Earth was lost. How half the planet's population had died before the 'culturists and water miners had managed to establish the United Provision Syndicate as a functional and effective body. She watched tapes of the complete ruin of Paros and Sagan, of the refugee camps, little terror shows of light and shadow flickering across the temple screen. The pictures from Sagan were the worst, because that dome had been so big and had needed so much to survive. The albino priestess had talked about the seven sol war, when Sagan had raided nearby Barsukov is a desperate attempt to save itself by stealing from another failing dome. In the end, the skins of both craters had been breached, and almost everyone had died one sort of death or another, most quickly from suffocation and decompression. She had been taught that honoring the Seven and the Seven was the only way to insure that those dark seasons never, ever came again.

"The goddesses smile on us, and they hold the Four at bay," said the white-haired priestess, "but *only* through our worship and only through our conservation of their bounty, which we wring from soil, earth, and sky.

"Waste is the one evil in the world. All wrongdoing is waste, in one way or in another. We remember this against our undoing."

Thirty-two years on, Beáta still believes that, sure as she believes fertilizer stinks. But she pays as much respect to the scientists and laborers of the UPS, and never fails to pay her dues, even if it means the rent goes wanting.

" . . . or holl'er for the light."

A produce inspector makes his last obligatory rounds before the hymns that signal the march's commencement, and when he stops at Beáta's stall, she gives him a fat, uncarved gourd on the cuff, the pick of what she has left.

"Now, Beá, you wouldn't be trying to grease me, would you?" he asks, admiring her gift, turning it over and over in his thin hands.

"Ain't no need in that, sir, not seein' as mine's the cleanest on the street," she assures him, spreading her arms wide to indicate every vegetable remaining at her stall. "Not a yea big speck of the phako or scourge anywhere to be seen."

"Then you're as kindly and as responsible as ever," he says, tossing the gourd up and catching it twice for luck, one for each of the Seven. "Clean bill, Beá, as usual. And all the blessings upon you."

"As on you, inspector."

He tips his cap and moves along to the next stall over, a fellow she knows from her own neighborhood. He sells neatly bound bouquets of collards and kale.

Outside the dome, the sun sets, twilight spreading out and filling up the canyons of the Corprates to the west, washing over the plains and channels surrounding Balboa. Drowning the craters. Beáta is visited by and sells to a handful of stragglers, and all but five of her smallest gourds are purchased. She makes an offering, tossing them into the boulevard to be trampled beneath the feet of the mummers, then draws the awning, ties it down, and goes to find her place among the devout.

-2-

Before he switches off the electric, Jack carefully snaps the antique clip into the even more antique crank box and then presses the ON switch. The sound that leaks from the speakers isn't *exactly* music. There might be music hidden somewhere in it, but it was recorded—decades ago—to mimic the wild voices of the goddesses, the wail of the global perihelion dust storms, the shudder of the dome against the gales. Once the lights are out, there's only the flickering, dim glow from the peanut oil lantern. The darkness is heavy and warm and musty.

Of course, he's not alone in the attic. There must always be three and ideally no more than three. Miranda and Dope already sit cross-legged on the plastic floor, waiting for him. In their way, these three twelve-year-olds are enacting a ceremony as sacred and crucial to the community's safe passage through Phantom Eve as the coming procession. Here, on the night before the March, all the children below the dome must gather in thrices to do their part, a duty that must be performed precisely and in all seriousness. Each of the three has already sliced the tip ends of their index fingers and squeezed blood into the lantern.

Jack takes his place with Miranda on his left, Dope on his right, and he's wishing two things: that he hadn't drawn short this year, and that there was another boy in the attic with him. Isn't having to assume the role of teller bad enough without also being the only XY?

Miranda takes a deep breath and begins reciting the invocation to the Seven and the Seven, and when she's finished, Dope murmurs the ward against the Four. Dope hardly ever raises her voice above a whisper, because she stutters sometimes. Jack waits patiently, his eyes on the lamp's wick, his mind running over all the details of the tale he's chosen.

"Your turn," Dope murmurs when she does, and Jack glares at her.

"Don't you think I know? Think I'm simple?"

"Nuh-nuh-no," she whispers.

"Shit. Think I don't *know* my part?"

"I'm suh-suh-suh-"

"Stop it, Jack," Miranda scowls. "She didn't mean nothing by it. She's just nervous is all. Tell me you ain't."

Jack shakes his head. "Might be nervous, but I know my part."

In the lantern light, Dope's face is still pale as cheese, and Miranda's is nearly the same red-brown as the desert. He wants to get up and shut off the crank. Not because he's scared, but who wants to hear those noises? Who in his right mind? They've already worked their way beneath his skin and are coiling, cold and dense, down in his gut.

"Sorry, Dope," he says, even if he isn't, and then he begins the tale.

The crank sings its wordless, disharmonious song.

"Was back at the start of the Seven Sol War, see, and it isn't a coincidence that the Seven and the Seven took offense when Sagan turned on its sister. The Seven knew to the final hour how long the fighting would go on, see. They knew, and that pissed them off just about as bad as they ever get pissed off, because they saw how it would make the Four even stronger than they were already."

He pauses, watching the lantern, wondering if there's anything he can leave out without breaking the rule. There isn't, but that doesn't stop him from wondering, or from wishing there were.

"But they waited," he continues. "They waited until the cannons had done their worst, and the Saganites had breach the containment gates to loot what was left of Barsukov, even if that wasn't much. That was the irony. Most of what they came to steal they destroyed in the war, by their own hands.

"And there were the Four, slitherin' about the skin of Barsukov and getting in the souls of the invaders. Waste, you see, that's the only evil in all the world, just like they say at temple mass. And the militia from Sagan, what had they done but waste pretty much all of a larder that was meager before they showed up?"

"Even if that wasn't their intent," chimes in Miranda, because her family is descended from Saganite refugees, and she can get defensive. "It was desper—"

"Did *you* draw," sighs Jack. "I sure don't *remember* you drawing, but maybe I'm mistaken."

The crank box roars and titters from across the attic, and Jack wishes he'd turned the volume down a bit.

Miranda apologizes.

"So," Jack says, "regardless of their *intent,* the militia did the worst thing possible when, as it was, there was so little to go around. Before they got inside, they scorched the ground. They burst cisterns, fouled reservoirs, even burned crops and grain silos. Hell, by the time the looting started, hardly a rat's squat left in there *to* loot. This made them angry, those men and women from the north, and so they killed even more, so it wasn't only the battles that killed."

"I don't like this puh-part," murmurs Dope, but Jack ignores her.

"And that's when the Seven and the Seven swept down from their towers at the poles, and up from the wells, too. They'd foreseen it all along, how the invaders would do themselves more harm than good—though, even if they hadn't, the Seven would have come upon them anyhow. Waste is waste, if it's a human life or a stalk of wheat.

"Now, back on Earth, in the old days, there used to be these big snakes. Not like any old rock viper or hedge green. No, sir. These snakes, they were so big could stretch from one side of a dome to the other with space left over past the end of their noses. Got hungry, they'd squeeze anything to death they wanted. Anything. Can't recall what they were called, those snakes, but that's what they'd do."

"Boads and ambakandees," says Miranda.

"Pythons," adds Dope. "Them, also."

Jack just glares at them, then goes of with the tale.

"And that last night of the war, the Seven and the Seven came down and settled over Barsukov, and they wrapped themselves as tight around the dome as those big Earth snakes would have done. The Four, who'd been busy and distracted, what with feeding on the dead and dying and the bloodthirsty, saw too late the fate rushing over them. They didn't have a chance to flee before the goddesses began to squeeze in. That's when the dome busted. *That's* when the worst of the dyin' started."

There's a clacking noise from the crank, and Dope jumps, which sort of makes Jack feel better.

"After all, when the people under siege saw how they were going to lose, some of them burned their *own* terraces and ponics, poisoned their *own* water, just so the Saganites wouldn't get at it. And waste is waste, right, no matter who commits it. So, the Seven and the Seven, they went and squeezed like them giant Earth snakes, and the dome started coming apart. So ferocious was their anger, that of the goddesses, that the Four fled back to their caverns down deep below Arsia Mons, leaving the conquerors *and* the conquered to their fates. Was almost a full week before rescuers from the south reached Barsukov, and most those people who didn't die the day the dome came down, they'd already perished by the time help arrived. Only a hundred or so got into the bunkers, a few dozen more air-locked and radsafe in private shelters. Some of the wealth-off, in-clover folk, those few were.

"They say, and it's gospel, when the rescuers were still coming the Hydaspis, they actually *saw* all the Ladies, still swirling about the crumpled mess left of Barsukov, and they looked a thousand times more terrible than the Four. Rescuers almost damned turned back then and forgot the distress signals, 'cause sure the people must have had coming to 'em what they got, if the Ladies were so riled.

"They had to decide, weighing the lives of whoever—if anybody—might have survived against the will of the Seven and the Seven. We'd have done the same."

The clip and crank box squeals loudly enough that Jack has to pause until he can once more be heard over the cacophony. You can buy new clips, the sound clean and adjusted—same as you can buy new playbacks, instead of relying on half-century old cranks that should have gone to the reprocess plant before he was born. But Jack's family grows potatoes and cabbages, and there's never money for luxuries.

"Respect the grace of the Ladies," his mother says, "and be glad for what we have. Don't mope for what we don't."

And he tries.

"The captain of the team, he went so far as to halt the rescuers then and there, and was gonna be a vote, to go on or turn back. That's when the birds came flying overhead, those huge black birds died out long, long ago, and all we have are pictures. Ravens, so they were called on Earth. Shouldn't have been able to fly here in the thin air, naturally, and sure shouldn't have been able to breathe or—shit, you both know—but, still, there they were. And not ghost birds, neither. *Genuine* ravens, their ebon feathers shining in the sun. The rescuers figured had to be a sign, but was it a sign to turn back, or was it a sign to finish what they came to do."

"I'd huh-have turned back, you bet," murmurs Dope.

"Fine thing then you weren't the priestess who read the significance of those ravens. She met with the captain in this dragger, and she told him that—even in their fury—the Seven and the Seven were not without mercy, and by their hands had the miracle of the birds been sent from the past of Earth and the memory of man to beckon him and his team on despite the terror of the sight before them. He listened. 'Course he listened, because that's what we do when a priestess talks."

In the dark attic, Jack finishes the sacred duty imparted upon him by drawing short. He tells of the heroism and the pardoning of the surviving Saganites by vote of the dome councils. He tells of how the ruins were abandoned to winds and dune, and of the survivors of the war who didn't live to see the brassy foil shimmer of Balboa's skin.

"So it was the Ladies did show us how even in the most sour

crannies of our hearts is there something worth salvation. But to this day, to this very day, prospectors and surveyors and the like who have cause to pass by those ruins, they can hear the bombs, and the crash of the broken Barsukov comin' down. Worst of all, they tell of the shrieks of the dying swept too and fro across the flats."

He knows that maybe that last part's true, and maybe it isn't. But he also knows that Phantom Night is more than a celebration of the life that will return beyond the long Martian winter. It's reverence of the dead, and it's time to send a few shivers through the soul, as well. Fear is the twin of Determination, that they dance always locked arm in arm, and there will not ever be the one without the other. When his tale is done, the three children bow their heads, and once the clip has run out an the crank automatically shut off, they recite the janazah, the specific fardth al-kaifāya demanded on that night to insure the community will see another year and to beseech another ten score years farther along. It is the task of the young to pray for the future. When Jack and Miranda and Dope are finished, they quietly exit the attic, and Jack pulls the trapdoor shut behind them and locks it. The clip is in his pocket, and he'll place it beneath his bed, where it will rest undisturbed until the conclusion of the March and the festivities.

-3-

In the strictest sense, the temple wasn't built. Rather, it was found, and then made the *cradle* for an elaborate construction. At least, as elaborate as the dome could manage, post-cutoff. The temple began as a cavern, discovered beneath the northwestern perimeter of Balboa during the digging of a basement vault for a genetic repository by the local office of the Provision Syndicate. Unlike the caverns on the flanks of Arsia Mons, this one is not an ancient lava tube, but was carved through sedimentary rock by an underground river long before the first multicellular life evolved on Earth.

Scaffolding, catwalks, and stairwells—mostly built from bamboo and adobe—wind downwards from the surface, as well as forming various levels. On the uppermost are the plazas for public prayer and the classrooms. The monks and priestesses have their spartan dwellings on the mid-levels. And at the very bottom is the series of interlinked ceremonial chambers. As Phantom Night is the most important of the year, the central chamber is the largest and the one with which the greatest care has been taken. But it isn't ostentatious, as waste is the one evil in all the cosmos. In accordance with the holy writ of the Seven and the Seven, it is functional, sufficient to its purpose and no more.

As is the custom, this year's avatars have been chosen by the drawing of lots from men and women between the ages of sixteen and twenty-three. They are the ones who much enact the most critical of all the observances of Phantom Night. They are the ones who will tread the line between *waste* and *sacrifice,* a hairline that exists only in the heart of humanity.

Beneath the sandstone roof of the cavern, at dawn on the day of the March, the drums sound like an old clip recording of thunder and cannon fire. Their rhythmic tattoo bruises the air and batters the bodies of the avatars. Seven plus Seven daughters for the polar Ladies, and four men to represent the Four. Within a central ring, the men stand on pedestals that have been placed at north, south, east, and west. Upon a low dais of polished basalt, placed *precisely* at the center of the circle, the women stand hand-in-hand, a ring with their backs to the men.

In a bamboo cage suspended ten feet above the dais is a single priestess, the highest appointed of that year, the Junon. Unlike the avatars, she isn't nude, but wears a heavy robe of the coarsest jute and a cap of thistle vine.

Flutes and strings join the drums, and the braziers are lit. The chamber quickly smells of sage, coriander, clove, and burning stalks of wheat. The smoke is drawn upwards through the natural chimney of the temple. Those who live nearby are blessed with the scent before the scrubbers remove it from the air. The avatars chosen to represent the Seven and the Seven turn to face the avatars chosen to stand in for the Four. In unison, the women recite the Litany of Preservation, and then the men jeer and curse them. Now the hands of the Seven and the Seven hang at their sides.

Overhead, the Junon dips her left hand into a gourd and

sprinkles water upon the heads on the women. Then, with her right, she scoops up a mixture of fine dust from dunes near the poles and ground human bone, and this, too, she sprinkles on the heads of the daughters. She gazes down at the avatars, and her face is both solemn and angry.

"Until the coming of the fleets, the Four held sway over the world, and during the days of darkness did they bring upon us the full force of their wickedness and destruction.

"Until the coming of the fleets, the Seven and the Seven slept in their towers of ice, for there was no need of them. But we came from the stars, and we *brought* need. We came, it seemed, only to destroy ourselves, as we had done on Earth, and the Four gathered to feast upon us. But the Seven and the Seven were awakened by the cries of the righteous and the just, by those who cherished life above all else.

"They awoke and did do war against the Four, and drove them deep below, and bound them there."

Each of the women steps off the dais, taking one step towards the outer ring, four of them taking a step towards the men. The women bow their heads, and the men continue with their carefully rehearsed insults.

"Having delivered us," the priestess says, shouting now above the rising music, "but this covenant can last only so long as we remain true and show our respect, and squander nothing which is precious! And as *all* things are precious, we squander *nothing,* or surely the Four *will* be once more released to ravage the world!"

The women take another step forward, wait, and then take five more. Now four of them are very near the heckling men who stand at the rocks arranged at the Four Quarters. At the feet of those four women are daggers planted in the hard-packed dirt, blades of black volcanic glass and iron hilts forged in the temple furnaces. The women stoop and draw the blades from the floor, and the men fall silent.

"Here, in this sacred place and on this morning, we remember the battle the Ladies bravely and selflessly fought on our behalf. In this hour, we offer our gratitude. We do this with no hesitation and with no regret."

The Junon falls silent then, her part done. And the four women descend upon the avatars of the Four with the scalpel-sharp daggers. The only resistance offered by the men is pantomime, but their pain and screams are real. Their wails rise, as the smoke from the incense rises, though few above will hear them, so deep is the cavern.

A pair of monks emerge from among the musicians, each bearing a guttering torch, and they turn the Junon's bamboo cage into an inferno. Her robes, her hair, her skin, all drenched with oil, burn with flame as hungry as any of the Four, and her screams are added to those of the men.

The ten daughters who were not fortunate enough to draw the crimson tiles turn to watch the slaughter of their brothers. All but two among them are young enough to have another opportunity for that honor next year.

But nothing here is wasted.

Nothing.

After the four women have eaten, whatever is left of the men will be gathered by the monks, and—along with the Junon's ashes—will be dispersed among the people of Balboa to fertilize gardens throughout the dome. The four women kneel, and their ten sisters repeat the Litany.

Beneath every dome across the planet the ceremony is coming to a close, and beneath every dome the bells above temples ring out across an indebted populace.

-4-

The dead of Mars are not buried. In the living memory of all the inhabitants of all the domes and that of all those who live on the out farms, mines, and wellingsteads, have the dead been buried. Instead, carved stones are erected beneath the orange-blue sky, carved stones marking a birth, a life, and a death, but signifying the final resting place of no one. The deceased are not ever tossed aside, but composted and so resurrected—bone and sinew, blood and organs—to nourish those who will come after.

Honor lies only in continuation, and the only immortality in repurposing.

Almost a quarter mile beyond the dome's west gates and locks and cargo hatches of Balboa, on a low rust-colored hill, is the vast field of monuments. Always, the wind blows between the stones, but on Phantom Night it blows with the voices of the dead. Even if few have heard these voices for themselves, few doubt the truth of the tales.

One night each twenty-four months, the dead come awake. But not to *haunt* the living. One night a year the dead come awake to howl reassurance across the planum. To whistle and sing thin, papery songs. To be grateful that the heirs to their incarnations are faithful and have kept the covenant to insure the Seven and the Seven keep the Four at bay. This is how the dead celebrate.

The dead sing.

And the living tell tales of the ghost songs.

The sun sets.

On the boulevard, the March begins.

-5-

In their rooms three stories above the revelers, two women lie in bed. Earlier, they were among those visited Beáta Copper's stall to buy their gourd, and they are the mothers of a girl child named Miranda. The women do not number themselves among the believers, not in the strictest sense. For them, this all the expression of metaphor. They might even use the word *superstition,* in the company of like-minded individuals. But they also do not doubt the value of ceremonies. Life is nothing easy, and whatever eases the passage is to be cherished, so long as it doesn't encourage waste. Like the faithful, they find no greater wrong against humanity than waste. So, in their own ways they observe the night. For example, there are few greater affirmations of life than sex.

Beryl sits up and gazes towards the open doors leading out onto their balcony. She's a school teacher, and her partner is employed at the windworks. Together, they can afford a good room above the streets, and they can afford to raise a daughter. Beryl sits and watches the not-darkness of the evening outside. The revelers are chanting, laughing, cheering, and soon enough now the march will pass in front of their building. Miranda is down on the street with her friends, waiting to catch the sweets and baubles that will be tossed by the harlequins, and shudders at the towering marionettes.

"We should go out now. It's getting late," Beryl says, and turns to smile at her lover. "We don't want to miss the mummers."

"Are you very sure?" asks Aruna, whose skin is almost a dark as Beryl's is pale. "It may be we could show greater devotion to the Ladies if we had another tumble."

"It might be you ought get dressed," Beryl replies.

Aruna kisses the small of her back, then lets one finger trail gently up the length of Beryl's spine. "We can't have ours the only dark veranda, now can we?" she whispers.

"No, we can't," Beryl says, standing, pulling on a simple white shift with elbow-length sleeves. "It would be a poor example."

Aruna makes an off-color joke, but she follows her partner's example, gathering up her trousers and a gingham shirt, and they go together out onto the balcony. Beryl uses a pocket flint to light the tcandle set into the gourd, and then she hangs it from a hook on one of the doors. They sit together at the edge of the balcony, letting their legs dangle through the iron bars, as if they were as young as their daughter.

On this night all are young, as all are as old.

On this night all simply *are*.

When she was twenty, Aruna drew a crimson tile, though she never talks about that dawn in the depths of the temple. She never brings up the subject, and Beryl never asks, though she's known for years. Beryl secretly hopes Miranda will be so lucky, even if her mothers do not accept the Seven and the Seven and the Four as literal fact, and even if they have raised their child to believe likewise.

"I can't see her anywhere," Aruna says, but that's hardly a surprise. It would be almost impossible to spot Miranda in the throng lining the boulevard.

"She's fine. You shouldn't worry."

"I'm not worried."

"*You* worry," Beryl replies, and Aruna knows it is pointless to argue.

Below them, there is the warm glow of hundreds of gourds, and the facades of every home and business are adorned with at least one—and sometimes several—soul lights. The sight of it makes Aruna sleepy, despite the noise, or it may be that she was sleepy before they stepped outside, and the glow is only making her sleepier. She lays her head on Beryl's shoulder.

"Stay awake," Beryl says immediately.

"I'm awake."

"You're awake now. Doesn't mean you'll be awake in five minutes."

"Doesn't mean I won't be."

Beryl turns and lightly kisses the top of Aruna's head. "I know you."

The drummers come first, escorted by the rows of temple monks, and for the time it takes them to pass, most of the onlookers fall silent. Beryl presses her face between the bars for a better view. After the monks will come the council and then retinue of priestesses. The women who were fortunate enough to draw the fourteen select tiles this year will follow after, still nude and four of them still wearing the dried gore of their feasts. The Four will be on their heels, in turn pursued by the Ladies. By then, the crowd will be a cacophony.

But before the monks have passed, Aruna is dozing.

Beryl doesn't wake her, not even once the avatars have passed, the proxies of the Seven and the Seven, shadowed by the puppets.

The New York Times recently hailed **Caitlín R. Kiernan** "one of our essential writers of dark fiction." Her novels include *The Red Tree* (nominated for the Shirley Jackson and World Fantasy awards) and *The Drowning Girl: A Memoir* (winner of the James Tiptree, Jr. Award and the Bram Stoker Award, nominated for the Nebula, Locus, Shirley Jackson, and Mythopoeic awards). To date, her short fiction has been collected in thirteen volumes, most recently *Confessions of a Five-Chambered Heart, Two Worlds and In Between: The Best of Caitlín R. Kiernan (Volume One)*, and *The Ape's Wife and Other Stories*. Currently, she's writing the graphic novel series *Alabaster* for Dark Horse Comics and working on her next novel, *Red Delicious*.

FOR THE REMOVAL OF UNWANTED GUESTS

A. C. Wise

The witch arrived at precisely 11:59 p.m., just as September ticked over to October, on the day after Michael Remmington moved into the house on Washington Street. She knocked at exactly midnight.

The house was all boxes, and Michael all ache from moving them. He'd been sitting on an air mattress—the bed wouldn't be delivered for another week—staring at a crossword puzzle at least five years old. He'd found it in the back of the closet, yellow as bone, and peeled it from the floor—an unwitting gift from the previous tenant.

Michael opened the door, only questioning the wisdom of it after it was done. It was midnight in a strange neighborhood; he wore a bathrobe and slippers, and he'd left his phone upstairs, so if it turned out to be an axe murderer at the door, he wouldn't even be able to call 911.

"Hello," the witch said. "I'm moving in."

A suitcase sat on her left, and a black cat on her right. The cat's tail coiled around its neatly placed feet. It blinked at Michael, its gaze as impassive as the witch's.

Michael couldn't say how he knew she was a witch, but he did, deep down in his bones. The truth of it sat at his core, as inevitable as moonrise, or spaghetti for dinner on Tuesdays.

"Okay," he said, which was not what he'd meant to say at all.

But he'd already stepped back, and the witch had already picked up her bag and crossed the threshold.

"I mean—What?"

The cat dragged a silken tail across Michael's shins, following the witch. It felt like a mark of approval. A chill wind chased the cat, swirling fallen leaves; Michael closed the door. The witch set her bag down, turning a slow circle while remaining in place.

"This house should have a witch." When she stopped, she faced him.

Her eyes were green, like pine boughs in winter, or the shadows between them.

"A witch needs to live here," she said, sniffing the air. "Can't you feel it?"

Michael sniffed, smelling only the witch herself. She smelled of cinnamon and fresh-cut cedar. She didn't look like a witch, except that she did. Not that Michael knew what witches looked like. People, he guessed. Mostly.

She wore black, a loose-fitting sweater over a long skirt that seemed to have layers. It reminded him of petals, like a flower, hung upside down. Her shoes clicked when she walked.

Michael couldn't begin to guess the witch's age. When he closed just his left eye, she might be around forty, but when switched and closed just his right eye, she seemed closer to fifty. Either way, her skin was smooth, except for a few crow's feet around her eyes, and a few lines at the corners of her mouth. Her hair hung half-way down her back, dark brown like thick molasses, threaded with strands of honey, rather than gray, and she wore a lot of jewelry—most of it chunky, most of it silver.

"Okay," he said again, then, "why?" after he thought about it.

"The windows are in upside down." The witch pointed.

Michael couldn't see anything unusual, but considered he wouldn't know an upside down window from a right-side-up one.

"The board for that step," the witch indicated a tread halfway up the staircase, "comes from a pirate ship that wrecked off the coast of Cape Cod, near Wellfleet."

She paced three steps forward. The floorboards clonked hollow under her shoes.

"There's a black cat buried in the leftmost corner of the basement. Sorry." She addressed the last to the cat at her feet, not Michael.

"So, a witch should live here. I'll take the attic."

"But it's my house," Michael said. "I have papers and everything. You can't just . . . "

The witch lifted her suitcase: a small thing, battered at the edges, and held closed with two brass catches. She gathered her skirt, and Michael found himself following her up the stairs.

"I haven't even unpacked yet," Michael said.

"I'll help you in the morning. I get up at seven. Tea with honey." She rounded on him so suddenly Michael nearly tripped on his heels.

They'd come to the foot of the second set of stairs, leading to the attic. Close up, the witch's eyes were flecked with gold, like bits of mica in stone. Michael stepped back a pace, but was annoyed when he did. He could follow her up the stairs if he wanted. Couldn't he?

"Hoop," she said.

"What?"

"It's the answer to 47 across." She flicked the crossword puzzle, and Michael realized he still held the yellowed paper in his hand.

"All around, Robin's backward friend. Four letters. It's *Pooh* spelled backward. As in *Winnie the*. Sixteen down is *Marilyn Monroe*. That should give you enough to get started."

"Oh." Michael didn't know what else to say.

"You'll find the mugs in the third box from the left in the kitchen. For the tea. I'll see you in the morning." Halfway up the steps, she paused, and turned again. Her eyes were luminous in the dark.

"You'll want to shut the windows. It's going to rain."

Michael stared until the door at the top of the stairs closed. He listened to the witch's shoes clomp over the floorboards, and wondered where she would sleep. There was nothing in the attic except dust and dead spiders. Maybe she'd hang herself from the ceiling like a bat. Maybe witches didn't sleep at all.

"Okay. Goodnight. I guess," he said to the silence.

Michael went back to his room. He closed the door, and after a moment's consideration, closed the window, too. The witch's cat had taken up residence in the middle of his pillow. It opened one eye, defying Michael to displace it. He sat gingerly and when the cat didn't leave, he risked petting it. The cat rewarded him with a faint purr.

As if on cue, rain tapped light fingers against the glass. The house creaked, settling it bones around them. No, not around them, around the witch. A few moments later, the downpour began in earnest.

The witch came down the stairs precisely at seven, the cat at her heels. She seemed to be wearing the same clothes as the night before, only in the dust-laden light slanting through the kitchen windows they looked deep green, or blue, rather than black. Michael wondered if he simply hadn't noticed the subtleties of shading last night. He handed the witch a mug of tea.

She breathed in steam, be-ringed hands wrapped around the mug, which he'd found exactly where she said it would be. He'd found the tea and kettle there, too, and other kitchen things, which remained in the box, largely untouched. Michael sipped from a mug that had been chipped in the moving process; to his annoyance, he'd saved the good mug for the witch.

"You can't stay here," Michael said.

He'd rehearsed the words in the pre-dawn light, lying in bed before coming downstairs to make the witch her tea. In his mind, the witch had accepted them, and everything had been perfectly reasonable. Normal. In the bright sunlight, with the witch looking at him over her mug, he wavered.

"Look, you don't even know anything about me. I could be an axe murderer!"

"Are you?"

"Well, no, but . . . "

The witch's cat leapt onto the counter, a stream of black ink defying gravity. It twitched its tail, smug. Michael wanted to ask how long the witch planned to stay, and what her name was. Would she split the mortgage payment? Did she have a job? Did she expect him to take turns cleaning out the kitty litter? But the witch's even gaze dismissed all his questions before he could voice them. Maybe a witch *should* live here.

If last night was any indication, the witch mostly kept to herself. He'd certainly slept much better, as in sleeping at all, once she'd arrived. It was as if the house had been holding its breath, waiting for her, and when it finally relaxed, he could, too.

"Is there a problem, Michael Remmington?" the witch asked.

The question came so suddenly, Michael choked on his tea. He was certain he'd never told her his name. This morning, her eyes were amber. She no longer smelled of cinnamon, but of salt; it made him think of storms and shipwrecks.

"No. Yes. I mean . . . Look, I don't want a roommate. Or a cat. I just want to live a normal, quiet, happy life. In *my* house." He left unspoken the word *alone*.

The witch narrowed her eyes, as if she'd heard the part he hadn't said. The cat pushed its head against Michael's hand. Instead of shooing it away, he scratched it behind the ears. This time, there was no mistaking the purr.

A stray leaf, snatched by the wind, smacked into the window, making Michael jump. He had no reason to feel guilty. His name was on all the legal documents for the house. The witch had crashed into his life, invited herself in. He didn't owe her a thing.

"Look . . . " Michael said.

"Thank you for the tea." The witch set her cup down.

Her eyes had shifted color again, taking on the hue of burnt wood. Michael could almost smell smoke in the air.

"Give me your hand." The witch held out her hand, palm up. Her bracelets rattled.

She looked younger this morning, no more than thirty-five, at a guess, but Michael was tired of guessing.

"What? Why?"

"So I can be sure you're not an axe murderer," the witch said. Her smile suggested she might be laughing at him.

He gave the witch his hand. She traced the lines, and her eyes turned pale violet, inexplicably making Michael think of dragons. The witch pursed her lips. She said, "Hmmm." He couldn't tell whether it was a good thing, or a bad thing.

A line of concentration appeared about a third of the way across the witch's lip, like an old scar. Like a sudden flash of lightning in the dark, Michael knew things about her—all true down in his bones.

The witch had drowned in 1717, and burned to death in 1691. In the 1800s, she'd died with a rope around her neck. In 1957, she'd been murdered—a kitchen knife to the gut, and blunt force trauma to the head combined.

Michael sucked in a sharp breath.

"It's all true," the witch said, without looking up.

Could she feel him in her head? Or was it like a broadcast, and he just happened to be tuned into her frequency?

"Sorry."

"I don't mind," she said, and then, "I'll be staying until at least Halloween."

"What happens on Halloween?"

She let go of Michael's hand, blinking eyes gone the color of pumpkins. There was a flicker of disappointment in her gaze, as though she couldn't understand why he regularly failed to keep up. The connection broke, taking the witch's deaths, spooling away from her, with it. Which was just as well, because Michael knew somehow they'd been headed for a knife made of stone, and a blood-covered altar, and he suspected there were things in that death in particular he didn't want to see.

"That's up to you." The disappointment in the witch's eyes turned to something else, something deeper and sadder that made Michael's skin crawl.

An apology rose, and he clamped it down. Nothing about the witch made sense. He pressed his lips tight. He couldn't be sure, but he thought he heard her sigh. It reminded him of leaves pulled from branches by the October wind, of shortening days, and snow piling up behind the clouds.

"What do you want?"

Michael didn't realize he'd spoken aloud until the witch smiled, brief as a moth's wing. But the sadness hadn't left her eyes. She held up a hand and ticked off points.

"I want to live in this house. I want tea every morning at seven, with toast on Wednesdays. I want not to die until I'm good and ready." She lowered her hand. "The rest I'm still figuring out."

Ink threaded the gold of her eyes; Michael fought the urge to shiver.

He wished the witch would stop looking at him. But when her gaze moved away, going to the window, he felt lost and unanchored.

The witch's eyes were green again. They reminded him of a toad he'd caught by accident in third grade. He'd given it to his teacher, who'd explained patiently that toads were much happier living outside than in classrooms, and would he please release it back into the wild.

"You should unpack now," the witch said.

Her voice was very quiet, but it still made Michael flinch. He stared at her for a moment before realizing the words were a dismissal. Since he couldn't think of a good retort, he obeyed.

Michael didn't know where the witch went during the day, and he didn't ask. He could picture her flying around the neighborhood on a broom, or transforming into a flock of birds. He could just as easily see her curling up in the attic reading books on economic theory.

He still didn't know her name. He didn't know anything about her really, and sometimes he amused himself by making up little stories about what she was doing at the exact moment it occurred to him to wonder—horseback riding, bowling, waltzing with the Zombie King of Austria on a floor made of crystal teeth. It annoyed him when he caught himself doing this. He constantly had to remind himself that the witch was an unwelcome intruder in his house. He couldn't let himself get used to her. He couldn't let her settle in and simply take over his life. Things just didn't work that way in the real world.

In college, he'd tried to picture what his life would be like after graduation. He'd long since given up on the high school fantasies of being a rock star, or an astronaut. He was tone deaf, and he'd barely passed intro to calculus. He didn't know exactly *what* he wanted to do with his life, but nowhere had his life plans included living with a witch. Magic was for fairy tales. Real life was bills and deadlines, not spells and potions.

Yet, the witch stayed, and life went on as though she'd always been there, an inevitable fact as much as the bills and deadlines. He gave the witch's cat the name Spencer, one of several dozen secret names he imagined the cat had accumulated over its lifetimes, as cats do. Michael only ever saw the witch at seven in the morning, and then again after dusk, as though she ceased to exist in-between, which he knew was as just as likely or improbable as every other scenario he'd dreamed for her.

On a Thursday afternoon, Michael found himself at the foot of the attic stairs, listening intently. He didn't know what he was listening for, but it never came, so he climbed the stairs. The witch's door stood open. It was just past three.

Afternoon sunlight, already burning to deep gold, slanted through a window set angle-wise in the slope of the roof. What the light illuminated was certainly nothing that had been in the attic before. Either the witch had snuck things in without making a sound, or magicked them into being from dust bunnies and dead spiders.

A rocking chair sat tucked under the angle of the roof, next to a white-painted dresser holding a single, season-incongruous daffodil in a slender vase. A braided rug lay on the floor between the dresser and the bed, and the bed was covered with a neat, white duvet. There was a dress-form in one corner, a carousel horse in the other, an empty birdcage hanging from the ceiling, a cello leaning against one wall, and seven identical pairs of shoes lined up beneath the second window. A sea chest footed the bed, and Spencer sat on it, tail twitching impatiently in response to Michael's wonder.

From the cat's perspective, Michael imagined, it was all so obvious. A chandelier hung, unlit, near the birdcage. The crystals caught the afternoon light, casting rainbows, and tinkled softly. The only thing Michael didn't see in the room was the witch's suitcase.

If he came back tomorrow, he truth-in-his-bones-knew the room would be different—there would be an easel, a fish tank, a music box, an accordion, and a plethora of bookshelves. Spencer jumped lightly from the chest, and wound around Michael's ankles. Where the cat had been sitting there was a leather bound book, swollen slightly, as though the pages had been wet and dried in crinkled waves.

The cat slid past Michael, leaving him alone in a room that suddenly seemed to contain less air than it had a moment before. He shouldn't, he knew he shouldn't, and he still watched himself reach out, his hand hovering just above the leather cover. His fingers touched down. He'd been expecting an electric shock, but nothing happened. The cover was soft, like worn velvet; the book was just a book.

He let out a breath. Still knowing he shouldn't, he flicked the cover aside. The book fell open near the middle, as though its spine had been broken there again and again. The pages were handwritten, the script thin and spidery, the ink brown.

For the Removal of Unwanted Guests
Midnight frost, one cup, melted
Trametes Versicolor, one handful
One each: tail feather of raven, crow, and owl
Six windfall apples
Soil from beneath a ripe pumpkin
Candy Corn, the proper kind

Michael's breath caught. If he didn't know better, he might think the witch had left the spell, the recipe, whatever it was, there for him to find. It was a trick, a trap, it had to be. He glanced around, expecting to find the witch in the doorway, her eyes the color of steel. But he was alone. And that was almost worse somehow.

With his pulse racing, Michael slipped his phone out of his pocket, and snapped a picture of the page. Then he slammed the book closed, turned, and fled down the stairs.

On Sunday, he went apple picking. The place he chose also had pick-your-own pumpkins, which made at least two items on list from the witch's book easy. On the way home, he planned to stop at the store and buy candy corn. That was half the items right there. And that frightened him.

Driving home, jumpy and unsettled, Michael couldn't keep his eyes off the rearview mirror. He expected the witch to come bearing down on him at any moment, all blood and fire and vengeance. He pictured her in a storm cloud, lightning in her hair, her eyes the color of rain. He almost went off the road twice, and when he finally pulled into the driveway and killed the engine, his hands were shaking so badly he could barely pull the keys from the ignition.

What was he doing? The witch wasn't bothering him; he barely ever saw her. Why should he want to get rid of her? And what made him think a spell from a water-logged book would banish her? Fight fire with fire, and magic with magic.

Even if he could gather all the items, what was he supposed to do with them? Brew them up in the witch's tea like a potion, and trick her into drinking it? And if he did, what then? What if he chased her out and she died again? She had drowned and burned and hanged already. All she wanted was tea, to live in his house quietly, and not to die again. Was that so wrong?

He carried the items upstairs, and hid them under his bed. His heart wouldn't stop racing, and he couldn't get his breathing under control.

When he came back downstairs, he found the witch organizing the utensils in the kitchen drawers. Under the butter-warm light, her black clothes looked like an incredibly deep, dark red. The honey strands in her hair stood out. He couldn't even imagine what color her eyes must be. Spencer brushed against Michael's leg, and he nearly screamed.

After a moment, he scooped up the cat. Spencer purred, rubbing Michael's neck with its head.

"You're lucky," the witch said without turning. "She never lets anyone pick her up."

So, Spencer was a she.

"She's the one that found this place, you know." The witch's tone was conversational, but there was a hint of melancholy underneath it, wistful. "I could smell it, but I couldn't pinpoint it. She led me right here. She's got a better nose."

"Where . . . were you before?"

The witch paused, the knives, forks, and spoons stilling in her hands. Michael wasn't sure he wanted the answer.

"A long way away." The witch's shoulders stiffened.

Her words smelled of bonfires. They felt like dirt, filling his mouth. They tasted like Halloween.

His mind clicking over to her frequency again, Michael saw the witch walking barefoot along the side of a road, headlights sweeping over her through a heavy rain. Broken glass from a car accident cut her soles, but she didn't seem to care. She either walked to, or from, her most recent death, and it clung to her like a shadow. Whatever her death had been, or would be, it wasn't pleasant. Not that any death was ever pleasant, Michael supposed, except for perhaps dying quietly in your sleep.

"Witches don't die that way," the witch said, so softly he could barely hear her. He flinched, and Spencer squirmed out of his arms.

He should go upstairs right now and throw away the apples, the dirt, and the candy corn, pretend he'd never seen the list or been in the witch's room. But if he did that, he'd be admitting she could stay. Even if he never said it out loud, he'd be inviting her into his life, and nothing would ever be normal again. Magic would be real, and witches, too. A woman could drown and hang and burn and still be in his kitchen organizing his spoons.

Cutlery rattled softly in the witch's hands. Michael stared at her back. If she turned around, the witch's eyes would be the color of smoke, the ghost of a thousand violent deaths drifting in the black at center of them. Could he live with all that death crowded behind her eyes? Could he live with all her impossibility? Michael was glad she kept her back to him. While the witch counted spoons, he turned silently, and slipped from the room.

It snowed the day before Halloween. The last time Michael remembered that happening, he'd been about nine years old. His parents had bundled him off on a Boy Scout trip, up in the mountains. It snowed on October 30, and the Scout leaders cut the trip short after one night because it was too cold. They all came back on the bus with flakes still falling, and white dusting the ground. Michael's mother made him go trick-or-treating in a bulky snowsuit, so no one could tell he was supposed to be Spider-Man that year.

Michael stood in the open front door, coffee in hand, Spencer at his feet, watching the flakes fall. Carved pumpkins all along the street wore caps of white lace. It was peaceful, beautiful even, but Michael couldn't shake his deep unease.

He'd spent yesterday at a nature preserve, where he'd found the mushrooms and the feathers from the witch's list. At least half an hour of the excursion had been Michael sitting in the car with the heater going full blast, comparing mushrooms and feathers to Google image searches on his phone.

He still hadn't decided what he was going to do. He told himself to think of it as insurance. Just because he gathered the ingredients didn't mean he had to use them.

"You're letting out all the warm air." The witch's voice snapped Michael's spine straight, and he wheeled guiltily, accidentally stepping on Spencer's tail.

The cat yowled, and shot away; the witch glared. Her eyes reminded him of sea-wet stones, slammed by endless waves.

"It's my heating bill." The words came more sharply than he intended.

The witch pressed her lips into an even thinner line, breathing through her nose. She'd snapped at him last night, too, when he'd suggested tacos for dinner. Spencer had hissed indiscriminately, taking in both their bristled postures without choosing sides, and stalked out the door when Michael had opened it to gather the mail.

Did she know he'd found the book? And if she did, why didn't she come out and say something, or cast a hex on him? Or whatever it was witches did when they were angry. She could turn him into a toad, and the house would be all hers. She wouldn't even have to share. Maybe it was the same for witches as vampires, and he had to invite her in, or she couldn't stay. He had no idea what the rules were, if there were any.

The witch shifted without moving, strain showing in her clenched jaw. Now, more than sea-wet stones, her eyes reminded him of lightning trapped beneath a skin of dark clouds.

There was only one day until Halloween. The witch had said she'd stay until Halloween at least, and the rest was up to him. Did that mean he was supposed to make the potion? That he was destined to betray her?

"Why me?" Michael asked.

He hadn't meant to speak at all. The witch's eyes turned the color of certain snakes Michael had seen on a nature show—the kind that hid in the sand, and uncoiled all at once to strike.

"Because this house needs a witch." The witch returned words like a slap. "And I thought you needed one, too. But maybe I was wrong."

Even though she hadn't moved, she'd folded the space between them somehow. They were face to face, the witch leaning into him, her nose pointed at him accusation-wise.

"All I want is to live a normal life. Is that too much to ask?" Michael stepped back. Coffee slopped over the edges of his mug, barely missing the witch's toes.

"Yes." The door banged shut behind Michael, punctuating the word. Startled, Michael dropped his mug; shards of ceramic skittered across the floor.

The witch made an impatient gesture with her hand, and the ceramic shards flew across the hall and into the kitchen, pelting the sink like hail.

"Life isn't fair. Nobody gets to choose whether they have a normal happy one or not. If they did, do you think anyone would get sick, or have their hearts broken? Would anyone die? It doesn't work that way."

The witch's deaths were in her eyes again. And her eyes themselves flickered from moonlight, to toadstools, to tsunamis and flames. The heat of them, the cold of them, the shock of them drove him back another step. Michael opened his mouth, but the witch spun on her heel, and banged up the stairs.

The floorboards shuddered when she slammed her door, and plaster dust filtered down from the ceiling. Michael blinked, the grit catching in his eyes.

Something in him tightened, twisting. Her life wasn't fair, but her anger wasn't either. All he'd done was move into a house with upside down windows and a staircase made of shipwrecks. And he could hardly be blamed for that.

"Damn it."

Michael's slippers smacked at his bare feet as he climbed the stairs. Inside his bathrobe, sweat gathered at the base of his spine. He knocked on the witch's door, and it swung open.

"I'm sorry," he said to an empty room.

Michael gaped. The bed, the dresser, the chandelier—all gone. And the witch, too. A tired looking cobweb hung where the birdcage had been, stirring on a breath of wind. Curtain-less windows let in gray light, showing the desiccated bodies of arachnids in the corners. Dust puffed, gritty beneath his feet.

The sheer emptiness of the room shot through him, a current driven like a spike from his soles all the way up his spine. It was the worst kind of absence and it sent him running down the stairs in unreasoned terror. The witch was so thoroughly gone, she might never have existed.

The house bowed under the insubstantial weight of snow. No, it *mourned*. Down in its bones, the house was melancholy over the loss of the witch. Like a haunting, there were sounds and scents just on the edge of perception. Turning a corner, he would catch a whiff of the sea. He didn't dare touch the walls, knowing they'd weep salt-dampness against his skin. An un-played note on a harpsichord sighed and shivered its way from the roof down to the basement where a black cat lay buried in the leftmost corner.

He needed to get the witch back.

Michael set out an hour before midnight with a measuring cup, his hands jammed in his pockets. Halloween stood on the other side of the clock's tick, all gathered up with fallen leaves and bats' wings and clouds across the moon. The snow had stopped, but the cold had deepened. The whole year waited to pivot on this point; the world was thin. It wasn't just the house—this night needed a witch, too.

A black cat streaked across his path. It might have been Spencer, or a random stray, he couldn't tell. The cat didn't pause. Michael glanced furtively in either direction. When he was certain he was alone, he used the razor blade he'd tucked into his jacket to shave the frost from his neighbor's pumpkin.

He felt like a fool. It was Devil's Night. The cops would be on high alert. What would they think of a man with a razor—even if it was only a Bic disposable—lurking outside his neighbor's houses, paying far too much attention to their pumpkins?

But he didn't have a choice. He would make the potion, and drink it himself. He was the unwanted guest that needed banishing. Then the witch would come back home, and everything would be the way it was supposed to be. It wasn't rational, but nothing about the witch was. Deep down on his bones, he knew the truth of it. He had to bring her back, because if he didn't . . . Because if he didn't, there wouldn't be a witch here.

The logic was as faulty as the logic of witches in general. And so it stood to reason his plan would work. It had to.

He moved to the next house, the next pumpkin. When he reached the end of the block, the cup was a quarter full. By the time he'd gone another block, the measuring cup was half full.

His life had been normal and boring until the witch had shown up. Then she had to go smell like smoke, and the sea, and cinnamon, and make him see that life was terrible, and unfair. And it was beautiful, too.

Because the house settled around the witch, and the clomp-clomp of her footsteps over the floorboards comforted him. He slept better with her in the house, and Spencer curled on his chest kept the nightmares at bay. And because the witch kept coming back, no matter how horrible her deaths. The force of life itself, or her will to try again, to live on her own terms, wouldn't let her give up. It was undeniable, and inexorable. Like moonrise, and spaghetti on Tuesdays. Like witches and black cats. And that was something. *That* was magic.

The cup was full. Michael held it up, watching frost melt in the moonlight. Maybe, just this once, life could play along and pretend to be fair after all. If witches were real, wasn't anything possible?

On Halloween, Michael brewed the ingredients from the witch's list like tea. He poured them into a jam jar, and let them cool. The resulting liquid was reddish gold, the color of museum amber.

Michael held the jar. He expected it to hum with power, but it only sloshed as he turned it from side to side. The contents left legs on the glass, like good alcohol. He wanted to say he was sorry. He wanted her to come back, and tell him her name. He wanted her to explain herself, and he wanted the chance to do the same. And he missed Spencer.

Michael sniffed the potion. After all the things the witch smelled of, smoke and the ocean, wet rope, and crashed cars, the liquid in the jam jar smelled of nothing. Not the candy corn, or the soft, half-rotten apples. He screwed the lid on, and slipped the jar into his pocket.

Even though it was just past noon, Michael Remmington decided it was high time he got well and totally drunk.

Sometime after sun down, it began to rain.

Would there be any trick-or-treaters in this downpour? Instead of Spider-Man, they'd all be dressed as kid-in-raincoat. He snickered, but really, it was depressing. He pulled out the jam jar, watching the way the light slid through the liquid as he turned it round and round. He needed to find the witch. She needed to see him drink the potion. She needed to know he was sorry.

He pushed the chair away from the table. The front door was miles away, but he made it somehow, and stepped out into the pouring rain.

A jack-o'-lantern carved from a pumpkin he didn't remember buying sat at the bottom of the porch steps. The lid had been knocked askew, and rain had drowned the candle. Along the street, other houses were similarly struggling.

"Crappy Halloween," he said to no one.

He couldn't even call the witch's name. Liquid sloshed uncomfortably in his stomach and his pocket—the alcohol and the witch's brew. A few brave parents with umbrellas ushered kids from house to house. No one looked happy.

Michael made his way toward the main road and the hum of cars. He could picture the witch walking past the library, and the grocery store; she'd come to the end of the sidewalk, but keep going. She wouldn't be barefoot, but her suitcase would be clutched in her hand, and she wouldn't have an umbrella. Spencer, wet and miserable, would be close at her heels.

He spotted her up ahead.

Michael stopped, blinking water out of his eyes. The witch looked just as he'd pictured her, which made him suspect wishful thinking. Or maybe the alcohol had gotten the better of him. He broke into a run.

A sudden gust of wind pulled leaves from the trees, and slicked them over the sidewalk. Water blew sideways. Michael slipped, nearly turning his ankle.

"Hey!" The downpour stole his voice.

The witch didn't turn. Even over the rain, he could hear the steady clunk of her heels. She clutched her suitcase in both hands, and her black skirt clung to her legs, ink bleeding into her skin, bleeding into the sidewalk, bleeding into the dark.

If she reached the end of the sidewalk, she would be lost. Michael felt it as down-in-his-bones-true. Whatever rules governed witches made it so; those rules governed him now, too.

He kept going, half running and half limping. He reached for her shoulder. The witch whirled on him and shouted something, but it was torn away by the wind.

Tendrils of wet hair clung to the witch's cheeks. She swung the suitcase like a weapon, and Michael ducked. He slipped again, scraping his palm.

The witch stepped off the sidewalk.

His heart lurched.

A black shape streaked past him. Spencer.

Headlights swept around a curve in the road, bearing down on the witch. Michael shot up, rain-blind, drunk.

He might have shouted as he plunged off the sidewalk, chasing the witch, chasing the cat. The witch turned, mouth open, but he couldn't hear her. Headlights washed her out, and made her eyes the same color as the storm.

They collided in midair.

She pushed him out of the way, or he pushed her. Or they pushed each other. Brakes squealed, and over the noise, a sound like wings and all of October taking flight filled the air. Against all reason, he heard the jam jar as it slipped from his pocket and became tiny splinters of glass and a magic potion washed away by the rain.

A slew of water hit him in the face. Michael threw up an arm to shield his eyes, and the bumper of an ancient '67 Oldsmobile stopped inches from his leg.

"Jesus, are you okay?" The woman, soaked the instant she stepped from the car, left the Olds askew in the center of the road, door hanging open.

Something nudged Michael's leg. He looked down. Spencer twined around his ankles, dragging his sodden tail over Michael's pant leg. The witch was nowhere to be seen.

"My cat," Michael said.

He bent and scooped Spencer into his arms. The wet bundle of fur purred louder than he'd ever heard her purr before.

"What?"

"She's okay," he said.

The woman stared. After a moment she nodded, looking more frightened than concerned. She climbed back into her car and shut the door. Michael held the cat, listening to her purr, listening to the woman's engine purr. The rain slackened, still slanting through the headlights cutting the night. He realized he was standing in the middle of the road and limped back to the sidewalk. The woman, ghosted behind the car's windows, shook her head in confusion as she pulled away.

A shape lay on the far side of the road, which might be the witch's suitcase. He couldn't be sure. But he didn't see the witch. The car hadn't hit her, or him, or Spencer. He squeezed the cat harder until she squirmed in protest; he unburied his face from her fur.

"Come on, let's go home."

The witch would be waiting for them with a cup of tea. Or she wouldn't. But it was possible. And she hadn't died. Just this once, life had decided to be fair. The witch could go on living on her own terms. Anything was possible on Halloween.

"Thank you," Michael said to the night and the turning year.

Behind the rain and the dense clouds, he could sense the sliver of a crescent moon, waiting to break free. It felt like a smile.

A. C. Wise was born and raised in Montreal and currently lives in the Philadelphia area. Her fiction has appeared in publications such as *Clarkesworld*, *Lightspeed*, Apex, and *The Best Horror of the Year Vol. 4*, among others. In addition to her fiction, she co-edits the online magazine *Unlikely Story*. You can find her online at www.acwise.net.

ANGELIC

Jay Caselberg

And so it begins . . .

Clouds roiled across the darkened sky, whipped as though with the breath of angels, though angels they were not.

A hint: the taste of stone upon the air; the flavor of old earth mixed with the spattering frozen drops, slashing against his back and loud in his ears through the hood cinched tight around his face. The wind gusted, splashing icy water in his eyes. It dribbled in rivulets down his forehead and over his brow. Using the back of one hand, he tried to wipe it away, to clear his sight.

Storm water, storm watch, storm dreams. His hands were numb, his knuckles aching with the cold, yet still he stood, waiting, watching, resolute.

Behind, the old church, gray stone made white and black with age, the roof collapsed, slates tumbled, and the jagged teeth of burnt rafters mouthing at the wind-tossed sky. To one side lay the graveyard, headstones leaning, ancient stone crosses mottled with lichen. A mound, a sunken hollow, pooling water, and a confusion of weeds and grass gone wild. The fence, once solid, had rusted through in places, brown and encrusted with years. It had been hallowed ground once, a sacred place. Now it just cradled rotted memories of the dead. The dead stayed dead. It was simply what lived beyond them that did not. He knew the truth of that, knew it well, but he chose not to keep it foremost in his mind. It was the living that bore the deepest part of it, whether inherited or not. At least he thought that was so. From time to time, though, these days, he was no longer sure.

He stood there upon the hillside, waiting, watching the road. She would come, he knew it. She would come. She would be there for that special night but two days hence, the family celebration, the tradition. She always came.

Inside the remains of the old church, behind him, in darkness, a tortured Christ figure stared down upon a littered floor. Streams of leaf-stained water made brown tears upon its cheeks.

Martin watched the empty road for a while longer. Not yet. Maybe tomorrow. She would come. She would come: he knew it.

He had heard the voices. And so, he knew.

Step back. Consider.

The avenging angel with sharpened teeth.

We call it angel, because it makes it knowable, makes it familiar, though angel is only a word, not an explanation.

It swoops, confusing you with its lack of sexuality. It is man, it is woman, it is both and yet neither. It has eyes that pierce you, transfixing you. It will rend you, limb from limb and feast upon your flesh, though you lie there still and pale, untouched.

It does not laugh, for it is without amusement.

It merely rails against your living. Your heartbeat, your breath, the dampness of your eyes . . . all of these are an affront to it.

It does not understand remorse. It never will.

Consider it well.

It was ritual more than anything else, an old tradition that just happened to coincide with the other rituals. Halloween, All Hallows, Samhain, call it what you will—it just happened to be the time when the family got together and worked hard at not doing each other mortal injury during its passing.

Estella really didn't know why it was that time of year rather than any of the other high feasts, secular or otherwise, that other "normal" families observed. Regardless, she liked the season, the chill, the damp, the winds scattering wet leaves and memory across the landscape. The feeling of huddling inside warm clothes, big coats, and scarves gave a sense of protectedness that she found comforting. There was something else about the time of year too, something lurking beneath the surface. Nothing expressly tangible, but perhaps that was why she was comforted by that sense of protection. Ever since she was a child, Estella had felt that otherness lurking at the shadow reaches of her subconscious, though it was more a knowing than the dreamlike essence of that which was not expressly conscious. She knew, she sensed, and she was aware of it, but she chose, rather, to ignore it, to put it from her mind. It was like the town. If you'd grown up and lived for any span of time within the boundaries of Sangerville, you knew things—things that nobody talked about. Estella's family, the Hollings, had lived variously in Sangerville for five generations; long enough to accumulate and store those hidden memories in their own dark and secret places. There were family memories that . . .

Estella shook her head and peered through the spattering drops at the road ahead. On an afternoon like this, it was better to concentrate on driving than random musings. Not that there was much traffic around Sangerville, apart from the townsfolk themselves and there were few enough of those. There'd been a decline over the last few years, with the younger generations seeking their own fortunes further afield more and more as the opportunities in the town itself dwindled. The old derelict church at the top of the hill was testament to that. Not even enough of a congregation to support it, though Old Martin did his best to maintain some sort of order in the grounds. Some of the townsfolk said that Martin was not quite all there, a little slow, but he was harmless enough. Everyone called him Old Martin, though he was not that old, really. It just seemed as if he had been with the town forever and he was there as a fixture in Estella's memory ever since she'd been a child. Someone had to be paying for the upkeep of the grounds, but thinking about it now, Estella realized that she had no idea who that might be.

She pulled into the small main street, wipers slapping the large drops away from in front of her. There were other reasons for her trepidation and the closer she got to the old family home the tension wound tighter. Bill and Linda Holling. They were a classic small town couple, bound up in the minutiae of the day to day that comes with living in an environment like Sangerville. One of the reasons she escaped, really. And then, coming back each visit, each family event, it was no different. The problem was that she really didn't *care* about what they seemed to care about, but she had to show that animated interest that proved she was paying attention, that she was being a dutiful daughter. It was almost enough to make her eyes glaze over. Sure Dad, that's really interesting.

Estella took a left, barely missing one of the local residents decked out in gray rain slicker and hat, fading conveniently into the washed out background and making him barely able to be seen. Well, she assumed it was a him. In the pouring rain and underneath the amorphous weather gear, she had no way of knowing. She sighed, shook her head and drove the last couple of blocks to her own street, tree-lined, but skeletal in these months, with the empty branches clawing at the clouded sky. And there, at last, stood the family home. It was funny how her family never invested either the time or the money in Halloween paraphernalia. No grinning faces or colors. The house stood as it always stood. No one came out to meet her, not that she had expected they would. Perhaps they didn't realize she was here yet.

She took a few seconds listening to the wipers beat back and forth, breathing slowly and deeply, till she killed the engine, and taking one last deep breath, opened the car door.

Martin stooped, and with one hand wiped away some old brown leaves that were adhering to a nearby gravestone. The rain had eased a little now, but already the light was starting to fade. She was here now. The cycle was almost complete. He straightened, turning slowly to gaze out over the town, avoiding the crumbling walls off to one side of where he stood. He didn't need to see them. Below, one or two lights were already painting dark shapes with yellowish glow against gray. Down there, down in the heart of the little community, people moved, breathed, got on with their lives. Some of them knew. Some of them understood, but they kept that understanding to themselves. It was something you didn't talk about. Not that anyone really ever talked to Martin apart from the civil good morning and the silent nod of the head. He was as much a familiar presence as he wandered the streets as the hulking hill that he stood upon now—a fixture in their memories, something that you acknowledged and with that acknowledgement, fulfilled your obligations.

He crouched down in front of the headstone, peering at the lettering, the carefully incised names and words, the once sharp edges softened with age, crumbling a little here and there, bruised with the moss marks and lichen. He reached out and traced the name with one finger. He had known this one many years ago. He looked back over towards the town. That was where she had lived. Over there. Dupan Street. Now one of her children lived there, with children of his own.

He nodded slowly to himself, and pulled back his hand to wipe the wetness from his face.

They were not greedy. They only took what they needed.

Slowly, he got to his feet. It would not be too long now. He could feel their restlessness. It echoed his own, but she was here now.

Her mother was fussing about in the kitchen, busy with her preparations, already starting on the feast that would accompany the tradition of that family dinner, leaving Estella sitting at the dining-room table looking across at her father and waiting for the next pause in conversation to be punctuated by yet another Sangerville observation or other words that were simply there to fill the silence that habitually lay between them. The funny thing was, if she didn't come, didn't observe the ritual, her world would be filled with words. She had tried it once and had heard about it for weeks afterwards. How could she be so insensitive? Didn't she know how much it meant to them?

"I'm glad you're here," said Bill finally. "I hope Johnny isn't too late."

There it was—the subtle backhand implication that maybe Estella didn't rate as much as her older brother. Or maybe she was just imagining it, her expectations getting the better of her.

"Oh, don't worry. He'll be here soon enough." Her mother stood in the kitchen doorway, wiping her hands on a tea towel, a strand of hair falling down over her face. She blew it out of the way, gave Estella a brief smile, and then disappeared back into the kitchen.

Her father was watching her, nodding slowly. It seemed that he had aged significantly over the last year. She tracked the lines in his face, the sallowness of his skin, the faint cloudiness to his gaze. His eyes were watery, tinged with red, as though not too long ago he had been weeping, but she knew that he had not. She looked back down into her tea, and lifted the mug slowly to fill more of the space, taking a sip.

"Well," she said, placing the mug down again. "I may as well go up and sort my things out."

As she stood, her father simply looked at her.

"Right," she said.

There was something in his face as he watched her leaving the room. She didn't quite know what it was.

One by one, she climbed the steps, up into the hallway that led to her old bedroom. The need to sort her things out was no more than an excuse. She hadn't brought much with her. She never did. And after tomorrow night, she had no plans to extend her stay for any longer than she had to. Just enough to see her through the ritual. That was all.

Her old room was just the same as it was every year: neat, ordered, kept as if she had never left it, and full of memories that crept from the corners to greet her every year. The room would always be there, waiting, at least until her parents had gone and whatever eventually happened to the house when that time came changed it. She stood for a couple of seconds in the doorway, chewing her lip, and then, with a sigh, moved over to the bed and opened her pack, laying out the few clothes and toiletries she had brought with her. As she placed them into the drawers, there was noise downstairs. Apparently Johnny had arrived. Voices and the laughter came muffled from the downstairs rooms.

"Where's Estella? I saw her car outside," she heard. The response was lost as she closed a drawer and moved back to sit on the bed, looking around at the familiar wallpaper and the patterned rug that sat in the room's center, the small white desk where she had hunched, doing her homework as a kid. White lace curtains shielded the darkness and rain pattering against the windowpane outside. She had been such a *girl* growing up, shy, quiet, meek. She shook her head at her own memory of herself. How had she turned out as she had—one failed marriage that had lasted a mere eighteen months, no kids and no real plans to have any. It was almost as if her growing up had been merely marking time and despite her escape, here she was again.

Well, there was nothing for it. Time to go down and greet the brother, to hear about the latest successes of his kids, to make enthusiastic noises about his latest career move. That was the ritual, and this time of year was all about ritual, if nothing else.

Teeth. Pale skin. Wings flapping. A rush of decaying air. Eyes without sight, but seeing right through her. No, not teeth, more like needle-sharp fangs.

Estella started awake, her heart pounding. The darkness was solid. A dream. It was a dream.

They know you, she thought.

Who?

The remnants of the dream still clawed at her chest, her throat, ran skittering through her brain, through draped curtain of fading sleep, her pulse racing. The voice kept whispering, mouthing the words in her memory, hissing through the darkness.

They know you.

She threw back the covers, her breath still coming in short, halting gasps. Calm. She struggled to control her breathing, her pulse, and swung her legs out of the bed, hunching over at the edge, her palms pressed down against the bed's edge.

Taking a single deeper breath, she stood and padded over to the window. Everything was quiet inside, not even the usual creaks and shifts you'd normally expect to hear in an old house at night. The sweat was starting to cool on her skin and, gradually, her breathing was returning to normal. With one hand, she pulled the curtain to one side to look out to the darkness, to the rain slicked field and the few scraggy trees that clustered at the rear of the house. The naked branches shivered in the intermittent gusts. Her gaze roved across the bleak landscape and then stopped. Her breath caught again. Someone was out there. The barely defined shape stood as a dark smudge, but she could tell. A lighter stain in the darkness marked the face and it was watching her window.

Again, the voice whispered inside her.

They know you. They're waiting.

Her heart in her throat, she let the curtain fall and rapidly stepped away from the window.

What?

She took another backward step, her hand at her throat.

Soon, came the voice.

Soon . . .

After a virtually sleepless night, Estella stumbled through most of the following day in a semi-daze. She'd managed to doze in the early hours of the morning, but it was hardly sleep. All through the morning, she heard that single word, echoing silently. Images of the figure in the darkness haunted her. In the early afternoon, she managed to catch an hour or so on the couch, but only dozing. The clattering and noises drifting through from the kitchen barely cut through the haze, nor did the continued back and forth between Johnny and her father. Once or twice, her father drifted into the living room, looking at her with a concerned expression on his face. There was something else in his expression, but in her current state, she had no energy or any real desire to try to fathom what it was. As the day staggered towards evening and the ritual dinner, if anything, the feeling of moving through a syrupy haze increased.

Finally, the time arrived for dinner. To Estella, it seemed as if it had taken a century. The traditional dinner gong rang through the house, her father's hand enacting the ritual. Dinner was early, giving time for them to get through most of it before any of the town's children might show up for their own seasonal ritual.

Soon.

Together, they took their places at the dining room table, sitting quietly as her mother started ferrying the steaming platters out of the kitchen. The scents of good home cooking swirling into the room with each new plate. Once that was done with, her mother took her place at the table and her father filled each of their glasses in turn and then, moving back to the head of the table stood in place, his own glass raised high.

"To the tradition," he said. "Long may it last." One by one, he met each of their eyes, Estella's last. He paused there, his gaze fixed as if observing.

Together, they raised their own glasses, repeating the words. "To the tradition."

Estella sipped tentatively, not really committed to the toast. Her father looked at her with a slight frown, then glanced across at her mother, who gave a slight nod.

Just at that moment, there came a knock at the door.

"Geez, they're a bit early aren't they?" said Johnny.

Her father sat heavily letting out a deep breath. Carefully he placed his glass back down. "It's not kids," he said. He bit his lip, glanced once at Estella and then spoke. "It's time," he said. "Linda, you'd better let him in."

Her mother pushed her chair back and with a nod and a slight expression of resignation on her face, stood and quickly left the room.

"Who?" said Johnny. "Who is it?"

Her father lifted a hand to still him. His gaze was fixed on Estella—deep, piercing, his eyes no longer watery, his features firm. "It is time, Estella."

At the sound of someone entering the room behind her, she turned. Her mother stood in the doorway with a man next to her. It was Old Martin.

"What's he doing here?" said Johnny.

Old Martin's gaze fixed Estella, just like her father's.

"It is time," he said. "They know you. They are waiting." The words were simple, the voice muddy, but filled with something else. They were the words from her nightmare. It had been Old Martin standing out there in the darkness. She knew it now.

Johnny had gone silent.

Old Martin reached out a hand. "Come," he said.

"Estella, you must go with him now." Her father's voice.

Her mother stood in the doorway, not moving, not saying anything.

Without knowing why or how she knew, she understood that her father's words were indisputable.

"Come," said Old Martin. "They are waiting."

Slowly, slowly, Estella pushed back her chair, stood and reached out her hand.

Ahead, looming jagged against the sky, the old church, gray stone made white and black with age, the roof collapsed, slates tumbled, burnt rafters stabbing black against the blackness. Estella had not been up here for years. She barely remembered it, but somehow, the memory was there, strong, insistent, just as Old Martin's hand drawing her forward was. To one side lay the graveyard, headstones leaning, ancient stone crosses mottled with lichen. A mound, a sunken hollow, pooling water, and a confusion of weeds and grass gone wild. The fence, once solid, had rusted through in places, brown and encrusted with years. All of these sights, these snapshot images burned now within her vision, in her mind.

Still old Martin drew her forward.

"There," he said. "There. Here is the place."

He stopped gesturing at the empty darkness, the broken place where people had once congregated.

It was dark, yet it was not. A pale luminescence painted the edges, the lines with dull light.

Martin urged her forward.

"They know you," he said, his voice breathy with his excitement. "It is now. They wait."

"But what . . . ?" said Estella.

"Shhhh," said Martin. "Shhhhhh."

He dropped her hand and stepped back.

She felt it then, the stirring, the movement in her blood and her bones. Here, now. Here was the doorway. No longer was it *soon*. It was *here*. It was *now*. She was no longer marking time.

Estella looked up, her breath stilled and caught. Her blood sang in her ears.

The angels had come, though you could hardly call them angels.

Jay Caselberg was born in a country town in Australia and then traveled extensively while growing up. Returning to Australia, he had a successful sojourn in the groves of academe but, just before turning in his doctoral dissertation, stepped out into the workforce and was soon based in London. From that time on, he traveled extensively throughout Europe and Africa. He started writing in 1996 as James A. Hartley and later under his own name. Caselberg currently lives in Germany and works in the consulting industry on international projects. His short fiction has appeared in periodicals such as *Crimewave*, *Electric Velocipede*, and *Interzone*, and anthologies as diverse as *Dead Red Heart*, *Powers of Detection: Tales of Mystery and Fantasy*, and *The Thackery T. Lambshead Pocket Guide to Eccentric and Discredited Diseases*. His horror novel *Empties* has just been published.

EMERGENCY

QUADRUPLE WHAMMY

Chelsea Quinn Yarbro

Jenkins and Wadley were sitting in an area called The Canteen. Used by nurses and staff, it was a small room behind the admissions desk with two microwaves, a pair of coffee-makers, an electric samovar filled with hot water next to a bowl of tea bags, a three-quarter size refrigerator, a half-sized sink, and a small television patched into the hospital's cable service; just at present it was showing one of *The Incredible Hulk* movies with the sound turned off. The room had a slightly greenish cast from the old-fashioned recessed lighting, as unflattering as it was hard on the eyes. At the moment the two men were quite alone, having shown up early, prepared for what Jenkins had called "The double whammy night: Halloween *and* a full moon!" They wore scrubs, having secured their coats in their lockers.

"Triple whammy: it's Saturday."

"That, too," Jenkins allowed.

"Still pretty quiet so far," said Wadley, a young African-American only recently out of college, rangy, clever, and ambitious; he sounded a bit disappointed.

"It'll get busier, Jamal—don't get ahead of yourself. By eight we should have our hands full, if this year is anything like last year." Jenkins got up and refilled his coffee cup from the caffeinated pot; he was more than a decade older than Wadley, an experienced X-ray technician with a host of good reports in his file and a passion for old horror movies; his first name was Chastain, but no one ever used it. "Which," he added after a thoughtful pause, "I hope it isn't. Newsvans in the parking lot. No thank you."

"Yeah," Wadley said. "Well, my sister's kids are going trick-or-treating for the first time tonight. Making the rounds in the neighborhood. Should be okay. Couple of adults going with them."

"Good idea. These days they may get tricked instead of treated."

"And not just kids," Wadley said.

"You mean like year before last when someone spiked the Golden Hills Country Club punch with LSD? Or last year when the Cavalier Club went up in flames? That was a bit over the top, wasn't it? And that bus accident didn't help. SUV versus bus, what a mess. You worked on the victims, didn't you?" Jenkins asked, just before Alan Samson came in: he was in his early thirties, blond-haired and green-eyed, a pediatric nurse who looked like a football player, with big shoulders, a sturdy torso, and legs like tree-trunks; his voice was low and comfortable. "Hey there. I thought you were through for the day."

Samson's outwardly imperturbable manner was characteristically unruffled. "Overtime," he said at his most laconic.

"You planning to take care of the teenagers, along with the kids?" Wadley asked, trying to urge Samson into a discussion.

"Whatever Spink wants; she arranged for me," was Samson's abbreviated answer, leaving out the negotiating that her request required. He took his cup down from the shelf, filled it with hot water and dropped a teabag from his breast pocket into it.

"And what about Chin and Wieznieki?" Jenkins inquired as Samson sat down opposite him; Chin was the cardiologist on duty, Wieznieki was the orthopedist.

"Spink is pediatrics; so am I. If she doesn't need me tonight, I can take other cases, just like you, Jamal." It was impossible to tell if this calculated needling aggravated or amused him.

"There are five Docs on call tonight, and three extra on the floor," Jenkins remarked. "Almost as expensive as New Year's."

"Serves the suits right if we don't get much action, and them paying all this overtime." Wadley often saw the hospital as being stocked with two separate forces that constantly rubbed against each other, not like companions, but more like tectonic plates, their disputes jarring Herbert Blythedale Memorial Hospital between them at irregular intervals.

"Be nice to have it go that way," Jenkins agreed doubtfully, sipping his coffee. "But the night's young, and anything can happen." He chuckled.

"The shift will change in about fifteen minutes," Samson remarked to no one in particular.

Lois Barnes, the head of ER nurses for the night, stuck her head into The Canteen. "Any of you seen Annamarie Smith? Or Nancy Flanders? They're late, and that isn't like them. And tonight of all nights." She glanced at her watch. "Well?"

The three men told her no.

"If you do, remind Smith she needs to be at the reception desk right now," she said, and withdrew.

"Annamarie is usually a little early," said Jenkins, evincing no concern at this minor tardiness.

"She's got three kids—she may be taking care of them, getting ready for trick-or-treating, or they might need to join up with other kids." Wadley thought this over. "Maybe there's more traffic than usual."

"There was a stabbing down on Claussen Avenue," said Wadley. "Some kid was wearing a costume in a rival gang's colors."

"All of the above tonight," said Samson, drinking his tea.

They fell into an uneasy silence, each feeling disquieted by a disruption in routine on a night like this. Wadley was the first to get up from the table; he gave his mug a cursory washing in the small sink, then set it out on the counter to dry. "I'm off. See you at break."

"Yeah," Jenkins said, stretching. "I'll be out of here in a couple of minutes. Tell Pomeroy I'm coming; she gets antsy. She likes to be out of here as near on six as she can, but won't leave until I sign in officially."

Samson made a sound that seemed to indicate something similar while contemplatively blowing on his tea.

Wadley had barely left when Megan Hastings came in, her forty-year-old face looking a good bit older; she walked as if her feet hurt. "Just got a half-dozen partyers in. They were on a forty-foot cabin cruiser, more than twenty guests aboard, and the skipper rammed it into Boromeo's Wharf; about ten went into the drink. The Coast Guard got them all out, but they're cold, wet, and bruised, most of them, though the host of the evening got a gash on his arm, and one of his guests has a concussion; there are probably other minor injuries."

"I didn't hear sirens," said Samson.

"Most came in by private car; the fire department wants to hold as many ambulances in reserve that they can. The EMTs said most of the injuries from the partyers weren't serious and the guys were okay to drive. They all signed off on their driving, and agreed to get medical help within twenty-four hours if they didn't come here before going home. The gash and concussion came in the ambulance together, no siren, and another four arrived by car. They're all in costume." She sighed. "I can't wait to get home. It's building up; I can feel it. They're gonna need you, Jenkins."

Not wanting to get into a discussion about Hastings' feelings, "See you on Tuesday," said Jenkins, shoving himself up from his chair. "Have a nice rest-of-the-weekend."

"You, too," she said, opening the refrigerator for the last of her sandwich.

Samson studied her. "How is it in the waiting room?"

"It was about average, but with the boat party, it's gonna be busy for a while: X-rays and some guys waiting to drive the injured home." She gave a short, mirthless laugh. "They're all dressed as pirates, the swashbuckling kind."

"*Yo-ho-ho and a bottle of rum* pirates, or cutthroat?" Samson asked.

"*Yo-ho-ho,* by the look of them," Hastings said. "Like they all want to be Johnny Depp."

"Just guys?"

Hastings shrugged. "It was that kind of party; you know."

Samson nodded and stepped out of The Canteen, working his way through the change-of-shift crowd at the admissions desk, pausing long enough to sign in officially, then going on to the Pediatrics office, taking a moment to make sure his undershirt was properly tucked into the trousers of his blue-green scrubs. He could hear a child crying, more in anger than fear or pain, which he took to be a good sign. In the corridor he passed a bedraggled young man in an outfit of wet leather pantaloons tucked into high, cuffed boots. What manner of shirt he wore was concealed by a blanket wrapped around his shoulders; the fellow had a bandage on his right hand, probably from scraped knuckles, Samson thought, as he turned into Linda Spink's office. "Happy Halloween."

Doctor Spink looked up from the open laptop on her desk. "Oh. To you, too, Samson." She had iron-gray hair cut like a shining steel helmet, and wore scrubs the color of slate; at fifty-six she was considered the doyen of the ER. "It's going to be you and Flanders tonight."

"I saw on the assignment board," he said. "She here yet?"

"I haven't seen her. She usually rides in with Annamarie—"

He interrupted her. "—Smith. They aren't here yet."

"Huh!" said Spink, surprised. "They usually call in if they're going to be late." She looked at the file-folders sitting on the shelf next to her right elbow. "You want to sit?"

"Sure," he said, and plunked himself down on the futon currently in couch mode next to the door, and looked through the magazines and papers on the occasional table next to the futon. He found a two-day-old newspaper and opened it. "Says here it was supposed to rain tonight—it's clear and windy."

"The Air Force says that the Wednesday night UFO flap was a hoax." Spink said, pointing to the front page of the paper that was emblazoned with a night sky spangled with red and green glowing eggs.

"Of course they did," Samson said, bored; he closed the paper.

"Did you see the pirates?" Spink asked suddenly.

"One of them. He was kind of waterlogged."

"He fell in the bay."

Samson snorted a kind of laugh. "Damn silly, if you ask me."

"People do get silly on Halloween," she said. "And worse than silly. The full moon doesn't help."

"Saturday doesn't either." He picked up a magazine from the rack and began to thumb through it.

Two honks on the hospital's public address system announced the change of shift. There was a flurry of activity out in the corridor, as the day shift gave over to the six-till-two shift. Lockers were opened and closed, a cluster of nurses and staff gathered in front of the emergency entrance, cell-phones clapped to their ears. Over the next ten minutes, staff and nurses milled in the admissions area, then either left the hospital or went along to their assignments. The hospital settled into its usual weekend rhythm, the ER ready for early arrivals.

Linda Spink answered her summons, gesturing to Samson to come with her. "Two kids with dog bites. Cops are with them."

Samson set the magazine aside and got up. "Right behind you, Doc."

They heard the noise before they reached the triage desk; Spink gave Samson a signal to keep close.

One woman's voice, shrill and angry, penetrated the general babble coming from the cluster of people confronting Mitchell Doyle, the triage nurse, who was trying to sort out what was going on. "You people! Letting dangerous dogs out on Halloween!" She appeared to be addressing the EMTs and two cops; she was in her thirties, of medium height, spare, with lackluster hair and work-chapped hands. "Reece could have been killed!"

"Aw, Ma," said the gangly ten-year-old boy in a cheap, store-bought Spiderman costume standing beside her, a thick bandage wrapped around his hand.

One of the cops rolled his eyes toward the ceiling.

She shifted attention to her son. "What were you thinking, going up to an unknown dog?"

"I keep telling you, he had a collar, and he wasn't that big," the boy whined. "Hey, the dog came up to us, tail wagging."

The woman next to her was kneeling down, comforting a slightly smaller boy in a homemade Mad Hatter costume; this child was clearly in need of more help than his companion, so Doctor Spink started with her. The woman looked up, flushed slightly, and got to her feet. "Doctor?"

"Talk to the cops and the EMTs, Samson," said Spink, and turned her attention to the smaller boy, speaking quietly to reassure him. "Why don't you tell me what happened?" she asked, lowering her voice.

The younger EMT came up to Samson. "They 9-1-1-ed us about thirty minutes ago, and we had the boys in the ambulance, mothers included, in a little over ten minutes. Animal control has the dog. Looks like a smaller shepherd mix of some kind, maybe thirty-five pounds. The boys told us they went up to pet it, and something spooked the dog, so it growled and bit."

The nearer cop said, "Dog looked trained. It backed right off when we showed up. I think the costumes bothered him."

"Male dog?" Samson asked.

"Once upon a time," said the cop. "That's another reason I'm not buying the kids' story of an unexpected attack."

"I see," said Samson.

The second EMT nodded toward Spiderman/Reece. "That one started it; you can tell. I have a hunch they were teasing the dog."

"Me, too," said the older cop, having completed his report to Mitchell Doyle. "Though I think it was more tormenting than teasing." He nodded in the direction of the boys. "You're right: that Reece kid's the type to do it."

Spink rose, but before she could speak, Reece's mother announced, "I'm going to sue the dog's owner and the city for allowing such a dangerous animal to run loose."

"Oh, Mandy," said the Mad Hatter's mother wearily.

"You should join me, Eloise. Someone has to pay for what's happened to Jeff."

"Whatever you decide to do, do it later," Spink said in what Samson called her Official Voice, "right now though, Jeff needs a couple X-rays and probably half-a-dozen stitches. If Reece will let me have a quick look at his hand, I'll know what more needs to be done with him."

"You heard Doctor Spink," said Samson, using his height to add force to his words. "Let her take care of the kids, then you can decide on what's to happen next."

"I'm not letting Reece out of my sight," his mother declared.

"I'm not asking you to," said Spink.

The PA system announced three children arriving by ambulance, suspected of being poisoned.

"Will you go deal with the new arrivals?" Spink asked Samson, briefly looking up from Jeff's injuries.

"If that's what you want," said Samson, ignoring the glare Mandy shot at him, and the sigh of the older cop.

"Take them into Bay 3, in case," she said, indicating she was anticipating vomit and feces at the least. "Where's Flanders when I need her?"

"I'll see if Doyle's heard anything," said Samson as he left the cubicle, bound for the ambulance entryway.

By eight o'clock, Spink had treated thirteen children, four of whom had been sent home, eight had been admitted for overnight observation, and one had been sent into surgery for multiple fractures that had nothing to do with Halloween; there was a thick file on the autistic girl's so-called falls and clumsiness. The emergency room was unusually busy for all those on duty, what with a riot having broken out on the edge of a homeless encampment and a number of admissions for some kind of unidentified flu, which was bringing sufferers to the ER at the rate of eight or nine a hour, coughing and running high temperatures. The hectic pace all this demanded was starting to tell on the staff.

"Flanders still isn't here," Samson told Spink as they stood near the waiting room, each with a cup of caffeinated coffee to shore up their increasing fatigue. "I checked with Doyle about five minutes ago. The clerk at the desk called her house, but there was no answer."

"I don't like it," said Spink.

"Who does? Smith and Flanders are important and we need them tonight." He drank more coffee.

"Another six hours," said Spink as if she was reciting a prison sentence.

"Fewer kids than last year," Samson observed.

"So far," said Spink.

"Do you want a little time to yourself? Nothing much is happening just now." Samson kept his voice even, though he wanted to yawn.

Spink thought about it. "No. It'll leave me groggy. I'll do better if I'm a bit hyper."

She saw Doyle coming toward her, fretting. "What is it?"

"Ambulance coming in, twelve-year-old on a bike clipped by a car. The driver wasn't drunk, but there were a lot of kids going door-to-door, and he couldn't watch them all. A Batman on a bike was hard to see. At least, that's his story."

"What do the EMTs say?" Spink asked as she tossed the last third of her coffee into the nearest refuse bin.

Doyle said, "Better to talk to the cops than the EMTs about that."

"Let me know if the cops show up." Motioning to Samson to follow her, she went along toward the pediatric cubicles, saying to him over her shoulder. "Find Jenkins and tell him to set up for a kid. Then check to see if he's arrived. I'll want you ready."

"Okay. Anything else?"

"Not until I see the boy." She waved him away, and went where Doyle pointed out to her.

Samson gave a short sigh, took a last gulp of coffee, and went off toward The Canteen to find out if Jenkins were available. "Try the computer room," one of the younger nurses recommended. Samson took her suggestion and found Jenkins emerging from the men's room. "Spink has a kid hit by car while on his bike coming in."

"Just one kid on a bike?" Jenkins asked as he changed directions. "I'm pretty sure we've got a machine available; the last of the pirates is gone. D'you think she'll want a CAT scan?"

"No idea, and I won't try to second-guess her. She wants you standing by." They went down a slight incline in the hall, a reminder of how two buildings had been cobbled into one almost twenty years before. Once they were in the larger portion of the building, they went to a sturdy double door that required Jenkins' ID card swipe to enter.

"Kid, possible multiple fractures, en route in the ambulance," he said to the monitor on duty, hardly slowing his pace. "Probably be here in ten minutes or so."

"Take Room 5," the monitor said, making an entry on the laptop at the end of the counter. Unlike most of the hospital, this facility lacked a waiting room, and there were no vending machines; there were chairs in a large alcove down the hall on the other side of the double doors where families and friends could wait. Just at present, the alcove was empty.

"Five it is," said Jenkins, bound for a heavy door at the far side of the small lobby. "Come on, Samson."

Samson paused at the monitor's counter. "The patient is Doc Swink's. Notify her where they'll bring the kid."

"Will do," the monitor said even as he punched in more information on the computer and pressed a button to signal the ER.

Jenkins was in the X-ray control room—which was little more than a bay in the corner—checking out the console. "Did you ever see a flick called *Fire Maidens from Outer Space?*" he asked Samson.

"I can't remember if I have or not," said Samson.

"Oh, you'd remember this one. It's *terrible*." He grinned. "I usually watch it on Halloween. You want to come over and watch it with me when our shift ends?"

"Why'd I stay up to see a bad movie?" Samson asked.

"You might get a kick out of it." He shrugged and said, "You see the Air Force said the UFOs were a hoax?"

"Yeah."

"That's bullshit." He drummed his fingers on the X-ray table. "How long do we have to wait, do you think?"

"Doyle seemed to believe the ambulance would be here shortly."

"You know where it's coming from?" Jenkins asked.

"No idea," said Samson, and went silent.

"The kid with the dog bites was admitted? Jeff, his name is," said Jenkins.

"Yes. Spink's worried about shock, not just the bites on his shoulder and thigh."

There was a bang as the main doors were opened by a gurney heading into the X-ray department, and less than a minute later, the gurney arrived at Room 5, an orderly pushing it with practiced speed. "You ready for him?"

Samson looked at the boy in his ruined Batman costume, his head held in place by the neck collar the EMTs had put on him; though the room was dark, Samson could see the patient was badly injured. "We have to handle him carefully," he told the orderly.

"I'm not a beginner," the orderly said curtly. "The kid's barely conscious. Name's Winston Bradley Harrison."

Samson glanced at the papers clipped to the gurney. "Four foot nine, eighty-seven pounds, broken bones for sure, possible skull fracture."

"So much for the obvious," said Jenkins as he brought out the plastic foam bolsters to put the boy in place on the table. "Parents here?"

"Father. With Spink," said the orderly. "Said it's his custody weekend. Mother lives in Easton; she's driving in. Should be here in a couple of hours."

Samson adjusted one of the bolsters, asking as he did, "Speaking of here, is Flanders here yet?"

"Don't think so," said the orderly, handing a sheet to Jenkins to sign. "Didn't see her anywhere in the ER, nor Smith."

Jenkins went into the control room where he kept his pen while the orderly prepared to move out of Room 5. "Is there a bed for this kid?"

"Spink was arranging it as I brought him up," said the orderly, waiting for Jenkins to hand him the paper.

"Any orders beyond what's on the paper?" Jenkins asked as he emerged with the paper.

"Not that I know of," said the orderly as he took the paper and got out of Room 5 and the X-ray department.

"Full body, spine, left arm, right shoulder, left knee-to-foot," Jenkins said. "I guess we better get started. I'll need your help on this one."

The boy coughed once, and foamy blood spread on his lips as he began to spasm.

"Better tell Spink to hurry," said Jenkins.

* * *

Things had slowed down a bit by ten-thirty, when Winston Harrison's mother arrived, pale yet outwardly composed, and went in to see Spink, leaving Samson to put himself at the service of whomever might need an extra nurse, which is how Samson was one of the first to hear that there had been an accident and that Smith and Flanders had been involved.

"Are they all right?" Doyle asked the cop who had brought the news. "Where are they?"

"They're at the fourth precinct giving statements."

"You mean they aren't hurt?"

"They're shaken up, but no blood showing," said the cop.

Samson ambled over to the admissions desk. "What happened?"

The cop regarded him suspiciously. "And you are?"

"Samson. I'm a pediatric nurse; I often work with Flanders." He leaned against the counter, minimizing the impact of his size; it worked with kids and it worked with the cop.

"Huh," said the cop. "Well, Smith was driving, so the fault is hers, but Flanders says the guy—he was in a dark costume, something like a wetsuit, but with a kind of *creature* head, something like a hadrosaur's top-knot—stepped out from between two cars, where the staff parks. There was a light, but it was out. We checked, and it was—had been for a couple of days."

Samson was amused that the cop knew something about dinosaurs, and decided he must have kids.

"Are you telling me that Smith ran into someone?" Doyle asked, his voice rising half an octave.

"Looks that way. She was going pretty fast." The cop shook his head, going on as if he wanted to figure it out for himself. "The two women stayed with the guy after they called 9-1-1. They gave some first aid, put a blanket over him, put a light bandage on his leg where it was bleeding, but didn't move him. They were out on Golden Hills Country Club Road; they'd dropped off Smith's kids for a party; her ex lives out there, in one of those yuppie mansions. Smith said they were running late so she was speeding. Says she didn't see him at all until the right front bumper tossed him in the air. They had real trouble getting bars enough to call 9-1-1. Flanders walked almost a mile before she could get through. And then dispatch took over an hour to get an ambulance to them; there're a lot of them busy picking up what's left of the rioters, and it took more than half an hour to free one up to go get the guy in the costume. It'll be coming in here in about twenty minutes. I can tell you right now, he's gonna need X-rays and maybe surgery. You'll have to undress him; that costume of his really is skintight and tough; the ladies didn't want to mess with the costume. Really sophisticated. Probably cost a bundle. The EMTs didn't want to try to cut it off him either."

"Why?" Samson asked. "Because it's expensive?"

"They wanted to move him as little as possible. He's pretty banged up, and getting something that tight off—" The cop gave a sketchy salute.

"What was he doing out on Golden Hills Country Club Road?" Doyle was baffled. "What's out there for trick-or-treat?"

"That's another thing," the cop said. "The guy's not a kid. Maybe a little short, but in good shape under his costume. Got real muscular legs, and thick arms. He could have been lost if he was looking for a private party, or he could have been up to no good—you know, putting on a costume so he wouldn't be noticed? It happens. There are some pricey homes with some valuable things in them in that development behind the country club. If the guy pulls through, we'll have some questions for him."

Doyle was still taken aback by this news, and so said nothing to the cop as he turned to leave.

"Thanks," said Samson, and decided not to interrupt Spink with this news, not while Spink was explaining to Winston Harrison's parents the likelihood that their son had suffered brain damage and would need long-term therapy when he woke up, if he woke up at all. Out of habit, he wandered into The Canteen, where four nurses were gathered in front of the TV, and made himself a cup of tea. He had just sat down away from the television when Wadley came into the room, looking haggard.

"You hear about Smith and Flanders?" He saw Samson nod. "Doyle just told me they hit someone driving in."

"That's what I heard," Samson said.

"What an awful thing to happen." Wadley poured some well-stewed coffee into a large mug. "I'm glad we're on the down-slope for our shift. We've admitted sixteen rioters so far, and treated fifty-three. I hope that's the last of them."

"You hope," said Samson, remembering that they could be kept over the end of their shifts if they were needed for an emergency.

"You're on overtime already," said Wadley. He, too, sat down, choosing the chair opposite Samson, one that enabled him to watch the TV, now turned to some kind of Halloween gala in LA.

About ten minutes later, Samson heard his name on the PA system, summoning him to the ambulance arrival doors. Without speaking to Wadley, who was engrossed in the activity on the screen, he emptied out the last of his tea, rinsed his cup and left The Canteen to Wadley.

Doyle was waiting for him at the double set of doors. "Take the patient into Bay 14. Conners will meet you there. I want your report on the patient's condition as soon as it's determined."

"Who's going to cover for me?" Samson asked.

"Baker will," said Doyle.

"Let Spink know," Samson said, and went off to Bay 14 to await the arrival of the new patient.

"You got it," said Doyle, sounding jittery.

An orderly and a cop accompanied the gurney with the well-swathed patient as it was rushed into Bay 14, four minutes earlier than the cop had predicted; two minutes later, Doctor Richard Conners opened the drapes that enclosed the bay, saying, "What have we here?" He was taller than average, blocky of build, with thinning blond hair, a large broken nose, and great deal of pale body hair under his scrubs.

"This is the guy the two nurses hit," said the cop before the orderly could speak. "The EMTs said he had a rapid pulse and his temperature was on the low side. They left his costume alone."

Conners drew back the sheet that covered the injured man; he gave a slow whistle. "That's some costume." He fingered the slithery, gray-green fabric that covered him from head to toe, and stared for half a minute at the face, obviously a make-up appliance. "That head—it's like something out of the movies."

"Creepy, isn't it? He really did it up brown—or gator-green," the cop said as if glad to find someone who agreed with him.

"I'll say," Conners agreed, trying to find a pulse under the costume. "I think I'll go along with the EMTs. Let's get some X-rays before we start working on him. We don't want to make him more shocky than he already is."

"No, we don't," said Samson, and signaled to the orderly to bring the gurney and its passenger along to the X-ray department. "Any ID on him?"

"Not obviously," said the cop. "Like I said: he looks a little too old for trick-or-treat to me. A party, or something no good."

"Unless he went to the Halloween dance at the Metropolitan," said Samson.

"Then what was he doing out on Golden Hills Country Club Road?" the cop asked, then noticed they were at the elevators. "Someone will do follow-up on this, come morning."

Samson shrugged and pressed the button for the elevator. "That's the next shift."

"I'll get your number from the nursing office," the cop said, and stood aside as the gurney was shoved into the elevator.

"This is going to get complicated," Conners complained.

They rode the rest of the way in silence, emerging into a small crowd gathered around the elevator doors.

"Coming through," said the orderly, and began to move the gurney without waiting for compliance from the crowd.

"Hey!" Conners admonished him. "Please move aside," he told the people, who slowly took a step or two back from the elevator.

Samson motioned the people to move farther back, and as the gurney went past him, the patient's taloned hand reached out and grabbed his wrist. A few of the people saw it; one of them yelped in shock, and another gasped. Samson disengaged the eerie fingers, and slid the hand back under the sheet that covered the patient.

"Shit, man," one of the crowd expostulated.

"He's still in costume," said Samson with his habitual calm. "That's a glove."

A few of the people laughed nervously, but one of the three children among them shrieked.

An older man said to Samson, "Mother's having a cancer

operation in the morning. We were given extended visiting hours, you know, just in case. We're a little jumpy."

Samson nodded his acceptance of this apology, and followed Conners, the orderly, and the gurney to the X-ray department, where they were sent along to Room 12, and found Jenkins waiting for them.

"See if you can take a pair of full-body shots before we start getting him out of his costume," Conners said, his voice lowered in case the patient was able to hear him.

Jenkins laughed quietly. "Looks like the Creature from the Black Lagoon, only better face appliances. How long's he been unconscious?"

"Not quite two hours, give or take," said the orderly, flapping the yellow-tinted EMT report.

"Um," said Jenkins. "Okay, I'll do it." He motioned to the orderly, and to Samson. "Help me transfer him to the table."

Conners stood back to allow the other three men to work, saying only, "Turn his head; as long as he's got the costume on, we won't try for a full-on face, it'll push on his neck too much." He watched them lifting the limp figure with the sturdy drape the EMTs had used to load him onto the stretcher and into the ambulance. At one point, the patient made a kind of groan, but there was no other obvious response. The room was very quiet.

"Align him, Samson," said Jenkins. "Like he was a nine-year-old who fell off his skateboard on a curl."

"Will do," said Samson, and unhurriedly maneuvered the patient as nearly as possible into the preferred position for his X-rays. "Want me to take off his shoes? They're forcing him onto the balls of his feet."

"He's lying down. We can take care of it later." Conners glowered at the patient as he stepped behind the shield in front of the controls for the machine. "God, I hate Halloween. We work with horrors every day of the week, then along comes Halloween, glorifying it all, and people wonder why our ER is so busy on this night."

"Hey, get in here," Jenkins called from his shielded control room. "We'll try a first shot."

Conners and Samson obeyed, squeezing in with the orderly and Jenkins, who pressed a series of buttons; there was a buzz and a soft clunk, and an image emerged on the computer screen in front of him.

"Holy shit," whispered Conners. "What's *that*?" He pointed to what appeared to be a malformation of the skull.

"Fan-fucking-tastic!" Jenkins marveled.

Samson stared at the screen and whistled softly, while the orderly blinked.

"What *is* that?" Conners wondered aloud.

"It ain't one of us," said Jenkins gleefully. "Look at the bone structure. Well, let's figure those are bones and not something else. That's from Somewhere Else. Not even the Elephant Man had that kind of skeleton."

"It's a hoax. It has to be," said Conner.

"Or it's one hell of a trick-or-treat," said Samson.

"I told you the flap was the real deal," Jenkins said victoriously. "What do we do now?"

"We report this," said Samson.

"I'll do it," the orderly volunteered, hoping to get out of this small space and away from the unmoving figure lying under the X-ray machine.

"To *who*?" Conner demanded, growing more and more disbelieving as he stared at the computer screen. "What do we tell them—it's Halloween, it's Saturday, the moon is full, *and* the aliens have landed?"

"Well, one has; you can't pretend that's human," said Samson, peering through the shield at the still figure on the table.

"Audioanimatronics," said Conner suddenly. "It's gotta be."

"Except that it hasn't moved and it's silent," said Jenkins.

The orderly gave a nervous sigh. "Is it alive?"

"No way to tell yet," said Jenkins.

"Got to get it out of costume first," said Samson.

"Is that a costume?" The orderly goggled.

"Is it dangerous?" Conner asked the air.

"Probably some kind of pressure suit, or body armor," said Jenkins, relishing the moment. "Hot-damn!"

Conners shook his head. "We ought to call someone. We have to leave it alone."

"But who do we call?" Samson's repetition of Conner's question took the other two aback. "We can't just let it lie here, can we?"

Then Jenkins beamed at the opportunity. "Ghostbusters!" he exclaimed, and immediately shut up.

"Want me to find out who to notify?" the orderly asked, wanting to get away from the alien being lying on the X-ray table.

"I'll do it," said Conners. "God, think of the press! I *hate* Halloween. It's just a left over beginning-of-winter pagan festival turned into a fancy dress party," he complained as he left the control booth.

Before Conners reached the door, Samson said, "Yeah. An old pagan rite turned into a festival." He moved out of the cramped space to stand beside the supine alien. "Like Christmas."

Chelsea Quinn Yarbro is the first woman to be named a Living Legend by the International Horror Guild. She has also been honored as a Bram Stoker Lifetime Achievement by the Horror Writers Association, and as Grand Master of the World Horror Convention. She is the recipient of the Fine Foundation Award for Literary Achievement and (along with Fred Saberhagen) was awarded the Knightly Order of the Brasov Citadel by the Transylvanian Society of Dracula in 1997. A professional writer since 1968, Yarbro has worked in a wide variety of genres, from science fiction to westerns and from young adult adventure to historical horror. Yarbro is the author of over ninety books, more than seventy works of short fiction, and more than two dozen essays and reviews. Best-known for her Count Saint-Germain series, *Night Pilgrims* (2013) is its twenty-sixth book and twenty-fourth novel. She's just completed the next novel in the series: *Sustenance.* Her website is chelseaquinnyarbro.net.

WE, THE FORTUNATE BEREAVED

Brian Hodge

He'd been relentless about it throughout the whole of October, as only a six-year-old could be, worse by the day as the month went on.

"I want it to be Daddy this year." Cody was up to what felt like a hundred times a day now that the end of the month was here, and the night at hand. "We have to do a really good job so that it's Daddy this year."

Bailey had told him nothing about this night, ever, nor had Drew when he was alive. For a few more years, at least, they'd wanted Halloween, for Cody, to be nothing more than trick-or-treating. And maybe, minus one congenital heart defect, undetected until it was too late, that's the way it would have been. Or maybe what they'd wanted wouldn't have mattered anyway. All it took was one other first-grader in the know, and soon enough they all knew. Children shared secrets even more readily than they shared bacteria and head lice.

But knowing about it was one thing. Having such an enormous personal stake in it was something else entirely.

"It's *got* to be Daddy this year."

"Then let's finish picking what we want to leave to call him," Bailey said. "Let's make it good. Have you thought really hard about what you want to pick?"

Of course he had. He'd been consumed by it all month. For Cody, the problem would be narrowing it down to just one. Because those were the rules. If he could've gotten away with it, he would've emptied his room of memories, harvested the closets clean, filled his wagon and more with them, then hauled them to the town square himself, to dump them at the foot of the cross where the frightful thing hung, awaiting something that looked like life.

Bailey's own choice had been easier, made almost by default. Was it to be her wedding ring? No. For all it meant, it had none of Drew's essence in it. His razor, still in the bathroom even though he'd been eight months in the ground? Improbably, it had survived since the first day of his freshman year of college, and had contoured his face nearly every day of his life since. No, not that either. It was too prosaic, with none of *her* essence in it.

In prior years, she'd heard local widows joke that what they should've picked was the TV remote—if anything could call their men over from the other side, that would do the trick.

In the end, though, on this morning of the thirty-first, what she chose was Drew's favorite shirt for nights and weekends during the long months of autumn and winter. It was the king of flannel shirts, blue and white, checked like a horse blanket and thick to keep out the cold. She'd liked to wear it too, even though it swallowed her whole—adored wearing it because of smelled of him, an enveloping scent that was entirely male, entirely Drew. And he'd adored getting it back, once it smelled of her.

Just a shirt, but still, it was what love would feel like if you could wear an emotion. She couldn't imagine anything more appropriate to leave as his lure.

And Cody? She watched from the doorway of his room before he knew she was there, and saw that he'd narrowed his choices to only enough to cover his bed. It was progress. Toys and books and items of clothing and things dragged in from the yard, and it made her sad in a way she'd never been before to realize that she really had no idea what many of these things even meant to Cody in relationship to Drew. Six years old and already he lived half the time in a world of secrets, and it was only going to get worse from here.

"What's it going to be, champ?" she asked.

"This," he said, after one final deliberation that twisted him into knots, then he turned around holding his Pinewood Derby car. "We built this. We built it together. This should be right . . . right?"

One of the last great projects of the previous winter. Cody hadn't even been eligible for Cub Scouts yet, much less the race. He'd just wanted the practice, to be ready for the day he was. As he had wanted nothing else, he'd wanted to build that car. She never would've guessed how much pride and joy that a $3.99 block of wood and four wheels could bring a kindergartner and a grown man.

"It's perfect," Bailey said. "Now get your jacket and let's get going."

Dunhaven was the only town she'd ever heard of where Halloween was a school holiday, but then Dunhaven wasn't like other towns. It was the only place she knew where the night brought more than just trickery and mischief. In Dunhaven, genuine magic, dark magic, pierced the veil on All Hallows Eve.

This would come in its own time. For now, morning was bright with the golden light of a cool sun, and the streets were uncommonly busy. Everybody had business on a day like this. Along the seven-block walk from home, she saw neighbors and friends, fellow teachers from the high school, students past and students present, as well as people in from the countryside that she might not see again until next year.

Everyone had business with the dead today, or believed they did.

And she couldn't help but wonder: Who among them would die in the year to come, and who would be hoping to call them forth next October?

The town square was less crowded than she might have guessed, green and crisscrossed with sidewalks that converged at the fountain in the middle, and nearly empty. More sunflowers than people, more shrubs than visitors, vibrant with the yellow of goldenrod and beds of sedum whose close-packed blossoms looked like bright red slashes in the earth.

One presence, at least, was a permanent fixture, and if it was an illusion of life now, no more animated than one of the benches flanking the walkways, night would change everything. Darkness would remind people why they tended not to idle about while this thing hung waiting for a soul.

It was just clothing and straw, a stuffed burlap bag for a head with buttons for eyes and stitching for a mouth and a broad-brimmed hat to hold the horsetail hair in place. Affixed to a rough-hewn field-cross in the heart of town and looking as if it had gotten lost from the corn, drawing stares instead of frightening crows . . . yet even now, it felt possible to offend it.

She held Cody's hand tighter as they approached. Usually he squirmed and pulled away when she tried that. Not today.

It seemed to wait for them, the slumped head looking down as they neared. Too light to hang there sagging like the agonized Christ of a crucifix, its pose looked casual, its weathered denim arms draped wide over the crossbar like someone stretching with a yawn across the backrest of a bench.

On the bottle-green grass, before the towering fencepost that pierced the earth, they set down their summonses: the well-worn flannel shirt and the beloved Pinewood car. These joined other items left by other hands: a book, undoubtedly the favorite of someone's lifetime, and a baseball glove, and a folio of sheet music, and a Purple Heart medal from some war. The most unusual was a cake that looked not just frosted but frosty, as though until some time around dawn it had spent months in a freezer, never sliced and eaten, someone's happy occasion turning tragic before the plates and forks came out.

There were so many little stories here, each of them sad in its own way.

She would have to check later, though, to make sure that the shirt and car were still here. There was a strategy to this. Put your offering out too soon, and you were only prolonging temptation, increasing the odds that it might disappear. This day did not always bring out the best in people. Lonely people, bereaved people, who wouldn't mind sabotaging their neighbor's chance at a reunion if it meant improving their own.

Put your offering out too late, though, and . . . well, nobody could say for sure when was too late, when these pieces of lives left behind started being *noticed*.

By the same token, nobody could say with any certainty when this custom had even started, or how. The oldest families in town—the Ralstons and the Goslings, the Chennowics and Harringtons—all claimed some propriety in the matter, but none of their stories matched up very well with any of the others, so much so that blows had been struck over it in the past . . . at least one, ironically, fatal.

What was beyond denying, though, was that it had been going on for at least 162 years, maybe longer, from a time when the land they stood on was the town commons, bordering a cornfield whose earliest ownership would be forever disputed. The records had been lost well before the arrival of the twentieth century, in a fire that had leveled the county clerk's office.

Was it the land itself? Or something done *on* or *to* the land to forever change the spirit of the place? Was it something bound up in the people, their heritages and bloodlines, that would've followed them anywhere if they'd packed up the whole of Dunhaven and moved the town someplace else? The residents of both the town and the surrounding county, out to a distance of at least eighteen miles, had benefited from it, if *benefit* was really the proper word for such a thing, and there were many who argued that it wasn't. That it was not the blessing people thought it to be.

Which never seemed to discourage anybody from hoping to be the one whose call was answered.

The truth came down to this: Deeply ancient custom held that, on Halloween night, the cusp between summer and winter, the veil between the worlds of the living and the dead grew thin, so thin that spirits might cross over to wander for a night. Another custom—perhaps related, perhaps not, and not nearly so ancient as the other but old enough—held that scarecrows came alive on Halloween night. Dunhaven was the only place in which Bailey had ever heard of it actually happening . . . although for all she or anyone else knew, Dunhaven was the place where this legend had been born.

One night, one scarecrow, and the returned soul of one person who had died during the past year. Just one. Never none, never two or more, only the one.

The rite had inspired a deep legacy of secrecy. It had never been a thing to share with the outside world, beyond the town and surrounding farmland. Here, you grew up understanding the importance of silence even before you fully understood what it was you weren't to talk about with anyone from farther off.

In the early decades, when people journeyed by horse, and most not very far, Dunhaven had been sufficiently remote that the secret was easy enough to keep. But time brought paved roads and the vehicles that traveled them, so stronger measures were needed. Roads could be closed. Innkeepers could be persuaded to turn away potential lodgers. Lingering strangers could be made to feel unwelcome. For every threat, there was an answer.

Still, peoples' tongues were the first and last lines of defense. Most children grew up indoctrinated with tales of bogeymen who punished those who let secrets slip. By the time they were old enough to know better, they'd already seen enough each Halloween to fear that bogeymen might not necessarily be a myth. And as adults, the last thing they wanted was a tide of incomers desperately seeking assurance of life after death, driving up the property tax base in the process.

Whatever few stray whispers did manage to escape seemed to suffocate in the skepticism of the modern world, and so the sacrament remained theirs alone. It had been going on for so long they took for granted it always would . . . even though people never liked to dwell on how which soul came through got decided on the other side. One preferred to believe in the concept of rest and peace, not in cutthroat competitions to seize the last second chance you might have to say goodbye.

Trinkets, things that had special meaning, seemed to sweeten the odds.

After Bailey and Cody set theirs down, they stepped back, as she took another look up at the face gazing blindly down at them, the potential of personality trying to crawl past the burlap and buttons.

"What will you say to him, if it's Daddy?" she whispered.

Cody thought for a long time. "If he'll take me with him."

Just a few simple words, worse than a dagger in the heart. Her first impulse was to tell him, *command* him, to never say such a thing. Not the best lesson to teach, that he had to censor himself around her. Hadn't she just been ruing, not half an hour ago, the fact that he already had secrets?

"Wouldn't you miss me?" she said instead. "I'd miss you. I'd miss you with all my heart." *Every minute of every day*, she almost said, but didn't want to oversell. It wasn't Cody's kind of talk. "I'd miss all the fun stuff we do."

He still didn't seem to grasp what the big deal was. Just looked at the scarecrow as if it were his escape clause, the answer to all the problems. "Then I'd come back next year."

She stiffened, thought she saw where this was going.

"Let's get you back home and into your costume," she said. "Nobody wants to be late for a party."

In Dunhaven, Halloween ran according to a different schedule. As most of the world had come to recognize it, Halloween was a holiday for children, and a tacky one at that, all cheap scares and greed. There could be no abolishing this part of it—they were realists here—but they could at least see to it that the childish side of the day was over and done with before sunset, before things turned serious, when even the grownups took pause. Parties in the morning, trick-or-treating in the afternoon. It helped if the day's sky was grim, and after a bright sunrise, the clouds were starting to cooperate.

Once Cody was suited up, she took him to the gathering in the basement at St. Aidan's Episcopal and turned him loose into the clamor of his classmates and friends. She doubled-checked the time the party was scheduled to end, and then the next three hours were hers.

Hardly anyplace in town was more than ten minutes from anyplace else, but still, Troy's house seemed another world away. He met her at the door, and she did her best to leave her guilt about this back in that other world. It would always be waiting when she returned.

Five minutes later, she wasn't really thinking about anything at all.

She pulled and she pushed, rode and was ridden, and it was still easy to tell herself that none of this meant anything. It was just an itch that needed scratching, one she couldn't reach on her own. That was all. The first time, of all the sorry, sad clichés, had been alcohol-related, on a night six weeks ago when Cody had been on a sleepover, and in a purely unforeseen development, she'd ended up doing the same.

After Drew's funeral, she'd promised herself, and him, if he was listening, that she would wait a year, at an absolute minimum, before she'd even *think* of dating again . . . and here she had barely made it six months before skipping the pretense of dating altogether. She'd awakened that next dawn wondering how it had happened, and vowing that it wouldn't happen again . . . but it was too late. The groove had been greased, so to speak. The second time was even easier to agree to, sober, than the first had been after wine.

Troy was nothing like Drew at all, and perhaps that was what made this easier. Where Drew had been beefy, Troy was lean and hard. Where Drew had towered, Troy was compact. Where Drew's hair was black, Troy was fair all over. While Drew had been quick to laugh, Troy found the humor in subtler things. Whereas Drew had loved living in the heart of town, Troy liked it out here on the periphery, in a renovated one-time farmhouse that hadn't been attached to a farm for a generation, after Dunhaven had grown out to meet it.

To look at them, at least, she and Troy matched up much more readily than she and Drew ever had. But it would never go further than this. She couldn't imagine Troy as a father, much less a stepfather. And that, she supposed, was the safety valve here.

"Tell me the truth, would you," he said, once it was all over, one more time, and they were free to stare at the ceiling. "How are you hoping it goes tonight? Are you *really* hoping he comes through?"

How to answer without either encouraging him or sounding like a callous bitch? "If it wasn't for Cody's sake? I don't know that I'd be going through with this after all."

"Oh yeah?"

"It might be good for him," she said. "He wasn't there when Drew had his heart seizure. And I'm glad of that much, that Cody didn't have to see it. But it robbed him of his chance to say goodbye. He goes to kindergarten one morning and he's got a dad, and by the time he comes home he doesn't. So tonight would probably be good for him."

Troy traced a finger along the downy blond fuzz at her temple, which felt better than she wanted it to. "And what about you?"

She couldn't find the words, and of course, that spoke volumes.

"If you're ambivalent, I can understand that," he said.

"Were you, with Angela?"

"Yes and no. The circumstances, they couldn't have been more different. With her, there was so much we didn't know. There were so many questions we would've liked to have answered. Obviously."

Obviously. Like, *Who took you, Angela? Who killed you? And where's the rest of you?*

She hadn't known Troy then, not in person and barely by sight. The first she'd seen of him was Halloween three years ago, Troy joining Angela Pemberton's sister Melanie, the two of them kneeling beside each other at the foot of the scarecrow, in that first row that custom reserved for the hopeful. It had been someone else's night, though, Angela apparently choosing to remain silent then and forever.

To see Melanie afterward, her crushing disappointment, was to understand the cruelty of this night. Trying not to be obvious about it, Bailey had watched Troy console her, and he'd seemed so kind and attentive that she wondered at the time if he and Melanie might become a couple in their own right. But it had never happened, and now she knew how naïve that was. Death and bereavement would always be the foundation of the relationship.

So now she saw that night for what it really was. Troy had been sowing his seeds in her heart without realizing it.

"But," he went on, "you learn what happens here, or you grow up with it, and you think it's going to be this great experience. You think, wow, who gets this chance, how lucky this place is. And some years, for some people, yeah, I'm sure it does turn out to be everything they hope it will be. But a part of me was scared. I wanted it to happen for Melanie's sake, it was her sister and all, but for me? The closer the night got, the more I didn't want it after all."

Bailey hung on every word. This was it. *This* was the thing nobody in Dunhaven ever talked about, at least not publicly, even though you could see it in their eyes every October. You could see the trepidation, the misgivings. Could recognize the look of someone who was going through with an act even though they'd begun to have second thoughts. None of which they would ever admit to. For obvious reasons: Who wanted to be first to come out and admit to being an ungrateful freak?

"What scared you about it?" she asked.

"I'd gotten to a place where I'd accepted that Angela was gone," Troy said. "That she wasn't coming back. I'd gotten to a place where I'd accepted we might never know what happened to her. And I realized I didn't *want* to know anymore. I didn't want to know how she'd suffered. And then . . . "

He seemed to have trouble, but Bailey thought she might be able to take it from here. "And then everybody expects you to put that aside for one night, and it's not as easy as it sounds?"

Troy nodded. "That's it. You'd know, wouldn't you?"

"And because you just get them back for one night, how are you supposed to deal with the pain of having to let them go all over again?"

He laughed, very quick, very soft. "You've obviously given this some thought. It's like you've got a stake in this for yourself, or something."

"But I do want it to happen for Cody," she said with resolve. "That's the bottom line. That's all that matters."

"Then I hope you get it. I hope it's him." *Him*, Troy always said. He never called Drew by name. "Who's the competition, do you know?"

She didn't, not exactly. They could only recall who'd died in the past year, and who among them might match up with the anonymous gifts lain thus far beneath the scarecrow's perch. The glove and the sheet music, the medal and the cake.

"The Purple Heart . . . I bet that was Larry Hughey's. He would've won that in Korea. He's the only veteran I can think of who's died this year."

"Oh god," she said, and imagined the man's poor widow coming out to leave the medal on the grass. "Candace Hughey's got to be in her eighties. Seems like she should be the lucky one tonight on seniority alone."

"Absolutely not," Troy said. "If you feel guilty about that, stop right now. Every time it goes to the geriatric crowd, it's a wasted year. It's like old people winning the lottery, you know? They're going to be dead in another three years anyway, so what's the point?"

She didn't want to laugh at this, but couldn't help it. "You're going to Hell for that one, I'm afraid."

"And if you're all lucky, I'll come back and tell you what it's like there."

She wasn't laughing anymore, and wondered why she had at all. It wasn't just talk, not in Dunhaven. Say a thing like that, and it could well turn out to happen.

"'Hell is other people,'" she mused, for no better reason than that it came to mind. Then again, there was always a better reason for most things. "Did you ever hear that? I don't remember who said it."

"No. But whoever it was, I'd buy him a drink."

They dawdled some more, in bed and then out, and shared a bite to eat—breakfast for him, brunch for her. They ate in the little nook before a bay window, overlooking the fading trees of autumn, bare enough and tall enough to appear to scrape the bellies of the charcoal clouds. It was almost like being outside, in the chill and unpredictable wind, on this day when the spirits gathered to roam.

And when it came time to leave, she both wanted to, and didn't.

"You going to be there tonight?" she asked.

"Should I? Do you want me to?"

Who could say what spirits understood, or were prepared to overlook? If they saw you getting on with your life, when theirs had been over a mere eight months, was that, to them, another kind of Hell?

"I don't know if that would be a good idea or not," she said.

He nodded. "I'm sure I'll hear all about it tomorrow."

When she left, every step between his door and her car felt like a few more degrees of transition between worlds—this time back to putting herself second, because that's what mothers were supposed to do. Halloween was the perfect day for this feeling, for changing masks so many times, one after another, so quickly that she could no longer be sure which of them was most real.

Trick-or-treating was a supervised event in Dunhaven, the kids going out in groups overseen by at least one parent, or better yet, two. You had to love them, of course, and their excitement, all dressed up and everywhere to go, but you still didn't want them roaming at will, losing track of time. It was better for all concerned that they get in by curfew, before nightfall, when Halloween was taken over by more adult concerns.

Bailey had *wanted* to be one of the parents helping out to escort the kids around. She'd volunteered for duty again and again, but the other mothers and the few dads who pitched in wouldn't hear of it. Telling her no, of course not, you've got enough to worry about this year. Like they couldn't see that this was precisely the point—that today, of all days, was a day when she could use distractions instead of dwelling on what might or might not happen after sundown.

So after she'd collected Cody from the party at St. Aidan's, and gotten him into his costume, then dropped him off at the grade-school gym where the candy-fueled army teamed up and set out, there could be no going home. The last thing she wanted was to sit around listening for the doorbell so she could spend the next hours throwing miniature Snickers bars at other people's children.

It was time to check on the offerings they'd left this morning anyway.

She was relieved to find them still there, right where they'd been left, along with the rest, nothing tampered with. They'd even been joined by a few more items, one a stuffed teddy bear with the nose half-chewed away, and with this one it only took a moment to figure out the likely source: the latest generation of Ralstons, Ellis and Kristen, who'd lost a baby girl to SIDS last spring.

Oh, come on, Bailey thought. *She wasn't even a year old, she wouldn't have been speaking anything more than a word at a time, so what's she got to tell you now?*

For which she felt perfectly ashamed a few moments later.

This day, this weird day—it *did* things to you, none of them good.

She'd never appreciated what a merciful thing it was that only those who'd died in the past year were able to come through. This limitation kept the incivility contained. If anyone could come back any year, the whole town would be at one another's throats each and every October. There wouldn't even be a Dunhaven by now, she was sure of it. The place would have imploded generations ago.

It wasn't just the sabotage from your fellow mourners you had to worry about, someone snitching your offering away to thin the competition for their own dearly departed. It was the sabotage you *couldn't* foresee coming that had, other years, made things interesting.

You didn't have to be old enough to remember it firsthand to have heard about the year James Gosling was caught stealing a locket and other items set out to call a woman named Meredith Hartmann, for fear of what her spirit might've had to reveal about the decade they'd kept secret from their spouses.

And beyond any living person's memory was a year that had passed into local legend. One of Dunhaven's most disreputable sons, Joseph Harrington, was alleged to have salted the earth of the entire town square, and soaked the wood of the fence post in holy water, in an attempt to keep *anyone* from coming through. Several people had died that spring, on the same night on the eve of May, three in ways that, it was said, left their bodies so mangled they looked as though they'd gone through a combine—although no one ever needed to run a combine until harvest. Whatever had happened, Harrington had thought it better to incur the wrath of all of Dunhaven than let someone have a chance to say a word about what they'd been up to out in the woods and fields far from the heart of town.

Anywhere else, people would write that off as lore that had grown so much in the telling that by now the episode was more fable than fact. But here, given what everybody *knew* would happen each October . . . ? Here, you couldn't be so sure.

Either way, the dead had secrets, and sometimes the living had a powerful interest in making sure both stayed on the other side, unseen, unheard.

Oddly enough, the local police kept out of this part of it, stepping in only when deeds and disagreements turned violent. People complained, but Bailey got the logic behind this—it would be that much harder to keep the peace when people started thinking you played favorites when it came to pilfering and petty theft of things left in plain sight, on public property.

If we want the privilege of speaking with the dead, she thought, *we're on our own.*

So as long as she was here and dreaded going home, she decided to do her civic duty and take a turn on unofficial watch. She hoofed it a block away, to the Jittery Bean, where she bought a hot chocolate, and brought it back here to the square and settled onto one of the benches in view of the waiting scarecrow, to make sure it all stayed on this side of fair.

She could feel it already, while dodging people on the sidewalks to and from the coffee shop, and could see it now from the bench: the eagerness of morning giving way to the nervousness of afternoon. The day was darkening too soon, it seemed, the sun gone weak in the south, the clouds sinking lower over the town, like a roof to screen them from the eye of God. A deeper chill rode in on a blustery wind that rattled leaves and windows alike.

We should've moved, she thought. *We should've moved away before Cody was born, the way we talked about. Drew would still be dead . . . but we wouldn't still be waiting to see if he's coming home.*

From here, she could see the blue-and-white of the shirt, the red lacquer of the Pinewood Derby car.

Go on, she thought. *Somebody come take them already. I'll cut you some slack, sit right here and pretend I don't see you.*

Before long, she thought she might have had a hopeful prospect, a scarf-wrapped woman walking up to the scarecrow and giving the offerings a studious look without having brought one of her own.

She soon drifted toward another walkway, in no hurry to leave. In profile and from behind it was hard to tell who it was, but once she sat down on another bench, Bailey could see her clearly, and realized that it was Melanie Pemberton.

She should've guessed.

Come Halloween time, Melanie was a reliable fixture here, ever since the year of that grim business with her younger sister Angela. Came early, stayed late, would've swept the streets, probably, if they'd handed her a broom.

Melanie noticed her now, for the first time, and saw that Bailey saw her, and there came the awkward moment of being unsure whether they should go back to pretending they hadn't, or consolidate space. *Oh, why not.* Bailey pointed to the spot on the bench beside her, and Melanie came over.

She was dark-haired and the last three years had left her hard-faced bordering on severe . . . but Bailey thought she understood the ongoing need in her, and didn't judge. If Drew wasn't the one who came through tonight, she felt confident that that would be it. Free to move on. Not haunt the place year after year, seeming to hope for a replay. But, like Troy had said, with Melanie it was a whole different set of issues.

"Even as a girl, I always wondered why we leave stuff," Melanie said. "Leave *stuff*, and walk away." She was stressing the word *stuff* as though it were something unpleasant, like *hospital waste*. "*We* should be camping out here, instead. But no. We seem to accept it on faith that inanimate objects will do a better job calling back the people we're supposed to love than we can."

Bailey had never regarded it quite that way, and anyhow, who really knew what went into the founding of a tradition this old? Here, 162 years ago, if you weren't spending every waking moment of October bringing in crops and preparing for winter, you were probably going hungry and cold long before spring.

Mostly, Melanie just seemed angry. She had good reasons to be angry.

"You don't have kids, do you?" Bailey asked.

"And bring them into a world like this? Not likely. *Not* likely."

"I was just going to say," Bailey went on, "that before they get to a certain age, kids seem to see a soul in everything. Everything's alive, on some level. So who's to say they don't know something we all forgot? And maybe the ones who've died, they remember it. So they're just happy to see a familiar soul that . . . I don't know . . . loved them unconditionally, maybe?"

Melanie sat there taking this in. At least she wasn't chewing it up and spitting it back in Bailey's face.

"Unconditional," Melanie said softly. "That's hard, isn't it."

Bailey swirled her cup and drained the cocoa, now cold, to the last dribbles. "Chocolate, that's easy for unconditional love. Everything else . . . ?"

Melanie laughed a little, maybe just being polite. Then she fell back into the black hole. "The day she disappeared, Angie and I . . . we had the worst fight. We said the worst things to each other. Me, mostly. *I* said them." She bowed her head in a prayer to nothing, then snapped up again. "Of all the days, huh? Of all the days."

Bailey wanted to say something, anything, the kneejerk words that you thought nobody must have thought to tell her before now. But of course she would've heard them all, listened to them until she was sick of them, and sick of the people who kept spouting them at her like found wisdom.

Instead, Bailey kept her mouth shut and reached over to rest her hand across the back of Melanie's, until she nodded, the understanding between them in no need of words, and it felt like time to draw her hand back again. Melanie looked at the scarecrow, and if longing alone could've done it, the thing would have come down off its cross and danced.

"That helped, actually. What you said." She sounded surprised about this. "It really did. But you know? There's only one thing that could ever make me feel like I could finally put it all behind me."

"I know."

Melanie stood and straightened her scarf. "Good luck tonight," she said, a rare wish that could assume the form of such opposing outcomes.

* * *

Evening fell, and dragged the night behind it.

The streets began to fill well before dusk, permanently now, people staking an early claim for a good view instead of having to rely on hearsay filtering back through the crowd. Everyone Bailey had seen throughout the day seemed to return fivefold, tenfold, expanding out in a circle from the center of the town square. When the span grew too great for that, the latecomers were forced to clog the streets between the low brick buildings of downtown.

Hundreds, easily. Thousands? Probably. She felt their pressure at her back, their eyes and expectations. Cody? Oblivious. Like his father, he could tune out anything he didn't want or need to hear.

She leaned close to his shoulder, thinking of his stated intention this morning to ask Drew to take him along.

"Have you thought about what *else* you're going to say to Daddy, if he comes?"

Cody nodded, looking more pensive than a six-year-old should. "Uh huh."

"Wanna tell me about the rest? Run it past me?"

Cody thought it over, then shook his head no. "That's okay."

It stung, yes, shut out again, but it was a thing to be proud of, too. *Good boy,* she thought. *This day of the year, at least, don't trust anybody.*

Here at the foot of the cross, in the alleged position of honor, they were sitting on a blanket folded quadruple to keep from hogging space and, less effectively, to shield their bottoms from the chill of the moist autumn earth. On either side, all in a tight row, were the rest of the bereaved. Candace Hughey, eighty if she was a day, eyes fixed on her husband's Purple Heart. The Ralstons, Ellis and Kristin, their true north that sad teddy bear; Kristin looked as if she'd recently finished crying and could start again if so much as a raindrop fell wrong. Others, more than a dozen by now, everybody too close for comfort in this quiet rivalry.

Cody was an hour coming down off the high of trick-or-treating, costume shed and stuffed into new clothes in a bathroom at the gradeschool rendezvous. He may not have needed it, but she poured him a hot chocolate anyway, from the Thermos she'd had filled at the Jittery Bean, to keep the inevitable sugar crash at bay a little longer.

She leaned in close again. "You know Daddy loves you very much. If it's not him tonight, that doesn't change anything. It doesn't mean any different. You know that, don't you?"

"I guess," he said.

"Where he is now, we don't know what it's like there. How they decide things. We've got our rules here, but we don't know what theirs are. Do you understand?"

Cody looked at her with, of all things, suspicion. "How come we don't know? How come nobody's asked?"

She blinked, feeling that special kind of stupid that kids could make you feel. "Asked who?"

"The dead people from before. If it's happened all these other times, then how come nobody's asked one of 'em what their rules are?"

It was a good question. Maybe it was already on his shortlist of things to discuss with Drew, or maybe he was adding it now.

"I don't know," she said. "Maybe people mean to, but then they get excited and forget."

The mayor stepped up onto a small platform and said more than a few words, as the mayors always did. It wasn't an address anyone seemed to want. This had been going on for 162 years, for god's sake, so it wasn't like there were people out there who needed a refresher on what the night was all about. This had gone on long before him and, presumably, would go on long after he became eligible to bore people from the other side.

The murmur of hundreds of conversations filled the night, a subdued sound considering the numbers. Expectant and alert, she felt electrified when something jolted her from the inside, then foolish when she realized it was just her phone, ringer off and set to vibrate. She slipped it out to find a fresh text message from Troy:

Anything yet?

No, she keyed back. *Everything quiet as a tomb. Except Mayor Bob.*

Thought I heard the wind pick up.

What r u doing now?

Movie nite. Wishing u were here to hold my hand during the scary parts.

Probably not all u wish I was holding, she keyed, and couldn't believe she'd said it, sent it. This was wrong on so many levels. Sexting, here and now, of all times and places, like she was trying to psychically sabotage the very thing her son wanted most in the world tonight. The thing she wished she could want as much as Cody did, but couldn't.

It came down to this, she realized: She had eleven years of memories with Drew, most good, some exquisite. And she didn't want the final one, that desperate goodbye in the hospital, to be shoved aside by some new one, post-mortem, the man she'd loved now wrapped inside a creepy shell of straw and old clothes and burlap, struggling to communicate whatever he felt he'd left unsaid.

Something to dream of, Troy wrote back. *Turning in early. Thought I'd be OK with this tonite but now I just want it over. Want it to be tomorrow.*

Me 2 x 1000.

"Who was that?" Cody asked after she'd put her phone away. Looking vaguely annoyed with her, as if her lapse in concentration would cost him everything. She'd lost her game face.

"Just a friend." Great—on top of everything else, guilt and lies. "She wanted to wish us good luck."

The impatience grew, thick with apprehension, everybody here in the front row appearing to feel it on some level or another. Down on the far end, a middle-aged widower was doing some breathing exercise. Five-count inhale, five-count hold, five-count exhale—she could see him ticking it off on his fingers.

The chill plunged further and the courthouse clock tower chimed nine, the mechanical crash of the hammer into the bell sharp and deep and unnerving. The echo seemed to roll for miles, still lingering in the air when something else charged the night. Was it just her, or did everyone feel it? The crowd fell silent behind her for a moment, then a groundswell of murmuring picked up again, expectant.

Bailey looked up along the cross with the same dread that guiltier souls than she was might have felt for a headsman hoisting his axe. Although she felt no wind, the fingers of one stuffed glove began to twitch. Then the arm began to stir, sliding along the crosspiece that held the thing in place, and one leg started to flex, the heel of the boot banging against the post.

You could blame everything on the wind until the head lifted.

The other arm moved, the other leg stirred, the shoulders appearing to strain as it leaned forward and weakly, so weakly, tried to push itself away from the post. The head tipped back and looked to the sky, then around at the tops of the downtown buildings, and down again, down to earth, out over the rapt and waiting throng . . . and if the thing could be said to see at all, with its black button eyes, then yes, the sight appeared to hasten its sense of urgency . . . or of agitation.

It wasn't the fact that it moved at all that most unnerved her. No, it was subtler than that. Everything breathed. Women and men, cats and cows, birds and apes. Everything breathed. But not this. Its chest and belly were as still as a corpse's. She hadn't realized how *wrong* this mimicry of life looked until now.

Beside her, Cody knelt tense and wide-eyed, hands clasped at his chin as he nibbled on the tips of his thumbs. When she put her arm around his rigid shoulders, he gave no sign of noticing.

Above them, the scarecrow finally succeeded in flopping one arm free of the crosspiece, then the rest of it followed, the entire faux being tumbling to the ground, where it landed on its side with a rustle of cloth and straw. It stirred for a moment, trying to right itself with the slow, helpless squirm of an overturned turtle. Then its glove caught, and it pulled itself over onto its belly, to crawl forward on elbows and knees, toward the gifts of its summons.

It inspected them for a long time, longer than she remembered this taking in the past. Every year it was always the same—when the scarecrow took the gift, found the link, that's how you knew who it was. Up and down the row it crawled, seeming to sense that *something* was here, something it just wasn't finding.

Finally it lingered . . .

And chose.

The cake. The old cake that, this morning, looked to have come from a freezer. She hadn't known whose it was, and still didn't. Beside her, Cody gave a groan of disappointment, so she squeezed him tight to her. This time he let her, then buried his face into her side and sobbed. She glanced left, right . . . *and none of them were moving*. In fact, they looked to be growing as mystified as she was.

Then who had set it out there?

She looked again at the scarecrow. With its clumsy hands, it was now pulling the cake apart, and something about the sight triggered a wave of revulsion in her. It had no mouth, yet it was going to try to eat? No, that wasn't it—

Bailey became aware of a commotion behind her.

—it was ripping the cake apart to get to something *inside*—

She became aware of a voice trying to make itself heard above the swelling din of the crowd.

—pawing aside frosting and crumbling cake that had been packed around something inside, to pull out—

Melanie again. Melanie Pemberton, shouldering her way to the front of the crowd, past well-intended men trying to hold her back.

—a music box. Old, chipped, adorned with painted arabesques. A music box.

Angela? *This* was her sister Angela? Now, three years after she'd . . . ?

And then, apart from her own losses, maybe the most heartbreaking sight Bailey had ever seen: the scarecrow trying to wind the music box's key, to hear its song once more, but unable to, its gloved fingers not nimble enough, strong enough.

"You all gave her up for dead! Remember?" Melanie screamed at the crowd, as she broke free to take her place at the front. "All of you! That made it easier for you to stop looking, didn't it! 'Oh, Angela has to be dead by now! What can we do, life goes on!' "

Oh god, Bailey thought. *We just assumed . . .*

"Well, she's dead now! And that's on you! All of you!"

"Mom?" Cody looked up at her, his face pleading. "What's going on, I don't understand."

Nobody did, apparently. It was the noisiest Bailey had ever heard the crowd on Halloween night, confusion rippling back and forth, ricochets of resentment. It surged with unease, like an animal on the verge of being spooked.

How could this have happened? They'd found a blouse with Angela's blood; two days later, two of her fingers out by the highway. Then nothing. No word, no sign, no more evidence at all. Days passed, then weeks turning to months. The conclusion came by gradual default, spreading from person to person like a cold: The poor young woman was surely dead, the rest of her sure to be found someday.

But why the subterfuge? Why the cake, to hide something in plain sight . . . unless Melanie didn't want to set out something that she feared someone else might recognize. But if that was it . . .

No. No, the notion was too vile to entertain.

Cody tugged at her coat sleeve. "I want to go home."

By now, Melanie had managed to struggle around the end of the front row, circling to get to the scarecrow while pushing past the mayor, who must have thought he was helping by trying to stop someone he believed was making a scene. Melanie dropped beside the bundle of cloth and straw and burlap, touching it tenderly, as if anything more might drive her sister away, and it touched her back in recognition.

Bailey didn't have to hear the woman to know what was coming next. It would be the questions Melanie had been waiting years to ask.

Who took you?

Where were you kept all this time?

Who killed you?

And, you had to consider, *is he here tonight? And was there more than one?*

Though they were head to head, could Melanie even hear what her sister would say? That was why the quiet of the crowd was so important. It wasn't simply reverence or being polite; it was practical, too. Those who would know had told her that the voice of the dead sounded thin and faraway, as though it emanated from a realm within the scarecrow rather than from the thing itself.

Abruptly, then, there was no chance of hearing it, no matter how keen Melanie's ears, as somewhere close behind, in the packed and straining crowd, a string of firecrackers went off like a volley of gunshots. It was all the reason they needed to panic, a surge of bodies pressing forward from behind as people scattered from the rising cloud of smoke and flashes.

Bailey held Cody tight to her as she took a shoulder hard in the back and, along with others in the front row, went spilling into the empty space between them and the fencepost. Gifts were scattered or trampled, and she caught sight of Mrs. Hughey trying to snatch up her husband's Purple Heart, only to have her forearm snapped under an errant foot.

Worse, far worse, because it was deliberate, and like killing Angela all over again, was the second pack of firecrackers that an unseen hand lobbed toward the scarecrow. Melanie saw the fuse spitting and hissing through the air, then it landed on the effigy's back and erupted in an endless barrage of hot white pops. The first flames danced to life in seconds, then spread, feeding on shirt and straw alike. In moments it was a mass of fire, and Bailey was sure she saw the thing twist and writhe even after Melanie's hands let it go, unable to beat out the flames, forced to quit by singed palms and the shredding assault of the firecrackers.

Leaving Angela dead and gone for good, and her secrets with her.

Bailey got to both feet, pulling Cody with her, to her, and moved to the other side of fencepost, so they wouldn't be squashed against it. Cody wanted to go home, of *course* he wanted to go home, but for now they might as well have been trapped on an island, keeping to this makeshift tree in a patch of green, surrounded by the surging sea of an unruly mob.

Close enough to spit at, the scarecrow continued to burn, its head and limbs ablaze, its back a scorched black cavity. Just as close, but out of reach, Drew's flannel shirt and the Pinewood Derby car were crushed into the ground by lurching feet and sprawling hands.

And it seemed as if all of Dunhaven wallowed before her.

She looked out over them with growing loathing, this town that hid its secrets so well that captors and murderers could walk in confidence across the placid face of normal life. Wearing masks not just on Halloween, but every day of the year. Had she smiled at them at the market? Chatted with them in line for coffee? Let them go first in traffic? Had she taught their children in school, or driven past their homes never suspecting what may have been chained in their basements?

She hadn't known, hadn't *wanted* to know, and now felt as guilty as any of them.

I want to go home too, she thought, only now grasping the truth that home was someplace she'd never been.

From out in the street, Bailey heard a man's voice yelling above the rest, then another, and another, and realized they were shouting about Troy. Whether instigation or ignorance, it didn't matter. The thought spread effortlessly, viral: It was always the boyfriends, always the husbands. Living out there all alone . . . who knew what he got up to? They would set it right.

Good god, were they even thinking straight? Were they capable of it anymore? Troy had been looked at, investigated, cleared. She knew his home, knew his grief. But none of that mattered. Not tonight. Tonight was a night for scapegoats.

Bailey fished the phone from her pocket to call him, but after the first couple of rings, got only his voice mail. Tried again; the same.

Turning in early, he'd texted. *Thought I'd be OK with this tonite but now I just want it over.*

Yet again; the same.

Please answer, she begged. *Please. Please wake up . . .*

As she clutched her phone in one hand and her fatherless son in the other, confined by the mob to this tiny plot of earth, she remembered the adage she'd told Troy earlier in the day: *Hell is other people.* All around her, they seemed so intent on proving it.

The scarecrow was ash now, nothing left to burn.

Finally she understood what had eluded them all for 162 years: why there was only ever one. If Hell was other people, then the dead had already escaped it, and so maybe coming back through was, for them, no privilege. Maybe it was a curse.

Brian Hodge is the award-winning author of eleven novels spanning horror, crime, and historical. He's also written over one hundred short stories, novelettes, and novellas, and five full-length collections. His first collection, *The Convulsion Factory*, was ranked by critic Stanley Wiater among the 113 best books of modern horror. Recent or forthcoming works include *No Law Left Unbroken*, a collection of crime fiction; *The Weight of the Dead* and *Whom the Gods Would Destroy*, both standalone novellas; a newly revised hardcover edition of *Dark Advent*, his early post-apocalyptic epic; and his latest novel, *Leaves of Sherwood*.

Hodge lives in Colorado, where more of everything is in the works. He also dabbles in music, sound design, and photography; loves everything about organic gardening except the thieving squirrels; and trains in Krav Maga, grappling, and kickboxing, which are of no use at all against the squirrels.

Connect through his web site (www.brianhodge.net) or on Facebook (www.facebook.com/brianhodgewriter), and follow his blog, Warrior Poet (www.warriorpoetblog.com).

ALL HALLOWS IN THE HIGH HILLS

Brenda Cooper

Mel picked up the box of glass. Butterflies, flowers, and birds lay nestled inside of old newspapers he'd been saving all summer, picking up the freebies from people's driveways whenever it was clear they weren't actually going to read them. He knelt carefully, as worried about his right knee as about the box. "Everything's breakable," he muttered as he carried his work carefully out to the battered old VW van sitting beside his equally battered workshop.

Two more trips and he had secured a second box of glass and two fists of long metal rebar. He made a third trip to retrieve his coffee, a late afternoon cup laced with the tiniest bit of whiskey as medicine for his sore muscles.

In spite of the autumn leaves on the oak beside his driveway, a spear of bright sun forced him to pull his sunglasses off of the rearview before he drove out onto Laguna Canyon Road. Even though it wasn't yet four in the afternoon, he passed a woman with three costumed kids in tow. A princess hung onto a small indeterminate superhero's hand and a pirate swaggered behind the others. He wouldn't be missing them: it had been years since any trick-or-treaters made it all the way to his door. Over a year since anyone had visited at all. Justine had helped him unpack when he'd returned from the festival summer-before-last.

Five minutes later he pulled up in the artist's loading area of the Sawdust Festival grounds. There were only two other vehicles there—the night manager's battered green truck and Paulette's little Pinto, which might be the last Pinto on the road anywhere on the West Coast. The ugly rattle-canned deathtrap had been young when he was young, and it was possible it looked even worse than he did. Given that it had a flat front tire, maybe it felt worse, too.

He sat and finished his coffee, contemplating the tall walls and the fancy sign, now wedged with red and gold for the upcoming holidays. He'd been part of the festival for so long that the constant changes in the festival signage and walls had become the way he marked years. Some people did this by how old their children were, but he never had a family. There had been cats, but now he only fed the feral ones outside, afraid he'd die and leave a pet behind.

He used to have a key to the festival grounds, but now he was forced to pull the bell-string, which rang the night manager's cellphone rather than ringing a real bell.

At least Jack showed up in just a few minutes, opening the door, and offering a wide smile under his strange multi-colored eyes, which always appeared to Mel to be full of the blues and greens of the sea, touched by the gold of the sun, and full of mischief. "Was about to give up on you."

"I never miss opening day," Mel retorted. "I'm just old and slow." He opened the van door. "Care to help?"

Jack laughed. "Of course."

Even though Mel liked Jack, who wasn't quite into middle age, and seemed to be around whenever anyone needed help, he didn't quite trust him. An air of oddness clung to him, something more than just his strange eyes. He had quite a reputation with the ladies, although he seemed to love all of them—young and old, thin and fat, pretty and not so pretty—and they all loved him in return. Mel had never quite understood this, and didn't quite approve of it, either.

At least Jack was strong. He managed one box and all of the rebar, and still had to stop twice to let Mel catch up to him as they made their way along the wide paths to Mel's small booth huddled between two bigger ones near the back. The sawdust had all been laid down neat, and the whole place smelled like wood chips. Clean. Tomorrow there'd be hot dogs cooking and lemonade stands and pumpkin ice cream and a myriad of other smells, but for now there was only the new sawdust.

In the early years, they'd had to spread the stuff over mud. Now a company spread it over concrete.

Jack stayed to help Mel slide the fragile lawn ornaments onto the rebar and set each piece into the holder Mel had fashioned from strong metal grating years ago. "Is opening for the holidays going to help?" Jack asked.

"I don't much like the holidays."

"Not even Halloween?" Jack asked.

Mel frowned. "Not really, and besides, I'm not having Halloween. I'm busy setting up." He sounded like an old grouch. "Something's gotta help. I'm more than halfway through last summer's earnings."

Jack stopped, his big hand holding a bright yellow flower. "Already?"

"Medical bills." Mel looked away so Jack wouldn't see that it bothered him. He jammed a blue butterfly down too hard on the rebar, cracking off a glass wing. He cursed under his breath. "That was my favorite piece for this season." Mel held up the broken part. "See how this line of gold shoots all the way through the wing? That was pure serendipity."

"It is a pretty one. I'm sure you'll do more that are as nice."

"If I'm around for it. I'm going to die in my traces soon." As far as he knew, Mel was the last artist alive from the first year of the festival in 1965. After Justine of the long blond hair and bellbottoms had disappeared last year—her hair gray but still swinging in a long braid past her butt—there was no one else left of the old founders.

"Not yet, I think," Jack said.

Mel put the last bird onto the last rebar and cradled it in an open spot on the stand.

"The booth looks good."

"Lately, it hurts to hold the blowpipe up long enough to make these." Mel assessed the impression his booth would leave. Not bad. It was sandwiched between ornate house-cats fashioned of multi-colored wood on one side and mirrors decorated with bronze and beads on the other. The cats would draw a crowd. "At least there's no Christmas decorations up."

"Yet. Committee won't allow them before Thanksgiving."

Mel snorted. "But we are opening the day after Halloween."

"You could have been on the committee."

"They kicked me off ten years ago for being a curmudgeon."

"Can I buy you a drink?"

Mel looked at the broken butterfly. "I should take this back to the studio and fix it."

Jack offered a slow smile, his eyes catching the last bit of daylight. "Meet you at the waterfall." He practically sprinted off, leaving Mel to limp after him with a broken bit of blue butterfly in each hand. The place looked a bit eerie as the long shadows of dusk faded into each other and became part of the approaching night. Only the safety lights were on, small yellow sun-globes lining the paths somewhat irregularly.

Brighter light beckoned around the last turn, and Mel emerged just as the waterfall started flowing. Strings of tiny blue and pink lights had been embedded in the rock behind the water at each edge. The waterfall was about ten feet wide and seven feet high. It flowed down a rock face into a shallow pool where the water slid down a drain to be pumped back up to the top to start falling all over again. "Do you like it?" Jack asked.

"They look like fairy lights."

Jack thrust a glass into Mel's hand. "Come on, have a drink."

Mel sniffed. "Bourbon?"

"You can spend the night here. After all, it's a holiday."

Mel had drank himself through the whole night here before. "I've got a blanket in the truck." He took an experimental sip and sighed with pleasure.

Jack disappeared for a moment and came back with a bag of potato chips, two apples, and a half-finished round of mixed nuts. The salt on the nuts tasted like heaven, and went with the next sip of bourbon.

They drank in companionable silence. Food and a stiff drink and the quiet of his favorite place mellowed Mel. Jack poured water into the empty cups. "You know this is a magical night."

Great. Jack's mystical side. Mel had heard tales of nighttime séances and late-night parties inside the festival grounds that included some of the less-wrapped denizens of the small beach town. Well, big beach town these days. He could play along. "All Hallows Eve."

"And you know this is a magical place. You helped create it."

"Yeah." No point in disagreeing.

"Care to come with me to a better place to fix up your butterfly?"

Mel narrowed his eyes. "I shouldn't be driving."

Jack looked positively full of mischief. "And I can't leave the grounds."

"Well. Where's the glue?" Not that glue would fix it.

"Do you trust me?" Jack went all serious. Or as serious as anybody who'd just downed two fifths of good bourbon ever looked.

Mel's stomach knotted up and his head felt light and odd, but he nodded.

Jack picked up the bigger piece of broken butterfly and took Mel's hand in his. "I think this going to work for you."

The gesture scraped Mel the tiniest bit raw, and he stiffened. "I don't like men."

"Don't blame you. Girls are curvier."

Jack's hand was warm and firm. Mel couldn't remember holding another man's hand as an adult, but he let it be and let Jack lead him toward the waterfall.

Into the waterfall.

The bourbon must have been stronger than he'd thought. Jack disappeared, although Mel would swear there was no opening behind the water. You could see the whole rock face the water fell down when the pump was turned off, and it was mostly smooth. If it weren't for the pull of Jack's hand—and to be honest, for the bourbon—Mel would have stopped.

Instead, he closed his eyes and put one foot in front of the other. Just as he started to flinch away, sure he was about to get soaked, he felt the cool stream of water for just a second, and then a soft push as if he were moving through a wall of blankets. The push and the pull of Jack's hand, and the swaying dizziness of standing after eating and drinking and walking through a waterfall as if he were dreaming—Mel doubled over.

He opened his eyes, in full possession of both his hands and in a place he had never seen before. He closed his eyes, and tried again.

Same result.

He and Jack stood side by side with a small cliff-face behind them, the kind that's really just a flat area in an otherwise rolling hill. A path wound from under their feet along a cleared meadow, over a wooden bridge, and west into scrub oak, directly toward a sunset that hadn't finished yet here.

Jack let him take it all in for a bit, and then he said, "This is my home."

"No shit."

"I'm glad the waterfall door worked for you."

"You didn't know it would work?"

"Even when it's working, it doesn't open for everybody. If you try all by yourself, you might scratch your nose."

"How does it work?"

Jack merely shrugged.

"You come here a lot?"

"Some years I winter here."

The conversation seemed way too normal for what had just happened, but Mel couldn't think of anything else to do but go on the same way. It was that or scream or pass out or ask to go back, and he didn't want to do any of those things. "Do they trick-or-treat here?"

"Tricks might be . . . interesting . . . over here." Jack smiled. "There's a bit of magic in the High Hills."

"I don't believe in magic."

Jack laughed. "Come on, old man. Want to go to the beach?"

"There's an ocean?"

"The High Hills and the town of Laguna Beach used to be the same. Mostly the directions and the main physical landmarks are the same, except of course the modern one has decapitated some of the hills and built roads where we have paths."

"That must explain why Laguna's so New Age."

"California. Shasta is here, too. I think maybe everything, but I'm a west coast kinda guy."

"So you don't lie when you say you winter at Shasta, huh?"

"I never lie." He grinned. "I like the modern Shasta better. There's a ski lift."

"Did you bring the bourbon bottle over?"

"No." Jack started down the path, and Mel followed, both men still carrying bits of blue glass. At least this time they weren't holding hands.

The spears of setting sunlight made it hard to see, but mostly the hills seemed to be yellow with fall grass going to seed, and most of the trees were dark green and low scrub oaks. Here and there, the red branches of Manzanita bushes added color. Rabbits hopped through brush at the edge of the meadow, and hawks circled overhead.

The path wound through a small, empty town. "Do people live here?" Mel asked.

"Of course. They're all where we're going."

Mel's knee hurt, but he didn't want to admit to Jack that he couldn't go much farther.

After two smaller rises Mel had to struggle up, and a gentle turn, they met up with the beach just as the orb of the sun fell into the water. High clouds cherished the last bits of sunfire, just a bit less crisp than the yellow-white of a bonfire a few hundred yards down the beach. They stood right in the middle of Main Beach, although there were no parking lots or tall swings or lifeguard towers, and also no boardwalk. But the open beach gave way to hills and wave-worn low cliffs just like at home.

Horses and wagons and a few modern bicycles were scattered to the foreside of the fire, watched over by a pair of young women in tattered jeans and Death Cab for Cutie T-shirts. Five women and a man busied themselves at wooden tables, setting out food and drink. Closer to the fire, at least thirty people stood talking or lounged in groups on rocks or driftwood. The real Main Beach never looked this natural or wild.

He liked it this way.

Mel collapsed on the first rock he came across that had a wide enough space for him, letting out a sigh of relief to have his weight off of his knee. "Stay here," Jack said. "I'll come back for you."

Mel hadn't been willing to follow up on Jack's reference to magic with a question earlier, but now that he didn't hurt as much, he looked around. The people looked pretty normal. No Tolkien elves or vampires or Mr. Spock ears. Although Spock wasn't really fantasy, was he?

Half the people were dressed in modern clothes and half in a mix of more handmade looking stuff. They seemed to like bright colors. He counted five or six kids.

No one appeared to be wearing Halloween costumes.

Then he saw her.

Justine of the long hair and bell bottoms.

He blinked, sure again that he dreamed. Then the wind carried her laughter to him and he knew it was her. He sat and watched Justine talking in a small circle of other old women, her face glowing in the firelight.

A smile broke unbidden across his face.

They'd never been lovers, but they'd been friends for years. She'd cried on Mel's shoulder through at least three break-ups and helped him rebuild his studio after a fire in 1987. He didn't realize how much he'd missed her until her laughter made him feel light again.

He'd wait. His knee still throbbed, and besides, he'd told Jack he'd wait.

Maybe he was a little scared.

It felt like if he did or said the wrong thing, he'd wake up and he'd be in a dream and he'd lose the fire and the clean beach and Justine of the long hair.

Jack worked the crowd, stopping from time to time for a hug or a short whispered conversation. The last of the light faded just as he came up to Justine and planted a kiss on her cheek and pointed at Mel.

She sat so the firelight illuminated half her face as she followed the direction of Jack's finger. To his utter delight, she appeared as pleased to see him as he had been to hear her laughter, and then she was up and sprinting across the still-warm sand. She smelled of smoke and sea air. Her blue eyes were wreathed in wrinkles, and there was more vitality to her than he remembered. "I never imagined," she said.

He held at a bit of distance, confused, but still ecstatic to see her. "What?"

"That you'd come here. That you could get through the gate at all. You always made such fun of me when I talked about seeing things you couldn't see."

"I don't remember that."

She frowned and then wiped the frown away and touched his cheek. "I'm glad to see you."

"We all worried about you. Thought we'd find you someday."

"Dead?"

He swallowed. "What else was there to think? You left all your weaving behind."

"I just decided to stay here. I love the peace here. It's so quiet."

It wasn't. Not at the moment. Someone had started to sing, and three kids were laughing and skipping stones into the dark ocean and squealing from time to time. But there weren't any horns honking or sirens fading into the distance. He swallowed, off balance again at the strangeness of seeing Justine and at the roaring fire and the time shift. "I don't understand any of this."

She reached down and took the broken bit of butterfly from him. "Gisele can fix this."

"Who's Gisele?"

"I was just talking to her. Want to meet her?"

He swallowed. "Not yet. I'm not ready to move yet."

She smiled and put a hand on his knee. He could feel her warmth even through his jeans.

"What are you doing?"

"Just something I learned here. Sit still for a bit."

Whatever she was doing with her hand, he liked it, so he let her shoulder him sideways to make room for her to sit beside him. She left her hand on his knee, the heat of her penetrating like the heat wrap they'd put on him the last time he let the girl at the doctor's office do physical therapy on it. "Wait a bit, and then you can get up."

"You live here?"

"I built a little house. I'll show you when we go to fix the butterfly."

"I have to go back. The festival's open for the holidays, starting tomorrow."

"I'd hate all that Christmas retail."

He smiled at how she felt just like he did about the whole thing.

"I still weave. That cloak that Gisele's wearing, that's mine."

He couldn't see much of it from where he sat. "You do all right then? You have enough?" She'd been like him, always running on the far edge of anything like security, showing up at the free Thanksgiving feeds and sitting through the Hare Krishna temple's silly dances in trade for hot lentil soup and flatbread one Sunday every month.

"I have more than enough. I miss the modern version, but maybe you pay a price for every good thing in life." She looked at him, a question in her eyes. "You could stay, too."

He stared at the fire. "It wouldn't be any easier to make glass over here. I'd still be old."

"There won't be time, now. You can't stay tonight. But we can take parts of your studio through over the summer."

"Why summer?"

"The door is open during the festival . . . and this one night. Rest of the year, even Jack can't come through." She set her head on his shoulder. She'd never done that in the real world. "I'm glad you're here. I didn't realize there was anything . . . anyone . . . I missed from back there."

For a long time he didn't say anything and he didn't move. He just watched the fire and the skipping stones and felt the warmth of her hand. He wanted to hold her, but he couldn't quite do it. He settled for saying, "I'm glad you're here, too."

She glanced up at him. "Do you remember the first year of the festival?"

"And the year off, when I sold stuff in stores, instead, and they took more than half my profits."

She laughed. "We'd all sworn never to do the festival again."

"And now look at it."

Her hair was unbound, and it looked even longer that way than when she braided it. She was still wearing bellbottoms, too. Retrowoman. But he probably didn't look different either, except older and more bent-over, and of course a little more hairless. He kept what he had left short now.

Jack and Gisele walked over to them. Gisele was an interesting woman, her face marked with sorrow and resolve and covered in more wrinkles than Justine's. He couldn't judge her age—she could be sixty or ninety. Her voice was stronger than an old woman's, and so melodious he wondered if she had been a singer once. "There's going to be a feast in an hour."

Justine held up the half a butterfly Jack had been carrying. "Jack wondered if we could fix this, first."

"Sure."

Justine had stopped leaning on him when Gisele came up, and now she lifted her hand from his knee and stood and held the hand out to him. "Are you game?" She looked almost like a little girl, excited and happy.

He stretched out his legs before he stood. They felt good. As he and Justine followed Gisele and Jack away from the fire, he leaned over and asked, "What did you do? My knee feels fabulous."

She grinned. "The small magics are the best."

He shook his head and kept his silence. The knee moved as well as the other one. No, better.

After a while they were back on the outskirts of the little town they'd come through on the way down, but near a building he didn't remember seeing. Gisele went through the door and lit a candle, throwing dim light so that he could make out bulky shapes. Then a light above a workbench bloomed on, making him blink and work to adjust his eyes. They stood in a workshop that smelled of sawdust and paint. Small wooden figurines filled baskets and bowls all over the shop—all animals of one kind or another.

He didn't see any way to way to heat glass. A regular fireplace sat cold and dark at the moment. He didn't even see small blowtorches. "How are you going to repair glass here?"

"I don't know if I am. I'm just going to try." Gisele reached out for the second half of the butterfly. "What can you tell me about this piece?"

"See that ridge of gold running through both of the wings? I'm trying to preserve that."

Gisele shook her head softly. She had both pieces now, laying on a high bench kind of like a draftsman's table. She had a tall chair, but she was standing and studying the glass. She looked more closely at him, and in the brighter light she looked even stranger to Jack, her face dark and the light throwing a halo around her head. "What did you feel when you worked on that piece?"

"My back hurt."

Gisele frowned, and then touched the break. "And its back broke. What else?"

"I always like to think of little girls liking my lawn ornaments." The words kind of surprised him, even though they were true. They just weren't the kind of thing he usually said. He kept going, too. "Everybody buys them, but I'm always happiest when a little girl buys them. Sometimes they walk out of the booth holding them up—they come on sticks, and the girls hold them up and bob them and their mothers tell them not to, but some of them do anyway."

"That's better." Gisele looked away from him and down at the butterfly, and then she opened a jar of paint and picked up a brush. "Watch," she told him.

She painted the thinnest line of blue along the break on one side, and then along the break on the other, and then she joined the two pieces.

"You should use a vise," he said. "You can't just hold them until the paint dries."

She opened her hands, and the butterfly flapped its wings twice.

He blinked at it. He looked back at Justine of the long hair and the bellbottoms. She was grinning at him, like someone who had just pulled off a surprise party. Jack seemed to be playing guardian of the door, but he looked happy as well.

Gisele just looked matter-of-fact.

The butterfly flapped three more times and turned toward him.

Gisele dabbed black paint where its eyes should be and Jack was certain the butterfly could see him.

She smiled.

He just stood still, the very core of him shaken by the glass butterfly's move.

Justine prodded him. "You could say thank you."

He opened his mouth and nothing came out. He closed it and tried again. "Th-th . . . thank you."

Gisele smiled. "You're welcome."

He swayed, feeling dizzy. Dream or not, this had become too strange. "I want to go home now."

Justine's face fell. "Don't you want to sit by the fire some more? Eat with us?"

"I think it's time for me to wake up."

She reached over and pinched him.

He yelped and stepped aside.

"Take your butterfly," Gisele said. "It's too heavy to fly, even here."

He picked it up and set it on his palm. It looked big and ungainly there, five inches of butterfly body and more of wing. The gold went through both wings really well now, and flared out at the top. Two gold drops had appeared on the long bottom of its wings.

Jack came up beside him. "You can choose whether to stay or not."

He swallowed, looking at Justine. There wasn't anyone waiting for him on the other side. "I might go crazy if I stay."

Justine looked hard at him, concern edging her mouth. "I didn't. I like it much better here."

"I . . . I'm not ready."

Gisele handed them both flashlights, but didn't go with them. She waved them off, telling Mel, "Good journey. You're welcome back if you decide to come."

"And good journey to you," he replied, and repeated "Thank you," because it seemed like that was needed. Gisele headed back toward the bonfire on the beach, and after she'd turned around he realized he couldn't remember the color of her eyes or how round her face had been (or not).

Jack and Justine walked him back to the cliff face. Justine was quiet until they were already over the wooden bridge, when she whispered, "Will you be back in the summer?"

"I don't know."

At the edge of the cliff, she stood on tiptoe and kissed his cheek, her lips warm and a little chapped.

He surprised himself by kissing her back, also on the cheek, although he felt like she would have accepted a kiss on the lips. He was the problem. He always had been. Always had withdrawn.

Of course, he was still her friend, and she'd left all of the other men in her life. Maybe he'd made the right decision. Maybe he'd never know.

"I'll be here if you come back," she said.

He nodded, all he could manage. He was blinking and his cheeks had grown hot.

The butterfly flapped in his hand. His grip had grown too tight.

This time he didn't have a hand free for Jack to take, so he simply followed him though the waterfall door.

On the other side, the butterfly was hard and cold and in one piece. The shape of its wings was entirely different than anything he could have done in his workshop. A water drop splashed from his eyelash onto the butterfly, next the new dark eyes.

"I'm going back," Jack said. "But I'll be here in the morning. Before anything opens up. And—happy Halloween, Mel."

Mel stopped for a moment, and then returned the greeting. "Happy Halloween, Jack." He watched Jack walk through the waterfall door. Mel put his butterfly down on a nearby bench, then went out to his van and retrieved his blanket. He curled up by the waterfall. Over here, his knee hurt all over again. When he checked the butterfly, it felt as cold and hard as the others, but it still looked alive. He would keep it; it made him smile.

The falling water made good background noise for sleeping. Maybe he would dream of Justine of the long blond hair, and maybe he would dream of summer.

Brenda Cooper is a technology professional, a science fiction writer, and a futurist. Her most recent novel, *The Creative Fire*, was published in 2012; its sequel, *The Diamond Deep*, which completes this duology, will be out in October of 2014. Cooper's short fiction has appeared in *Nature*, *Analog*, *Asimov's*, *Strange Horizons*, *The Salal Review*, and multiple anthologies. She lives in Bellevue, Washington with her partner, Toni Cramer, Toni's daughter Katie, and two dogs. She has an adult son, David Cooper, a firefighter/paramedic with Cowlitz 2 Fire and Rescue. Cooper blogs regularly at www.brenda-cooper.com and periodically guest-blogs at Futurist.com and other venues.

TRICK OR TREAT

Nancy Kilpatrick

"Malina, despite your resistance to change, I recommend you give the idea a try. Change is what life is all about. The Goddess is here to help and protect you."

"But, Guin, I'm not sure—"

"You never are! But, think about it. You've been coming to see me for a year and while your confidence has increased in certain ways, you've taken few risks regarding social contact."

"It goes against—"

"—the grain. Yes, I know. You've said this before, need I remind you."

Malina felt her face redden. Yes, they'd been over this ground many times, enough that even *she* was getting bored. Maybe Guin was right. Maybe it was time to find the energy and the courage to try a different approach. Be a bit more open to the world. Wasn't that why she'd sought out a New Age healer in the first place? A modern witch—oh how Malina's mother would have laughed at *that*!

"I think this is why you came to me in the first place," Guin said, and Malina bowed her head in a respectful nod to this wise woman, whose intuition had proven itself time and again.

"It's a trust issue," Guin continued, touching Malina's hand,

"and it always has been. You have to trust that all the messages you received in childhood are just the views of people who were angry, paranoid, and resentful. They had only one way to look at life and that was a skewed view. This is a welcoming planet, when the earth goddess travels with you. There are other ways to experience the world and frankly, Malina, the world has changed considerably. It's a much more open place than your mother, for instance, could have imagined." She smiled. "You've made good progress here. You're ready for the next step, a practical step in our philosophy: checking out reality!"

Guin raised her eyebrows, lovely reddish-gold brows, perfectly shaped over innocent yet wise blue eyes. So unlike me, Malina thought, thinking of the darkness of her hair and eyes, the olive tint of her skin, of her shadowy soul. Darkness had shaped her view of herself and the world's view of her. No, she reminded herself, catching that negative thought as Guin had been teaching her to do, not the *world's* view of me, what I was *taught* was how people see me.

Suddenly, Guin tossed an orange crystal and by reflex, Malina snagged it with her hand. "Nice catch!" Guin said, her full lips turned up, nothing like the thin downturned mouth Malina had inherited from her bitter mother and grandmother. "It's carnelian from India. It will bring you joy. And protect you from demons, in all their forms."

"How did you—?"

"It was on your face, the instant scowl of disbelief. And in a split second, a flash of understanding that it was *just* a belief, nothing more, not reality." She smiled again, her face emitting that glow so like the sun.

Guin picked up both of Malina's cool hands and held them in her warm ones. "You've changed, you really have. It's time to take another step up in consciousness. Praise be to the Goddess!"

As the session ended, Malina felt pretty good about herself. It was a feeling that had grown over time. She *was* stronger, ready to put these new ideas to the test.

She slid the carnelian into the little pouch she wore around her neck, adding it to the many tiny pieces of black onyx, hematite, and black jade: dark stones her mother had made her promise she would always wear. Stones that Guin explained symbolize fear and death and dark forces in the universe, said with a hint that they should be gotten rid of. Malina wasn't quite ready to part with the dark stones. In fact, the idea brought on a new fear—the unspecified outcome of losing touch with the stones, which would bring about something awful. That spoke volumes about her witchy mother's influence!

But that challenge was for another day. Today, she felt good, so good that on the way home she decided to buy a pumpkin. She selected a large, plump one, then spontaneously she bought a bunch more, little ones. *Pumpkin children*, she thought, laughing, which made the older clerk look at her strangely, but Malina said quickly, "I've never carved one and thought I'd better practice." It was a bold thing to say to a stranger, and she *never* talked to strangers. But never was a long time, and this little public confession elicited a shift on the face of the man behind the counter.

"Well, you'll need a big, sharp knife. The skins of these little suckers is tough. And make sure you scrape out all the seeds. Some dry 'em and eat 'em, but I never had a taste for that. You can take out the pulp and make a pie," he suggested, receiving her money, and she didn't hear the rest of it, she just smiled and nodded and felt . . . normal. Yes, that was the word. *Normal*. Just like everyone else. A regular person, not a strange person suspect in the eyes of the world, distrusted, feared. A regular woman buying Halloween pumpkins from a regular store clerk.

The man didn't seem to notice that she was smiling like a lunatic. And once he'd handed over her change, he offered to help her load the pumpkins into her car. He lifted the big one out of the cart and she handed him the small ones, two at a time. He placed them all in the back seat, like an adult surrounded by thirteen children. Malina laughed aloud, thinking that maybe she should seatbelt them all in.

The man swung his head quickly at her sharp laugh, a questioning look on his face. Should she explain it to him? She wasn't sure, but this new-found openness needed testing. "I was just thinking how they look like a bunch of children with a parent. Maybe they need seatbelts."

As she said it, it sounded stilted. Silly. An odd thing to say. But the man suddenly grinned. "Could be," he said, then closed the back door and began to walk away, saying, "Happy Halloween to you, Miss. I guess I should say Happy Mischief Night first!"

No one had *ever* wished her a Happy Halloween before. She wasn't even sure how to respond, but finally said, "Yes. You too!" He didn't turn so maybe he didn't hear her.

She drove home in a cloud of optimism, finding parking on the street quite close to her house, another good omen. She lifted out the big pumpkin and one small. She'd have to come back for the rest.

This was one of those times she wished she didn't have thirteen steps to climb to the old house she'd inherited. Out of habit, she counted them all in the rhyme her mother had taught her: *A baker's dozen, twelve plus one, none will see the rising sun. One . . . two . . .*

Maybe she should hire a carpenter to build a fourteenth step, to break the cycle. She felt positive about breaking cycles now.

Three more trips were needed to retrieve the other small pumpkins that she hauled to the kitchen. She brewed a pot of herb tea and sat looking at her acquisitions for a while. She hadn't realized it when she was picking them out, but the little ones were all shapes and a variety of sizes. Some were taller, others wider, perfect rounds, and misshapen gourds with curiously odd stems. Even the colors were slightly different one from the other, She rearranged them first by size, then by pale to dark orange, drinking her tea and thinking that this was going to be the best Halloween ever. Nothing like the ones she'd lived, caught in terror of the night and those who walked it and the torment they inflicted. And especially that last Halloween before her mother died. Her determined and cruel mother who liked to force dark thoughts inside Malina's head, stirring up anxieties about a vicious world of "normal," those who didn't like "our kind." Mother had been a darkling raised by another darkling of a mother and Malina hesitated to call them "evil" but the word was right there, in her mind if not on her tongue. As Guin said once, "Both your grandmother and your mother were women who drove their husbands away, apparently, and would rather have destroyed their daughter than to change."

Malina was not going to be like her mother. Not *ever*.

She stood abruptly and spread a heavy dark tarp over half the table, placed the pumpkins haphazardly onto it and then covered the rest of the table with the tarp.

She had seen carved pumpkins, of course, and had watched them being carved on TV, but had never done that herself. And she knew the history—of the hideous faces used to scare away demons, or offering those very same demons a home for the night when they breeched the veil between the world of the living and the world of the dead. In her childhood there had been no pumpkins at the window or on the porch. Her mother said they didn't need them; demons were always welcome in their house.

Malina picked out a large carving knife from the knife rack and walked to the table. She touched her fingertip gently to the blade edge. Instantly, a line of blood appeared on her finger. Before she could move her hand away, blood dripped onto the thick skin of the large pumpkin, the three bright red drops sliding down the orange shell. Something about that troubled her and she raced to the sink to get a cloth. But in those short moments when she'd turned, the pumpkin had absorbed the blood. She couldn't believe her eyes. But then, she could. She had seen many strange things in her life, why not this?

She spent the better part of the afternoon and early evening carving pumpkins. Something in her was determined to finish them all. She ended up with a mess of pumpkin "guts" spilling over the table and onto the floor, seeds and the stringy bits everywhere, some clinging to fragments of hard pulp. She decided to use a shovel to clean the floor and ended up folding the mess in the tarp and tossing it into the trash.

Once the cleanup had been done, she gathered every candle in the house, seven of them, all black, and cut them in half so she'd have enough for all the jack-o'-lanterns.

The sun had set and while the sky still held streaks of paleness, she turned off the kitchen light to looked at the mother and thirteen babies—as she had come to think of them—with their glowing and flickering eyes, noses, and mouths. They really did look amazing. And horrifying. Instinctively, she had managed to carve frightening faces. Well, that was normal, wasn't it? That's what normal people did.

On impulse, she opened the pouch around her neck and dumped the stones into her hand. Besides the orange, there were thirteen black ones. One for each, she thought, and placed a black stone inside every small pumpkin and the orange stone inside the large one. This would test her mother's theory. And maybe it was a first step in parting with them.

Then, carefully, she moved them one by one onto the front porch, lining them up on the long weather-worn carpenter's bench, the mother in the center, six babies to her left and seven to her right, ordered by height, all of them aflame inside.

She backed up to the top step but needed a better view, one that everyone else would see, so she went down the steps and backed along the path. Yes, they looked spectacular. Hers was the only house in the neighborhood with so many pumpkins, she was sure of it. To confirm this, she turned and glanced at the porches and windows of her neighbors, seeing a pumpkin here, a fake pumpkin there, no pumpkin in the next, and so on, until her eyes scanned past her car . . . and then went right back to it. The car windows were smashed!

Malina hurried down the walk and raced around the car, stunned, not believing what she was seeing. The side, front and back, the rear window, and the other side were broken through, glass shards littering the seats and floor. The windshield had spider-webbed, with a hole that had to have been caused by the huge rock sitting on the hood. Even the driver's side mirror was shattered. She picked up the gray rock that was as big as her two fists and at the sound of laugher spun around, unable to determine from where the wind had carried the sound, but able to make out the words, "Witch!" repeated over and over like a chant.

"Brats!" she shrieked. "You'll pay for this!"

She sounded to her own ears like her mother, shrill, loud, evil. *I don't care*! she thought, her new-found optimism crushed by cruelty for which she had no recourse.

She rushed indoors, still holding the heavy stone that had

damaged her car, envisioning pulverizing heads with it, but mostly aware of how much this stone had wounded her. She sat with the cool rock resting in her palms, trembling, and soon tears gathered in her eyes and rolled down her cheeks until she was sobbing. It took some time, but finally she was able to make the call.

"Calm down," Guin said, "and tell me everything."

The events were repeated, from the enthusiasm of buying and carving pumpkins to the shattering of hope for a new way of living "in this rotten world! They're so cruel, Guin. I can't stand it! Maybe I should just do what my mother would have done and—"

"Malina, stop! Just stop."

She struggled to hold her emotions in and the effort produced a loud, low moan, something that didn't even sound human to her own ears, but Guin said, "I know you're hurt. And you're afraid. But, calm down, Mal. We'll deal with this together."

By the end of the long conversation Guin had convinced Malina that what happens on Mischief Night is not personal, and she shouldn't take it that way. Yes, children can be cruel and the word "mischief" doesn't really cover the extreme damage to her car, but if Malina was friends with the neighbors, she'd probably discover that things just as terrible had happened to their cars or houses or gardens too. For some reason, it was tradition for children to do bad things on Mischief Night, hence the name. "Mal, this was very wrong. But, you can call the police. And you have car insurance for vandalism that will pay for the damage. Hold on, okay? Tomorrow night is Halloween. Those same kids will be ringing your doorbell, begging for candy. And that's when you have the biggest opportunity of your life to change. You can tell them from a vulnerable place just how hurt you were by what they did."

"Tell them?"

"Yes. It's part of healing, expressing from your most vulnerable self exactly what you feel. It's the place that touches others and allows *them* to change. These children can see the error of their ways and you can help them. Oh, and don't forget to also give them a piece of candy, to show you're human."

"Am I? Human?"

"Of course you are! If you weren't, you wouldn't feel wounded by this. And, by the way, your little pumpkins sound delightful. I'm busy tomorrow, and tomorrow night I'll be giving out candy myself, but leave those pumpkins out and I'll drive by the day after Halloween and have a look. That's quite a creative idea, you know."

They talked a little more and while Malina didn't feel happy when she got off the phone, a fragile scab had formed over the bleeding rawness within and she was able to pull herself to her feet and begin making the candy apples she'd planned as giveaways, deciding to *not* call the police, at least not until she calmed down. She had the bushel of Granny Smiths, bought a week before from the same vendor from whom she'd purchased the pumpkins—when she had been too terrified to look him in the eye! When he virtually ignored her. And hadn't offered to help her carry the basket to the car.

Malina decided to keep busy—that was the best way to take her mind off the remnants of the destruction. At least that was one thing her mother had taught her that made sense.

She pulled out the large blackened pot that had been her grandmother's and placed it on the stove top, taking up two burners. It was an easy recipe, one her mother had made several times, though once not as it should have been done. The year before her mother died, she made candy apples and placed the tiniest tip of a razor blade inside one of the apples. So many people gave out candy apples that year her mother had not been caught, but it was in all the news, especially stories of the little boy who'd received stitches and a tetanus shot. At school, the other kids had been suspicious and directed their accusations at Malina and her mother, and that made her life hell for months. In her head, Malina could still hear the cackle that resonated through the house as her mother recounted the event with fondness. Oh how mother wished she could imbed *every* treat with razor blades *every* year. Or perhaps the tips of needles. Anything to inflict pain—that would bring her such joy.

She had no intention of hiding anything in the apples that would cut the children, even if those same children had cut her emotionally. Guin was right. Tell them how much their actions had hurt her. Give them a chance to learn to be better people. That was the key.

Into the large pot she poured white corn syrup, water, sugar, and a colorant that turned the mixture a brilliant red. When the ingredients reached the right temperature, she coated the skewered apples, and then placed them onto a waxed sheet. Thirteen, that was the number she made. There were thirteen children in this neighborhood, as she recalled from the year before. A baker's dozen. And she marveled at how that number seemed to be everywhere tonight. It was like an omen of some kind, but she didn't let her mind travel far along that path, a rocky road of pitfalls that her mother had dragged her down far too often.

October thirty-first dawned with a foreboding in the chilly air. Dying leaves pirouetted from the wind, twirling in a graceful dance macabre, or so Malina thought of it as she stared out the window, her emotions flat-lined by the events of the night before.

She'd woke in fits and starts from nightmares, but only rose at noon, still overcome with exhaustion. Now it was late afternoon, headed towards evening. She sat in her grandmother's rocking chair by the window, a pot of herb tea on the little table, watching the sun struggle to get down the sky until it gratefully disappeared behind a house across the way and ultimately hid below the horizon.

Malina heard then saw the first of the children at the end of the street. Wearing their costumes, holding small, dim flashlights so they could see in the encroaching darkness, each with a bag slung over an arm or clutching a little plastic bucket to receive treats.

The first three were quickly joined by another three and then another four and finally there were thirteen of them, all shapes and sizes, moving as if they were one unit, one being, and Malina thought they looked like a pulsing, throbbing single-celled life form, many parts joined together and coming apart but ultimately remaining together, and the word "parasite" came to mind with a new understanding.

They went from house to house, crossing the street, back and forth, laughing, pushing and shoving one another, waiting for doors to open then shouting in unison "Trick or treat!" Malina watched as candies were placed into bags, and more were demanded until the giver met their demands. One householder even offered the bowl—

the greedy children grabbed handfuls of whatever was in it until the bowl was empty.

Once they reached her house they paused at the curb, pointing at the pumpkins she had lit earlier on the porch, no doubt discussing the wisdom of knocking on the "witch's" door. A couple of the more brazen ones pointed to the car and laughed, admiring their work of the previous evening, the destruction bolstering their courage, no doubt, and Malina felt a fury rise in her which she quickly shoved down.

Finally, she heard the tallest boy say, "Don't be chickenshits! Let's do it!" and they moved as a group along the cement to the thirteen steps and climbed them, the youngest and shortest in the front, staring at the jack-o'-lanterns as they made their way up.

Malina rose from her seat and went to the door, waiting for the bell to ring. When it did, she opened the door without hesitation. The dim yellow porch light and the glow from the pumpkins offered the only illumination as she stood at the entrance of her home surrounded by darkness peering out at the costumed group. There were no presidents or princesses among them, no superheroes or pirates. Every single one wore the mask and costume of a supernatural, but to her eyes, they were all resembled demons.

The darkness that enfolded Malina stopped the chatter for a moment, and as she scanned the little mob she could see in the mask holes the eyes of the youngest ones reflecting something akin to fear. But as she examined them by age, the older they got, the more the fear turned to confusion, then questioning, and finally to blatant arrogance.

The oldest, a boy in a skeleton suit and cape, holding a wooden-handled scythe, the blade made of plastic, said in a snarky voice, "Trick or treat, witch!"

The others laughed. This gave them courage and a chant rose up that started with a few of them until all thirteen were shouting in unison, "Trick or treat, witch!" over and over.

Whatever confidence Malina had felt became submerged in her own fear. She tried to tell herself through Guin's voice in her head: *They're just children. They can't hurt you.* But then she remembered vivid stories her mother and grandmother had repeated about the burning days, their kind being tormented, tortured then tied to a stake and set on fire. Terror surged through her and she shook her head rapidly to clear it of the horrific images.

The oldest boy mistook the head shake for a *no* and shouted, "Then we'll trick you, ugly witch! Again!"

A survival instinct rose up and Malina blurted out, "I have treats!"

"Let's see 'em?" yelled one of the younger ones, a bloody-fanged vampire, the voice so coldly demanding she could hardly believe it came from such a fragile-looking being.

"Yeah, where are the treats, ugly witch? Bring 'em, or we'll torch this place!" The boy, a hairy lycanthrope, snarled at her and gnashed his teeth, making the graveyard ghoul next to him giggle.

"Right here," she said, turning sideways to the tray of candy apples she'd made. She tried to still the trembling of her arms as she held the tray.

The younger ones started to reach into the darkness with both hands, towards the apples, but the oldest, the reaper, said, "Wait! This isn't candy from the store. How do we know there aren't razor blades in them?"

"You'll just have to trust me," Malina said in a calm voice. Then, "Despite what you did to my car, which wounded me quite a bit, I want to celebrate Halloween with you as it was intended to be celebrated. Here are the treats. Help yourselves, but *only* if you feel you really deserve them after what you did to me."

By now, the youngest had each grabbed an apple by the stick and soon the waxed paper was empty as the last, Reaper boy, took his. They stood there, watching her like ravenous animals eying meat, ready to pounce, and she wanted nothing more than to slam the door in their collective faces. But she also wanted to see how this would end. They thought they deserved treats, after what they did. She'd given them the option to own up to their cruelty, but none had taken that route.

The standoff was over when the eldest glared at her one last time and said, "Stupid, ugly witch! Whatever you get you deserve! Come on," he told the others. "We're outta here!"

He turned and started down the steps, and one by one the children turned and followed, the youngest of them already a third of the way into her candy apple, the red coating smeared over bloodless ghost lips and chin, staining the white sheet costume.

Malina stayed in the doorway listening to them discuss going to another street and trying their luck there, and one of them wanted to visit the cemetery and overturn tombstones. She watched them disappear into the darkness, leaving her house in peace, her life intact, her car utterly destroyed. Their insulting and hostile tones still ringing in her ears.

The autumn coldness finally penetrated her bones, but the wind had stopped and the night turned calm and quiet. A sudden urge overwhelmed Malina. She stepped onto the porch and picked up the large rock that had damaged her car, raised it above her head and brought it down hard onto the smallest pumpkin, crushing it into pieces. She stared at the remains for long moments, then in a fury swept what was left off the bench with her hand. The remains bounced and split and splattered further. Demonic energy possessed her and one by one she bashed in each pumpkin, sending the flesh crashing onto the steps. She felt in a trance, ecstatic, breaking their little heads, spewing their guts across the thirteen steps, destroying them utterly! She moved fast, smashing each until all thirteen were pulverized, leaving only the one large pumpkin intact. All the while a cackle split the night that she realized came from her. She didn't stop until her energy was spent and by then she was breathing hard, covered in mushy pumpkin guts.

The pumpkins, one for each, with the dark stones inside, had drawn the young demons to her. The outcome depended on whether her mother's reality made the most sense or Guin's did. The thirteen could be real monsters or fake monsters, that didn't matter to Malina. If innocent, as the youngest probably were, they would be fine. And those who felt true remorse would not be affected either. If they didn't, well, then, they wouldn't survive the treats because of the trick.

"*Razor blades!*" She laughed aloud. Mother was always so obvious. So dramatic. *So* uncreative. Witch's blood, *that* was the most powerful ingredient in any spell aimed at the unrepentant. And, as it turned out, witch's blood was also the best colorant for candy apples!

Nancy Kilpatrick is a writer and editor. She has published eighteen novels, one nonfiction book, over two hundred short stories, five collections of short fiction, and has edited twelve anthologies. She writes dark fantasy, horror, mysteries, and erotic horror, under her own name, and her *noms de plume* Amarantha Knight and Desirée Knight. Kilpatrick has been a Bram Stoker Award finalist three times, a finalist for the Aurora Award five times and, in addition to winning several short fiction contests, won the Arthur Ellis Award for best mystery. She lives with her calico cat Fedex in lovely Montréal in a dwelling that features Gothic decor, which suits the sensibilities of both residents. When not writing, Kilpatrick travels in search of cemeteries, ossuaries, catacombs, mummies, and *danse macabre* artwork.

FROM DUST

Laura Bickle

"We reap what we sow," my mother would say. "No harvest is gained without surrendering something of value."

I don't think that I believed her. Not then.

Maybe it was because I was too young. And too much in sunshine. I grew up on land with straight ribbons of Kansas road that extended from horizon to horizon, never any traffic on them. Those horizons stretched farther than I could fling my arms, the blue glass bowl of the sky stretching over me. Our fields were green, green from the start of spring when the crop would be tall enough to tickle my ankles until harvest when the crop reached over my head. For two weeks in glorious autumn, the sunflowers would open. Hundreds of thousands of sunflowers under the turquoise fall sky. They'd track the morning sun in the east, turning their heads in unison to follow the sun until it set late at night.

Those two weeks were my glory, every year. I'd watch the sun rise from my upstairs window in our old farmhouse. The white clapboard house dated back to the first settlers in this area, my mother had said. It still held memories of our family, long gone. They dotted the walls in dusty photographs: women in calico dresses, wide toothy smiles, and shoes with no stockings. I saw my mother as a baby and my grandmother and aunts, women I'd never met in person. And there were sunflowers in the pictures. Someone had even colored the sunflowers yellow with some sort of watercolor dye. But the women were black and white and gone. And no men among them.

We had everything we needed, materially and more. My mother was always conscious not to be boastful of the things we had. We kept our old icebox and mended our socks, but there was a fine industrial-size washing machine in the basement as well as a fancy refrigerator that had been imported on a truck from Missouri. My mother kept a jewelry box of sparkling gems she never wore. We used a set of fine china for our everyday dishes, but hid them in the cupboard when the neighbors came. Visitors were always served on cheerful chipped yellow ceramic dishes.

"Why do we do that?" I asked, carefully drying the silver teapot we used for our afternoon tea. We used it so often that it had no chance to gather tarnish. I often felt I was playing at being a princess here, albeit a secret one.

"Why do we do what?"

"Why do the neighbors get the yellow dishes?"

My mother paused to think for some minutes, soaping the delicate teacups in the sink. Water licked at her patched apron. I began to think she'd forgotten my question. But she answered me finally: "Because it is always best to blend in, my dear. No good ever comes of rubbing good fortune in another's face."

"But shouldn't we . . . " I wasn't sure what we *should* do. Share? Be honest?

"Jealousy is a wicked emotion. A very human emotion. And such emotions caused wealthy women to be burned in ages past."

"Burned?" I tried to understand a human burning. I supposed it was not so different than any other creature . . . we were meat, but . . .

My mother kissed the top of my head. "Be quiet, be humble, and keep your treasures well-guarded."

The sunflowers were our treasure. They always grew, through drought and cold and rattling wind. When our neighbors' fields of wheat withered under the sun and died, our flowers were always lush and green. We never told them that we didn't water. My mother would murmur something about underground springs and offer them another glass of iced tea.

I would sometimes wander to my mother's jewelry box and take out the pieces to gaze at them. She would never stop me from playing dress-up with them as a girl. I would struggle to work the clasp of a pendant on a heavy chain, a yellow diamond as large as a bottle cap. It wasn't until I was sixteen that I was able to actually work the clasp and get it to hang properly over my heart.

My mother watched me, smoothing my hair back from my ears. We looked very much alike: blond and sun-freckled, but with eyes so dark they were nearly black, like wet tea leaves. "It's yours, my dear. It was your grandmother's. From the old country, where women knew the earth well."

I touched the cool stone. I knew that I'd never be able to wear it outside. The fear of losing it was enough to stop my heart. Never mind what the neighbors might say . . .

My mother lifted the chain and tucked the pendant down the top of my dress. The stone felt cold against my skin, hidden.

I closed the jewelry box on my mother's gold rings and pearl necklaces. My mother's wedding ring was there. She didn't wear it anymore. The ring she wore daily was a plain sterling silver band that made her finger itch. She was never without a ring in public, not at the market nor in town. Though my father was long dead from our house and my memory, she did not return the admiring glances of the men. She always stared straight ahead or into her shopping basket.

It was not as if the men didn't try. The fellow we hired with the cultivator to come every fall, Mr. Mauer, tried to linger a bit too much after a day of labor and polite iced tea. My mother would never call him by his first name and would gently shovel him out of the door with an envelope of cash. Our nearest neighbors, three miles away, often tried to set my mother up with the husband's brother, but she always refused.

"I'm happy with our life," she would say as she hung our wash out on the clothesline. "There's no reason to change it."

I half-believed her.

I believed her most in those last two weeks of October, when the sunflowers were at the height of their glory. The sun was warm against my face, but dimmed from summer. I could feel it as I slipped into the fields, the sticky stems of the sunflowers prickling against my clothes. The leaves at the bases of the stalks were growing yellow, a harbinger of winter. The backs would grow brown and the seeds would blacken before harvest at Halloween. And the sun set earlier now than in summer, filling me with a pang of sadness. I could imagine the howling winds of winter rattling our door . . .

. . . but not today. I was awash in a sea of blue and yellow as I waded through the fields. I was certain that I could avoid any human being who I might encounter.

Though I was never alone this time of year.

The crows were always with us.

They'd arise early in the morning, cawing to each other. The crows would descend into the fields in pairs and then in great numbers. They'd balance on the bobbing sunflower stems and peck at the faces of the flowers, devouring the seeds in greedy gulps. Their black wings would flash among the yellow of the sunflowers and blue of the sky. Our fields would seethe with wind and sun and feathers, like a vast living thing.

I was a part of that. I'd stand in the middle of the field, with the sun on my face and the breeze rippling through the stalks, filtering down to my fingers and nipping at the edge of my dress. If I closed my eyes, it seemed as if my feet were not touching the earth, as if I could fly. My hair worked free of its braid and tendrils would stick to my mouth, tasting bitterly of green sunflower-sticky-stalk. The cawing of the birds formed a deafening cacophony around me, a swirl of motion, sun, and shadows. At my feet, black feathers and empty sunflower hulls would litter the ground. Feathers would stick to my hair, and I'd save them, tucking them away in the wooden frame of my bedroom mirror. When I looked at my reflection in the mirror, it was surrounded by those feathers.

My mother respected the crows . . . no, she did more than that. She honored them. There were never any scarecrows on our property. Each year, she'd instruct Mr. Mauer not to run the combine close to the house. With red ribbon and stakes, she'd mark off a strip about three hundred feet wide of sunflowers on the western edge of the house. Those were to be left standing. She'd stand there with her arms crossed, daring Mr. Mauer to run them over.

And he wanted to. "It's a perfect waste to let sunflowers go to seed there, Carol."

"I don't want dust kicked up that close to the house, Mr. Mauer." She stroked the wheat-blonde hair on the top of my head when I was small. "And Jeanie loves the flowers. Leave them be, for her."

I knew my mother cared nothing for dust. And she would have left the flowers if I asked.

When Mr. Mauer had shaken his head and climbed back into the combine, I looked uncertainly up at her. "Thank you."

She bent to kiss my cheek. "They're not for you, sweet one. They are for the crows. They are a sacrifice, for a good harvest and a good life. Always leave them their portion."

I glanced back at the house, brow furrowed. My mother had bought us a pair of pumpkins to carve for Halloween, and they sat against the step, full and waiting. "Are these for the birds?"

She chuckled. "They're for us, too. We use the shells, and they take the seeds. Like the sunflowers."

And the crows were always pleased. They would descend upon that little garden that remained and pluck the seed heads clean within a week. As the rest of the fields were stripped forlornly away by the machine, the brittle stalks would stand, like sentries, until we cut them down in the spring to plant anew.

Every year was the same as the last. Until the autumn I turned sixteen.

The sunflowers opened as they always did, brighter than the sun. I slipped away from my chores to go walk among them. I had much to think about. The neighbor's boy, Sam, occupied a great many of my thoughts, and I wanted to be alone with them. Not necessarily him—I was too shy and unsure of what I felt. But I knew that it seemed like sunshine on my face. I idly braided my hair as I swam in the flowers. I reached up to bend down one of the faces to mine, plucking the seeds to eat. They were almost ripe, dry and warm with daylight on my tongue. I spat out the seeds onto the ground.

A crow fluttered down to the bent sunflower stalk. It stared at me, fluffed up its ruff, and cawed. I stepped back. The crows never looked at us humans with any particular interest, but this one continued to caw, raising its wings in a hooded fashion. Wind ruffled its tail and it bobbed up and down at me, shrieking with all its might.

It was as if it was trying to tell me something. Something that came from the very marrow of its light bones.

Something cold and fearful rose in my throat. I turned and ran back to the house. The leaves and stems of the sunflowers slashed at me as I fled, raising welts on my arms. I put my head down and ran. I fled until I burst out of the shadow of the field and into the bright sun of the yard. I surged across the grass and up the steps, across the worn boards of the porch, shivering the wind chimes. The screen door slammed behind me and I stood in the parlor. My hands fluttered to my chest, as if I could keep my heart from leaping out of my ribcage.

I knew at once something was wrong. I knew it deep in the darkness inside my chest. I knew it when the silence of the house greeted me, and not my mother's voice. I knew it when I saw the puddle of tea spreading on my mother's immaculate linoleum floor.

I lurched into the kitchen. My mother was sprawled on the floor in front of the sink, surrounded in shattered glass. The water was still running.

I fell to my knees in the glass, reaching for my mother's shoulder. I shook her. "Mom?"

She was still breathing. I turned her over. Her mouth was slack and her eyes were closed. I cupped my hands around her throat. I could feel her pulse beating there. But she didn't answer me.

I skidded backward on the floor. The glass had made my knees red and sticky.

A crow perched in the kitchen window, peering down at me, the sunlight edging its silhouette. The bird made no sound, but I could hear the crows outside—scores of them—cawing in a raucous cry of alarm.

I ran. I ran, as hard as I could, to the neighbors' house, three miles distant. I was down the dirt road before the screen door slammed behind me.

A black cloud followed me.

My hair sucked into my mouth, sticking to my lips and ragged breath as I turned. A squawking, churning mass of crows followed me. My fists pumped hard against my sides. I ducked my head and forced my feet into the dust, my skirt tearing at my legs. My vision was blurry as I spotted the neighbors' house behind shriveled wheat. It bobbed and jagged with my breath.

Sam saw me staggering up to the yard. He ran to me, the straw hat flying off his tow head. He grasped me by the shoulders, looking at me with eyes the color of cornflowers.

"What's wrong?"

It took me three tries before I could pant the words out: "My mother."

Sam shouted to the house. His father charged down the steps, tugging on his shoes.

"My mother," I rasped. "She needs a doctor. Fast."

Sam's father paled. He scuttled to the green pickup truck, motioned for us to get in the back. His wife piled into the cab with him. The sleeves of her blouse were rolled up, and tomato spatters dotted her apron. Her hands were red. I dimly assumed she'd been canning.

"Come on," Sam said. He jumped into the open tailgate and pulled me up behind him.

I clung to him in the back of the truck as it kicked up plumes of dust. That seemed to keep the crows at bay. I couldn't see their shadows through the thick yellow miasma. My fingers dug deep into Sam's arm, but he didn't wince. He just smoothed my sweaty hair from my face. If he said anything, I couldn't hear it over the roar of the engine and the sound of gravel kicking up on the oil pan. The metal bed of the truck scorched the pale flesh of my legs, but I didn't care. I just kept visualizing my mother on the kitchen floor.

Sam and I scrambled out of the truck at my house. Sam's mother climbed out and slammed the door. It echoed loudly. The sound of the truck engine drained away in a plume of sallow dust.

It was then that I realized my ears were ringing. There was no other sound. No crows. Not even the tinkle of the wind chimes on our porch.

I rushed into the house, with Sam and his mother behind me. I skidded into the kitchen. The water was still running in the sink. It overflowed now, water dripping against the floor with the shattered glass.

My mother wasn't there.

My fingers clenched. "She was just here . . . " I whispered.

Sam's mother gathered me to her, a reflex. She buried my head in her shoulder. I felt Sam and his mother exchange heavy glances over my head.

My mother was gone. And so were the crows

Sam went to search the parlor, calling for my mother.

I pulled myself free of his mother's grasp, mumbling that I would look upstairs. Deep down, I didn't want the neighbors to see my mother's finery, squirrelled away from view. I hoped that she had crawled off to her bed, that she had fainted. But the quilt covering her bed was as smooth as she'd made it this morning. The bathroom was empty.

I saw Sam's mother at the top of the stairs. I saw her looking at me, then past me, at my mother's silk drapes. I'm not sure what she thought, if she thought anything.

I opened my mouth to speak, not knowing what to say. I don't know if I meant to mumble some excuse about the drapes or to start crying.

But Sam shouted from below. "Come here! Come outside!"

I flew down the stairs, out into the yard. I circled around behind the house, to the swing in the cottonwood tree in the back yard. Sam was kneeling over a limp figure at the edge of the line of sunflowers. I recognized my mother's cotton dress. Her feet were bare.

I fell to my knees beside my mother. She lay sprawled upon the grass, gazing up at the sky, unblinking. Her arms were covered in fine red scratches, as if a murder of crows had tried to pick her up where she fell. In her left hand, she held a sunflower with all the seeds culled out of it.

A crow stood at her head, gently plucking at strands of her hair in a worried fashion. It only flew away when Sam shook his hat at it. But I could feel its eyes on us from deep within the field.

* * *

The doctor said my mother was suffering from exhaustion and a weak heart. After spending many long minutes listening to her heart with a stethoscope, he sent her to bed. I was given a bottle of laudanum to administer to her at sunrise and sunset. Sam's mother helped me dress my mother in a ruffled dressing gown—she owned no plain ones—and tuck her in bed under her fine linens. Sam's mother's rough hand lingered on the embroidered edges of the sheet.

The figure that lay there after everyone had left was not my mother. She lay there, thin and cold and staring up at the ceiling. When she slept and when she woke, she rambled on about the crows and the flowers and storms and strange shadows. How the crows had come to rescue her from her rattling heart and take her away to the sky. None of it made any sense. Her eyes were far distant, looking through me and through the thick plaster walls to the sky beyond.

She stayed that way for days, neither awake nor asleep. She was between worlds. I bathed her as one would a child, daubed the scratches with antiseptic, and pinned her hair up. I saw streaks of grey in it now that had never been there before. The neighbors came by to bring casseroles and to offer any assistance they could.

I thanked them and asked for them to get word to Mr. Mauer that the harvest was ready to be taken in. It was almost Halloween, and my mother had always been insistent that this task be done by then. I did not let anyone see her. I did not want them to gawk at her in this oddly unanchored state.

I slept beside her at night, listening to her shallow breathing. I was afraid that she would somehow stop and slip away if I quit observing. I laid my hand to her breastbone and felt it rise and fall, all through the night, night after night. I would finally fall asleep near dawn, exhausted, when the rays of sun filtered in through the silk drapes. I spiraled into strange dreams that I hadn't had since I was a little girl. Dreams of flying, of seeing the land from far up above, with our house a postage-stamp-sized speck in the fields.

One morning, I awoke to the sounds of machinery. I pressed my head into the pillow, wanting to drain a few precious moments' more of sleep from the sunny day. My mother was sleeping quietly. I pulled the quilt up over my shoulders, my muzzy thinking circling around whether I would prepare eggs or biscuits for breakfast with bacon.

But my mother lurched bold upright in bed, eyes wide open, and shrieked.

I clasped her arms, pressing her back to the bed. "Mother, it's all right!"

Her skin was glossed with sweat, and her eyes were wide and unseeing. "Don't let him take the sunflowers!"

I smoothed a dark curl from my mother's face. "Mr. Mauer is doing as he always does. He's harvesting the seeds. Today is Halloween. Remember?"

My mother shook her head hard and balled her hands into fists. "No. He must leave some for the crows." Her fists became claws, tearing at my arms. I cried out as her nails drew blood.

I extricated myself, peeling her hands away and pushing her back to the bed. I felt her fear pressing against me, like humidity. It felt like a shimmering, tangible thing.

I backpedaled out of the room, dove down the stairs and out the door, into yard. Above, the sky was a sickly yellow. I could see the combine making its last orbit, near the house.

I ran after it, shouting at Mr. Mauer to stop. He couldn't hear me above the noise of the machine; his sunburned neck didn't even turn. The machine plowed down the sunflowers near the house, chewing them up like some terrible locust. Dust roiled in his wake. There was nothing I could do.

The combine turned left, left in its orbit back around the field. It left me standing among the splintered, stubbly stalks piercing the earth.

I heard the solitary call of a crow. I turned, seeing a crow perched on the gutter of the house. He watched me with dark eyes, cold in an almost human wrath.

Something had changed. I could feel it.

I tried to placate my mother. I drew the drapes and lied to her, telling her the sunflowers were safe. I told her that when she felt better that we could carve our pumpkins. I knew full well that our neglected pumpkins had caved in on themselves on the porch and had the musty scent of rot about them. I placed a cool cloth on her head and gave her laudanum to help her sleep. She still tossed fitfully. It was as if she could sense the nudity of the earth.

I could sense it, too, the way the wind rose that night and scraped through the remnants of the field. The wind howled so hard that it leaked around the panes of the bedroom window and moved the drapes like ghosts. Once or twice, I went to the window and tried to peer through it. But the glass was covered with dust and bits of frass and brown petals from the ruined sunflowers.

I had never felt afraid in my own house before. I had never felt compelled to make certain that all the windows were latched and that the doors were locked. Maybe it was the way the glass rattled in the sashes and the way that the wind sucked down the fireplace, but it sounded like a breath over a bottle. Hollow. Alive.

Something scratched at the front door. My breath congealed in my throat. It was not the rhythmic digging of a dog coming home. This was a thin, prolonged scratching, as if someone drew a rake over the door.

I hoped it was a broken tree branch shoved by the wind, that it would simply stop. But the scraping continued, deliberate, rhythmic. Perhaps it was a Halloween prank perpetrated by the older kids from town . . .

I turned my head to gaze at my mother. I don't know if I expected her to protect me, as she always had, from bees and taunts to fevers.

But she was beyond that, now. Her eyes were squeezed shut, and sweat glossed her face. The drug and the fever had finally brought her into silence.

My hands chewed at the blanket. Deep in my chest, I knew that I would have to protect her.

I fought the urge to pull the blankets over my bed. I drew the covers back and forced my bare feet to the floor. I reached underneath the bed for the loaded rifle my mother kept there.

With quaking hands, I clutched the gun to my chest. I crept toward the door, past it, out into the hallway.

I stared down the stairs, at the back door. The scratching was clearer now, drawing down the wood. Through the stained-glass panels at the top, a shadow moved, shadows against shadows. I heard no giggling and whispering of children.

My heart pounded as I descended the steps. I lifted the stock of the rifle to my shoulder. My hands shook and my skin was slick with sweat.

"Who's there?" I demanded. I meant it to come out as a fearsome roar, but it came out as a whisper.

Whatever was out there heard me.

The scratching halted, and I sucked in my breath.

A great fluttering sounded behind me, like thousands of bird wings. I pivoted toward the fireplace. Wings hammered against the chimney and against the flue. In an explosion of black wings and yellow dust, birds exploded from the fireplace. Hundreds and hundreds of black-winged birds.

I screamed. I screamed and crouched down, clutching the gun. Claws and feathers tore past me, churning darkness.

And the door imploded. It ripped back on its hinges, slamming against the wall and breaking out the glass. Wind and dust and debris tore into the house. I curled my hand over my tearing eyes, as I struggled to see . . .

. . . struggled to see the silhouette framed in the doorway.

At first, I thought it was a man. But it seethed and moved with black feathers. It walked across the scarred floorboards toward me with the clawed feet of a bird, the claws leaving terrible scars in the wood.

I clutched the gun, ratcheting back the slide. The shadow swept over me, yanking the gun from my grip. I sprawled before it, my hands balling into fists.

It loomed over me. I was given the impression of a cloak of feathers, but the creature wore the face of a man. His face was pale and angular, hair long and black.

And the eyes were what stopped me. The eyes looked familiar. Dark as tea leaves, like mine.

The bird-man regarded me with an inscrutable expression, cocking his head.

"I'm sorry," I blurted. "I'm sorry for the sunflowers."

He spoke to me then. He spoke to me in a voice like gravel, the hoarse voice of the crows. "Every boon demands a sacrifice."

"Don't hurt my mother."

"Your mother . . . "

He reached toward me with a pale, clawed hand. I screwed my eyes shut, certain that he intended to rip my throat out.

I felt pressure around my neck. The chain on the diamond pendant snapped. I gasped, my eyes snapping open.

The crow-man held the yellow diamond in the palm of his hand, head cocked, staring at it. He reminded me of one of the crows looking at a bottle cap, entranced by the shininess.

He reached forward then, pushing a tendril of hair behind my ear. I was reminded of the crow standing in the yard over my mother's hair. It was an oddly tender gesture that rattled my teeth with its familiarity.

He stood. Without another word, he turned and swept out of the doorway that howled with dust and wings.

My mother died the next morning. All Souls Day. She died without ever waking up. I found her with her face pressed to the pillow, her jaw slack like a small child's. She was pale and gaunt as a skeleton of a bird as I washed her and dressed her one last time.

I knew that the crows had taken her from me. As a sacrifice.

I sanded and painted the scratches in the door and the floor. I swept the dust from the parlor and gathered each feather from the house. I found them for a long time afterward, jammed in lampshades, drawers, and even between cushions.

The work kept me busy. I opened the windows to air the smell of death from the house. But it only brought in the scent of fresh-turned earth from the hole dug for my mother's grave underneath the cottonwood trees. She would lie beside her mother and all the women who had come before, under a simple stone marker.

I had occasion to think about things, about all the mysterious material things we had. I used to think that we had them because we deserved them.

No, we had traded for them. And I had violated our end of the bargain.

The dust storms came in after that, stripping all the seeds from the earth. It chewed the paint from the side of our house and ruined the neighbors' crops.

It was as if something unholy and hot descended upon the land, like a desert. Walking to meet Sam, I would lose track of the dust-covered road, my head wrapped in a scarf to keep from tasting the dead earth.

"We're moving away," Sam said when spring brought the worst storms yet. "West. To California. Where there's work." He reached out to take my hand. "Come with us. Come with me."

I shook my head. "I can't leave my home."

"There ain't nothing here but dust and wind," he said. "Nothing living."

I shook my head. My mother loved this place. I would stay. I stood on my front porch and watched as the family went down the road with all their things packed in the back of their pickup. Sam sat in the back, his legs dangling over the tailgate.

I watched until the truck was a speck on the horizon.

I felt truly alone, then.

I saw to it that the field was planted thick with black seed. Mr. Mauer said it was no use, that nothing would grow this year, that all the yellow dust blown in had ruined everything. There had been no rain for months. But I insisted. I paid him. Money was one of the only things that talked, these days. And I still had some.

I watched the fields, waiting, not knowing if anything would grow. The crows were mysteriously absent.

I sat at the edge of our field . . . my field . . . on the dry and ruined grass.

I knew, deep down, that this was not enough. I had an oasis, an enviable life. The women in my family had made a bargain with the crows. One that I had unwittingly broken. I didn't know what I could do to fix things. What sacrifice could I make to bring it all back?

I clambered to my feet and ran back into the house. I gathered all our fine things: the jewelry, the dishes, the silverware, the crystal. I brought these treasures and a shovel to the edge of the field. I jammed the shovel into the pale amber earth, turning it up. I dropped a handful of pearls into it. I covered the hole, dug out another two paces away. I tossed a dinner plate into it. The china shattered into shards, cutting my bare foot. It didn't matter. I kept on. I kept planting the only things I had to give: the shiny baubles and the fragments of the riches we enjoyed. Anything . . . anything to call back the quiet, satisfyingly bucolic life I'd led before my mother's death.

"I'm sorry," I whispered as I worked. "I didn't understand."

My tears speckled the soil, along with blood from my foot. I worked until the sun set, burying all the fine treasures my mother had so carefully passed down to me. Coins, watches, paper money . . . it all went into the earth. It had come from the earth, and I gave it back.

Even my mother's wedding ring, though now I doubted if there had ever been any man here with her, only a shadow with feathers who perhaps smoothed her hair the way the crow had in the yard.

When it was accomplished, I fell to my filthy knees beside the disturbed earth. "Please!" I cried to the darkness. "Please bring it back . . . all of it."

I pressed my forehead to the ground.

Nothing answered me.

I think I must have passed out there, in the dust. The cut on my foot was more serious than I'd thought. I only know that I woke in the morning with my cheek pressed against the cool soil. I reached up to rub dirt from my eyes.

When my eyes cleared, I spied a crow pacing in the distance, along one of the furrows, pecking for seeds. Small green sprouts reached like fingers up from the furrows.

Rain began a soft patter along my back, sticking my dress to my skin, like a caress. I pulled myself to a seated position. My arms were covered in small red scratches, as if I had tried to hold a dozen angry cats. A crow feather was stuck to the shoulder of my dress, glossy and black as obsidian.

I turned my face up to the gray sky, where crows swirled, and I smiled. I reached up for my hair, finding it neatly tucked and twisted behind my ears, knotted and braided. Feathers prickled through, feeling stiff where they had been carefully wound in my hair.

I had sown. I would reap. I would begin again and carry on as my mother had, in a new cycle and a new season, with the old earth.

Laura Bickle's professional background is in criminal justice and library science, and when she's not patrolling the stacks at the public library she's dreaming up stories about the monsters under the stairs. (She also writes contemporary fantasy novels under the name Alayna Williams). Laura lives in Ohio with her husband and five mostly-reformed feral cats. *The Hallowed Ones*, her first young adult novel, was published in 2012; its sequel, *The Outside*, will be out in September 2013. For more information, please see www.laurabickle.com.

ALL SOULS DAY

✝

Barbara Roden

"I want to see the haunted house."

Debra had smiled when she'd seen Richard's text, following hard on the heels of the announcement that the following year's World Conference on Disaster Management would be held in Toronto. *I'm guessing this means you'll be at the conference* she'd texted, to which he'd replied with a smiley face.

Typical Richard; and typical of him to recall a throwaway comment she'd made once, about her grandparents living on the same Toronto street as a haunted house. That had been at a conference in San Jose, four—no, five—years earlier. She hadn't known Richard then, but he'd been one of a group of them sitting at a table on the outdoor patio. A sudden wind had sprung up, and someone had asked where that came from, and she'd been amazed to hear someone say, in a soft Texas accent, "Where I come from, we'd have said someone whistled for it."

"M. R. James!" she'd said in delight, to the bemusement of almost everyone else at the table. The one exception was a slim, dark-haired man sitting three places down from her, who grinned. "*Quis est iste qui venit?*" she'd added, and his grin widened.

"I can't tell you how many times I've used that line. You're the first one who's ever recognized it," he said. "A group of us are planning a trip to the Winchester House tomorrow, before the conference starts. I think you'd like it. Want to join us?"

Just like that, before they even knew each other's names, a friendship was born. Long distance, as so many friendships were these days, what with Richard in Atlanta most of the time, and Debra in Vancouver. They kept up via e-mail and text, sending each other links to weird and wonderful news stories. She sent congratulations when his eldest daughter was named valedictorian of her graduating class; he sent condolences when her father had a heart attack. Each twelve months they met up in whatever city the annual conference was held, picking up their friendship as if they'd seen each other last week, not last year.

"There was a haunted house on the street my grandparents lived on in Toronto," she'd said at the Winchester House, as they both gazed up a stairway that led to nowhere, and he reminded her of that now.

"I'd love to see it, if there's time," his e-mail read. "After all, how many chances do you get to see a real live (no pun intended) haunted house?" She'd replied that it wasn't much to see: "It was a very ordinary house, not at all the Charles Addams-style mansion I'd half-expected. I think I was a bit disappointed when I first saw it. Besides, I don't even know if it's still there. It must be thirty years since I was in Toronto."

She wasn't trying to put him off, not really, and he knew that; which was why they found themselves, some months later, purring down Bloor Street in Richard's rental car. Debra had a map spread out in front of her, just in case. "It's not that I don't trust GPS," she said, "just that . . . "

" . . . you don't trust GPS," said Richard. "I hear you. It looks a pretty straightforward route, though."

And it was. Debra gazed out the window as they drove, searching for anything that looked familiar. For a time there was nothing, merely shop front after shop front, the same mix of chain stores and coffee bars to be seen in any urban centre of North America. As they left the CN Tower behind, however, the mix of shops grew less homogenized, more eccentric, and the buildings gave way from hard-edged steel and glass to softer brick, mellowed with age and softened round the edges.

The first thing she recognized with certainty was High Park, and soon after that they crossed the Humber River. Then buildings began to come into focus, one after another, little islands of familiarity. A green sweep of trees and grass appeared beside them, and Debra said "Next left," folding up the map as she spoke.

"What's this, another park?" asked Richard, flicking on the turn signal. "I didn't know Toronto had so many."

"Not a park," said Debra with a grin, and Richard took a better look.

"Holy crap! A haunted house *and* a cemetery! Is there an abandoned crypt too? That would just about complete the set."

"Not unless they've added one in the last thirty years or so," said Debra, as they turned. "Oh," she whispered.

"What is it?"

"It's—well, nothing's changed. Nothing. It looks exactly the way it did in my mind, picturing it from when I was a child." Now that they were out of the traffic on Bloor Street, Richard had slowed down, and she gazed round her. "Except the trees," she said finally. "It was always summer when we visited. I'm not used to seeing them bare."

The cemetery was on their left, and neat brick houses set back from the road were on their right. The lawns and gardens were uniformly tidy, trees and bushes neatly pruned, the paths clear of leaves. Everything was peaceful and quiet, and Debra could almost believe that nothing *had* changed since the last time she had been there.

Until, that is, she asked Richard to stop the car, and peered at the house directly to their left. It was the first house beside the south fence line of the cemetery, and Richard looked at her inquiringly.

"My grandparents' house," she said. "My dad grew up there." She shook her head. "Now that *has* changed. That whole addition next to the driveway is new, and the siding is different. I wouldn't have recognized it if it wasn't for the location." She laughed. "I guess the old saying is right. You *can't* go home again."

Richard pulled round a corner and parked the car. "So where's this haunted house of yours?" he asked, pulling his top-of-the-line Nikon from the back seat. "I've come a long way to see it."

"This side of the street, up about four blocks," replied Debra. She glanced up at the sky. "I hope the rain holds off. It's not looking very promising."

"Adds to the atmosphere," said Richard, locking the car. "Lead on, Macduff."

They strolled along the sidewalk, sidestepping the occasional pile of soggy leaves huddled against the grass border. Apart from the odd car passing them, all was silent, and there were no signs of life in any of the houses they passed.

"You Canadians are trusting souls," Richard said as they crossed another side street. Debra looked at him quizzically. "Look at all the houses we're passing. Notice anything?"

"No, not really. Nothing out of the ordinary, anyway. What do you mean?"

"I mean if people on our street had left their Halloween pumpkins out after Halloween night, they wouldn't still be sitting on front porches. They'd be smashed all over the road."

Debra looked again, and realized he was right. Every house they passed had at least one pumpkin on the front porch, their bright orange faces one of the few notes of color to be seen. "I wonder why they're still out," she said, puzzled.

"Canadian custom?"

"If it is, it's one I've never heard of. Most people clear them away as soon as Halloween night is over. So they *won't* end up smashed all over the road. We're not as polite as people make us out to be."

Richard shrugged. "Maybe it's some neighborhood street party thing," he suggested. "Or someone's filming here and they've asked for the Halloween stuff to stay out. Looks nice, whatever the reason."

"You think so?" said Debra, and Richard glanced at her. "I think it's a bit depressing, now that Halloween's over. The same way the Christmas tree just doesn't look the same after the twenty-fifth of December. Kind of—deflated, somehow. Like it's lost its reason to be there."

They were halfway along the block, and Richard stopped. "Look," he said, pointing to a house that was in the process of being torn down. The yard was ringed with a temporary fence of chain wire, and what was left of the yard was a torn-up mass of dirt and rocks and bits of brick. There had obviously been a small peaked roof over the front door, but it had been pulled away, exposing fresh-looking brickwork behind it. Yet even this house had a carved pumpkin on the front step, incongruously perched beside a pile of bricks.

"That makes a change," said Richard. "Builders with a sense of the season. Usually they just leave empty pop cans lying around." He took a few pictures.

"You're obviously still into photography in a big way."

"When I get the opportunity. I'm trying to put together enough for an exhibit at a biggish art show next spring. Wish me luck." He slung the camera back over his shoulder. "Okay, on to the haunted house. It can't be far."

Debra was looking at the house numbers. "It should be that one, on the next corner," she said, and they crossed one more side street. She consulted a piece of paper she pulled from her pocket. "Yes. This is it."

She was conscious of a sense of anticlimax as they stopped in front of it. It was a very ordinary-looking house indeed, and there was little to set it apart from any of the other houses they had passed, except that where the others were all open to the street, this one was ringed with a tall hedge which almost completely obscured it from view. The only place they could find that gave a glimpse of the front was a small gap where the hedge bordered the front property line of the house next door.

"Well, this is what you traveled however many thousand miles to see," she said. "I'm sorry it's not more impressive."

"Oh, I don't know," said Richard, snapping off some of pictures. "There's certainly an appropriately gloomy aura about it. What's supposed to have happened here?"

Debra shrugged. "Some people who lived here heard noises in the attic—footsteps, and then banging, as if someone was trying to get out. When they went up to investigate they saw a glowing orb near the window—that one there, on the front, I expect." She pointed to the single top-floor window, which was obscured by curtains. They did not quite meet in the middle, and as the window itself was open they blew slightly in the breeze, giving the impression of someone standing behind them.

"And?"

"And that's about it. They called in some psychic investigators, who put flour and tripwires down on the attic floor. It didn't stop the noises, but apparently there was no sign of a disturbance when they checked it out. They never did figure out what was going on."

"Typical true-life ghost story," said Richard with a laugh. "No beginning or end, just a rather inconclusive middle section." They walked back the way they had come and turned the corner, so they were at the side of the house. The hedge only extended halfway down the property here, and they had a better view of the building, which looked empty.

"No one at home," said Richard, taking a few final shots. "Not even the obligatory pumpkin. The neighborhood beautification committee will be having a few words with the owner. I think *that* house is safe, though." He pointed to the neat bungalow across the street. "Now there's someone who really gets into the spirit of Halloween."

Debra saw what he meant. Whereas a handful of the houses they had passed had sported more than one pumpkin near the front door, the owners of this particular house had more than a dozen pumpkins lining the front walkway, and another four perched beside the door itself, two on either side like guards.

"I think we have a winner," said Debra. "If someone's awarding prizes, I hope they get a good one. They deserve it."

"They're supposed to keep evil spirits away," said Richard as they rounded the corner back on to the main road and began walking towards where the car was parked. "Back in the old days, I mean, when they were carved out of turnips."

"We tried carving a turnip once," said Debra. "I almost sliced my hand open."

"Did you go in for Halloween in a big way when you were a kid?"

"Oh yeah. It was a big deal all right. Pumpkins, decorations, sound effects, the lot. What about you?"

"Pretty low key," said Richard. "My brother and I each carved a pumpkin, and that was about it. We were more interested in the candies."

They had drawn up opposite her grandparents' old house. Debra crossed the street and stood on the sidewalk. "Could you get a picture of me standing on the front path?" she asked, handing him her camera and walking to the front door.

"Hope the people who live here aren't home," said Richard. "They'll think we're burglars, casing the joint. All right, smile and say *Cthulhu*." He snapped a couple of shots. "Uh-oh," he said in a stage whisper. "We've been spotted."

The front door had opened a crack, and Debra turned to see a woman's face peering out at her above a stout chain which prevented the door opening any further. She said nothing, merely stared at Debra with a look that was—what? Scared, more than anything. Debra smiled, and adopted her most reassuring voice.

"Hi there. Sorry if I startled you. I hope you don't mind me getting a couple of pictures of the house." The woman still said nothing. "My grandparents used to live here," she added, "and my dad grew up here. I used to visit when I was a kid. I haven't seen the house for years, and since I was in town I thought I'd pay a visit."

Still the woman said nothing, and Debra's voice trailed off. *Maybe she doesn't speak English*, she thought, and was just about to apologize again and turn away when the woman spoke.

"Where did you come from?" she asked.

"Vancouver," said Debra. "And my friend here"—she pointed at Richard, who gave a small wave—"came from Atlanta. We're here for a conference."

"Conference." The woman nodded. "That's all right, then. I thought that you . . . " She shook her head. "It doesn't matter. You take care of yourselves. Take care." And she closed the door.

Debra stood for a moment, staring, then rejoined Richard on the sidewalk. "What a strange woman," she said. "I wonder what she thought we were."

"Jehovah's Witnesses, probably."

"Well, you've seen your haunted house," Debra said, "and a little piece of my family history. What's the plan now?"

"I'd thought maybe some lunch. There's a neat-looking brewhouse restaurant downtown that sounds good." Richard was one of the few people she knew who could say "neat" and not make it sound affected, and Debra smiled. "But would you mind if we checked out the cemetery first? Not to sound ghoulish or anything, but it looks like a great place to get some pictures. *Very* atmospheric."

"The rain helps," said Debra.

"It's not *actually* raining," Richard answered, holding his hand up as if testing the air. "Not quite. And if it starts then we make a dash for the car."

"All right," said Debra. "I'm glad I wore sensible shoes," she added, as they started down the sidewalk.

"What do you know about this place?" asked Richard, gesturing over the fence to their right.

"Not a lot. It's very old; my dad says it was here when he was a boy. His mother's parents are buried in there somewhere, but I never found the grave. I used to spend a lot of time in there when we visited my grandparents," she added, by way of explanation. "There wasn't a lot else to do, and the park down the road was kind of boring, so I used to come here and wander around. It was lovely and cool in summer, and there were lots of squirrels to watch. And I had the place pretty much to myself, as you can imagine."

They had reached the gates, which were wide open, and turned in at the drive. A few yards in the road split into three narrow tributaries that snaked off into the cemetery, twisting amid the headstones.

"Which way?" asked Richard, pausing in front of a small stone building which was clearly an office of some sort. Two cars were parked in front of it, but there were no lights on inside.

"Straight on?" asked Debra. "Then we can get a better idea of where we are, and what there is to take pictures of."

They wandered along the roadway, keeping clear of the puddles that dappled the uneven surface. Above them bare boughs rubbed together in the slight breeze, and a few leaves skittered in front of them, tumbling over themselves before coming to rest in the grass. Richard peered at the grave markers crowding in on them from both sides, stopping now and then to take pictures of the more elaborate headstones.

"A lot of Ukrainian names, it looks like," he said. "Is there a big Ukrainian community here?"

"Must be. There're a lot of Italians in Toronto, I know that. There's a big section of Italian graves in the back corner there." She pointed. "I remember a lot of the gravestones had photographs inset in them, in ornate frames. I'd never seen anything like it before."

"Here's one," said Richard, pointing, and they moved closer to look at it. "Guiseppe Gagliano, 1902–1957," he read out. "Not very old. Wonder what he died of."

Debra studied the picture inset in the tombstone, which showed a heavy-set man with close-set dark eyes. "Nothing that involved wasting away, if this was taken near the end of his life," she said, and Richard made a *tsk*-ing noise.

"Now, now," he admonished, "*de mortuis* and all that. He might be listening."

"Stop it," she said. "This isn't the opening scene of *Night of the Living Dead*." They stepped back onto the road, then had to step off again in a hurry as a car swept by. Debra felt her feet sink, and looked down to see mud welling up over the sides of her shoes. She scraped them off as best she could, and they continued on their way.

"I always thought, when I was a kid, that it was funny to see cars driving through a cemetery," she said.

"I guess so," said Richard absently. He was eying a vista of gravestones and trees and grass stretching away from them, the markers sweeping in an undulating wave over the hills and curves of the lawn. "Hang on a sec, I want to get a picture of this."

Debra waited while Richard took his shots, glancing around the cemetery. Gray clouds scudded above the trees, and she shivered. The rain was still holding off, but just barely. "A Scotch mist," her mother would have called it, that sodden air halfway between vapor and full-scale rain. *If the skies open we'll only be half-soaked by the time we get back to the car*, she thought. It didn't comfort her much.

She noticed movement out of the corner of her eye, and she turned. A couple were standing a short distance away, gazing at one of the gravestones. Her gaze rose up and past them, and she noticed more people beyond them, and still more farther off; small groups of one or two standing among the markers. She went over to where Richard was standing.

"Doesn't this place seem a bit crowded to you?" she asked, and he looked at her for a moment, then swept his eyes round the cemetery.

"Now that you mention it, yes," he admitted.

"Kind of odd for a mid-week morning, don't you think?"

"I guess so." He thought for a moment. "What day is it?"

"Thursday."

"No, I mean what's the date?"

"November second. Why?" He started laughing, and she looked puzzled. "What is it?"

"You're obviously not a Roman Catholic. Well, neither am I, anymore, but I still remember a lot of it." She still didn't understand, and he explained. "November second. All Souls Day. Also known as the Day of the Dead because it's supposed to be when souls in purgatory can return to the earth and pray for release. The living honor their ancestors by placing candles and flowers on their graves. You can even invite them into your home, if you want to, by leaving a door or window open. Of course, if you don't want them in you leave a light burning outside, which gave us jack-o'-lanterns. Because they're souls in purgatory you can pray for them, to help them pass on. It's called a plenary indulgence. Not quite a 'get out of jail free' card, but close."

She looked skeptical. "And that works? I mean, it helps someone get out of purgatory?"

Richard shrugged. "It's supposed to. Look, I don't make the rules. And as I said, it's been a long time since I considered myself a Roman Catholic. I've probably got a couple of the details wrong, but that's the gist of it." He looked round. "There are a lot of Europeans buried here, it looks like. I'm guessing there'll be a lot of visitors here today. Old traditions from the old country, that sort of thing."

By now they had crossed through the heart of the cemetery and come to where the road split into two, heading left and right. "I just want to walk along this way for a bit, and get a couple of shots looking back over the cemetery toward the gates," said Richard. "Aren't you going to take any pictures?"

"I guess I should," Debra replied, pulling her digital camera out of her pocket. "Knowing me, it's the only time I'll have my camera out all week. I don't know why I bring it along to these things."

Her little Canon looked insignificant compared with Richard's camera, and he was clicking shot after shot, not bothering to check them for quality. Debra raised her camera to her face and peered through it, trying to frame a decent picture. *If only all those people weren't milling about*, she thought. *Not very atmospheric.*

She clicked a shot, and the glare of the flash going off made her sigh. She still hadn't quite got the hang of the settings, and she ran her eyes over the buttons on the back, trying to figure out how to turn the flash off. As she did so she saw the picture she had just taken, framed in the screen on the back. It was only there for a second or two before disappearing, leaving a view of the road and her left foot that shook slightly as she tried to process what she had just seen.

She looked up at the scene before her: gravestones, bare trees, muddy grass, and several people standing among the gravestones, most with their heads bent as if in prayer. She took a deep breath, then pushed the button that would scroll back and show her the picture she had just taken of the same scene.

And there it was. Gravestones, bare trees, muddy grass, all slightly overlit because of the flash. But—and it took her brain a few seconds to comprehend it—there were no people in the shot.

None at all.

She looked up again, blinking. There they were, plain as day. Dressed in black, as befitted people come to mourn the dead, say prayers for their souls.

Or dressed in black, as befitted people who had died and been laid out for burial.

She shook her head. This was crazy. As if to prove it she raised her camera and fired off two quick shots, then looked down at the screen.

No one.

This was wrong, all wrong. Richard had finally stopped taking pictures and turned towards her, and she saw a look of concern sweep over his face. He crossed to where she was standing and took her arm.

"Hey, are you all right? You look awful. Do you want to sit down somewhere for a minute?"

She fought to keep herself under control. "Richard, could you do something for me? Just turn and tell me how many people you see."

He looked confused, and started to say something, but she cut him off. "Please, Richard, just do it."

He turned his head and she heard him counting under his breath. "About three dozen, at least in the immediate vicinity. I don't know how many others there might be. Why?"

"Could you just take a picture, trying to get as many of them in the shot as you can?" she asked. Her voice sounded funny to her own ears, and she tried to keep it steady. "Just take the shot, and then look at it."

"Yeah, okay." He lifted the camera up to his face, fiddled with it for a moment, and then pressed the shutter. She heard the sharp *click*, then watched as he turned the camera in his hands and pushed a button.

"Jesus Christ."

So it was true. Debra didn't know whether to feel relieved or not. Relieved, on balance, until she looked up and realized how far it was back to the gate, and where their route would take them.

"What does it mean, Richard?" she asked. "Who are they?"

"I don't know," he replied, and they both knew he was lying. "But I think we need to get out of here." He took her arm. "Stay close," he said quietly, "and don't look to the side. Keep your eyes on the ground in front of you."

They began walking as quickly as they could, keeping to the middle of the road. Even though she kept her eyes down, Debra was conscious of the figures on either side of them. Was it her imagination, or were there more of them? No one had passed them save the one car, and a quick glance ahead, measuring the distance to the gate, showed there were still only two cars parked in front of the office. *They didn't all come in three cars, and there was no one else on the street*, she thought. Then, *No wonder the office is closed today. I bet they couldn't pay anyone* nearly *enough to work here today.*

They were getting closer and closer to the entrance, and Debra tried to work out how much farther they had to go. As she did so she stumbled over a slight dip, and would have fallen if it weren't for Richard's firm hand on her arm, holding her up. She turned to thank him, and her gaze fell on a man standing at the side of the road, turned towards them. He was beside the marker they had stopped at earlier, the one for Guiseppe Gagliano, and his heavy-set face and close-set eyes were expressionless as they passed him.

If Richard noticed, he said nothing, other than "Not much further. We're almost there." Then they were past the office and at the gates and through them, out on to the sidewalk beyond.

It had started to rain at last, but neither of them noticed as they made their way back to the car. As she stood by the passenger door, waiting for Richard to unlock it, Debra glanced across the street toward her grandparents' old house. The woman she had spoken to earlier was standing inside the front window, looking out at them, her face expressionless.

"I think all the pumpkins will stay out until midnight," she heard Richard say. "Then it'll be safe to get rid of them."

She said nothing, just nodded her head. All the way past the long expanse of cemetery to their right she kept her eyes fixed on the road ahead of them, and did not breathe deeply again until they had turned onto Bloor Street and left the cemetery far behind them.

Barbara Roden lives two hundred miles northeast of Vancouver, British Columbia, in the heart of ranching country. Since 1994 she has been joint editor of *All Hallows*, the journal of the Ghost Story Society, and in that same year co-founded, with her husband Christopher, Ash-Tree Press. Roden has edited or co-edited seven anthologies. A World Fantasy Award-winning editor and publisher who has, since 2004, been turning her hand to writing: her story "Northwest Passage" was nominated for the World Fantasy, Stoker, and IHG Awards. Some of her short fiction has been collected in *Northwest Passages*. Her fiction has appeared in publications such as *Apparitions, Blood and Other Cravings, Chilling Tales, Exotic Gothic, Poe,* and *Subterranean Online.*

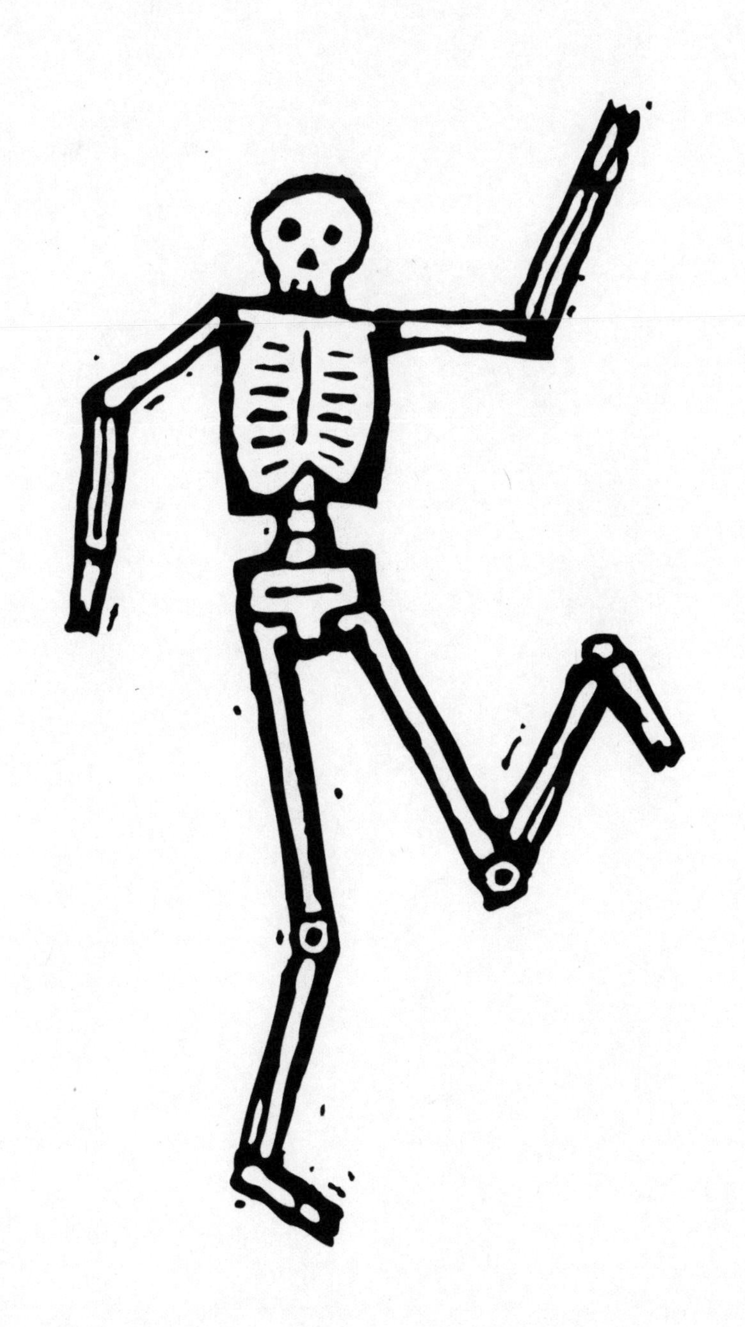

AND WHEN YOU CALLED US WE CAME TO YOU

John Shirley

It was a hot afternoon and her fingers were slick with sweat as she worked the shears along the edges of the glaring face. Today and tomorrow, it was Chun's job to cut the faces from the dangling sheet of rubber.

Some factories had machines that did all the trimming, her cellmate Bao-Yu had told her. *"But here we are the machines."*

Bao-Yu was across the room from her touching up the masks with spray paint. Chun wished they could talk while they worked, but she wasn't allowed to leave her station for hours yet.

They were in a Shen Yang labor camp, after all, not a regular manufacturing site, though in truth conditions weren't much better in an ordinary factory. People got paid a little more, and they worked perhaps twelve hours a day instead of the fifteen Chun and the others worked. And they weren't likely to be beaten.

There was a hand-operated machine in the main work shed that pressed out forms for the Halloween masks, before they came here to Chun and Bao-Yu and the other girls; here the masks were trimmed, and connected to the straps that held them on the wearer's head. The masks, it was said, were for the American custom of Halloween, and sometimes they reminded Chun a little of the images displayed during the Festival of Hungry Ghosts, to placate the lost ghosts of ancestors. But the American Halloween seemed to Chun to be something else entirely. This mask, intended for export to America, didn't have the plaintive, pitiful look of a hungry ghost. This monster's face was angry, cruel, wild, and absurd all at once. It was a furred man, partly wolf, its mouth agape to show fangs, its pointed ears tufted, the deep lines of its face suggesting it was straining with all its will to leap into the real world and kill whatever stood in its way.

She would have to trim more than a thousand of these today. Yesterday it had been a green-faced demon with bright red lips; the day before she'd assembled the plastic bones of dancing, mockingly hateful skeletons with glowing red eyes.

Today she seemed to feel the three years she'd been imprisoned here, and the three more years awaiting her, like crushing weights. Her arms ached; it was mid-afternoon, a long time till the twenty-minute dinner break. Her mouth was dry. The Halloween masks were not just made of rubber, there were other chemicals in them too, and working around them for five days made her skin red, her fingers swollen. The painting the others were doing in the same poorly ventilated room made her eyes burn; she coughed sometimes and it was often hard to catch her breath.

Sometimes when she was feeling tired and sick it seemed to her that the Halloween masks sensed her vulnerability. Then, from the corners of her eyes, she could catch them looking directly at her, waiting for her weakness to increase. As if they were waiting for the right moment when they would snap their jaws at her . . .

The wearier Chun grew, the sharper the smell of rubber and chemicals grew, till she thought she might throw up. But last time she'd vomited on the job the supervisor had shouted at her, slapped the back of her head and said to stop malingering. If she slowed down her work too much, or went to the bathroom more than once a shift, he would jab her in the belly with his baton.

Did the people across the sea know how these masks were made? Did they know about the labor camps, and the factories where other such decorations were made? Where those strange horrible bearded "Christmas" figures were sewn together, with the blow-up man in the white and red suit and black boots: the "Santa" who lived inside a transparent plastic globe, seeming to delight in a perpetual blizzard? Or the eyeless reindeer made of blinking lights? Did the Americans know about the people who worked so long, worked until they sickened, for so little, making these bizarre trinkets?

Chun reached up with her clippers to trim another face free of the sheet, feeling her joints grinding with the motion. She snipped it out and laid the limp, bestial face on the worktable, face down, so that its inverted inner face watched her. She started to attach the flexible straps . . .

And then everything darkened, shrank to a murky picture at the end of a tunnel. She felt herself swaying, close to falling. She heard the supervisor shouting at her, telling her to stop pretending or he would get the electric shocker and really wake her up and . . .

She tried to focus her eyes. She was rushing down the tunnel, toward the mask on the table; toward its wide-open black mouth.

She didn't really believe in the old ancestral worship her grandfather had practiced. But she didn't believe in the People's Republic, either. She had no one but her grandfather to call upon for help. No one but grandfather, and the ancestors, the lonely ghosts who looked for a chance to help so they would be set free from this coarse world . . .

So she cried out to them.

Use your strength, grandmothers, grandfathers—your strength is great! Use your strength to defend me!

Flying through whirling darkness, Chun called with all her soul, all the energy of her anger and all her frustration. She called to those who wait beyond the darkness . . .

The tunnel ended. She was back in the shed, still standing, staring at the face on the table.

Its mouth was moving. It was speaking to her . . .

"You have been heard. For many years they have called to us, without knowing it. Now your call has lifted their voices, so that we hear them clearly; it has lifted their masks of summoning. Oh how they tantalized us! Their icons cried out to us, but we could not respond. It was never quite enough. Something more was needed.

"But now we answer. You have given us what was needed. And now we will respond. You have called us and we will come to you."

The Ouija board was a big-ass fail. Just a tired old disappointment. Maura got annoyed when Julie tried to force the planchet to form messages from her ex-boyfriend who wasn't even dead. Apart from that zoggy bullshit nothing happened with the Ouija board.

"Ohhhh well, let's do shots," Gwen said, but that was pretty much her answer for any boredom challenge.

They were in the basement of Maura's house, with the lights out and candles lit. All three of them in their lame costumes, sitting with big ol' Gwen, the hefty goth girl—not really fat, exactly, just *big*, with the bulk of a linebacker. And little Julie, a Filipina girl who was almost small enough to be a midget.

Cliff had said, "You could fit two Julies in a Gwen, you totally should, and have two friends in one, and save on ticket prices and shit." Then he'd made that donkey sound he called laughing.

Mom had gone to a Halloween party, one that Maura so totally did *not* want to go to, at the Stephenson's house. It would be mostly middle-aged people playing old Alice Cooper songs and wearing costumes rented from shops. And anyway, Maura didn't want to see her mom get drunk and whorey. Especially not at a party. Mom waited exactly one month after the divorce to start whoring around and sloppily draping herself on guys at parties. It was *gross*.

Then Mom would be hung over and insist on their going to Sunday mass so she could skulk into confession. Anybody within ten yards of the confessional could hear Mom crying in there. A real drama queen.

No, uh uh, not that party. But this wasn't much better. Three teen girls wishing they were with three college boys instead of each other. Maura stuck in her Green Man costume, tights and a plastic mask with some fake plants stapled to it. The costume was left over from the school play, where they'd said, "You're going to be the Green Man" and she'd said, "Can't I be the Green Girl?" and they said no, that's not the legend.

"We have lame costumes," Maura said, looking at Gwen's. "Julie's is kinda okay but . . . mostly just lame." Everyone was sick of zombies by now . . .

Gwen had wedged herself into a ridiculous Catwoman outfit from *Batman Rising*, a costume she'd mostly made herself that was only going to make guys snigger behind her back. And Julie was in her Evil Fairy outfit—she looked like Tinkerbell gone all zombie. They were drinking Jagermeister shots, which always made Julie sick. "If you drink enough shots, Julie," Maura said, "you could throw up on yourself and it'd make your costume better."

They all laughed at that. But somehow today Maura couldn't feel like she was part of anything even while she was laughing along with her friends. Gwen and Julie both looked so *loser*. Julie was so eager to try to be "edgy" with them but really she was just another Catholic girl, planning to go to Community college, have a job in a dentist's office, and then get married and have kids.

Who's the losiest loser here? Julie asked herself, thinking of the song by Princess Doggie.

Who's the Losiest Loser here
Who's the one with facebook fake up
Who's the Losiest Loser here
Who's the one with fucked up makeup

"Maybe me," Maura said, taking a shot of tequila from the bottle sitting on the Ouija board.

"Maybe you what?" Julie asked.

"Maybe I'll get sick from mixing Jagermeister and tequila." She did a shot. "Oh yuck, that didn't go down good." Her stomach felt like some hand was wrenching at it.

"What if your mom comes home early?"

Maura shrugged. "So what? She'll be so drunk she won't notice what we're doing. Or she'll pretend she doesn't."

"We could find a party, there's some, um, somewhere," Julie said.

"Where?"

"I don't know. But there have to be. We can call around. There's that Laura Ginsler party, but she's such a Miss Thang snobby-ass."

"She is, too," Maura said. "All T no shade."

"I've still got half of that Hawaiian hesh ciggie," Gwen said.

"Ciggie? Who calls them ciggies?" Maura said, rolling her eyes.

"You're, all, like, in a bad mood," Gwen said, rooting around in her pocket-sized black taffeta-trimmed purse.

"Yeah I am in a bad mood. You should like that, you being all goth and stuff. Goths dress like bad moods."

"No, that's not what it is." Gwen ran her stubby fingers through her red and black streaked hair. Then she went into one of her jolting changes of topic. "Oh! Let's go on the roof!"

Julie blinked at her. "The roof?"

"Yeah! We can smoke up there and watch people on the street. We could throw water balloons at people. We might get some guys to come and check it out."

"Oh God, listen to her," Maura laughed. "You're a worse whore than my mom."

"Not worse than mine."

"Your mom just sleeps with your dad."

"Uh, hello, that's what you think. Do you have a ladder?"

It was a little cold on the roof, but it wasn't raining, and was, actually, pretty tight up there, Maura thought.

There was just one cloud in the blue-black night sky. "That cloud is shaped like a Band-Aid," Gwen said. And it was. The thin dirty-looking cloud was stretched over the blister-like moon but didn't hide much. The cloud gave the moon a red halo, like blood on a bandage, and seemed to make the face of the man in the moon stand out more sharply, so you could see every bit of it, even the crinkle lines at the corners of his eyes . . .

Or maybe it was just the Hawaiian weed making it seemed that way. She saw the lips of the man in the moon move, then. Yeah, the hesh, probably.

She sighed and turned to look at Gwen and Julie. Gwen's four water balloons were sacrifices made from the four condoms she kept in her purse. She'd carried them for months; hopelessly, really, so not much of a sacrifice. Gwen and Julie sat crosslegged just above the front edge of the roof, their feet right by the rain gutter, looking down at the street. Across the street two groups of small children were walking along in costume, shepherded by parents and older siblings. The children tittered and waved their plastic candy bags. Some of them ran, and skidded to a stop when they were reined in by their parents. Orange glows studded the row of houses irregularly, where people had put out jack-o'-lanterns. Across the street the Castlemans had a more elaborate display, with Styrofoam tombstones and one of those dancing skeletons with the wanly glowing bones and hot coals for eyes.

"What if they dug down under those fake tombstones," Maura said, "and found real bodies under each one?"

"Ha-a-a," Gwen cackled. "That'd be awesome . . . "

"Awesome . . . "

"Who said that?" Maura asked, looking down in the bushes. She half expected to see Cliff there, trolling them.

"Said what?" Julie asked, looking at her.

"I thought I heard a man's voice say *awesome* after Gwen did."

"She's going crazy crazy *cra*-zyyyyy, " Gwen chanted, making a scared face and pointing at Maura.

They all three cracked up at that. When that calmed down, Maura said, "That hesh is good. Is there any left?"

"Just a whatsit, what my dad calls it . . . a roach." Gwen held it up in her black gloved fingers and looked at it so close her eyes almost crossed. "Teensy."

"That skeleton can dance, like on a motor," Julie said. "I didn't know they could do that."

"Oh yeah, they got all kinds that move around now," Maura said, suddenly bored again. "Skeletons that come down on strings and shit. Wish I hadn't mixed Jager and tequila. I'm like, about to spout orange goo."

"You feel sick?" Julie asked. "You should drink a glass of water." Her mom was a nurse and some of it had rubbed off.

"You could suck the water out of one of these condoms," Gwen said seductively, holding up a water-bloated oblong of blue latex that sloshed in her palm. Condoms were their water balloons.

Maura laughed and then said, "Don't make me laugh, I might puke."

But that made them laugh more.

Maura looked back at the dancing skeleton Halloween decoration, and saw it was now dancing to the edge of the Castleman's yard. "Wow, it can move forward and backwards too, look . . . "

They stared. Gwen said, "Whaaaaat? It must be on a rail or something."

"Wow, that's a good illusion," Julie said. "Really really good. Looks so real."

"I think you said the same thing three times, Julie . . . Oh! Here comes Cliff, get the condoms ready . . . "

"Eee-ewww, with *Cliff*?" Gwen asked, screwing up her face.

"I mean the balloons, retard."

"I know you did. Here's one balloon for you and one for you."

Cliff was walking down the sidewalk toward Maura's house. He was tall and awkward; he had narrow shoulders and wide hips and the sagging pants he wore, to be all hip-hop, just made his hips look worse. He had his hair teased up in a faux hawk and he was wearing his worn-out Oakland Raiders jacket open over a Necro T-shirt. He had one hand in his coat, where he concealed a bottle in a paper sack, probably a forty of that horrible ale he liked. As he walked, Cliff kept staring at that dancing skeleton in the Castleman's yard. The Halloween decoration looked like it was making little warning runs at him, as if it was preparing to rush him. He just looked at it and laughed. Even from here Maura knew he was stoned, the way he gaped and stared and laughed.

"He hasn't seen us," Julie said.

Gwen put a finger over her lips to signal for quiet, and then crept across the roof, hunched down, toward the porch, carrying the condom water balloon. She raised the balloon; it jiggled obscenely in her hand as Cliff walked across the lawn, just missing a patch of dog waste, toward the front door.

Then Julie giggled and Cliff looked up—he saw her. "Whoa, are you guys having a—"

Whatever stupid thing he was going to say was cut short by the impact of a water balloon, hitting him just above the crotch and bursting nicely. "My aim is truuuuuue!" Gwen shouted triumphantly.

Maura and Julie were throwing theirs; Julie missed, was probably not really trying to hit Cliff. Maura got him in the left leg as he backed away, hollering, "Oh that *blows*! You guys buh-*low*!"

"Trick or fucking treat, Cliff!" Maura yelled, laughing.

Then, backing up, he blundered right into the dog poo, and knew it immediately. German shepherd poo. Big. "Oh fuuuuuuuck! That so blows! Oh my fucking God! You bitches made me step in dog shit!"

The girls laughed, Julie with her hand clamped over her mouth, Gwen almost falling off the roof in her mirth.

"Use the hose to wash it off!" Julie shouted, tittering between words, pointing at the hose by the front door. "The hose!"

"No way! You guys are gonna nail me again!"

"We're out of condoms, you're safe, retard!" Maura yelled.

"If we're out of condoms we're *not* safe," Gwen said, as Cliff went to use the hose. "So sad. So sad."

As if Gwen ever needs one, Maura thought.

She looked at Julie who was automatically covering her braces with her hand as she laughed at Cliff—he was hopping around on one foot trying to use the hose to spray the poop off a shoe.

A few minutes later, Cliff was on the roof, sitting with them, hugging his wet legs, his forty of cheap ale beside him. He'd gotten most of the poo off so he only smelled a little and the cloud of smoke from the marijuana he'd brought made it go away. He passed them his pipe; Maura and Gwen took a hit. Julie said, "Nuh uh, I had enough already. I would but I'm afraid I might fall off! I mean we're on a *roof*. . . "

" 'She paid the price of smoking dope,' " Cliff brayed. " 'Girl falls off roof, news at eleven!' "

He and Gwen laughed and Julie smiled, covering her braces with her hand again, but Maura was feeling depressed and cold all of a sudden. She looked down at the Castleman's yard. Something was missing. No skeleton. "Where's that skeleton gone? Did they take it in?"

Gwen looked at the house where the skeleton had capered. "Must've. He's gone! That sucks ass. He was the cutest guy around here."

Julie laughed and said, "Don't be mean to Cliff . . . "

She said something else too, and Cliff replied, but Maura wasn't really hearing what any of them said, now. A feeling of weight was spreading, pushing down on her from above, as if the atmospheric pressure was suddenly all mad heavy; sounds were hushed and distant, as if they couldn't fully make it through the thick, laden air.

A movement drew her to look, with difficulty, to the left—and she saw the skeleton from the Castleman's yard climbing up onto the roof of the porch.

Hallucination. The dope.

But she didn't believe it was the dope. Especially when Gwen yelled, loud enough to penetrate the thick air. "How'd they make that thing climb up here!" Even that shout came out muted, like a voice heard when you're swimming underwater.

As Maura watched, the skeleton pulled itself up like a gymnast from *Cirque du Soleil*: up and then a flip and it landed neatly on the roof—but it didn't come at them, though Cliff and Julie were screaming and Gwen was laughing hysterically. It kept going upward. It jumped into the air, spinning around, a perfect ballet pirouette, its bony fingers waving like ribbons in a wind, singing to itself in some forgotten language. It sounded like some guttural old language from Europe, like you'd expect Vikings to talk.

Up the wicked skeleton went, dancing its way into the air, defying gravity. Was it a flying machine, a balloon?

She knew it wasn't. Something was whispering to her . . . something was explaining . . .

She heard Cliff shout, "Awesome, fucking awesome!"

And the whispering male voice said, as it had before, "*Awesome . . .* "

But it meant something else. Maura felt awe when she saw those the skeleton summoned.

She stood up to watch as the air filled with dark forms, shapes in black and red and bone white, glittering eyes and clutching hands . . .

And a thumping came from somewhere and everywhere, regular as a dance beat. The summoned throng descended, and they capered in dance.

All around Maura's house, the dark spirits danced. And Maura, standing now, simply watched, swaying to the beat from the drum that was a thrumming of the air itself.

"Oh," she said. She couldn't hear her own voice. But she was saying, "Oh. Oh."

The skeleton's dance was a summoning, every turn drawing ever more furies from the stunned and sickly air, the pregnant density of the atmosphere birthing cannibalistic witches and vicious, sparklefree vampires and icy-eyed slashers in ski masks and masks of human skin and hockey masks. Demons formed and slid down the sky, as if sliding on invisible stalactites; white-winged angels turned black-winged and cruel; friendly ghosts became hatefully unfriendly; wolf-faced men gnashed and howled.

A great, swelling crowd of lunatic figures danced around Maura—figures that had once been ornaments on Halloween lawns, and had once been costumes, and had once been images in movies and in posters and in books, dancing now in mad Samhain glee; in Dionysian delight: obscenely, profanely, mockingly, satirically, but in deadly earnest, surrounding her house. Some detached from the crowd to chase a car down the street, leaping on it, covering it, tearing open the steel roof as if it were thin cardboard, laughing at the screams from within as it crashed, jigging in the flames rising from the burning car . . .

She looked over at Gwen who was standing, mouth open, shaking her head as she stared at the thronging masquerade of dark spirits, smiling and then frowning and then smiling and then frowning again. Clinging to Gwen, Julie was weeping, her shoulders shaking.

The thickness was still pressing in on Maura, and she felt it whisper urgently to her.

"Give them to us, and thus sign your pledge. Give them to us, before we rise and take them. Give them to us and you may join us."

Maura thought about her mother, and that party and the priest who'd put his hand up her dress when she was twelve, and her father not returning her calls, and her teachers who wanted the class to be over even more than the students did, and her friends whom she didn't really like much . . .

"Okay," she said. She could barely hear her own voice. "Sure."

"*You know what to do.*"

"Yes."

She moved toward Gwen and Julie, finding it hard to push through the thick air, but she came up behind them, Julie turning a questioning, startled face toward her—

She shoved them both. Julie had a good grip on Gwen, and they both went quite neatly off the roof, falling into the macabre throng.

His face squeezed into its own Halloween mask of terror, Cliff was just getting up, swinging a fist at her. It hit her glancingly. She hardly felt it.

She squatted, grabbed the forty by its neck, smashed it on the roof, swung the broken end up into Cliff's belly. She felt it cut through his shirt, his skin, his muscles . . .

Not a killing blow, but it didn't matter, he staggered back, mouth open, a red hole yowling . . .

And he fell into the throng.

Maura looked down, saw the dark crowd tearing at Julie and Gwen and Cliff, pulling their limbs off as cruel children pull wings off flies.

Then the air thickened even more, crushing in around her, squeezing . . .

And it squeezed her out of her body. She felt herself fired up, into the sky, like a pressed pip, flying upward, arcing down—and then rushing headlong into a flying cannibal witch, that was opening its mouth wide . . . wider, and wider . . .

She flew into that rubbery maw, and down, spun about inside.

Then she found she was in a new body, a form corporeal and incorporeal at once; a body that flew as she willed it to, upward, along with many other dark spirits, sweeping into the sky, heading to the East.

It was not quite dawn, but Chun was awake. Something had whispered to her.

"*We are here,*" it said in Mandarin.

"Who?" she asked hoarsely, getting out of bed, to stand in the weakening darkness.

"Those whom you called! The ancestors heard, and brought your cry to us, and now we descend, because of your merit and trueness, and because the Earth and the planets turned within the lock of the sky to open the gate. But your cry was the key. And when you called us, we came to you. Now—come and see."

Chun walked stiffly to the door. It should've been locked, but as she approached it, the door swung open, all on its own.

Muscles still aching from the previous day's work, she walked through the door, though she wore only threadbare pajamas, and went barefoot out into the gray dawn.

She came to a sudden stop, freezing in place with a mingling of horror and exaltation when she saw the throng in the sky; it was like a gigantic flock of starlings, swirling and turning in the air, but the dark spirits had replaced the starlings, and she saw many faces amongst the spirits she knew; faces she'd clipped from their rubber backdrop. But now they were not empty masks. They had been given form.

The throng's chorused shrieking woke the guards, who came clamoring from their posts and their barracks, guns in hand, some of them firing erratically and uselessly at the laughing nightmares who swooped down upon them . . .

Chun watched, gasping, as the dark spirits swarmed over the guards; as they ripped and bit and killed . . .

Then the spirits rose from the ravaged corpses, spreading wings of ectoplasm and shadow to sweep over the camp; they darted down, and broke locked doors with contemptuous flicks of their hands; they knocked down gates. Then they flew up, and into the nearby city, to lay waste to any who would keep Chun and the other prisoners from their freedom.

As the dark throng departed, Chun sat herself on the cold ground, to wait, and watch. Others came out, murmuring, to gaze about them in wonder.

Not quite a full hour later the throng reeled away from the city, and up over the half-shattered buildings. Chun saw the spirits depart, ascending in the distance: a tornado of cruel laughter, into the sky.

She stood, and went stiffly to put on her clothes. Then, with Bao-

Yu and the others, Chun walked into the burning town. Chun wished to find one of the few old shrines that the Republic still allowed, so that they could thank their ancestors.

John Shirley is the author of numerous books and many, many short stories. His novels include *Bleak History*, *Demons*, *Everything Is Broken*, and seminal cyberpunk works *City Come A-Walkin'* as well as the A Song Called Youth trilogy of *Eclipse*, *Eclipse Penumbra*, and *Eclipse Corona*. His collections include the Bram Stoker and International Horror Guild award-winning *Black Butterflies* and *In Extremis: The Most Extreme Short Stories of John Shirley*. He also writes for screen (*The Crow*) and television. As a musician Shirley has fronted his own bands and written lyrics for Blue Öyster Cult and others. His two-CD album of songs, *Broken Mirror Glass*, was recently released from Black October Records. His most recent publication is *New Taboos*, from PMPress/Outspoken Authors. It features both nonfiction and a novella. Novel *Doyle After Death* is forthcoming from HarperCollins.

About the Editor

This volume and the almost simultaneously released *Once Upon a Time: New Fairy Tales* will be the third and fourth "original" anthologies edited by Paula Guran; her twenty-second and twenty-third anthologies altogether. As senior editor for Prime Books and Masque Books she also edits novels and collections. Guran has a website (www.paulaguran.com) which she has yet to actually do much with, but you can find out more about her there.

The website, however, won't give you information like this: Even if she does nothing else for Halloween these days, she still plugs in a green light bulb that illuminates a ceramic jack-o'-lantern her mother made over fifty years ago.

Guran used to do more for the holiday. As the mother of four, she devised many costumes over the years and decorated the house in an appropriate manner. (At various times, her basement and yard were turned into "haunted" attractions by offspring. To her knowledge, no money exchanged hands for those who visited.) One son and daughter-in-law are graduates of Ohio University, home of the internationally infamous Athens Ohio Halloween Block Party. Another son attended Miami University in Oxford, Ohio, where a large portion of the town shuts down for a smaller, but equally notorious Halloween celebration that results in arrests of (mostly) out-of-town Ohio State students.

Guran lives in Akron, Ohio, where, on 31 October 1993, Nirvana played the James A. Rhodes Arena at the University of Akron. Kurt Cobain dressed as Barney and chugged Jack Daniels through the costume's mouth. Pat Smear dressed as Slash from Guns N' Roses, Dave Grohl was a mummy, and Krist Novoselic wore white makeup and had *P. C.* written on his forehead (for "politically correct"). On 31 October 2012, President Barack Obama appeared in the same arena. He did not wear a costume of any sort nor did he drink Jack Daniels.

Guran wonders if anyone ever reads these "abouts" anyway, and figured she might as well have fun with this one. Trick or treat!

Acknowledgements

"Black Dog" © 2013 by Laird Barron.

"From Dust" © 2013 by Laura Bickle.

"Angelic" © 2013 by Jay Caselberg.

"Pumpkin Head Escapes" © 2013 by Lawrence C. Connolly.

"All Hallows in the High Hills" © 2013 by Brenda Cooper.

"We, the Fortunate Bereaved" © 2013 Brian Hodge.

"Thirteen" © 2013 by Stephen Graham Jones.

"Whilst the Night Rejoices Profound and Still" © 2012 Caitlín R. Kiernan. First published in *Sirenia Digest #83*.

"Trick or Treat" © 2013 Nancy Kilpatrick.

"Long Way Home" © 2013 Jonathan Maberry Productions, LLC.

"The Mummy's Heart" © 2013 by Norman Partridge.

"All Souls Day" © 2013 Barbara Roden.

"And When You Called Us We Came to You" © 2013 John Shirley.

"The Halloween Men" © 2013 Maria V. Snyder.

"Lesser Fires" © 2013 Steve Rasnic Tem and Melanie Tem.

"Unternehmen Werwolf" © Carrie Vaughn, LLC.

"For the Removal of Unwanted Guests" © 2013 A. C. Wise.

"Quadruple Whammy" © 2013 Chelsea Quinn Yarbro.

Illustrations preceding stories:

"Thirteen": © 2013 Ron and Joe; used under license from Shutterstock.com.

"The Mummy's Kiss": © 2013 John T. Takai; used under license from Shutterstock.com.

"Unternehmen Werwolf": © 2013 Ron and Joe; used under license from Shutterstock.com.

"Lesser Fires": © 2013 Ron and Joe; used under license from Shutterstock.com.

"Long Way Home": © 2013 Ron and Joe; used under license from Shutterstock.com.

"Black Dog": © 2013 Ron and Joe; used under license from Shutterstock.com.

"The Halloween Men": © 2013 Montebasso; used under license from Shutterstock.com.

"Pumpkin Head Escapes": © 2013 Ron and Joe; used under license from Shutterstock.com.

"Whilst the Night Rejoices Profound and Still": © 2013 Ron and Joe; used under license from Shutterstock.com.

"For the Removal of Unwanted Guests": © 2013 Ron and Joe; used under license from Shutterstock.com.

"Angelic": © 2013 Ron and Joe; used under license from Shutterstock.com.

"Quadruple Whammy": © 2013 Ron and Joe; used under license from Shutterstock.com.

"We, The Fortunate Bereaved": Xonk Arts; used under license from iStockphoto.com.

"All Hallows in High Hills": © 2013 Ron and Joe; used under license from Shutterstock.com.

"Trick or treat" © 2013 Ron and Joe; used under license from Shutterstock.com.

"From Dust": © 2013 VladimirCeresnak; used under license from Shutterstock.com.

"All Souls Day": © 2013 Ron and Joe; used under license from Shutterstock.com.

"And When You Called Us We Came To You": © 2013 Ron and Joe; used under license from Shutterstock.com.

Dingbats: Ill October by Hybrid Space, Evilz by N Plus, FireStarter by Gaut, Butterflies by Typadelic Fonts